Seadogs and Criminals

BOOK ONE

Alex Fisher

Grosvenor House
Publishing Limited

This book is published by
Grosvenor House Publishing Ltd
Link House
140 The Broadway, Tolworth, Surrey, KT6 7HT.
www.grosvenorhousepublishing.co.uk

This book is a work of fiction. Any resemblance to
people or events, past or present, is purely coincidental.

A CIP record for this book
is available from the British Library

ISBN 978-1-83975-342-8

For my family
and
For anyone with a taste for adventure.

Acknowledgements

I would like to thank my family and Katie for their continued support throughout this process and for giving me guidance when I needed it most.

I would like to thank Nik from Book Beaver for creating the covers for my books, listening to my ideas and giving the covers a professional identity.

I would like to thank Grosvenor House Publishing for taking my work on to be published and for guiding me through the process. You have opened doors for me and my writing career.

Prologue

Tapping his pen against the paper, Charlie Munson left small dots that quickly turned into fat splodges of ink as his fountain pen began to resist the sudden jerking motion of his frustration. Ink began to splatter from the tip, ruining the blank featureless page below his hard work. The words and paragraphs he had been trying to construct began to blur in his vision, becoming a meaningless clutter of nouns and verbs. His foot tapped against the floor, accompanying the angry tapping of his inky pen until he could take no more. Tearing the page up from the table, he scrunched it into a ball and threw it into the roaring fire in front of him, already fuelled by his previous failed attempts at creating a masterpiece.

'Throw any more paper on that fire and you're buyin' the night's round at the bar, alroight? I can barely think it's so hot in here from the amount you've stoked the bastard up!' Alex Drayson exclaimed in his thick Australian accent from the other side of the room. His best friend and writing partner, Alex was always honest.

Charlie sighed and scratched his brown hair, exasperated. 'Of all the things I could've got a job in, why did I choose to be a writer? We wrote that one book together that turned out to be good and now I've got to live out the rest of my career waiting for ideas. Christ, I've got enough fuck'n blocks to make a church wall jealous.'

Alex smiled as he got up from the table to open the window of their office with sweat rolling down his face; his long sideburns feeling matted. His shirt had stuck to his back and the patches under his arms were widespread. Charlie wasn't the only one feeling the blocks, he had been too; a sheer lack of inspiration had gripped him and whenever he looked down to a blank sheet of paper, instead of seeing a story through his mind's eye, he saw menial jobs he had to do around his house and what to eat for dinner. Anything and everything decided to enter his working mind to keep it distracted; procrastination caging his focus in bars wrought of unbreakable boredom. As he breathed in the cool air, one idea suddenly came to mind: the best idea they'd had in hours. 'You know what a series of blocks call for,' he turned around to Charlie's tired eyes, knowing they were about to lighten up. 'Beer!'

No persuasion was needed. Slipping their jackets on to fend off the evening's chill, they locked the door behind them and passed horses and carriages as they headed down to the local pub where the candles on the tables were already alight and the punters were already stumbling. All types of personnel were enjoying themselves, from workers to dockers, businessmen to brokers; one of the only places in town where all social classes could share a common interest: the intoxicating contents swilling in a pint glass.

The two writers slowly jostled their way through the crowd to reach the bar where Charlie ordered them two pints of the good stuff. They found a spare table and drank and laughed, giving their blocks a good rinsing; lubricating the cogs of their minds to get them whirring as soon as sobriety had dug in its solemn claws and made them care of things again. It was not long before three more pint glasses stood foaming and empty on their table with ruddy faces looking at them with bloodshot eyes. It was then, heeding their merry spirit, that they decided it was time for another round.

The evening turned into night and the night turned into morning, and in gradual trickles the pub began to empty of its swooning drunkards and the raucous din was replaced by a sobering chatter around candles running short of wax and wick. With his shirt half unbuttoned and his hair, usually combed with a parting, tousled drunkenly, Charlie leaned back in his chair and finished his last pint. 'So, how're you and Marie gettin' along now? Getting used to the married life?' he asked, wiping the foam from his lips.

Alex looked down into the foamy dregs of his last pint glass before gazing up into the distance, deep in thought.

'I know that look. What is it? What've you thought of?'

He gently shook his head. 'Not thinking. Listening.' In a subtle motion, he turned his head and looked at the table behind them where a group sat in silence, listening to a man with dirt on his shirt and a golden tooth flashing in the candlelight. He looked to be a prospector, and the words coming from his mouth made those at the table feel like they'd struck gold too.

'They trudged through the jungle, they told me, trudged through seeing monkeys and bats, butterflies and wonderous things until they got to this crack that led deep down into the bowels of the earth. None of them wanted to enter but they had no choice and so they walked in, worried and confused, following a boy that spoke barely any English, until they came through into a cavern. Through cracks in the roof of the cave, daylight speared and lit up this mysterious cavern; a cavern filled, packed to the brim, they saw, with diamonds bright and colourful and twinklin'. The most beautiful thing any of 'em had ever seen. Why, just hearin' about it sent my old digger's hands shaking! Although, some told me they saw even more beauty than that, with one saying that it stirred somethin' deep inside and "awakened a part of his soul he didn't even know was there", he'd told me. "Jack," says he, "beauty is always there. You've just got to know where to look, and when to appreciate."' He took a swig from his pint glass. From the look in his eyes, Alex could tell he was being honest; this wasn't the ramblings of a drunken man nor the brags of one being boastful. This man was sober and was telling the truth.

'It's incredible what they did, what they saw,' he continued, 'half o' me didn't believe it, I mean, how often is it that you hear of people doin' something like that? A group of hopeless backstreet urchins from the big smoky city managin' to get themselves out and away, seekin' fortunes and freedom. I still run it all through my mind, rattled as it may be, and I'm still baffled by it all. If anything, it gives me hope where there wasn't any before.' He paused, 'I feel honoured to be a part of their journey, their tale, if it is only a small part: they've had such an impact on me. I've never known people like 'em, and I doubt I ever will again. Determination, or endurance, I should say, can pay off.' He picked up his glass and drained the rest of his beer.

Alex turned back to Charlie, completely sober and with eyes alight with wonder and fascination. 'Did you hear any of that?!'

Charlie's chin was resting on his chest as it rose and lowered in relaxing rolls with a small string of dribble hanging from the corner of his mouth, but Alex was too excited to be angry. He turned back to find the man, only to see an empty chair and an empty pint glass. The man had left, and the group he was with was getting to their feet and beginning to leave.

Getting to his feet, he hurried over to one of the men. 'Excuse me, sorry to be a bother, but who was that man? I need to talk to him.'

The man looked barely awake with his eyes squinting and bloodshot. The few too many had taken their toll. The next man helping him toward the door, though, fared a little better. 'Jack Potts is who he is. Why? He owes you money too?'

'No. I need to meet him. Where can I find him?'

'Ah, he lives a few streets along in one of them new houses. Look for the green door, he'll most probably be in if he isn't out diggin'. Old Jackie loves a dig, just as much as he loves tellin' that fuck'n story. I mustah heard it four times now.'

He nodded a quick thanks before turning back to Charlie sleeping in his chair. Rousing him gently, Alex realised Charlie was worse for wear and required a helping shoulder to drape from to get him through the door. The fresh air was revitalising, though, and helped to sober Charlie enough to ask, 'what was it you were sayin' in there?'

With determined eyes, Alex looked straight ahead. 'We're going to meet someone tomorrow, ol' cobber. Best clean yourself up before we do.'

The morning air was warm and bright with a clear blue sky. The day had barely begun and already workers were closing their doors and heading out for the next shift, including two writers who had donned their jackets, waistcoats and bowler hats. They'd also brought along their leather cases full of blank paper ready to be filled. Charlie shielded his eyes from the bright sunlight, as pale as a passing cloud. 'What *are* we doing up at this *ungodly* hour?' he groaned, feeling the burden of the night's shenanigans weighing heavily.

'We're going to find Jack Potts. I've got a feeling he's got the answers that'll get rid of our blocks.' Replied Alex with a keen stride and firm grip on the handle of his case.

'And what answer moight that be?'

'Inspiration.'

Charlie nodded, trying to resist the urge to retch.

They didn't have to look far before they spotted a green door on a house that had been newly built along the expanding street; recently repainted, it was bold and bright against the dusty coloured brick. At once, Alex approached and knocked.

They stood waiting, before he knocked again.

The door opened a slither and an eye peeped out, then narrowed in confusion, before the door opened entirely. A tall man looked out to them wearing a loose untucked shirt and braces that were lopsided having been slipped on only a moment before. His face was handsome and narrow with dark stubble peppering his jawline, yet his bloodshot eyes appeared redder upon his ashen complexion; Charlie was not the only one struggling this morning, it seemed. He squinted as he tried to recognise them, then rubbed his eyes tiredly, before giving them a smile. 'G'day to you foine lookin' gentlemen. I would ask who you are, but I think a more important question to ask roight now is what on earth you call this hour?' Picking out a strip of paper and a pinch of tobacco, he began rolling a cigarette.

Charlie looked to Alex, 'I've been thinkin' the same thing myself mate.'

Alex pulled out his pocket watch, 'seven o' clock. Sorry to wake you, Mister Potts, but I was wondering whether we could talk?'

A passing look of confusion moulded Jack's face, turning into concern. He put the cigarette between his lips and lit it with a lighter. 'To talk about what, kind sirs?'

'We were at the bar last night and I couldn't help overhearing you talkin' about a tale you played a part in, an adventure of sorts concerning a group of people. It sounded fascinating and we're intrigued to know more. We're writers, you see, and telling tales is part of our job description.'

A strange smile spread over Jack's face. 'Writers, y' say? Well then. If a grand tale for eager ears is what you're after, that's exactly what you'll get. An adventure of fates and freedom to reach a fabled chest called the Lost Loot.'

'Lost Loot? I heard that was only a bedtime story you tell your kids.'

Jack smiled, 'exactly. A fabled chest, indeed. Or so I thought. By the end though, you'll understand what I mean when I say it gives hope where none seemed possible. A rekindling of faith. The amount they saw and endured; it's a remarkable journey.' He paused, blowing out smoke, 'I'm sorry to disappoint you though, but I'm not the man to tell this, not how it should be told. The man you're looking for is Joseph Winter. He's the one that set it all off, that got the journey on its feet. He's the one you need.'

'Joseph Winter.' He said, remembering the name. 'Where can we find him?'

Jack pointed, 'next town along. Ask around and people can point you the way to their house.'

'Their house?'

He nodded, 'oh yeah, he's a married man now. Lives with his wife. What a good couple too; they do eiverythin' together. Actually, you moight want to talk with her as well.'

Alex and Charlie nodded and held out their hands, excited to get going. 'Thank you, Mister Potts. You've been a great help. Sorry again for the early start.'

Shaking their hands, he shrugged lightly, 'Ah no dramas. I had to face the hangover sooner or later. You'll loike old Joseph, as honest as the sky's blue. Safe journey boys. G'day to you's both.' He said, waving after them as they walked down the street, heading in the direction of his pointing finger.

Before they left, they hurried to their homes to let their wives know their plans and, for Charlie, to bid his children goodbye. At the edge of the town, they found all the hansom cabs were busy and, as Charlie adamantly said, 'I will walk over hot coals before I walk to the next town in this state,' they looked for an alternative. Soon, they found a man with his horse and a full cart packed with goods who was heading in their direction, and they paid him well for a seat on the back which he happily agreed to.

Taking off their hats and jackets, they sat on the back of the bumbling cart with the morning heat beating through their shirts. Taking off their neckties, they popped open the first few buttons and adopted the appearance of casual travellers instead of wealthy businessmen. Amid the clopping of hooves, rumbling of the cartwheels and creaking of the goods they sat against, Alex asked Charlie, 'what do you think then, cobber? Worth the early start, eh?'

Charlie gave a smile with a red flustered face, 'definitely; there's somethin' there. Thank god you were soberin' up last night to catch Jackie talking about it. I just hope I feel better by the time we get to their house, the rockin' of this cart isn't doin' the old insides much good.'

The horse and cart rumbled on down the dirt-track road for the next four hours, passing fellow travellers and couriers as well as a lush green meadow filled with the native bouncing fauna. At last, civilisation came into view and the town was in walking distance. 'Ee-yar, fellas. There's the town.' Their driver said with a nod of his head.

They collected their belongings and jumped off, thanking their driver for the ride, before setting off for the town. Thankfully, the distance didn't take too long to travel, and they entered the town in the afternoon, stopping off at the local eatery for a meal and to refresh themselves.

As it turned out, Joseph's house wasn't too hard to find as nearly all the townspeople knew of him and his wife, with all the people they asked having nothing but kind words to say about them despite not knowing where they came from. 'It's loike they dropped from the sky,' one shop owner confessed, 'they just appeared and bought a lovely little house with a lagoon at the back without a quibble about the price. I mean, it was an expensive property, a proice people would've scoffed at, but they agreed to it straight away. They didn't look loike people of business or wealth, but they mustah had somethin' stashed away, I guess. Don't get me wrong though, they're a lovely couple; always happy, always smilin', perfectly content, you know.' Walking out of the shop, the two writers found the case of Joseph Winter even more intriguing and shrouded in mystery, only adding to their burning desire to meet him.

Eventually, they found the abode on the outskirts of the town down a dusty road and saw it to be a small house with a large beautiful tree standing out the front. Their house looked moderately new, not a mansion by any means, just a simple, humble home. It was tidy, appearing to be well looked after; cosy and inviting with flowers and plants potted around the base of the house's front. Upon a latticework trellis standing before the porch, honeysuckle flourished, growing through to the porch where their colourful vines and blooming flowers overhung the top of the front door where Charlie and Alex approached. With a buzzing anticipation, Alex knocked.

The door opened a moment later, and a woman stood smiling. She was tall, youthful, and had a slender, pretty face with luscious light brown hair tied up to get air to her neck after this hot day. She wore a bright floral dress covering a modest pregnancy bump. 'Hello,' she started, 'can I help you gentlemen?'

'G'day. We were hoping to talk with a Mister Joseph Winter, does he live here?'

She nodded, 'he does. Although he's at work right now, but he'll be back later. Is everything alright?'

They nodded. 'Everything's fine, Missus Winter, no need to worry. We'll come back later if that's alright?' Charlie said.

'Of course,' she smiled, 'see you later.' She closed the door and both men walked away, already eager to return.

A few hours passed where they visited the bar in town and had a drink, and as the afternoon turned into evening, they decided they'd try again. A strange nervousness crept up on them as they approached the front door and it was with a clammy fist that Charlie knocked upon it.

There was a moment's delay before the door opened to reveal a man who looked to be in his thirties. He had a healthy glow of tanned skin from working outside and a slight hint of weathering upon his face in the form of crow's feet wrinkles, but that wasn't to say he didn't take care of himself. His brown beard was cropped and neat and his hair was short and tidy, with small patches of grey around his temples and flecks within his beard showing signs of former stress. He wore a cotton vest, but from his exposed shoulders and arms they saw he was muscular and had lived an active life, which was also what his eyes told. Those greens were clear and sharp, honest and attentive; they had seen much, and, right now, those eyes looked at the two writers patiently, curiously. At last, Charlie began. 'G'd evening sir, moight you be a Mister Joseph Winter? My name is Charlie Munson and he's Alex Drayson, and we'd loike to ask a few questions about some things to do with a remarkable journey you've been on; we were told it had the power to give hope where none seemed possible.'

The man gave them a look of passing confusion. 'I am Joseph Winter, but might I know who told you all this?'

'A Mister Jack Potts.'

A smile found its way to Joseph's lips, as if the memory of Jack were a pleasant one. They noticed then that he had a golden tooth in amongst his molars. 'I might know of the man. Come in. We're just eating, so if you wouldn't mind waiting, we can talk about this after.'

'Of course.' They followed him through the front door and into his home which was, indeed, as cosy as they'd guessed. Straight down the corridor was a kitchen illuminated by the evening sunlight spilling through the window, and a dining table where Joseph's wife sat eating. Along the wall were framed photographs of their most recent travels and people they'd met. In the corner between the room to their left and the kitchen ahead was a potted houseplant with large fronds, and it was this left room that Joseph led them to.

The drawing room was large with a comfy sofa against the wall facing the window with a large fireplace and oaken mantlepiece to the sofa's right. Beautiful jewels and ornaments lined the mantlepiece and a piano sat against the wall opposite the hearth with a framed photograph standing upon its top next to a small purple orchid. Joseph offered them a seat on the sofa and quickly made a small fire and lit it for them to fend off the evening chills, before leaving them to finish his meal. Whilst he was gone, they inspected a photograph of their wedding day and the incredible jewels upon the mantlepiece; they were unlike anything the two men had ever seen, especially one which was long and smooth and seemed to glow purple and move from within. Although, this one was perplexing and they quickly moved away from it, unsure of what to make of it.

Soon, the scraping of cutlery finished, and Joseph entered the room and sat on a chair under the window where the last light of day poured through. 'Is your wife available for a chat too? We were told Missus Winter had a part to play as well.'

He nodded, 'of course.' He then called to her and she walked in a moment later.

'Hello again sirs. Sorry about the mess, I'd have tidied up beforehand.' She smiled her radiant smile that made Charlie and Alex agree that these two were a fitting couple.

'Don't worry yourself, there's nothing to tidy.' They smiled in the glow of the flames as the evening darkened outside, where Charlie then began. 'Now you're both here, we were wondering if we could talk to you about an adventure; a journey you both, and others, endured, to find a fabled chest; a Lost Loot, I think it was called, that turned out to be very much real. Is this correct?'

They nodded, 'why do you ask?'

'We're extremely interested in your tale. Mister Potts tells us it's a tale of fates, and a passage to freedom. We are writers and we were hoping to take notes and eventually write a novel about it, with both of your permissions, of course? It would be a work of fiction, written in third person perspective, yet it would be authentic and visceral, as if the reader were there.' Alex Drayson asked politely.

Joseph looked to his wife who lightly shrugged, and they nodded, 'I can't see a problem with that,' he replied, 'it's a . . .' he paused and took a breath; they could see events, memories unfolding from his eyes like reflections upon the surface of a pool of clear water. He was going to struggle with some parts of this, they knew, but they were prepared to wait. They would wait for as long as it took, however long he needed. In the pause, they wondered if he was considering what this was to be: a story, a biography, or maybe even a confession. Joseph blinked, before making his decision. 'It's a long tale to tell. Have you the time?'

They reached into their leather cases, reaching for their paper and pens. Alex smiled at them, 'all the time in the world . . .'

Joseph nodded, then went to collect the table for them to work on. Once everyone was settled, he pulled his chair up and reflected, wondering where to start. 'I'd heard of the Lost Loot, Scott's Trove, but had never believed in it.' He began, 'it was just a story, a fantasy to give excitement and wonder to those who ever dared to dream. Little did I know what it would become to me, who it would influence, what fates it would shape.

'Before it all began though, before the adventures and the legends, I was a different man. A man of London's streets, born and bred. A man that never left a trace . . .'

Chapter One

Victorian London

Heaving in cold morning breaths, Joseph Winter bolted through the dirty cobbled streets; one hand clutching his bulging jacket pocket, the other gripping a felt black bowler hat. He ran fast, his pace constant– endurance was key in desperate times like these; the body had to be ready for a quick dash, a swift escape, if he wanted to stay out of that godawful place again. By now, Joseph didn't mind the running; after years of it he quite enjoyed the exercise. One thing he enjoyed more though was the thrill of the pursuit, and even better, the art of the steal.

'Stop!' they called out behind him. 'Stop right there, criminal!'

Joseph shot a glance behind. The peelers were close but were not as fast as him; clearly, they were not expecting such a flying response when they'd spotted what he'd done. He would've chuckled to himself if he had the air to. Quickly dashing around a corner, he slipped down an alley choked with strewn litter and waste.

That job had been easy, almost too easy. *You've been in this game long enough, old boy, maybe you're used to it.* Or perhaps their security just wasn't tight enough, especially for things so valuable; he'd have thought they would've been more guarded. Not that he complained, if anything, he took it as a compliment. It was just as Mad Vinny had said when they'd met in prison all those years ago: *"yer only as good as the things you steal, and yer only as fast as yer feet can carry you. Don't go stealin' pretty things if you can't outrun the people tryin' to chase you!"* Truer words had never been spoken. Mad Vinny had been right, as always, and it was advice that Joseph had held biblically close ever since. There was irony in it, he found, that the one place meant to "redeem" and "rehabilitate" him was the sole place that inspired him into a life of more crime.

In all honesty, his attraction to pretty things couldn't be helped. Things of worth, of value, anything that had a high price; he had the eye of a magpie you could say, spotting the shiny and glittering from afar. It was natural. It was a skill he took pride in; that, as well as being able to read and write, giving him advantages many did not have. Surprisingly, he even had a mild interest in law– the wrong side of the law, no doubt, but its obstacles kept him sharp and constantly needed jumping over– or running from. Intelligent and quick on his feet, Joseph loved these horrid streets; despite their usual abhorrent stench of decay and faeces and the sweeping swathing clouds of pollution, they were his rat-runs and he knew almost all of them. Very handy when in need of a quick getaway.

His boots clopped against the undulating stone, pressing into the patches of soft London Mud until he burst out onto a road before a busy market, nearly colliding with the trunk-like thigh of a horse pulling a hansom cab. Eyes darting and sweat running down his blushed cheeks, he narrowly skipped around it feeling the scornful glare from the driver and ran into the market square where he stopped. Stalls were set up in a crowd with the owners loudly flogging their wares, competing with the cacophony of a busy urban market. People walked, bought, browsed, talked; an endless stream of bartering, it was too crowded to run through, but he needed to keep pace. He could hear his heart thundering; he had no choice. *Hide! I need to hide!*

Breathing heavily, Joseph looked at the detail within the frontal scene, scouring anything that gave an opportunity. Stalls were propped up everywhere, parting often to let customers wander through the narrow paths. He spied tables of vegetables, tables of apples, tables of fish; eels; nuts; tables selling meats, pork; beef; lamb; chicken. Tables watched by onlookers, customers bartering, buying and pointing and laughing. Beady-eyed children with a light touch and no money slithering through the thrum waiting for vulnerable pockets. Open boxes brimming with food, large upturned empty wooden boxes no longer needed by the owner of stalls; wicker baskets hanging from women's arms. Suddenly, he saw his answer.

Glancing back, he saw the peelers were entering the market.

There's your answer. It was a risk, but he was used to taking them.

Joseph jumped around a pile of dirty cloths next to a stall, turned over an empty box and sat against it. He ruffled his hair, muddied his fingers and rubbed his face, wrapped one of the cloths around his head covering an eye, opened a few of his shirt buttons and started chewing tobacco to blacken his teeth. He was in the centre of the marketplace; his eye peering, heart thumping, waiting.

A range of people walked by; kitchen-maids, mothers, a few men and couples browsing for their supper that evening and buying goods from trusted sellers. Out of everyone though, his eye was drawn to the poverty-stricken children; thin with dirty, tattered clothes scampering around wandering legs begging for money with open palms streaked brown from skulking in the grime of the cobbles. Sometimes not begging; finding money for themselves without permission. He watched on as three children took the attention of a well-dressed couple whilst the other two snaked around their pockets and bags. Joseph smiled faintly, remembering the days of his youth when he was just an average pick-pocketer. A pang of sympathy rushed to him, a rare feeling indeed. Ever since old Robert Peel had become Home Secretary and remade the police force, thieving was not as easy as it used to be. It had certainly eliminated majority of the weaklings; over half would probably end up in those overcrowded prisons now. Joseph, however, had been there and was not a weakling anymore; he couldn't help but smile at the better jobs and new opportunities he'd been getting because of the arrests. *That's right Mister Peel, you keep clearing up the streets, get the old trouts out the way to make way for the bigger fish.*

His eye moved on through the crowd, sifting, waiting. Suddenly the children disappeared, darting away like a pack of rats that had just been discovered skulking around the dinner table. Joseph looked on eagerly and heard the approach of heavy black boots. The peelers slowed to a stop near his box, completely out of breath. People bustled by them, not giving them any mind. 'Where'd he go?' one asked the other irritably.

'He came this way, I'm sure! I saw 'im!' the policeman huffed, 'come on, let's keep looking.' They both trudged on through the busy square, passing him completely.

Exhaling, Joseph smiled with pride and knew the law had passed him by once more. Peelers were a problem in his line of work, but with a light foot and a little initiative one could easily blend into a crowd, especially with these streets full of people. After years of honing, he'd learned the tricks of the trade. Camouflage, rendezvous and sanctuaries were a must, as well as a fast wit and light feet– that, and a large empty wooden box. Reaching into his pocket he pulled out a handful of jewellery a man of his social status wasn't meant to have.

The collection glittered and twinkled, appearing even more bright against the grubby background. Necklaces and diamonds and rubies and rings, all perfectly crafted; a wonder to behold. His scheming and timing had paid well as he marvelled with a twinkle in his eye. All the jobs paid well, mind; his career had been a successful trajectory with an abundance of money and rare ornaments he fancied for himself. This stunt had been almost too easy, but nevertheless he knew Mad Vinny would be pleased with the result.

Slowly rising from his crouch, he stood and surveyed, making sure the policemen had truly gone. Fortunately, they had but the children were still hidden up and, he noticed, were now watching him from under the tables. *This'll give the poor robins something to look at.* He took off the cloth, winked and slid off his dirty pockmarked jacket. He brushed it down . . . and folded it inside out.

The children watched in amazement as his old jacket, aged and faded with stitches in places, stains brown and smears green, turned into a black expensive-looking tailor-made garment with a velvet collar. Removing a clean handkerchief from his pocket, he rubbed the dirt and sweat from his face, quickly smoothed down his sideburns and brushed his trousers, boots and waistcoat and combed his hair to a parted wavy bounce. He whipped out a length of fine material and tied a necktie to his starched high collar before picking up a matching black bowler hat that was at his feet and placing it gently on his head.

In that one minute, Joseph Winter transformed from a lower-class vagabond criminal to a wealthy-looking businessman, and nobody had even noticed. Except the wide eyes underneath the tablecloths. He raised a finger to his lips and shook his head; a secret they had to share. The children nodded, smiling and giggling. Joseph smiled back, tipped his hat politely and strolled on through the market heading for the Back House, his hands dug deep into his pockets to avoid any loud jingling.

In some respects, Joseph Winter was a master of his trade. A lifetime of stealing, burglaries, gaining contacts and rising through the ranks had honed his skills into that of an expert thief, a burglar whose tastes varied beyond the simple coin– indeed, he was interested in finer things than that. Jewels, horses, women, expensive clothing and other things a working-class man shouldn't even be seeing– these were his forte, his main level of expertise. Shops were raided, stocks were swayed, businesses were hijacked all in the name of prosperity. Money was a material he was in contact with frequently; enough to love it rather than depend on it, toying with it in ways to develop its growth. Gambling it and laundering it to earn from it; he played a big game. To a horticulturalist, money was his plant and he spent his days watering it regularly. He wasn't a wealthy man, yet his wallet was far from empty. He wasn't a famous man, but he was sought after. At thirty years old, at the top of his chain, Joseph had become widely known around the backstreets as Trace– because he never left one.

Taking an exit from the market, he walked the streets with his nose in the air as a man of wealth would do, acting as if the only things in life that should be taken care of was how full a man's pocket was and how grand he can keep his property. People reacted differently instantly, keeping their heads down with those of a higher class beginning to sniff a new fish in their small pond. *Let them look, let them all look, but whatever you do, do not roll up here.* Already he could feel his chest beginning to tense and his fingers jitter; the temptation to pick out his tobacco and light a strip of yesterday's newspaper was almost too much. *Keep it together, wearing this jacket I should be smoking a cigar– not a strip of yesterday's news.*

His pace was brisk as he marched past a bakery, inhaling as he did so; the smell was bliss compared to the hazy concocted mist of coal smoke and horse and human waste alike. Moving hastily past a pair of women strolling and nattering, he crossed the road, narrowly dodging a hansom as it trotted along the cobbles beside him. Onto the pavement, he strode with an air of wealth, politely nodding to others who knew the game who passed by, knowing to keep quiet when he was working. A pair of peelers then approached– they wouldn't recognise him of course, his disguise offered him a false appearance of importance that the peelers dared not to touch but then a sudden panic gripped him as one slowed, eyed him up . . . then walked past giving a polite nod. Joseph nodded back. *If only they knew who they'd just walked past.* Not for the first time this morning he could have laughed, but then his attitude changed as he felt eyes prying– eyes he could not see but could see him. Anxious, this façade was tiresome. *I've got to get off the streets.*

Spotting the next turn off, Joseph darted down another street off the main thoroughfare but this one was even more cramped full of people going about their daily business. He walked around a trio of men rolling barrels full of beer to the brewery and skirted around a woman selling barely edible fish. Children ran around, ducking and dodging and disappearing into the crowd, past the workers playing dice and crabs in their break. Women passed by with baskets laden with groceries and gypsies sat smoking in their patterned bandanas, watching the lively street with a keen eye.

Sounds of London life filled his ears; there was no escaping it. It was everywhere. Around every corner, every shop, every street there were people bustling and moving; he gently shook his head, he could remember a time when the influx of people was just an inkling, a steady stream before this industrial boom had turned the stream into a fast-flowing current as more people abandoned their rural setting in search of new work in the developing city. Joseph shrugged to himself; *more people, more belongings, more work for me.* In all honesty, he wasn't complaining; he liked his job– it gave him a thrill. He didn't need to do it, but in a way, he did.

A left, right and left again brought him to his destination: The Back House. The central hub of activity for people like Joseph– a place to trade, exchange and gain insight into likely hotspots vulnerable for a pilfering. Joseph peered up at the wide wooden warehouse squeezed between two other buildings; to the flaking white paint peeling off the sliding doors, to the old wood that needed a varnish. It certainly didn't look like much, but to Joseph this place was a second home. He knew too well not to use the front door– it was only a ruse that led into a storage facility for the local wool factory. The *actual* place of importance lay below ground, down a hidden staircase around the back wherein lay large vaulted wine cellar; the doors to which were concealed by a thicket of holly bushes.

Excited to be back, Joseph hurried between the buildings away from the drone of sound and came to the back of the warehouse where rubble lay strewn. Weeds poked from the ground here and rats skirted through the mess. It was perfect. It looked awful, which paradoxically was great. The less attention, the better.

He found the holly bushes growing up against the back wall and moved the boards beside them, another distraction, to find the wooden doors underneath. Lifting the doors outwards, he walked down the first few steps before closing the doors behind him. Descending, he came to the door at the bottom where he knocked, was inspected, then allowed to enter the Back House.

Dense stagnant air clogged his nose at first and a fusty aroma of cheap beer, cider, wine and mildew lay heavy in his lungs and but after a few breaths the smell was comforting, like stepping through your front door at the end of a long day. He breathed it in deeply and listened to the constant noise that the Back House always came with. Men and women alike talked business in private booths and on the tables with beauties on their laps, laughed with old friends over pints of cheap ale and either had their fortune read behind one curtain or briefly loved an open-legged woman behind another. A sandy pit in the centre of the floor made grand entertainment for cockfighting as well as a makeshift unlicensed boxing ring. Today, boxing was on the stubs and crowds were gathered around the ring, cheering on the bareknuckle punters to win their bets.

Despite the hubbub and cloying smells, the atmosphere was always merry, like an extended family gathering welcoming strangers and old-timers alike. True, the Back House wasn't much, but it was a secret place to lie low for a while to recuperate and relax from the watchful eye of the ever-growing laws. Everyone was in the same boat here, it was an equal playing field; no one was rich, anyone was welcome, and everyone knew how to make the best of things. People knew how to get by. Joseph gave time to let his eyes adjust to the dim orange glow of the candles, setting the scene in a faint mellow hue.

A cheer went up, 'Eyy! Trace's 'ere!' Men and women sitting at the tables over to the far right were looking at him raising their jugs of ale in greeting, calling to be heard above the din from the fight. Joseph smiled. The "usuals" were always here, although he wouldn't exactly call them reliable; they were criminals just as he was: crafty and meticulous, light of hand, they were the magpies of London in their constant search for the silky and the shiny. Either way though, they were friendly characters. He didn't trust a single one.

He lifted his hat and called back, 'good to see you.' Even though it wasn't. None of them questioned his fine-looking attire, nearly all knew of his little jacket trick just as he knew some of their tricks too. As in the gaol, this place was common ground to share ideas, yet Joseph rarely shared. You didn't get far by doing that often. His eyes were drawn to the fight in the ring. It was bloody, and the topless boxers were tiring; their fists bleeding, hearts beating to the shouts and cries of the forceful gamblers.

'Come over 'ere, my man! My old possum, eh? Let us get you a pint o' the strong stuff, get some neck oil down yer!' A man cried to him, beckoning him over. Joseph considered; he was strictly here on business as he scoured the large cellar, past the brick pillars in search for the man he had to see, the man with the brand Mister Vinny Jenkins. Unfortunately, he wasn't at the tables and as Joseph scoured the main floor, he saw he wasn't there either, neither was he in the crowd of gamblers nor at the kegs filling a pint. He huffed, glancing around to the left where beds of straw had been made for vagabonds in need of comfort. *Not there either. Might as well have one.* He skulked over to the table where John sat, his tight-corseted prostitute on his lap. Other friends were around the table too, punters pretending to be hard cases. Joseph pulled up a chair. 'Alright, John? How are we all?'

John nodded; he had a square chin, flat face and a scar and had a lopsided grin that showed he was up the pole. Despite sitting on his lap, the fancy girl kept her gaze on Joseph and licked her lips, twiddling the loose curls from her chignon. Joseph didn't know of John's friends, but he nodded to them all from under his bowler hat. Keeping the peace. 'Ah, you know, keeping free, Trace, keeping free.' John replied, 'beer and skittles, mate. By the by, thank'ee for sorting out that hit. Done us a real favour, and it looked like a perfick accident! That old codger's dead and gone, out o' my hair at last. Done to a bloody turn, I don't know how yer do it!'

He shrugged and smiled, picking out his tobacco and strips of newspaper, rolling up and lighting it with a match from his book. He took a drag, a beautiful drag, and billowed out the smoke. 'I do what I can, just trying to raise as little question as possible. Whilst we're on the subject, *by the by*, you still owe me some shin plasters for that.'

'Yes, yes. Course. I an't forgot, old John never forgets. Yer'll be getting yer sovereigns soon enough me ol' possum! What brings you down 'ere?' John asked, nodding to the ring as he lit a cigarette of his own. 'Fancying a fight?'

'Nah, you know I only fight when I drink. I'm here to see the Old Boy himself. Got some things he might like. You don't know if he's about, do you?' He looked around to the ring and felt his stomach clenching with an unquenchable thirst for a brawl.

'Oh, course, course. Forgot. The Mad Vin is busy, but the lovely girl here can let you know when he's free.' He took a swig and a drag, 'well it's a shame yer not up for a fight; bets a' flowing today and I got a drink right here to tickle one's innards.' He slid over a pint of cheap cider with a sly glint in his eye. 'I tell you what, if you get in that ring, I'll set me stubs on you to win and all the winnings are yours. If you lose-'

'-then you'll pay me double. I an't here to be bonneted, John.'

A pause, 'Yes. Yes. Course.'

'And if you don't pay up, my skilmalink friend, a couple of hornets will be coming your way, sending your rotten soul down to the Old Scratch.' He faked a smile, and picked up his pint, smelling the strong cider as it neared his nose.

Don't do it, Lucy will know. Just put it back down. The edge touched his lips and he took a long gulp, then put the cigarette back to the crook of his mouth and inhaled with a smile, taking off his hat.

Loosely moving his fists, his feet were light on the sand as his ears were filled with cries and cheers of the hardy outlaws banging the wood of the ring. His face throbbed and he felt blood trickling warmly down the side of his face, mixing with his sweat. Eyes ahead, he watched the movement of fists from his dancing opponent: a brute of a fellow with a barrelled chest and a head like a potato. Already his nose was crooked from his other fights, although Joseph had made it bleed as well as his lip.

The man came at him, swinging his fists in powerful practised arcs; experience played on his part and his bare knuckles delivered blow after crunching blow to Trace's stomach and ribs, pulverising his muscles, making him wince and cry, then another hook around the head sent showers of stars raining down his vision. Trace backed up, falling to the border with pain licking its flaming tongues around his body; his head spinning wildly. He grabbed the wood and pulled himself up, his hands quivering as he put his cigarette to his lips and took a deep drag. When he took it away, blood was on the butt. *The ratbag's bloodied my fag.* Turning, he jumped to his attacker and blew the smoke in his face before using his smaller frame to his advantage and landing blow after blow with rapid pace.

One to the head, two, three, four. One to the stomach, another to the ribs; antagonising his lungs, then another to his stomach. A slap came next, then a punch, cracking the cheek bone. Blocking wild desperate swings from the barrel, his eyes darted down to stop his leg from raising to a kick, then hooked an uppercut to his chin that clamped shut his jaws like a safe door. His balance amuck, Trace shoved him hard sending them both to the ground where he straddled him and delivered a volley of violence using fist and elbow to the man's head, mashing the potato to the thrum of the onlookers banging the side of the wood until his knuckles were cracked and bleeding.

Once the man was unconscious, Trace got to his feet and coolly bowed like a showman to the cheering crowd, his sweaty brown hair falling over his forehead. He placed his cigarette in his lips and took a drag, watching the orange ember shrink. It was one of the few times he loved these people, when often he thought of them only with contempt. They were, after all, competition in this unruly game of street life scrounging. '*Trace! Trace! Trace!*' The crowd cried as he walked out the ring brushing himself down and collected his pile of paper winnings from under the squinting brow and hooked nose of the judging umpire.

Slipping past the excited crowd, he pocketed his wad and walked over to the table, slipped on his shirt, buttoning it halfway before clipping his braces back on and adorning his waistcoat. With his jacket under an arm, he shook his head at the missing chairs. John was nowhere to be seen. *Well would you look at that, the hornswoggler. Johnny boy's done a runner. Looks like you've opened the hall my pigeon-livered friend.* His eyes squinting angrily, he made his way over to the makeshift bar, 'pint of the apple lady, George. As tender as you can tame her.' He ordered, wincing at his sore muscles. A glass was placed in front of him brimming with a sweet cider.

'This 'uns on the house, for the win.' The barman said with a wink.

Do one thing to entertain them and they love you. Trace gave a bloodied smile and lifted the glass to his lips and took a long swig. 'George, you're a diamond.' He said, wiping the froth away. A tap on the shoulder then made him turn and he was greeted by a pretty woman with whom he knew of very well, knew of very . . . intimately. 'Surely Trace hasn't come all the way here just to drink and smoke and fight?' Charlotte said coolly as she slipped beside him, his lover's eyes lighting up. He never had the heart to tell her he was already courting a woman, but she didn't need to know that. Honestly, he wondered if she'd even care. *All she wants is a fat purse at the end of the night, and a few privy moments with the mighty Trace,* he reminded himself as he felt his loins stir at her smile and low-set corset revealing the top of her petite rounded bosoms. 'Or were there other things on his mind?'

He leaned against the bar and looked the other way, 'I'm waiting to see Vinny, love.'

She leaned against the bar beside him, her long brown curls falling past her shoulders. 'Perhaps I could offer some horizontal refreshments to go with that cider whilst you wait?' Charlotte suggested softly, stroking his chin and neck seductively. A wagtail: she knew how to play him.

'I an't really got much time to spare, my dear.' Although his loins told a different story.

Turning to him, her smile was like melting butter. She took his hand, 'don't worry, there's more time to spare than you think.'

Pulling the curtain aside, Trace exited the booth buttoning his shirt once again and slipped his braces and waistcoat on, out of breath. Wiping the sweat from his forehead, he turned and spoke into the candlelit gloom, 'lovely to see you again, my dear.'

'The pleasure's all mine. See you soon.' Came the reply and he smiled, pulling the curtain closed. Taking another gulp of his drink, he walked over to another closed curtain, *blimey, busy man today Vincent.* He stood by waiting for a minute, watching the wretches of this industrial city drink, gamble, whore and smoke. Midgets and dwarves were here too, he spotted, alongside other crutch-bound people with amputated limbs from the Crimean war and shrivelled limbs from episodes of polio. There were black people with skin like soot and bushy-bearded Indians; people of all races and religions enjoying the buzz of the Back House. Joseph held his tongue, tiring of the crowd, beginning to long for something else, something more.

The curtain was pulled aside, and two gentlemen walked out putting their hats back on. Quickly, Trace slipped inside the dingy booth and closed the curtain, where a big man sat at a table with a pint in his hand and a cigar between his lips, a branded V flickering in the candlelight. Everyone in this part of London knew the tale, knew why Vincent Jenkins had earned his title– and very few could forget it. Back when he was a young man, a lowlife vagabond, Vincent had got involved with a gang of thugs who ran the streets bullying and thieving until he got caught by a peeler by mistake. On the way to prison however, he knocked the policeman unconscious, took his uniform and roamed the streets for four days pretending to be a man of the law. Upon his capture, Vinny had been whipped through the streets and burned through the ear as punishment. After gaining leadership over the gang a few years later, he almost strangled a peeler who tried to arrest him for stealing food for a helpless child, and then wore his uniform through the streets until he was captured again, flogged and branded with a V on his forehead. V for vagabond so no one could mistake him as a lowlife, but others who respected him thought of it as V for Vinny– the man who defied the law to help the poor, the man who was utterly and loveably mad.

Trace sat on one of the chairs and looked at the bald stocky man in an old and faded chequered jacket sitting opposite. Despite his waistcoat buttons desperately struggling to hold together, his weight had never concerned him. A stern look crossed his rounded face, 'Well, well. In 'ere he comes; uppity Trace, swaggering with that fancy jacket to come and see me: the frousy jollock.' Slowly the sternness morphed into a friendly smile. He chuckled, 'Dash my bloody wig. Do yer really think yer gonna come in 'ere and not greet an old friend properly?!' He stood and walked around the table, minding his rotund waist, and held out his hand.

Trace grinned and stood up, grabbed his hand and pulled himself in to give a half embrace and a slap on the back. Choking his nostrils, Vinny smelled of sweat, ale and tobacco– the usual fragrance. 'Good to see you, old cod. Cheers for that tip on the jewellers. Quite a haul I got there. And speaking of big hauls, that's quite a belt you've got, big man Jollocks.' He smiled.

Mad Vinny laughed heartily, 'you leave a man and his appetites alone! You should be thanking me, not insulting me Mister Winter! I heard about it and thought it might be a job for a slippery-fingered crook like yourself, so I sent the word out. Plus, you an't been 'ere in a while and I wanted to see my old chuckaboo in the flesh, and to know he was still in business.'

'Oh, well an't you the sweetest!' Trace sat back down, and Vinny did also with a sigh. 'Prices for selling this stuff have risen, then, I hear.' He said with a sly look.

He took a swig from his pint and almost spurted it out in laughter, 'Risen! The cheek of it, yer bastard!' he calmed himself, 'Ah. Nah. Business can wait a few, I want to know how yer've been getting on out there in the runs?'

'Not too bad, keeping busy as always. Few jigs set up, coins made, coins lost. You know what it's like.'

He nodded, sucking on the cigar, 'too well I'm afraid. You mustn't have been doin' too badly mate, you an't been back 'ere in a day and an age! And from the looks of it you've had yourself a good time. Win a match, did yer?' He looked to the cuts and the lipstick haphazardly rubbed off, 'And riding with a Dutch gal, I see.' He smiled, 'thing's an't going too well with the ol' gel Lucy then? No rings given or promises made, bumps under a blouse?'

Trace smiled and looked away, 'nah. Not yet. Blimey, I'm already chained to a life on the streets, why would I want to clamp myself in another manacle? I do love her; we both work hard but I . . . I don't know, I just think sometimes we don't understand each other.' He spoke the truth, yet the details were finer than that. He loved and hated her simultaneously, just as he loved and hated his career and reputation, as he loved and hated himself. To give the job up meant a dull life doing what everyone else did, buying the same things and joining society as a valued honest member. *Christ, I couldn't imagine anything worse.* The whole charade of society's whims was a disgusting repetition, following the norm to look the same as everyone else to keep the status quo, until it became a mindless flop of wasted days and a lifetime of recycled glob. In a way, he was running from society's pressures as well as the law. Where was the raised pulses? Where was the spontaneity? *The streets are where I belong, not in a marriage, no matter how many people pester me about it.*

Vinny shrugged, 'that's courting for yer. There's love and there's hate, then in between there's a balance; it can take a while to find.'

Trace opened his palms, 'alright Mister Gypsy, put down your crystal ball. I thought we were here to talk about business and a few fine things you might like, but if you wanted to talk about courting and the like then I guess I can take my deep pockets elsewhere.' He feigned turning and getting to his feet.

The big man laughed, '*Walk-er*! Sit down yer ratbag! Alright, alright. Let's get to it. Two necklaces, five rings and four rubies and some diamonds. You manage to get 'em all?'

Reaching into his pocket, Trace pulled out his shining haul and laid it on the table. Even in the light of the dip, the colours twinkled and gleamed as if he has just pulled out a handful of fallen stars. Their beautiful light sparkled in Vinny's face. He stared at them; transfixed and bewildered as if he'd never seen anything so clean and pure before– and never had it so within reach. It'd always been behind glass, around a porcelain neck or stuck on a soft finger, not on a table in front of him. *He looks like this every time he sees jewels and diamonds,* Trace observed, *even though he deals in pawning these off every day.*

Eventually, Vinny smiled. His own thieves were good, but they left traces. This man did not. 'Trace . . . you really are one skilful little bugger. Those fingers of yours might as well be feathers, and those feet might as well be wings. Well done, my man!' He plucked his case from beside him and placed it on the table, unclasped it and handled the stolen jewellery, tucking it all inside, ready for the next step along the pawning chain. He pulled out a large pouch from the case and laid it in front of Joseph to take, as well as a banded roll of sheets. The jingle of the pouch was different from the pocket full of jewellery, but it played the same lovely note. 'That's as much as I 'ave. And if all this sells well, you'll be getting more of where that comes from.'

'Hunky dorey.' Trace took the pouch and noted its heavy weight. This, combined with his winnings, was to be a very profitable day. The money was one reason why he liked this line of work, but it was more for the rush; in other words, he had found his place in the underbelly of London: the money wasn't legal but it was well-earned and rates seemed to be rising. His earnings today would tide him and his girlfriend over for quite a while, yet that wouldn't stop his fingers from getting itchy. He tucked the pouch and band away in his pocket. 'Now that's out the way, how've things been with you Mister Jenkins?'

Vinny shrugged, exhaling out cigar smoke. 'Mad, as always.' He tilted his head back and chortled loudly, then took another gulp of ale and rubbed his rounded face. Trace noticed the scarred V on his forehead seemed to shine in the candlelight. 'Nah things have been good, just the same old life of a same old vagabond. Business' slackened a bit, especially after the rise in the peelers roamin' the streets picking off the foozlers, but they can't get rid of us all and I doubt they ever will.'

Trace raised his glass to that, and they clinked. 'Well it's still good to see you're still up and going.'

'Course I bloody well am, Jesus, Trace I an't that old y' know!' he laughed again, but then his laughter died down and he went quiet. A serious tone found his voice. 'I've 'eard of a new job that's come about though if you're interested?'

Trace's ears pricked up. *A new job? From Mad Vinny himself? This one must be good.* Usually jobs were passed through the grapevine, tips of where to raid next. To hear it come from Vinny's own lips though was odd. After a pause, he nodded. 'Where?'

'A house. Big one. Big district.'

He nodded, knowing where that meant.

'The price?'

'Same as the jewellery. Its valuable.'

Trace's interest spiked; his fingers twitched. He leaned closer, 'What's on offer?'

The big man pulled a fold of curtain and peeked through the gap to make sure no one was eavesdropping. Satisfied, he faced forward and spoke in a soft tone. 'Believe what you will, but I've 'eard there's a treasure map hidden inside. A treasure map leading to the Lost Loot itself. Scott's Trove . . .'

A pause. 'Balls to that! *Walk-er!* You could make a stuffed bird laugh with things like that.' Trace exclaimed and sat back and laughed, 'treasure maps? Those times are gone, Vinny. They were about when my old grandfather was alive! No way they're about nowadays. All the treasure there is now is hanging around the necks of fine rich ladies or stuck around the fingers of fat rich gentlemen: those are the treasures *we* hunt, Vinny.' He chuckled, 'If you want to believe in maps and lost treasures, you really must be as mad as everyone says.'

Mad Vinny pointed a fat finger at him, 'Oi, 'nough of that. Do you want this tip or not? If not, I'll just give it to someone else and they can go and find it.'

Incredulous, Trace huffed, 'you really believe there's a treasure map in there leading to the Lost Loot?'

Vinny seemed to give it some thought before answering, 'I do. The house is an old one y' know, and old houses keep old secrets. Secrets even the owner may not know about.' He paused, 'plus, it's an interestin' thought, an't it, that somewhere out there there's that chest o' treasure waiting to be found.'

'Well, yeah, it's an interesting thought, Vinny, I'll give you that, but come on, these are just thoughts; that's all they'll ever be. How did you even find out about it?' Trace sipped his oil of gladness. The apple lady was sweet to him this evening. Despite his disbelief there was still a side of him that desperately wanted to believe– for what man could say no to a treasure hunt? Yet his fear was more convincing, and the caution was too great. It was a leap of faith that he wasn't sure he was ready for. This wasn't burgling jewels or valuable expenses; this was for a mystery map leading to a treasure that he couldn't be sure was even there. It was called the lost loot for a reason.

'I've heard whisperings down the line, Trace, whisperings tellin' me of the map.'

'*Reliable* whisperings?'

'From the maid that works in the house, yes, I'd say they're bloody reliable. What's all the dilly-dallyin' about anyway? I thought you of all cons would jump out at a chance like this, especially with your family history an' that.'

Sighing, Trace gazed down at the foaming dregs of cider in his glass. Everyone in his family had had to live with that burden, and near enough everyone in the lower-working classes knew the tale of his grandfather; the explorer who sought fame and fortune like James Cook, hunting endlessly for his own land to claim but never finding it. Even though the hot climates of the far-off countries did not melt Frederick Winter's passion, his desperation, hopelessness and lack of satisfaction eventually did and after years of searching his health deteriorated until he could explore no more and in time, Winter turned bitterly cold; forever tormented by the failure of his lost and fruitless expeditions.

Trace looked back up to the brand on his forehead, then to Vinny's hazel eyes looking at him intently. 'It's just a risk. A big risk. Say I do go to this house, break in and find the map, who knows if there's going to be any treasure at the other end anyway? Someone might've stumbled across it first without the need of the map. It *is* a *lost* loot anyway. I don't know. I just don't want to jump into it only to find out the X has already been marked and spotted.'

There was a pause.

Vinny shook his head, 'you don't ken the tale of it, do yer?'

Trace tilted his head curiously, 'what tale?'

The old vagabond cleared his throat, taking the cigar from his lips. 'Back in the olden days of pirates and seadogs sailing the seven seas, a man and woman met and fell in love, then suddenly found a treasure chest and kept it. Took it with them wherever they went. They weren't only a mister and missus; they were partners who kept the treasure hidden with them so well that those who knew them rarely heard them speak of it, yet alone see it.

'Their love for the sea kept them riding the waves and over the years they sailed on many ships across many oceans, exploring and travelling, lookin' for the perfect place to bury their treasure. Then one day their ship hits some rocks and wrecks, taking half of the crew with it. They were some of the lucky survivors but the land they got shipwrecked on was so vast and empty I doubt whether I'd call them lucky at all with the suffering they must 'a went through.' He took a gulp of cider, 'legend says they died in that mysterious land, along with the other survivors, but not before they buried their treasure . . . and left a map for it to be rediscovered one day. No one's ever found it though, earning it the name of the Lost Loot. Some people believe it, some don't. What say you?'

'Hmm.' Trace frowned and sat back in his chair. 'How come they never spent their treasure? Why'd they keep it to bury?'

'Apparently it must've been too good to spend, but just think Trace; how much money d' you think that chest would be worth? It was worth a lot then, just imagine what it would be now! Sometimes age does come with benefits. An old penny is worth more than a new one.'

Trace agreed, knowing the trade too well. 'So, what does this have to do with the map? Is this the map from the legend?'

'It might well be Trace, but I was just using that as an example that not all treasure in history is found so soon. Some of it is still out there, buried somewhere.'

He sighed, unable to deny that the persuasion was working. He finished his cider and spun the edge of the glass on his finger in thought. *It could still be out there, buried somewhere in London, in England, in some other exotic country.* It was a possibility that he was acquainting himself with, the idea sounding preposterous, as well as dangerous and stupid.

. . . and yet . . . there was a part of him that wanted to believe.

'What yer say then, Trace? Fancy being part of a legend?' Vinny spied him eagerly. It was no wonder the old coot had managed to get out of some sticky situations– his skills in persuasion were slick as oil.

Eventually Trace looked up. 'I have some questions. What's the house like? Is it tight? Secure?'

'Trace, you've just come in 'ere with a handful of stolen jewellery from the famously secure jewellers and you're asking me if this *house* is alright to burgle?'

'Point taken but I'm serious! I need to know mate, come on.'

Mad Vinny sighed, 'it's not too bad. I've had a gander past it once or twice. There's gates out the front with a padlock then stairs leading up to the front door.'

'What about people? Who lives there?'

'Old couple; must be in their sixties, wealthy; she likes her tea parties and knitting clubs and he has the average gentleman's interests of port, cigars and fancy girls who like a few pennies in her little back pocket. They're home Monday to Thursday. Come Friday they're both out and it's only her that returns at night– whilst *he* stays out a little later enjoying what he shouldn't.'

Trace nodded. Sometimes the wealthy were even more coy with their hobbies than the criminals. 'Is the front door the only way in?'

Vinny shook his head. 'I hear there's a hidden entrance in the alley nearby– leads down a tunnel to a trap door somewhere in the house. You can get in from there.'

'What am I looking for in the alley?'

'There's a metal grate in the ground near the wall. Looks like a small drain but I hear there's some small hidden handles in the ground around it that you can lift to fit through.'

'Right. Any other tips?'

'Hmm.' He leaned back and scratched the first of his chins. 'Maids and butlers are workin' there every day, they might spot yer so be careful.'

'Vinny. Come on. What am I known for?' A smile spread across his face.

Mad Vinny smiled and laughed. 'I don't know why I even bother tellin' yer anymore.'

He laughed, 'You're getting soft, you mad ol' crook.'

Vinny belted a chortle before quieting and rising to a stand, holding out his four-fingered hand, 'Good luck to you, Mister Winter. Keep those feet o' yours light and your fingers lighter.'

Trace stood and shook his friend's hand, smiling. 'And you stay out of trouble, Mister Jenkins. Good-bye.' He pulled the curtain to one side and made his way for the exit, tilting his hat to Charlotte as he passed.

Once outside, he looked out to the rubble with steam billowing from his mouth. The evening was chilly, the air sharp to breathe. Digging his hands in his pockets, he brought his left hand out again and opened it up . . . to look at the shine of the diamonds and silver rings he'd intentionally kept in there. He couldn't help but chuckle, 'I always do keep my fingers lighter.'

Chapter Two

Dusk brought light to the links that dotted along the streets, yet their illumination was barely enough to penetrate a thick swathe of smoky mist that had crept in. Joseph slowly walked back to his through-house, mulling over the conversation again and the possibilities of what might occur. Concerns always nagged at him when he took on a job but never like this; usually he thought about timings and escape routes, refuges and prices– this time he had to contemplate whether the goal even existed. Even sitting at their dining table, staring at his plate of food, he contemplated, seeing but not taking it in. His mind was elsewhere. *Vinny wouldn't make things like this up, an honest man he is. A trusted friend, too. I've said yes now anyway, there's no backing out.* Once Joseph Winter took on a job, he never quit from it. On the outside he presented an air of confidence, but behind the façade he was an overly cautious man; meticulous and prepared– it was one of the reasons why he was so good at his job. That, and the reversible jacket Lucy had made for him.

Speaking opposite from him, Lucy Bolts decided to end the silence. 'Joseph, you've barely said a word since you came in and hardly touched your food. The devil's the matter?'

He looked up, awakening from thought and smiled. 'Sorry, my mind's been elsewhere.' He cut a slither of cold meat and ate it, chewing it slowly. The fire crackled in the hearth, heating a kettle and casting flickering ambers and oranges against the walls where rare paintings hung, and shelves of fine expensive ornaments decorated.

She sighed, tiring of his double life. Ever since meeting him and falling in love, she knew he was complicated, but the attraction was there; he was bad which made him an interesting character.

Yet enough time had passed where she knew the difference between himself and when he'd been playing up. 'You've been at it again, haven't you? You've got another one lined up?' she asked, her brown eyes inquiring.

The look on his face answered for him.

'Joseph! For god's sake!' She exclaimed, pulling her chair from the table. 'How many times, how many?! You told me that last job was it. Once you'd finished that one, you'd stop the cabbaging and pilferin' and start looking for real work. A real job where you're not ripping people off and you're earning money honestly. Like a normal person. What was it today, eh? Loaves of bread? Horses? Money? Gambling? Setting up hits?'

Joseph swallowed a chunk of potato that felt like a boulder and pursed his lips, guilty but there was a small buzz of excitement at being caught. Sipping some water, he replied. 'I'm sorry, Luce'. It was a job I couldn't turn away from, it was too easy, and it paid well. What does it matter where the money comes from anyway? We still got food on the table and a roof over our heads . . . and whether it matters or not, it was jewellery. Since you ask.' He reached into his pocket and laid his sparkling bounty on the table. The clarity of the gems seeming to brighten the dark wood they lay on.

Lucy stared at the stolen goods, mesmerised for a moment at the beauty she should've never been able to see on her own dining table. She'd seen goods like this before, valuables he'd laid his hands on, but it was still a wonderous sight. 'Good lord. I saw these at down in Mayfair.' Her gaze shifted to his, her long black hair tumbling prettily over her shoulders in loose curls. She wore a cloth gown, yet her soft features made even this simple robe resplendent. 'That wasn't all, was it?'

He shook his head, 'I took a handful, but these are the things I kept for you. I thought you'd like them.'

Admiring them with wide eyes, Lucy was baffled. 'Course I like them! But think for a minute, will you? When can I wear them without being noticed? I work for a few bob a week; I'd have to save up for years to afford things like this. These would shine too bright against my poor skin that's for sure.' She paused, 'where did the rest of the handful go if that's what you'd kept?'

Joseph coughed, 'Mad Vinny.'

The glare he got chilled the air; he almost shivered. 'You were at the Back House again?' she asked coldly.

'Yes, only to pick up the earnings.' He reached into another pocket and pulled out the pouch of money.

'And to fight from the looks of it. And drink. You've got cuts and bruises on your face and I can smell cider on your tongue, how in Christ's name did you think I wouldn't notice? Are you trying to bonnet me?'

That's not all my dear . . . he gulped and showed his winnings, 'I won the fight though. It wasn't all for nothing.'

Lucy sighed exhaustedly and slipped her head into her hand, covering sight of him. She'd lost her appetite. 'You know how I feel about you going back *there.*' She hissed, 'how many times have I told you, *implored* you to give it up and get a proper job? You can read and write and you're good with numbers, surely that's got to be worth something? But you just can't stop killing that canary, can you? We just keep running in circles like a mongrel dog after its tail. You love it all too much, that's your problem. You love it more than you love me, if not you would've listened to me by now. Listened to my advice. We would be married by now if you'd just give it up . . .' She paused to gauge his reaction, but after getting none, she continued sternly, 'it's a dangerous game, but the more you keep taking the more you keep playing. Those people in that place won't do you any good; they're dangerous and they'll rat you out as soon as they get the chance.'

Of course, she spoke the truth and he agreed but he couldn't let her know that. 'They're good people, mind! Hard-working and friendly. Look, Lucy, I know what I'm doing, alright? I just have one more job to do and then-'

She looked up abruptly, '-that Mad Vinny gave you?'

His pause was enough.

Her face turned to stone and the temperature in the room plummeted even though the fire burned in the hearth. The kettle began to steam and bubble, ready to be poured. 'All right then. I'll play along. What's this job for now? Tell me.' Lucy pried, folding her arms.

A part of him didn't want to tell her, he just wanted it to be his possession alone. It was *his* job, a one he'd been given. Yet another part of him wanted to play her game, regardless of her reaction. Eventually the latter won over, it usually did. He leaned in over the table and covered the basis of his job.

Carved from granite, she gave nothing away for a time. Then there was a slow shake of the head. 'You fool, Joseph Winter. You absolute fool.' She pushed clear of the table and exited the room, leaving him in an ugly silence.

'Bitch the pot, love.' He said light-heartedly, glancing over to the two empty mugs, but there was no response and the kettle continued to steam.

The silence spread through the night. Hardly speaking to each other, she read the newspapers whilst he watched the flames until they went to bed. He didn't like to admit it but he had to: their relationship was toxic, like a confused thermometer it could work so well that nothing could intercept their love for each other but when things were bad an iciness frosted their company, chilling it to a bitter and unpleasant gloom. He knew that was what courting was about: he'd had his fair share but recently this one seemed to be riding up the rocks frequently; they were different people there was no denying it. Patiently, he awaited the day when their ship could wreck for him to be free amongst the driftwood.

The next morning Joseph woke early, washed the grime from his face, shaved around the cut to his lip, leaving his long sideburns and donned his tailored jacket, picked up two hats and walked out the door.

A swaddling cloud of coal smoke filled his lungs, making him cough, and the London Mud smelt ripe on the roads. *Bloody hell! I've come out here for fresh air and I get a lungful of this shite!* Litter and browning waste piled the streets where mongrel dogs sniffed in hope of something edible. Hooves clopped on the dirty cobbles as horses trotted by. Children chased them, and the streets were already beginning to wake to the cries of the sellers of food and news. *Another beautiful day in the rat-runs.* He thought as he rolled up tobacco in his newspaper strip and lit it, filling his lungs with yet more shite.

The morning sun would hopefully clear the air yet with such a density of pollution it usually struggled to penetrate through. He buttoned his vagabond jacket up to the neck and wrapped around his comforter as he expelled clouds of steam and smoke. Adorning his newsboy cap, he slipped the bowler hat under his jacket until he needed to switch.

He had left early but the burglary couldn't happen yet, after all, it was only Tuesday and the owners were in. However, there were still things that needed attending to if he wanted this task to be fruitful. True, he had burgled houses before but never without a few days' preparation; something which most common thieves didn't seem to understand. *No wonder the prisons overflow, these fresh fish just can't wait for the right moment.*

A whiff of freshly baked bread reached his nose. A wondrous scent, giving a moment's respite. His stomach gurgled, reminding him to breakfast. Following the scent around the corner the baker-boy called, *'Bread! Fresh loaves! Come and get 'em whilst their hot!'* and immediately the sweaty aproned baker spotted him and smiled. Joseph returned the expression, *a friendly gigglemug– yes, you beautiful baker, I'm interested.*

The baker left his table and made his way to Joseph. *That's it, come to me.*

'Good morning sir, care to try one of our fresh buns?' he said and began to revise his lines for the morning. 'These 'ave traces of honey and seeds in 'em; new recipe I made this morning. Freshly baked. Yer won't find any other like these around the streets, or the city.'

And I'm sure you won't be the only seller to say that today. Joseph walked between him and the table and turned, keeping the arm closest to the table slightly outstretched with his fingers ready. With his other arm, he patted the shoulder of the baker, drawing his attention to the touch and to Joseph's green eyes. 'Not today my ol' possum, but I'll come back tomorrow with a threepence and a friendly smile.' Slyly, his light fingers pinched a honeyed bun from behind him as he moved past the produce.

'See yer then. Have a good day, sir.' The baker nodded, smiling as the thief began to walk away completely unconscious to his stolen goods.

'And to you, good man.' Joseph tipped the rim of his old hat and moved on, making sure his arm was in front of him.

A moment of guilt gave his mind a pause, but it was not enough to stop his legs from walking. Passing around the next corner, he took a bite from the roll. It was still warm, and the hint of honey was a refreshing treat on the tongue and the seeds gave a light hint of savoury to balance the sweet. 'Blimey, he an't wrong. I probably won't find this anywhere else.' He said, taking another satisfying bite.

An hour passed before he spotted the signs letting him know the area, but he didn't need them to know where he was. The atmosphere and general architecture fluctuated from long rows of dismal grey and brown Victorian townhouses with little greenery to splendid grandeurs sporting pillared entrances and front gardens, all protected by a row of gates. Walking the pavement, he noticed the number of homeless and disabled decline as well as the bustling workers; the clothing people wore graduated from dirty work shirts and stitched up botch-jobs to expensive tailor-made waistcoats with shoes primly shined. People became less unkempt and more well-kept. A few people walking around were poor, Joseph could tell, but the general population of this part of the city were the wealthy lords and ladies. *Oh yes, I'm here.* His eyes glistened with the light of opportunity.

Slipping into an alley away from the busy streets, he switched his jacket to the suave version and took off his hat to replace it with the bowler. He combed his hair, parting it from the centre with a moderate wave and tied a necktie around his high collar. This, combined with the waistcoat, completed the look. The last thing he needed was strange looks and odd glances from the locals as he assessed the chosen house. He wanted to look like a fine gentleman admiring the architecture of his neighbour, not a penniless crook eyeing up his next job.

Joseph took to the streets again but with a more elegant nature this time, and even managed to gain a nod of acceptance from a fellow gentleman strolling down the pavement with his finely clipped moustache under his rising top hat. He tipped his hat politely in return, 'good day.' *Appearances and quick judgements. That's what it's about. Who's got time for anything else? As long as you look rich, they'll accept you as one of their own.*

With a brisk pace and a keen eye, he found a row of glorious houses that could only be bought by the illustrious or inherited by the rich; somewhere people like him could only dream of. For what it was worth, the architecture was grand; the very age of the bricks of every house ripened this street to another level of value. Greenery was trimmed, pavements were swept, gates were freshly painted– suddenly Joseph suspected money was not the only importance within these places. No, it was also the *image* that had to be upheld. If you didn't keep your house tidy, then obviously you weren't supposed to be living here. He tutted; all the streets of London rife with rampant poverty, disease and death and the people with the money were only spending it on the upkeep of their own presentation. It was a different world, fortunately it was a world Joseph Winter was familiar with.

His eyes flittered from one house to the next, strolling at a fair pace but keeping it casual until he caught sight of it. It was just as Mad Vinny had said. There was a padlock on the gates and a path that led through a front garden leading up to two stairs to the front entrance. Two potted trees stood sentinel on either side of the large oak door, standing sentinel within the porch. The front bay windows were illuminated orange where the glow of a fire and gaslights lit the room and silhouettes could be seen wandering through. The owners were in and the servants were tending to their needs. It was Tuesday; he had three days to prepare until the house was empty. Then, he could begin.

Like a mental notebook, his mind immediately flipped open the first page. It was time to get to work.

All day he stuck around the area, taking occasional strolls to see the comings and goings of the community but mostly to see if anyone were to accidentally pass by and witness his doings.

At four in the afternoon when daylight began to wane, he walked down the alley next to the house and checked there were no windows overlooking the drain which could give him away. There wasn't. *Check.* He pace was slow, his eyes searching, finding, finding . . . found the drain buried in the cobbles next to the wall. *Check.* He stopped over it and looked left and right– it was clear, no one was watching. Digging his hands in his pockets, he peered at the ground, making sure Vinny's tips were indeed factual. After a moment of looking, he discovered they were. *Check.*

Two small handles lay buried in the ground, hidden amongst the stones, and lay a shoulder length apart two feet away from the drain. Narrowing his vision, he spotted the line of separation where the ground did not join. It was very well concealed; any passer-by would have missed it. Joseph on the other hand, knew what to look for, and now knew his way into the house. A sly smile hooked the corners of his lips, his fingers twitched, and his hands began to sweat. Now his excitement began to dwell; the job was plausible but now it was possible.

As the night fell into its dull gloom and a slight fog swept in amongst the burning links lighting the streets, Joseph Winter walked home smoking a cigarette and prepared for day two.

Wednesday passed without much change except from a few new faces taking a morning stroll. He stayed out later, watching, making sure nothing unexpected happened. Then he tracked a complex route away from the house that included a refuge. It was his protocol, a back-up failsafe in case things turned sideways in the middle of a job– in case he had to abort and hole up until night came. Nothing happened to report, and he returned home feeling confident and ready for day three.

Thursday, Joseph prepared further and sought other escape routes and possible sanctuaries, inspected the area further and scoured for anything that might intercept, although nothing of the sort presented itself. He sighed, relieved. Since all was ready, he was clear to go.

There was only one thing left to decide, and that was when to begin.

'It's tomorrow, an't it? When you're going to do it.' Lucy spoke up as she walked up to the fire where he sat reading the newspaper beside it, smoking with a mug of tea. She had a tone with her voice that Joseph did not care for right now. 'I can tell you know. I *do live* with you.'

He looked up. She had hardly spoken to him all week, obviously knowing there was no changing his stubborn mind. He cleared his throat, 'I had planned for it, yes.'

Her eyes looked down, 'Joseph, please don't do this. I know we don't see eye to eye sometimes and we manage to pull through but this, your work, it's got to stop. It an't right, and all this for a poxy treasure map– it's . . . it's mad. Preposterous.'

Joseph put his paper down not intending it to be forceful, yet it was anything but. 'It *will* stop. I won't take on as many jobs after this.'

'You said that about the last one and the last one before that!'

'It's as you said Lucy, we've always managed to pull through. How come this one is different? Besides, it's a bloody bit of paper somewhere in the house. It's not as if I'm cabbaging her pearls!'

'That's why you shouldn't go along with it, if it's not much you're stealing then why bother stealing it in the first place?!'

He could see her point, but it wasn't enough. 'Vinny said there'll be something there, as valuable as a pot of gold– all I have to do is find that pot of gold.'

'If Vinny told you to jump off a cliff 'cause there's some shiny coins at the bottom, would you do it?' she folded her arms.

He paused to think about it.

The frustration was growing, Joseph could see it in her face. She nodded with pursed lips, 'you know what, I'm done.' And she left the room.

Joseph took a deep breath ready to call out for her but then exhaled and left her to walk away, not wanting to cause another argument. He was sorry, truly, he was, although his apologetic feeling was short-lived due to the philosophy he lived by– to live within the moment. What happens, happens. Plus, he never started something without an intent on finishing and already this this escapade had begun, and he intended on completing it. Besides, everything had checked out; what could go wrong?

After a restless night's sleep, he woke early and, grabbing his costume, was heading for the door. The only reception received was a cold glare as he slipped on his jacket and grabbed his cane, then she walked away without saying a word. 'I'm sorry,' he called out to her, 'this is my job, this is what I'm good at. I'll be back later.' She didn't understand, she wasn't a part of this game; the game which Joseph Winter was a professional. Dangerous and morally wrong, he couldn't help but to be attracted to its flaws, addicted to the intensity. Yet, as he walked out a pang of guilt pulled his face down. *I'm sorry Lucy, I hope you'll forgive me soon*, he thought but didn't say. It would only start off another conflict and that was not what he needed on a day like today.

Closing the door behind him he took to the streets with a roll-up between his lips, puffing smoke into the murky morning. The links were still alight, yet their glow was hazy through the thick cloud of smoke, as was the glow from shop windows. It was cold and penniless vagabonds warmed their holey cotton-gloved hands against fires burning in metal baskets.

Nerves began to take hold on the walk; his stomach twisting itself into knots and despite trying to keep a clear head, his thoughts strayed and frayed like fibres at the end of a rope. Taking a calming breath, he walked around to the bakers again where he slipped a warm pastry in his pocket for the journey. His mind was clearing, that didn't mean his stomach had to be too.

Walking steadily past skittering skinny mongrel dogs and people wrapped in long coats and comforters, his feet had been taking the directions for him and when he looked up, he saw he was nearly there. Slipping his jacket off he switched into the wealthy businessman and prepared himself. The only thing he'd forgotten was his handkerchief. Other than that, he was ready.

Walking past the houses of the district, his palms began to sweat, and a ball lodged in his throat making it hard to swallow. Passing the neighbouring houses made his muscles tighten with the suspense; the air suddenly felt thicker. He flicked the butt of his cigarette away. Approaching his chosen abode, he suddenly felt a flicker of enlightenment: a glimmer of the thrill, the feeling during and after the climax. It was only this bubbling apprehension that warped him in tension, and he knew it, which was why his feet kept walking and the target closed in.

Suddenly a kitchen-maid exited the gates, locking them behind her and began to walk his way toward the market, crossing the entrance to the alley and approaching him. His stomach churned; his face dropped. *She's not due out for another hour!* His pace faltered slightly, he stumbled and coughed; it was enough for the young maid to notice. She eyed him strangely then remembered her manners. 'Good morning, sir. Are you alright?' she asked as she slowed down in front of him.

Joseph quickly coughed and mumbled a, 'morning, yes, I'm fine.' And tried to be on his way but she spoke up again.

'Begging your pardon for being so bold, sir, but we've been noticin' you around here the past few days and was wondering what your business might be, and if I could be of any service?'

The conman stopped walking and paused, *she's only a kitchen-maid and she thinks you're a wealthy businessman, she'll believe anything you tell her right now. Remember your character.* He turned back, 'how well do you know this area?' he asked in the finest accent he could muster.

She paused a moment. 'Sir? I don't understand.'

'I asked if you know this area well?' he repeated.

Eventually, she nodded, her bonnet tied neatly into her dark brown hair. 'Yes. I've lived here for several years.'

Joseph nodded and smiled, leaning on his cane to emphasise a wounded foot in explanation for his faltering step. 'Excellent! Charles Pettering, how do you do?' he held a gloved hand out for her to shake. *A gentleman wouldn't do that! What gentleman wants a shake from a kitchen-maid! You fool!* Nonetheless, she shook it and he rambled on, 'I have recently transferred here from Birmingham and am currently living with some colleagues of mine. Alas, seeing as my work is looking to be of a more permanent nature, I've decided on investing in another dwelling and was considering moving-' *no, buying! Buying! Not moving!* '-or buying a property around the area. It seems nice enough from the outside, but one can never be so sure these days,' he uttered a shallow chuckle. 'Tell me, what is the neighbourhood like?'

A glimmer of a smile appeared on her face, then she snatched it away to retain her professionalism.

She's sold.

'It's quiet and friendly. The people keep mainly to themselves. What part of the district are you looking at, sir? If you don't mind me being so bold?'

'Hmm.' He feigned a thought, 'this area, mainly. My heart is drawn to peace and quiet whereas my eyes are drawn to finer things. The architecture around here is rather beautiful, I must say. A certain grandeur you can only get in a capital city.'

'Yes, the houses here are quite lovely.'

'Indeed. Are there many for sale, pray tell?'

She paused in thought, 'not that I know of. Most of these properties were bought a long time ago and are to be inherited. I would suggest looking down the neighbouring district, the last I heard there were some properties selling over there.' She hesitated, eying him suspiciously, 'forgive me sir, but you don't seem to have a Birmingham accent.'

Shit! With a quick wit, he spooned another lie, 'I was born and raised on the outskirts of this city actually. I've lived in Birmingham for the past year, but it was not enough to secure a strong accent. Besides, I never was one for that particular tongue; it was not kind to my ears.' Feigning a thought, he swiftly changed the conversation. 'When I do move here though, I'm unsure as to how many servants to employ, since previously servants have been granted to me forthright. Might I be so bold as to ask how many your master and mistress employ?'

'Of course, sir, there are eight altogether.'

He smiled, 'Ah, that sounds just the right amount.'

Suddenly he felt her eyes on him again, spotting the cuts and bruises he'd tried hard to conceal. Gulping, he pursed his lips, 'I know. Awful, isn't it? I happened to be ambushed the other day by a group of rowdy vagabonds and they tried to rob me. I tried to defend myself, alas they were too quick. I'm sure the criminals of this city seem to be getting wilier.' *Perhaps too wily.* He pulled out his pocket watch and clicked the crown and feigned a sigh, 'I must be going. Thank you for your help. Good day to you.' He tipped his hat politely and gave a charming smile.

She nodded in return, giving a slight smile, 'you're welcome. Good day to you, sir.'

They parted ways, Joseph feeling confident his ruse had worked in his favour, now knowing the exact number of servants in employment; the exact amount to look out for and evade. He suddenly felt a slight guilt for the poor kitchen-maid, she'd just allowed him to burgle the house she worked in– luckily for her she wouldn't know a thing; he'd be in and gone by the time she returned.

Strolling down the alley, he scanned the ground and found the handles. Looking left, there was no one coming or going, watching or spying. Looking right, there wasn't a soul in sight, the streets were quiet, the air was ripe with anticipation. 'Time to get to work.' He muttered to himself and crouched, gripping the handles and pulling them upwards, heaving the large slab of stone and mortar up from the rest, breaking the hidden seal and revealing a dark tunnel underneath. There was a reason why he brought his cane; today it was to become a prop.

He slipped the cane underneath and propped up the slab before ducking under and taking to the stairs below. Turning, he took his cane and slowly lowered the slab back down.

By his calculations, he had an hour and a half before the maid returned and anyone would notice.

An hour and a half . . . beginning now.

Chapter Three

A darkness engulfed him; dank and sickly. A smell of trapped moisture smothered his nose and made him cough. It stank, the air was tainted with the thick mossy aroma. It had been a long time since anyone had been down here from the thick wedges and green fluffy pillows sprouting green slime from the walls of the drain and coating the stairs. He took out his watch and by the light of the drain above he marked the time at twelve noon– promising to remember to check every so often. Time was of the essence. Reaching the bottom of the stairs, he passed through the shafts of light from the drain above into the tunnel beyond, his shoes clopping on the solid stone ground and echoing through the empty void.

His pace was brisk, he didn't slow or stop even when a family of rats scuttled under his feet, squeaking as they scarpered away. The rats in the dark didn't frighten him– running out of time did.

The tunnel stretched until the light of the drain had shrunk in his vision. *I must be somewhere near the house now, surely!* Just as he began to wonder where the tunnel led to it suddenly presented itself with a dead end; a complete blockade of three tall walls.

Joseph spared no time with panicking that this was a true dead end; he instead confided in logic: if this was an escape shaft then it must be connected to the house; there must be a way in and a way out. Or in his case, the way *out* was *his* way in. With outstretched arms, he felt the walls around him until his hands brushed upon a piece of wood; quickly sweeping over it he discerned it as an object– an object with purpose, giving a possibility. He smiled in the dark and pulled the ladder out and leaned it against the wall.

With a trying test of a foot, the first rung felt sturdy enough to hold his weight; he took to it and climbed to the top where he felt the ceiling of the tunnel in the dark. A hard surface knocked against his fingers and running his hands along it, he felt planks: it was wood. He felt further and found hinges. If there were hinges, that meant something could swing open. If something could swing that meant he had found a door.

Placing both palms on the ceiling he gently pushed and felt movement, he lowered back down again. He pushed harder and felt the wood pull apart from each other, the hinges squeaking, but no shaft of light ushered its way in. 'Hmm.' *That's odd.* He pushed the door up and open and climbed up out of the tunnel and into a dark room. Carefully, he closed the trap door behind him and took a breath. A spicy aroma intoxicated his nostrils and a musty smell accompanied the inhalation. *Dark room, spicy smell; I know where I am.* At once the answer came to him. *I'm in the pantry. The cupboard for spices and salts.* But then a more important thought overtook, *I'm in the house.*

A fleeting thought gripped his mind; to run out, search each room, spot every corner, scour every nook, scan every cranny, turn over tables and turn over furniture, looking and searching and eyeballing everywhere for the item until he found it. Then the moment passed . . . and instead he allowed logic in to conjure an intricately woven plan, never forgetting to leave his trademark: nothing. There was no trademark. Never leave a trace. Never let them know of another presence. *As of now Trace, you're a ghost.*

Closing his eyes, he mused. *The most common place to keep something hidden would be . . . somewhere secret, somewhere only the owner would know. Somewhere random but somewhere personal so if ever forgotten it could be remembered there.*

Possibilities could be . . . bedroom, drawing room, parlour, attic, cellar. Hidden somewhere in something to keep it out of sight.

And if the owners don't even know they've got it . . . then it'll still be in the same place as it was left when this house was passed down to them.

Which means . . . it could be anywhere at all.

It's got to be somewhere. Somewhere safe, somewhere dry, somewhere unthought of. Come on Trace, think outside the box. If you had a treasure map, where would you hide it?

He concluded an answer half out of a rough guess, half out of basic logic. *A personal place, like my bedroom. And in this case the bedroom would probably be upstairs, on whatever floor, far away from the entrance, keeping everything private.* Trace wasted no time in quibbling thoughts any longer. Every minute he spent thinking was less time doing.

Quickly now, he removed his jacket and hat and placed them under a shelf; they would restrict movement. He took off his necktie and undid the top button; he needed free unrestricted breaths. His cane he lay over the top of the folded pile and took his shoes off: experience had shown him socks were helpful tools; no noise, no mess, no trace at all. The ground beneath his feet was cool and dry. He took a breath in . . . and out. He was ready.

With a light touch, he reached out for the latch, unhooked it and pushed the door slowly outwards, making sure the hinges did not squeak. He poked his trepid head out and glanced left and right. Left was a corridor leading further into the kitchen and scullery; the walls smooth and painted white, and to the right was a closed door. A smell of cooking wafted down the walls and clouded around his nose; the chef was at work, and that meant the housemaids and scullery maids were washing clothes and dishes, or upstairs dusting and sweeping. But then there were also the butlers to consider. The kitchen-maid had said there were eight altogether. *Curse the bloody rich with their bloody lot of servants!* As for immediate sight, though, it was all clear and he was free to move.

He stepped outside and closed the door behind him, making sure to remember which door he had emerged from and opened the door to his right, darted up the stone stairs where he reached the top landing door and stopped. Above him was a descending jagged wooden ceiling, telling him he was beneath a staircase. His heart pounded loudly in his head. Everything was silent except for that constant thump. *Control it, don't let it control you.* He took a deep silent breath and slowed his heart down, the last thing he needed was to be running around this house panting like a hot dog.

He lifted the latch to the door and carefully pulled it to him, peeking through the gap to check the coast was clear, before stepping through.

The bottom of a staircase descended above him, leading to a grand entrance hall with an intricately designed carpet beneath a great chandelier; an impressive welcome to whomever strode through the front door directly ahead. In the patterned walls either side of the front door were closed oak doors, leading to the drawing room and dining room, he supposed. *Blimey so many rooms for just one house! No doubt they've got one of them new fandangled toilets that can flush too.*

Stealthily, he stepped out from under the staircase and walked into the hall spotting two houseplants potted in fine china vases in the corners of the room, before spying a large painting through the staircase banister; its golden frame boldened by the patterned burgundy wallpaper it rested against. It depicted helpless survivors holding onto the fallen mast of their wrecked ship as angry waves bellowed rage in the dying light of a setting sun. Trace recognised it; he'd seen it once before in an art pamphlet given to him a few years ago, which turned out to be a wonderful reserve for his tobacco when he ran short on newspaper. Nonetheless it was an interesting creation; the colours were bright, vivid and inspiring yet displayed such a stressful, unforgiving scene– a rare dichotomy of light combined with dark; brutality of life combined with the circle of life; hope to the hopeless. *The sailors don't have much time left,* he observed, *and neither do I.* He could almost feel the seconds ticking against his chest on his pocket watch. Looking around the room it was clear, so he quickly checked and vaulted up the carpeted stairs to the next floor.

He reached a long corridor with more houseplants in fine china vases upon small decorative tables dotted between three separate doors, and upon hearing muffled sounds coming from the door immediately ahead, he scurried to the next and nearest door and, upon checking the coast was clear, slipped through it.

A luxuriant room filled his vision. *Good Lord. All that poverty out there whilst they're tucked up in here. Not a bad spot.* The entire wall to his left was a bookcase housing numerous books and ornaments, dusty busts and clasped volumes, whilst two luxurious sofas, a chaise longue and numerous tables with candles waiting to be lit surrounded the lavish fireplace in the opposite wall. There were cushioned footstools and another table holding a decanter of port and two clean glasses. He stepped in, feeling the carpeted floor beneath his socks and spotted more paintings hanging on the furthest wall. *A reading room, of course. It wouldn't be in here. I need a bedroom. I need to get higher.*

Once the sounds of the passing person had faded, he backed out of the room carefully, closed the door and stepped over to the door directly ahead of the stairs. Opening it quietly, he saw the staircase ahead switched back on itself to become a U-shaped staircase and wasted no time in climbing it to the next floor where another corridor stretched to his right. Pursing his lips, he wondered; there were five doors in total: one of them had to be a bedroom. *I can't try them all. Look closer.*

Each were wooden and expensive; he didn't even need to hazard a guess to know that the doorknobs themselves would cost more than a worker's wage. He looked for one in particular though; one with a lock. A lock meant privacy, and privacy meant personal space, which meant a bedroom.

With feet barely making a sound upon the patterned rug, he shuffled to the doors and found what he was looking for. A lock. Turning the knob gently, he prayed for the lock to not be in use. It wasn't.

The door was open, and Trace peeked inside.

A large room opened before him, and to his relief it was a bedroom. A king-sized bed complete with spiralling oak pillars and an expensive canopy with heavy decorative drapes rested in the middle-left wall of the room opposite a grand hearth. The duvet and pillows were scuffled; *the maids haven't been in yet. Tut tut.* Mahogany night tables stood on either side of the bed with crystal-bottomed paraffin lamps on them. Paintings of plants hung on the floral wallpaper and a large oriental rug adorned the varnished wooden floor. A decorative padded and patterned chair sat serenely in the far-right corner of the room next to a window where heavy floor-length curtains were closed, and daylight struggled to illuminate through; it was dim and translucent but just enough to see by.

He entered the room trying to keep his heart below his throat and closed the door behind him. *The map could be anywhere in here.* There were a few possibilities; under the bed was a classic, locked in a drawer was another thought, hidden in a chest would just be perfectly appropriate. *Hmm.* As quietly as he could, he walked into the room . . . and noticed the duvet was not just scuffled . . . but occupied. It was clear now why the maids hadn't come in to clean. The lady of the house was still sleeping.

A fresh bead of sweat trickled down his brow; a new level of stress twanged the nerves up his spine. *Curse you Vinny! Curse you!* What was she still doing here?! She was meant to be out along with her husband leaving a house full of servants. With her here, the chances of this escapade being a success were very slim indeed. And with him entering the very same room she was sleeping in to find the hidden map made the chances of success even slimmer. His chance wasn't even a wedge in thickness now. It was a thin, measly ration runt of a chance. *But it's still a chance.* He gulped; *I must be even quieter.*

In the murky light, he spotted a bottle of opium and a cup on her night table. Now he understood; she was ill, a factor he hadn't considered in his planning. An expert like him should've taken it into consideration; it was an amateur's mistake, a mishap that would cost him everything if he made a sound. The situation had turned very delicate indeed, as delicate as the fine china vases this house was riddled with.

Come on Trace, you still have a job to do. Get looking. He glided to the bed and crouched low, holding his breath and lifted the curtain that covered the bottom of the bed. Disappointment came in the form of balls of dust. There was no treasure map here. Biting his lip, he turned and sat against the bed and looked over at the decorative chair, to the expensive chest of drawers in the corner, to the walnut dressing table decorated with numerous necklaces and rings.

The magpie within was suddenly drawn to a fine necklace and pretty ring and before he knew what he was doing, he made his way over to it. He picked them up from the rest; they were shinier, prettier; valuable. His hands looked pale, ghostlike in the mirror as he held the shiny jewellery. *Compensation, if nothing is found,* he shrugged and slipped the jewellery into his pocket. He stepped back toward the door contemplating other possibilities.

Suddenly a floorboard underneath him squeaked, sounding like a bomb exploding. Startled, he froze, daring not to move another inch. Not to breathe. A murmur was heard behind him, and a scuffle of movement. Sweat ran in streams, his shirt clung to his back.

The woman had turned over . . . and was now facing him. He struggled to supress the urge to vomit.

Time seemed to pass rigidly, each second pounding as the second hand clunked, but the scream and frightful reaction he was expecting never came. In a glacial motion, Trace turned his head.

Her eyes were shut.

Relief rained over him like a shower. She was still asleep. A surge of adrenalin hit, suddenly he wanted to breathe and run and fly, but he couldn't– all it would take was for her eyelids to open, that was all. Then it would be over, and he would be dead and buried. Yet he was still in the game . . . for now.

Glaring down to the floorboard that had nearly given him away, he cursed it to the high heavens until something caught his eye. There were no nails in the section he'd stepped on. It was lifting slightly. To the owners this was nothing more than damp wood expanding, lifting and creating a nuisance; but to Trace, this was an opportunity, a tiny chance.

Crouching again, he slipped his fingers under the floorboard and pried it up higher to fit his hand beneath. It slipped up easily; no, this was not just damp wood. He felt around, probing the mysterious opening for anything of worth but only a piece of string managed to give him any satisfaction. There was nothing else down there but the string. If he could've sighed and swore, he would of.

Joseph pulled the string from the opening and noticed it was longer than he thought and ran through the slit where the floorboards joined. With interest rising like a curling wave, he pulled the string up and discovered it ran to a tiny slit in the bottom of the wall and with a slight tug a small folded piece of parchment appeared.

At first Trace had felt curious, but now the situation had nipped his interest, grabbing his attention and twirling it in a waltzing dance. Indignant to his sudden turn of luck, he untied the string and unfolded the corners, examining it enthusiastically, feasting his eyes upon . . . a torn-out page of a book. It wasn't the map, but it was something important. Why else would it have been placed there?

The top of the page identified its belonging to *Paradise Lost,* a book by John Milton. *What on earth? What is this?* He saw it was from Book Nine. He'd never read the book, but if he had he'd have learned of Genesis: the fall of mankind from the Garden of Eden. He frowned and scanned further, noticing some words had been underlined– random words that formed a sentence:

. . . all . . . is not lost . . .

. . . have . . . courage . . .

. . . never to submit . . . or yield . . .

It's a hidden message, my god. It's telling me to not give up. His eyes landed on the bottom of the page where a footnote had been written, although this was not a footnote; at a second glance this became something else, something separate, something for who-ever came across this piece of paper.

Written in handwriting against the rip near the tear were the words:

Find me and ye shall find

The message and the quotes clicked.

Trace folded the page and slipped it in his pocket before swiftly exiting from the room. He already knew where to go. Checking the path was clear, he darted back down the corridor, flew down the stairs to the one place he knew it would be. He reached the door at the bottom of the stairs and opened it ajar, checked, then skulked out from it and slithered to the door of the reading room where he found it gloriously empty.

Paradise Lost is up there somewhere. The thief stared in awe at the sheer size of it, a great archive stretching from floor to ceiling. There must've been a hundred volumes there, over a million pages, over a billion words; and only one book of importance. One book that mattered. He stalked to it, eyes scanning over the shelves to different volumes, genres, titles, works, chronicles, epics, some leather-bound, some hardback: a treasure trove of information. Works beginning with Z were at the bottom shelf, he spotted, and gazing up the shelves he saw Y, X and W scattered along next to each other. *They're alphabetised, which means that . . .* P was on a higher shelf, beyond his reach.

A ladder was attached to the bookshelf and offered movement via a wheel and track mechanism built into the middle shelf. Trace saw it and smiled, it was not just a ladder, but a prayer answered. He hurried and pulled it along to section P as carefully as he could without creating noise and immediately began to climb. Tilting his head, he flicked through the titles, sifting, searching, until he saw it. There, in between two leather-bound books, was *Paradise Lost.*

Trembling with excitement, he gulped a dry chaff throat and slid the book out as carefully as he could, tucked it under his arm and descended the ladder before hurrying over to the nearest table and opening it. Some corners were folded over and the pages were yellowed, faded with age but the ink remained bold enough to read. Flicking through the chapters, he reached Book Nine and began to turn each page individually in rapid flits, searching for what should have been there.

Where is it, where is it, where is it, come on . . . another bead of nervous sweat trickled down the side of his face and into his sideburns. Another wave of nausea breached. He hadn't checked his watch in a while; the maid would come back soon and if she entered the house, she would recognise his face and see straight through the lie he'd fed this morning. The image made him shudder. It would be the end of him.

Suddenly he found a tear in the centre between two pages and his green eyes gleamed. *The missing page!* But to his great dismay, there was nothing there. Just the ripped segment of a torn page.

Trace frowned. *What? This can't be it, surely* . . . Digging his hand into his pocket, he pulled out the folded page and opened it up, placing it back in the book where it should've been . . . and there, a revelation was found.

Turning the page, Joseph saw that those six words added onto the paper were in fact half of a sentence. The other half was written up the base of the page, where the message would be hidden in the crease of the book. Only those who looked for it would have seen it; it was so simple, yet so effective.

Trace read the words again then turned the book to read along the base of the page.

*Find me and ye shall find... the next step of the hunt.
Seek where I came from.*

His eyes shot back to the empty slot where *Paradise Lost* had been. *Up there!* Snatching the page back, he closed the book and ran to the ladder where he climbed to the gap and considered the gloomy opening. Nothing was there; it was empty. He stuck a hand into it, groping the wooden shelf for anything extraordinary . . . and brushed against something small and hard.

As gently as he could, he picked it up and pulled it out. It was not what he was expecting, although he was not sure what he expected at all. To his surprise, he found between his fingers a small pink and cream conch shell no bigger than his finger. Eyebrows furrowing in confusion, Trace was befuddled. *What's this got to do with anything?*

Keeping to his policy, Trace slotted the book back into its place, climbed down the ladder and wheeled it back to where it had been. Now he had a chance to fully examine. It wasn't the map, but it was so random he classed it as coincidence– or purposeful? He turned the shell over in his palm.

A bell rang from somewhere in the house. Footsteps could be heard brushing over the rugs and carpets and muffled voices made him look up in alarm. *As long as they don't come in, I'll be fine.* After a few tense breaths, he exhaled and looked back down to the conch shell . . . when suddenly the doorknob turned, and daylight flooded in. Like a rat he scarpered out of sight behind a sofa, not sure whether he was quick enough.

Footsteps scuffled toward the bookcase and stopped as the servant examined, then pulled out a book and scuffled back to the door, closing it behind them.

Trace sighed through his nose, letting out the tense breath he'd been holding. The servant had almost seen him! Thankfully, his reactions had been rapid, and the sofa was large, allowing him room to hide. Now that problem had been sorted, he looked at the other problem in his hand.

The conch shell stared up at him innocently, its whitewash colours perfectly blended around its twisted shape. Small spikes moulded up from the main cone, enabling it to sit on his palm. He still didn't understand; this linked with nothing, certainly not *Paradise Lost* and certainly not to the next part of the hunt. *Maybe this is nothing, just an accident.* At the thought, his hopes dampened slightly. Still, it nagged at him. *What would a shell be doing there?* He picked it up and peered into the shell itself with eagle eyes.

There, rolled up and tucked in the tight space, was a small piece of parchment.

His fingers fumbled with anticipation; he struggled to pick it out, yet with focus he pried it from its slot and rolled it open.

> *Always cease to look behinnd,*
> *Look ahead to future tymes.*
> *Back here, back there againn,*
> *Up until thee very end.*
> *Don't wave this moment goodbye.*

Alright . . . what? Trace read through it three times and still didn't understand. Was it a poem? A riddle? A clue? The errors made it impossible to understand. *That's why it's a perfect clue. Read it again.*

Examining, suddenly the first words of the first three lines made their own sentence. *Always look back up.* Trace pursed his lips.

That can't be it. Look harder. This time he picked at the errors; "behinnd" should only have one N. "Tymes" should've been spelt with an I as if referring to time, which it appeared to be since it mentioned the future. "Againn" should have been spelt with one N. *And thee? What about that?* Sometimes holy scriptures mentioned "thee", but he wasn't sure about this one; somehow it didn't seem to fit. *In that case the "the" has an extra E.* Trace looked up, lost. *This doesn't make any se–*

Suddenly he saw it. It wasn't just a clue. It was a puzzle.

The errors were made deliberately.

Together, the extra or misspelled letters formed the word: NINE.

Nine. *What in the name of Mister J Christ does that have to do with anything?! Nine what? Letters? Clues? Bloody conch shells? What?!* He read it through again and suddenly the last line caught his eye. There were no errors in it.

Don't wave this moment goodbye.

No errors? Perhaps it's to do with Nine? Maybe Nine can be applied to it? His mind whirred. *Nine goodbyes? Nine moments? Nine waves?* His mind clicked.

Nine waves? The Ninth Wave. The Ninth Wave! The randomness of the conch shell was suddenly clear to him. It was a seashell . . . and The Ninth Wave was a sailor's phrase of the biggest wave after the build-up in a storm. It was also the name of a specific painting of the sea. An angry sea under a beautiful sunset. Suddenly the link between the clues became apparent.

Shoving the note and shell in his pocket, Trace bolted for the door. He stopped and checked. It was clear. He closed the door behind him; stopped, checked, clear. He ran through the corridor and descended the stairs halfway, stopping to view the wall on his left. The painting. *The Ninth Wave. That bloody pamphlet came in handy after all. I was staring at the clue earlier on!*

He stared up at the large painting in wonder. The colours appeared even brighter now as if they too were eager to reveal the truth they had been hiding.

Trace stepped to the frame and peered into the edges, checking nothing was tucked into them. There wasn't. He checked the painting itself. Nothing but careful brush strokes. *Behind it?* Placing his fingers on the edge of the frame, he gently pried it from the wall and peered behind . . . and saw a piece of paper poking out from the back.

Like a child at a sweetshop, he quickly plucked the piece and held it out to the light. It was a small piece of torn newspaper. If it had ever fallen out it would've been mistaken for rubbish, but in it, Joseph saw an importance that could not be missed, especially when he noticed some words had been underlined to form a sentence.

Look

> **For**

> **Length**

> > **Of black and white and**

> **See**

> > **Flatly.**

Look for length of black and white and see flatly? Once again, his mind was picked up and thrown away; this didn't make sense either. *It's not going to make sense, you fool! It's meant to make you think!* He started on the only thing that did make sense: the length of black and white. *What's black and white?* He looked back to the message again and suddenly he saw the answer. It was right there all along. Right there in his hand. The piece of newspaper. A length of black and white.

I need to find some newspapers! Rapidly, he ascended the stairs, taking two at a time, his socks skimming the carpet; stopped at the top; checked; the coast was clear, and he ran back to the door and entered the reading room. He searched but could only find recent newspapers piled neatly into a stack. He picked up the top one and scanned the pages; they were the news stories he had read yesterday and had torn from for a fresh supply. *Christ, I could do with a smoke.* Despite his efforts, nothing jumped out at him. He pulled the newspaper up to his eye and looked against it at a horizontal angle to "see flatly" and scanned up and down the page. Still, nothing came to him. Then logic returned. *These are too recent; this hunt must've been laid out long before yesterday. I need older papers.* He was about to make a dash for the bookshelf when he stopped himself. Why would the owners keep newspapers from an age before they were even born, or whenever this course was set? They wouldn't, they would throw them out or stash them away, it was all old news. They wouldn't be on the bookshelf anyway, not where the popular material was. *Something an't right.* Suddenly the answer of newspapers didn't seem to fit anymore.

It had to be something else.

Length of black and white and see flatly? Nothing came to mind.

Length of black and white and see flatly?? His mind was blank.

Length of black and white and see flatly?! Frustration squeezed his mind, making it impossible to think. *I need answers!*

Suddenly he heard more bells and a collection of footsteps coming down the stairs from above. More than one pair this time. There were mutterings; a woman was talking, and a maid was answering. The lady of the house had awoken and was coming down to the same floor.

I am not getting trapped in here. Abort. Trace wasted no time.

Before the lady and her servant reached the door at the bottom of the staircase, the thief bolted from the reading room and swooped down the stairs heading for the door that led back to the kitchens and pantry where his jacket, hat and cane lay waiting. He wasn't going to risk everything for the sake of agitation, stubbornness and a problem he could not solve. His reputation, although supported, was fragile if word slipped of being seen. No, it was not worth it. He was escaping, aborting; time was up. The lady was awake; servants would be crawling around this area now. It was a hopeless and reckless quest to sneak around unnoticed. *I'll try again next week . . .*

He reached the bottom and ran into the hall about to turn for the door leading to the kitchens when suddenly it began to open. In a mad dash, he changed course and vaulted through the door to the hall's right and entered the drawing room.

It looked so similar to the other rooms Trace wondered where their creativity for interior design lay. With nervous eyes, he spotted more houseplants, more luxury rugs and furniture, patterned wallpaper, heavy floor-length curtains and padded sofas surrounding the fireplace. *Jesus what is it with the rich and their damn cluttered rooms and patterned wallpaper. Give it a few years and it'll all be out of fashion.* The only difference was the grand piano standing in the centre of the room used to entertain guests. Its black sheen glinting, it had been recently dusted and polished.

Trace halted abruptly and gulped, wiping the sweat from his forehead. Slowly, he stepped over to the piano and scanned its impeccably clean keys. A length of black and white . . . a possible answer. The most probable he had. Was it reliable enough? *The keys, it must be something to do with them.* They gleamed at him boldly. A proud, neat line of black and white, capable of creating a messy jumble or a legendary masterpiece if ordered correctly. He scratched his head. Symbols were engraved and varnished into the solid black wood above each of the keys. He hadn't a clue what any meant, yet he knew they made beautiful music when approached properly and they had strange markings, a hash and a small b, above the letters to clarify what tone they played. His eagle eye scouring, he spied the engravings and noticed there were notes classed as "C". His eyes widened as possibilities broadened.

He'd read somewhere that the small markings meant a sharp tone or a flat tone.

Realisation slapped him around the face harder than any hand could.

His heart thumped in his head. His clammy palms were slick, the knots in his back entwined and suddenly, with a glint in his eye, Joseph Winter understood the riddle and could now see flatly.

In a split second, he made his decision. He was too far in this hunt now to call it off and come back another day; he had to see the end and hopefully collect what he'd come here for, but now it was going to be harder and the risk of getting caught even higher. Not only because the lady of the house was awake and the servants were flittering back and forth to care for her whims, but because the next clue could only be unlocked by playing a musical note which drew profound unwanted attention. A ghost never left traces and never made a sound; a piano would.

There was a way to play the note and still get away unseen though, if only he could treat time as if he were holding a large glass chandelier– with the utmost of care, consideration and respect. One slip, one drop, one step in the wrong direction would cost him and cost him dearly and his fates would come shattering to the floor. As he stood at the piano listening to his heart thump loudly, he wondered how loudly it would play. True, the door was shut but with servants coming and going, he wasn't sure whose ears would prick up to the sound of a rogue note. It was a risk.

Trace stretched to get a view inside the instrument, then looked down at the piano keys. His pulse a drum roll, he saw a C flat symbol engraved beneath a B key. C Flat, that's what he guessed it to be, and decided the C Flat key he had to press was the middle one, central to the piano. He wasn't sure, but he had to be. There was only one chance. He wiped his sweaty hand on his shirt and took a tense breath. *Just do it.*

He lowered his finger to the C Flat key and pressed down hard, holding for a few seconds.

The contraption behind built into the piano was set into play; strings pulled, chords struck, and the note rung out loudly into the drawing room– perfectly tuned and surprisingly loud. His eyes were drawn to the one damper that kicked up in reaction to the key being pressed . . . and there, underneath the small wooden object, was a small key.

Immediately he pulled his finger up. The sound ceased and he scrambled around to the edge of the piano and leaned in, finding the damper. Reaching over, he pushed his hand in between the contraption underneath the C Flat note until his fingers caught hold of the key. He pulled it out, clutching it tightly in his palm and now understood. It was ironic, *the one key I need hidden amongst a long row of other keys.* It was so blindly simple it became covert.

The seconds ticked on. He hoped no one had been close enough to hear. Trace opened his palm to see the small key and saw attached to the hoop was a small label. This time there were no riddles, no notes; only one word.

Attic.

Strangely, he found himself waiting for someone to come in to check the noise. Unlike his usual confidence, he found himself stalling. *Go, Joseph, go now!* Stepping to the door, he opened it and checked; no one was there. He slipped through and closed the door behind him. Then, as quick as a hare darting from the hunting fox, Trace darted for the staircase across the hall as fast as his socks could manage upon the woven rug. He clambered up the stairs two at a time and reached the top, stopped and peered to check the corridor was clear, before opening the door, checking again, then scurrying through. He vaulted up the staircase, turned, vaulted up the next set before stopping at the corridor of the third floor to think on the best way to the attic, and to let out his tense breath. *Places like this wouldn't have a hatch, they'd have a staircase. There must be another one.*

Wasting no time, Trace hurried to the closest door, checked, and was delighted to see another U-shaped staircase. *How much bloody room do these people need?!* He ran up them as fast as he could manage, the wooden stairs barely giving any sound as his feet whispered over them. He entered another floor that was sparsely furnished and cold, a row of basic beds lined the cracked walls and small windows made the room dingy; servants quarters, but he didn't stop to browse, he continued to climb until he reached the very top: the darkest and dustiest room of the house.

The attic was as creepy and murky as it was cobwebbed and moth-eaten. Clutter clung onto the sides and grew steadily like growing mould. He found a candle and picked out a match, lit it and then lit the candle, his eyes already scouring through the dim yet penetrative glow of the candlelight. He took a step and saw boxes, a table, a rolled-up rug with a couple of large books sitting beside. *Come on, where is it?* Frowning, Trace scanned further and eventually kneeled, moving another box out of the way only to find a bundle of old clothes, damp and moth-balled, and an empty box. As he moved the box out of the way it slipped from his fingers and toppled over . . . and a dull clunk thumped from within.

Cringing, wincing; he hoped no one heard. Peering down to the box, he allowed himself to wonder; those eagle eyes hungry for the one sight he wanted to see. Pulling the box up, he lifted the lid off . . . and saw a small object inside.

Breathing deeper, Joseph reached in and pulled out a small chest. A small key . . . for a small chest.

It was ornately designed with the metal framework welded onto the wood in a web-like fashion. Two metal handles gave easier handling, and the small lock peered at him with its one dark eye.

He sat the candle down and looked at the key in his fingers, and slowly inserted it into the lock and turned, hearing a soft click. The chest was unlocked, and Trace gently pulled back the lid.

A scroll of parchment lay inside, along with a compass. A compass he recognised. A compass given to him by his grandfather once, a compass he'd pawned to feed himself and his mother. Stunned, he hadn't seen it in years.

Carefully and mostly in shock, Trace reached in and pulled the two objects out with trembling hands. Indignant, the compass seemed like it was meant to be here with this scroll; and he was meant to find it, just as his grandfather had used it all those years ago on his expeditions. *This is fate, this treasure hunt is my destiny.* Slipping it in his pocket, Trace wasn't sure how to react, so he moved onto the second item. It was old paper; he could feel it. Its rough texture was like wrinkles on an aged face, lips waiting to tell secrets from a bygone era. As gently as he could, he rolled the paper back to see the contents.

Instead of a waving dotted line leading up to a bold X, a letter was waiting for him.

𝔚𝔥𝔬𝔪𝔢𝔳𝔢𝔯 𝔦𝔱 𝔪𝔞𝔶 𝔠𝔬𝔫𝔠𝔢𝔯𝔫,
𝔍𝔣 𝔶𝔬𝔲 𝔥𝔞𝔳𝔢 𝔣𝔬𝔲𝔫𝔡 𝔱𝔥𝔦𝔰 𝔩𝔢𝔱𝔱𝔢𝔯, 𝔱𝔥𝔢𝔫 𝔶𝔬𝔲 𝔥𝔞𝔳𝔢 𝔞 𝔠𝔥𝔞𝔫𝔠𝔢 𝔞𝔱 𝔟𝔢𝔦𝔫𝔤 𝔞 𝔭𝔞𝔯𝔱
𝔬𝔣 𝔞𝔫 𝔲𝔫𝔣𝔦𝔫𝔦𝔰𝔥𝔢𝔡 𝔩𝔢𝔤𝔢𝔫𝔡 𝔲𝔫𝔱𝔬𝔩𝔡 𝔱𝔬 𝔱𝔥𝔢 𝔞𝔤𝔢𝔰. 𝔗𝔥𝔢 𝔣𝔦𝔫𝔞𝔩 𝔭𝔞𝔤𝔢𝔰 𝔫𝔢𝔢𝔡

writing, and adventure awaits – only if you are worthy enough,
courageous enough and desperate enough to fill in the blank and
give it the ending it deserves. Treasure lie waiting . . .
If you can find it.

Seek far and seek wide,
to the heavens above, to earth's lapping tide.
Sail the seas, travel and learn,
Perhaps it's time to take your turn?
Hope is something you must not lose,
For only in this life can you choose.
If you are strong enough – then you can,
Set foot off the map to unchartered land,
Where the moon is welcomed and the sun is below,
Perhaps you'll chance upon her glow.
Days turn and turn, lost dates and dead-weights
But the days will not illuminate,
Under the stars and under the hills is where you must locate.
The end of days is what she seeks,
The edge of horizon is where Polaris weeps,
Bleeding in the black, crying in the night,
Wishing for the idol that lost its light.
Seek far, seek wide, lose yourself
. . . and find.

Trace looked up from the parchment, the hairs on the back of his
neck tingling. This was a poem, a treasure map– no, his thoughts
gave a clearer description; *this is an invitation.* An invitation to
seek a lost treasure, to be part of a legend lost to the ages.

He smiled.

He'd already accepted.

Chapter Four

The handle of the wicker basket dug in the crook of her arm as kitchen-maid Sylvia Brooks topped the pile of fresh vegetables with a bundle of carrots, their green stalks long and fresh. *That'll have to be the last of it,* she grunted with effort, her arm aching. Nonetheless, she felt she'd done well with the short amount of time she had. *I must start making a move back to the house.*

Other than the vegetables there was also some wrapped up meat for the evening meal, another bottle of opium for the lady of the house and a small bag of iced buns she thought would be a nice treat for the rest of the household when she returned. It was a Friday after all, and the master of the house was out. Not that he would mind the iced buns, however, unless they were for him; but as every Friday came and went Sylvia always brought a few treats back for the maids and butlers – they were always treasured and never noticed – there was never a crumb left, not a trace.

'Thank you, sir.' She smiled at the grocer and started making her way through the busy crowd. It bustled and was cacophonous, but it didn't bother her; she liked the feel of people around. The bustle of life made her feel a part of it and made a change from the same faces she saw everyday around the house. A few new faces could not stop looking at her though, as she passed a stall and felt the eyes of the fishmonger following her; she wanted to look back, to get a smile from the man, but she decided not to. Being only twenty-five and a pretty woman, she was used to getting looks from men in the markets; but for now, her duties lay with serving her master and mistress– Sylvia had worked too hard to give up her job for courting.

Despite all the faces she saw wandering around the market, looking and browsing, smiling and talking; her mind flashed back to the prominent face she had met earlier on, and her own face blushed. That new face; *Charles Pettering; that was his name*, had been a handsome one. Not only that but he was friendly to her, unlike her master or many of the neighbourhood that lived around the district. *He spoke to me like an equal, a friend.* She suddenly found herself hoping she'd see his face again, he said he was moving to somewhere around the area so perhaps she would– and she looked forward to it.

Sylvia exited the market and began her walk back carrying her laden basket. The mist of the morning had dissipated, retreating up to the thick clouds above, and a faint white sun slid across a gap squeezed between the buildings and timing came across her mind; *how long have I been gone?* Picking out her watch, she saw she needed a faster pace. *I've nearly been gone an-*

'-hour and a half.' Trace gulped, cursing his stupidity. After entering the tunnel at noon, he calculated he had five minutes remaining.

I've got five minutes to get out before the maid gets back! Joseph tucked his pocket watch away, his muscles tightening with the tension. The air in the attic suddenly felt sluggish and hard to breathe. How could he have been so careless? He should have checked sooner. *Never mind that now, focus on getting out!*

He rolled the parchment back up and tucked it in his back pocket, rolling his shirt over the top before slipping the compass in his pocket, picking up the boxes and placing them back where he'd found them. Blowing out the candle, darkness enveloped him; the only light he had to see by was from the staircase. Hurriedly, he stepped over to it and descended the first set to the servant's quarters where he checked the coast was clear, before descending further as quickly as his feet could manage. Upon reaching the door to the corridor, he stopped to catch his breath and to run through everything he'd touched and moved, making sure everything was back where he'd found it, looking just how he liked it: with no trace he'd been there. *You're a ghost, Trace. An apparition. Nothing more.*

That belief would become harder to keep to though. Ghosts floated and could move through walls; he could do neither.

Trace cracked open the door, checked, exited and closed the door behind him then ran across the landing to the next staircase where he stopped, casting a glance over to the bedroom where this hunt had all began; the door was open; she had not returned to it. *Damn.* He scurried down the stairs and stopped at the door, his heart hammering in his chest. *She's not in her room so she's got to be somewhere down here. Reading room, maybe drawing room, with servants crawling all over; oh Trace, you never make it easy, do you?*

Prying the door open by a slither, he peeped through the gap to find the landing empty and was just about to make a dash for the stairs ahead when a uniformed maid came climbing up the final steps, carrying a tray of freshly baked biscuits and a pot of tea. The smell of the biscuits was irresistible and triggered his stomach to gurgle; it was only then he realised how hungry he was. Food had to wait. Everything had to wait, including his future as a free man. It was in these next few moments that his future rested against. Once again, Trace found himself holding that glass chandelier, only this time he had less fingers and stood on one foot.

The maid reached the landing and turned right heading down the length of the corridor. *She must be in the reading room, why else would the maid be taking tea and biscuits that way?* Opening the door further, he took a gamble and peered out to look down the corridor. The door to the reading room was open and voices could be heard from inside. He winced, knowing he was going to have to be extra careful. Taking a deep breath, he forced himself to step out, close the door and slowly take each step down, one at a time, when all he wanted to do was thunder away in a whirlwind.

Passing the painting, he carefully descended to the bottom and into the entrance hall where he peered around to the door to the kitchens with a straining neck. Every muscle was tense, a bead of sweat ran down his face and his shirt clung to his damp body. He saw it was clear and shifted quietly over to it, listening to the voices above, when suddenly the door to the drawing room opened and a butler strode out.

Trace froze near the doorway in the shadow of the landing above. His heart in his throat, he wanted to double over and vomit; yet the startled shriek and cry of surprise never came. In the corner of his eye, he saw the butler heading for the staircase with his head low, eyes to the floor and his mind elsewhere. The butler stopped at the bottom, his back to the hall, waiting for someone descending. With his keen hearing picking up a slight rattle of fine china upon a tray, Trace guessed the maid was returning to the kitchens to refill the teapot. Eyes wide, he knew she'd be coming his way. *Go, go, go!*

Giving up with cautious steps, he flew to the door in a flurry, opened it and bolted through, closing it behind him. The stairs were empty: the ghost couldn't believe his luck, but he wasted no time in basking in it. Trace darted down to the bottom step where he stopped and checked; there was no one around. He wiped the sweat from his forehead and tiptoed to the door where he opened it slightly and peeked through. The stairs were clear; the corridor down to the kitchen, though, he couldn't be sure. He breathed shallowly, barely eking air into his lungs.

He could hear talking and laughing from the cooks and servants and gave ear to the clattering pots, although they reached his senses in more ways than one; their smells comforted his nose and wetted his tongue in a longing crave. Smells of bread baking and food cooking also intoxicated him, reminding his stomach of its emptiness. Matters of such had to wait though, for the tunnel was clear and his golden moment was now.

Trace opened the door and wisped into the pantry, taking care to close it without a sound. The familiar musty scent hugged his nostrils whilst the spices and salts gave them a tickle; he welcomed them back with relief. He collected his belongings from under the bottom shelf and slipped on his shoes. Lifting the wooden trap door, he bundled everything under an arm and descended the ladder as quickly as he could, pulling the door down after him.

Reaching the floor, the quiet of the tunnel was deafening with his heart pounding behind his ears. For the next few passing seconds he stood in it, collecting his senses, then the rush of adrenalin hit him and he nearly gave into its pumping rush by jumping in excitement and yelping with triumph but having a care; he knew he was not finished yet. Those sensations could wait until he was home, or at least until after he was back out again. He tied his shoes with jittery hands, donned his jacket and unscrewed the top off his cane revealing the hollow in the centre; the second reason why he brought his cane today. Reaching for the scroll, he pulled the paper from his back pocket and pushed it into his cane, screwing the top back on when he was finished. Donning his hat, Trace moved the ladder back against the wall and sighed.

You're done, Trace. You've done it to a turn; in and out without a sight. Slyly, a smile formed as he began the walk back through the darkness heading for the shaft of light from the drain at the other end. With each step Trace took he felt bones reform within, then muscles and tendons reattach, nerves and organs knitting his body together to be covered by a human skin. No longer did he need to be a ghost. At last he could enjoy loud breathing and the sound of his footsteps again without concern of being heard. He was floating no longer; now he was walking, walking away from the house with victory in the shape of a rolled-up piece of parchment and his grandfather's old compass.

A relieved smile tugged at the corners of his mouth and he clenched his fists in exultation at the result of the job. As he moved, though, torment naturally niggled the back of his mind; whispering of the authenticity of the scroll; questioning it, deeming it to be more of a myth rather than fact. That surely the treasure of the Lost Loot would have been lost or found or ruined from when the hunt was set through the house.

That torment was soon pushed away when the gravity sunk in; he had it. He had it in his possession. Real or fake, discovered or undiscovered, it had been another successful day. He had a map, a series of clues that all led to one final and valuable conclusion; the large X at the end of the long-dotted line. It was all there, perhaps not in the clearest of forms but what treasure map was *clear?* It had to be difficult and tough so that only those determined and worthy enough could go out seeking what had been lost. Already his mind began to thread the needle and spool ideas to knit together, but first he needed another look at the map in full. It was an overwhelming concept though, a one he was not like to get over soon. *Fortune, a lost chest of unfathomable worth. The Lost Loot! Scott's Trove!* With twitching fingers, his eyes glittered with the image of falling coins and twinkling gems.

Trace walked through the tunnel, drawing ever closer to the light at the end. *Lift the hatch, walk home and tell Lucy the good news. She'll be pleased, I know it. She won't believe me at first, but she will, oh she will. This is the real deal now, surely worth a decent pint of the good stuff.* His thoughts jumbled with excitement, he felt out of breath. Despite the dark murk of the tunnel, he saw only the light, the joy and thrill, it was intense; a feeling he loved.

This time the light from the drain reached him in no time and in all honesty, he couldn't even say whether he walked or ran through the tunnel, he just wanted to get out. A sickness of skulking in the shadows had begun to haunt him. Trace longed to be Joseph Winter again; craving for the light of day to bask, to revel, to absorb in the glow of new ideas, new possibilities, new adventures. New fortunes. He skipped up the stone steps where he reached the top and pushed up against the drain; the stones feeling wet and cold against his palms. The weight of the stone felt heavy, exhaustion had taken its toll, but he pushed with strength and released the seal, lifting the door upwards.

Daylight broke through, throwing colourful spots over his stinging pupils. He squinted. Then the trapdoor suddenly raised from his fingers without him pushing, as if it had done it on its own accord.

Or as if . . .

No. No, that's impossible.

. . . Someone had . . .

No one knew, no one except Lucy and Vinny.

. . . Lifted the trapdoor.

The air tasted fresh and sweet in his lungs, perhaps too sweet, perhaps too fresh. Fresher than earlier, like the freshness of lemon zest. Was that what freedom tasted like? He couldn't remember; in all actuality it stank of vile waste with patches of smoky fog, yet it seemed anew after the stuffy air of the house.

Slowly he opened his eyes . . . and blinked several times to make sure what lay before him was in fact reality.

'No matter how many times you wash rats away,' said a familiar voice, 'they'll always keep crawlin' back up the drain.'

It was reality. A harsh and horrid one.

Five policemen surrounded the trapdoor, cutting off all escape routes down the alley or anywhere else he could go. Two were the policemen that had chased him from the jewellers earlier on that week; their faces were smiling, as if they'd finally trapped the vermin that had been infesting their home. An ugly truth had to be faced; they had. And they knew it.

Joseph gulped and his mouth hung open, saying nothing. Thinking nothing. Doing nothing. There was nothing he could do.

He'd been scrupulous about detail, planned everything to a dot, kept out of sight and left no trace. Not one. Nobody even knew what his intentions had been; only Lucy . . . and Vinny. *Vinny wouldn't do that to you, he's a close friend. But* . . . One solid and icy notion sheared through him, a one that chilled his soul and broke his trust in two words. *Is he?*

Vinny Jenkins . . . set me up. This was a sour tip.

Without giving a second thought, he made a dash for it and tried to break free from the circle, but hands grabbed him with a vice grip, too many hands; overpowering hands. A surge of panic swelled within, he felt like crying for help. *No, you can't! They can't know you've been snagged! It would be the end of you!* Instead of writhing in a struggle, he subdued with dignity and let them pat his pockets. 'There an't nothing in there, that's a promise, boys. Found nothing. Now, how's about you let me go and I give you a few sovereigns each to put a button on those lips, eh?'

They continued their search, deaf to his bribe. He found himself wanting to vomit again, wanting to be the ghost once more. 'Alright, alright. No sovereigns; too low. How's about a few shinnies then? Buy the wife something nice, enough to pay for a turkey this Christmas, eh? What's the verdict? Eh?' his bribes were beginning to sound like desperate pleas and were not helped by one of the policemen pulling out the lady's necklace and ring he forgot he'd taken. *Oh Joseph . . . what have you done?*

'Well, looks like we've got a rat *and* a thief on our hands.' One of them said and smiled, 'try not to squeak now, Mister Winter.'

Joseph quickly shut his eyes.

Smack! A baton powered into his belly, taking the wind from his lungs; he doubled over. *Crack!* A baton beat down onto his back; he cried out in agony and collapsed to the cobbles. Cold and hard, the stones would not help him; all they could do was hold him whilst he endured.

A boot kicked him in the stomach. Another hit him in the face. Another landed in his back. Blasts of fire pelted his body from the batons and still the volley continued. Joseph curled into a ball, wishing for it to be over. Wishing for the pain to stop. Praying for this horror to pass. He felt a hand grasp his collar and pull him up, only to receive a blow to the face that sent forks of pain fizzing around his skull. He fell to the floor again, blood drooling from his mouth and from splits on his puffy face, teetering on the edge of consciousness.

With ears ringing and hearing fuzzy, it was difficult to discern the identity of the voice that spoke but in that moment of hesitation it sounded deep and miraculous, like the voice of God. 'Alright. Alright that's enough! He's had enough now don't yer think? Betty fang 'im anymore and we'll kill the bloke!'

'He's a dirty thief, Bill, and has made a fool of us for so long. He's had this coming to 'im!'

'That may be, but I reckon yer've made your point. The mush can 'ardly bleedin' breathe! What's he gonna' think if we bring him in lookin' any worse than this?' The voice of Bill said.

'He threw us a few punches whilst we were gettin' him,' another voice spoke, 'we did that to him in self-defence; that's all there is to know. Now hurry. Let's get him up. Grab his hat and cane.'

Hands grappled around him and hauled him to his feet. They held him up whilst a cloth wiped the blood that oozed from his nose and out the corner of his lolloping mouth, but nothing could stop his face from throbbing as heavily as it did. One eye felt worse than the other; the swelling had already begun; he could feel its heated rising waves. They sat his hat on his head and tipped it low to hide the worst of the damage and began to drag him through the streets as if he were a drunk.

The next two hours he could not account for, except darkness; a black pit his mind had shut him off to for his own safety. For the first time in his adult life he felt lost in these streets he called home. Disorientation spinning his senses on an axis, his senses jumbling in a chaotic mess. How long he'd been unconscious for he didn't know, but for now his systems were rebooting for an awakening.

Afternoon light slipped through the slight crack in his left eye, his only good eye for now; he quickly shut it again and winced at its brightness. Sounds came and went, but it was hard to distinguish anything through the crumbling white noise his ears were providing him with. *Curse the bloody peelers! Curse the fuckin' mutton shunters! Curse the . . . where am I?* Curiously, he opened his good eye and gently pulled himself up against the stone wall he leaned against. A whiff of human filth made his nose wrinkle, the abhorrence leaving a nasty tang in the back of his throat. He peered around at his surroundings, praying to the mighty lord above that he was not where he thought he was.

Men of rough appearances, hard case bricky men, walked and talked in tight-knit groups; some were sitting on tables and benches, some were throwing a rotten onion to each other. Some were heavy-set, others were thin and weedy with scraps of a beard; some were overly hairy and scarred, some had one eye or were missing a limb. There were a lot of them; women were here too, women that looked malnourished and as pale, thin and as delicate as snow, yet with the strength of steel. Children were here, dirty and darting through the crowds, joining the gangs, finding their places in the pecking order. All wore clothes torn and dirty with hair ragged and unkempt, their teeth yellowed stumps with brown in places. They seemed content, relatively happy amongst the piles of faeces and dead rats. Positive, which was odd seeing as there was a large thick brick wall containing them, separating them from society. The only interruption in the tall drab wall was a great thick wooden door manned by two guards. *Oh no.* Panic began to steeple through his veins, *no, no, no. Not here. Not now.* His good eye darted left to right and, turning, he looked over to the other side where the great wall ran and connected with the building behind him, the building he was leaning up against.

A corner was next to him, he saw, and he peered around it to see more people bustling, more drab grey smoky bricks reaching new heights and shapes; windows were dark and blotted and barred, doors were heavy and cumbersome and metal was commonplace. Metal studded the doors, metal lined and barred the windows, metal crowned the great damned wall in a row of sharp spikes. A tough place was emerging. *Metal and bricks, a hard place for hard people.* These sights were nothing new to him, however; in a way, he was back home after a long absence. Pursing his lips, he looked to the ground in thought. Lucy had been right; she always had a way about things, it was only in stubborn spite did he choose not to heed her; *you and your bloody pride, you damned ratbag foozler.* Just then he felt a rush of affection for her and looked forward to holding her again in his grasp, knowing he could get out of here; he'd escaped before, he could do it again. For now, though, prison was welcoming him back with a cold and unloving embrace.

The thought of having to endure another trial, another administration, another jail cell and another shuffle finding a place in the hierarchy made him want to retch. *You should've been more careful; something had slipped and now you're in here with the rest of these miserable parasites.* Memory then served as well as the reason why he was back in here. *That bloody house . . .*

The stone was cold against his back, as well as his arms and head; he shivered, breathing out puffs of steam and realised his jacket was missing along with his hat. And cane. Suddenly it struck him; his cane was nowhere to be seen. *That cane is the only reason I'm in this mess!* All his items had been taken, stolen by the criminals he was locked up with, probably being passed along and inspected or reclaimed as their own. Anger flared within; *I've got to find it!*

'Ello. You're awake then.' A voice said from his left.

Joseph jumped, his swollen right eye not being able to see the person sitting next to him. The criminal turned and looked at a boy with fine down of fluff coating his red cheeks and chin; a boy, a teenager, although Joseph could see his eyes were that of a man after the things he must've seen and done to land him in this hellhole. Children were not children for long in this day and age.

'Stealin',' he said nodding, as if he had read his mind, obviously he was asked frequently the reason of his presence. 'Tryin' to run off with a lady's bag but didn't see the peeler round the corner. Foolish, I know, but I'll admit to it, unlike some of these lying crooks in 'ere believing their cleaner than a vicar's whistle. But what's a man to do, eh Trace?' he smiled, 'got to keep running.'

'Do I know you?' his voice was croaky; he could still taste blood.

'No, but I know you. I've seen you a few times in the Back House before, but never on the streets; it's impressive.' The lad grinned, he had a tooth missing and had a forehead of acne under his mop of brown hair. 'Most people know you, Trace, *and* know your tricks.' The boy held up his jacket and hat.

Joseph smiled and sighed with relief; not only at seeing his possessions hadn't been stolen but for having friends on the inside too. As a returning criminal, he knew this meant a chance at surviving. He took his things back and thanked the boy, then his smile faded as he remembered, 'wait . . . my cane? Where's my-'

'Oh yeah, sorry,' the boy handed it to him, 'thought I'd take them before anyone else could. For safe-keepin', like. I'm Robert by the way. Robert Epping. People call me Rob, or Hare.'

A surge of relief overwhelmed him then and he slumped against the wall, swallowing the raw taste of blood; *it wasn't all in vain*. It would be a silly thing to check for the map right here though, he knew from past experiences that eyes followed everyone everywhere. Prisons were wrought with their own gangs and criminal societies and underlying businesses; always looking, always inspecting a new face or a returning one like his. He could already feel eyes peering at him, wanting to pick him to see what his soul had to offer. He sat his things by his side closely, taking out his tobacco and paper and rolling a cigarette from his jacket pocket. He lit it and inhaled, tasting the relief as it filled his lungs. 'Hare?' he asked.

Rob smiled, 'everyone used to say I could run as fast as one, especially Mother . . . well, not anymore, but the name stuck.' Joseph could relate, as soon as one person started calling him Trace everyone suddenly did. 'Guess they won't be calling me that anymore now that the Hare got trapped.'

A man walked by them then and they both stopped talking. He wore a thick comforter wrapped around his neck, a large tattered jacket and a holey bowler hat scuffed and splattered with dirt; a scar ran from his forehead down to his cheek. He glanced down at them with a white cloud of an eye; his fingers twitched, then he moved along without a word. *Snitch*, Joseph observed, *he's scouting for fresh fish for his gang which is* . . . he looked through the crowd of people and saw a group gathered, occasionally glancing around to their snitch who'd just walked past . . . *over there.* He'd had his run in with snitches before, thankfully he was a wiser man now. It was a dangerous and desperate role within the ranks. Joseph looked back to the lad, sucking on the cigarette, 'you're only as good as the things you steal and you're only as fast as your feet can carry you.' He recited Vinny's words proudly, then remembered what had happened. The memory stung hard.

The lad smiled, 'Gospel truth. Shame we weren't as good as the things we stole, Trace.'

Joseph was about to retort a clever boisterous reply about how Trace never got caught, until he realised his situation and slowly nodded in reply, remembering the necklace and ring from the house. The *compensation,* but now he thought about it those items had turned into his downfall, a major regret. *They'd still have got you anyway, they were waiting for you outside; they knew you'd be there. And the jewellery you gave them another reason to give you the ol' black and blue.* He held the cane close to him; the real reason why he entered the house in the first place, yet instead of it giving him strength he felt hollow and vulnerable inside. *Was it worth it in the end? For a piece of flousy parchment?* Maybe it was the brick walls around him causing him to doubt, giving him a reason to pity himself for the first time in years; maybe it was because the tenacious Joseph 'Trace' Winter had finally been caught and cuffed.

Suddenly he felt alone, shameful, even remorseful, but surprisingly not sad for he knew he would be back out within a few days; he owed no debts and would be a good boy. The old boys in here like good behaviour and he knew he could win them over. Despite their hardened exterior, they were soft yolks within and from the looks of these overflowing confines, they'd *want* him out. Besides, he only committed a small crime: thieving a necklace and a ring. Criminals in here had done atrocious things– *they* were the real convicts, not him. He lifted his head up and looked forward to returning home.

A bell rang from the other side of the grounds. Its cold clang was a sad reminder of his previous incarcerations; its chime giving him a reason to frown. All heads turned to the sound of the bell and bodies began to jostle and move toward the doorways and metal gates to the yells and hollers of the guards. It was a tremendous flood of people; Joseph didn't remember this many before. The tales he'd heard were true: the prisons were overcrowding. *No wonder they keep carting loads off to the colonies down south.* He pushed himself up using his cane and a helping hand from Rob and winced loudly at the sharp pain crackling from his ribs and back. His stomach hurt to tense and his head began to pound but he got to his feet and slipped on his jacket, placing his hat gently on his head.

'You'll have to go over to the guards and get yourself signed in for a shared cell. There an't enough cells for one each.' Rob told him.

He turned back, his head thumping, 'don't you worry old possum, I've been here before. Thanks for the hand.'

Rob smiled and nodded then parted from him, heading toward his own shared cell. Joseph watched him leave, hoping his new cellmates would keep themselves to themselves and not give him hassle. He remembered his first cellmates, two of whom had been let out along with him; the other two had managed to attain freedom at the end of a rope, becoming the hosts for the entertainment of a public hanging. *Poor old sods.* Turning back, he hobbled toward the nearest doorway, looking at the bricks and metal and dark grimy windows; a nest for the rats not shrewd enough to keep on their runs.

A thief this morning, a ghost this afternoon and a rat this evening; who will you be tomorrow? With luck, a free man once more.

Following the crowd, Joseph entered the prison door.

Chapter Five

'Name?'

He sighed, 'Joseph Winter.' It was the same man at the desk from his last visit here, except this time his narrow jaw was decorated with sideburns and a moustache. Even then it had not been his first incarceration; he'd been acquainted with cold bars twice before during his youth but when he last strode forth from these doors, he'd vowed it was going to be his last time behind them. *Was* going to be his last. *My own vow's been broken, as well as my face, and god knows what else.* His pride was one he could count for a start.

The man glanced at him then did a double take, scrutinising his malformed face, almost seeing the thought behind it; *Christ almighty, what in the devil happened to you?!* For a passing moment, Joseph thought the man recognised him from before, yet this was a stretch. His eye was a ballooning blue, his cheeks were swollen and bruised, his lip was cut and weeping as well as a cut above his eye and he was leaning on his cane, wincing with every breath. No wonder the man didn't recognise him; if Joseph had a mirror, he didn't think he would've recognised the man staring back at him either. Nonetheless, the gaoler filed his name and gave his routine dribble, 'yer'll be collected for the magistrates in two days. Yer lucky yer in time for the Lent session else we'd be keepin' yer in 'ere until the summer. For now, get yerself over to D Block and the gaoler will give yer a cell. We'll come and get yer when yer time's come.'

'To court?' he asked, perplexed.

'Yeh, that's usually where it 'appens.'

'I only pilfered a few bits, a quarter session wouldn't be worth it, surely? I doubt majority of the people in here have had a case filed.' He coughed harshly, hacking up a glob of blood. *That's not good.*

The gaoler looked nonplussed behind his desk, 'majority don't. But it says 'ere *you* have to. In two days. Now skedaddle over to D Block, *Trace.*'

Joseph forced a smile. *Of course, it's the reputation they're trialling, to smear the name. Get another story in the evening wheezes. Bloody Robert Peel with your bloody new fandangle laws.* Wiping his mouth, he nodded and politely, almost sarcastically, tipped his hat and hobbled down the corridor, making his way slowly to D Block where a guard stood by the entrance, keys in hand.

He addressed the guard in a dull tone, looking the guard in the eyes with his one good one.

The guard stared at him unwaveringly through the shadow of his overhanging brow. His chin was square and chiselled below a squashed nose and his shoulders were broad, making the uniform a tight fit. A block of wood with legs. Barely even noticing Joseph's injuries, there was no pity in those small deep-set eyes; but he guessed that was because he was used to seeing abuse like this– after he'd inflicted it. The ox grunted and unlocked the door, opened it and walked through with Joseph hobbling behind catching sight of five rats scurrying back to their holes.

Immediately a choice of smells hit him. Dank moisture, musty straw, filth, rot and the foul aroma of stewing excrement stuffed themselves up his nose before he had a chance to prepare. It caught in his throat and he coughed, wanting to retch, squinting with a watering eye at the torchlight flickering up the stone walls in their sconces. It was barely evening but D Block looked like it was a place of permanent darkness: a blot of ink on the building plans.

It wasn't much to look at; the architect seemingly shrugging his shoulders when it came to its design. Its large rectangular area had two floors of cells running parallel to each other with each cell not too far apart from the next. There was a table and chair on the bottom floor at the very back where a candle burned displaying a bale of straw in the corner. Hanging on the rear wall were instruments from what Joseph could distinguish; there was a whip as well as chains, manacles and a coil of rope. From the smell of the place the bale of fresh straw had not been opened, but desperately needed to be. He'd heard things of D Block in his last visit, things that needed to be repressed if he wanted to cope here, but walking past the cells and spotting the torturous equipment, he could not help an increasing dread.

Suddenly shouts and yells from the inmates began to spread from one cell to the next. Three to four shadows appeared from each cell, with five in a few, and were peering down to see their new inmate. Old, young, tall, short, black, white, fully limbed or not it made no difference; they were bundled in together, cramped and condemned.

'*Fresh meat lads!*' he heard one yell. '*Fresh fish!*'

'*Bring 'im in here Dennis, come on! Let us 'av the mumbling cove!*' Joseph looked around but couldn't find the man who'd said that.

'*Bugger me! Is that Trace?!*'

'*Looks like Trace has left some traces after all!*' There was laughing.

'*Food, bring us food!*'

'*We need a doctor in here! Bring anyone! Anyone you can!*'

'*Let me out, I'm innocent I swear it!*'

'*Get me out of here! I'll kill the whole fucking lot of 'em, I don't care!*' Voices were crying out for one thing or the other, bouncing from wall to wall, bar to bar, until the gaoler had had enough.

'*ENOUGH!*' he bellowed, '*if I hear another sound, so much as a squeak I'll come and rip your worthless heads from your shoulders and stick 'em on spikes for the world to see! I don't care for you, any of you! You all an't nothing to me but scum! Scraps from the London Mud!*' the guard looked up and around at the now blank faces. Every mouth closed. Every prisoner silenced. The flicker of flames sounded loud as the torches burned within their sconces, now the only sound daring to be heard. The guard had a powerful voice, Joseph noted, and noted not to get on the wrong side of him if he didn't want another black eye. *Lovely man, a true angel.*

'I'm an't scared of you Dennis, you ol' mongrel gibface!'
A brave voice shouted out from one of the cells. The rest were quiet and did not join in. A bad sign. Joseph winced. Was this courage the man had, or stupidity? Either way, the man had a death wish and he did not want to be him.

The guard looked up at a cell, knowing exactly who had spoken. In a calm sinister tone Dennis replied, 'just you wait there, Frank, I'll be up in a minute.' He glanced around to Joseph and motioned him to follow.

They walked the length of D Block until the guard stopped and peered in a cell, and he turned to him, 'this one's got three in it. You can be the fourth.' He nodded to the bars coldly.

Hobbling up, Joseph looked inside to the shadows of two cons looking out to him with wide eyes, but he couldn't tell whether that was curiosity or anger looming in their stare. Behind them, there were two sets of bunk beds screwed parallel into the close walls, a metal pail squatting in the far-right corner and a small barred rectangular window near the ceiling. A sprinkle of straw was strewn across the floor along with some earthly deposits littered in places. A rat squeaked and scurried away.

The gaoler unlocked the cell, swung it open and shoved him inside.

The bars slammed, and the key turned, locking him in. A *thief – a ghost – a rat – a fool and now a locked-up convict. The list continues.* He limped over to the wall and leaned against it. *It's only for a few days, Joseph. Your trial will come, and you'll slip out and away and back to your house, back to Lucy. You managed it before you can manage it again. This is only a temporary stop in a life of adventure, just wait out these few days.*

Heavy footsteps clopped back down the walkway and thumped up the stairs to the cell. There was a jangle of keys, a lock turning and a sharp squeak of the cell as the bars opened. 'Come 'ere then Frank, you scummy bastard, how many times 'av I told you what trouble that mouth can get you in?' There was a *'wait, hang on now-'* then a shout, a tousle, then a smack. The bars squeaked shut, the key turned, and the heavy footsteps thudded back down the stairs, followed by another lighter set struggling against the force of this oxen of a man. '*No!*' Frank cried, '*No! Let me be! I'll behave, I'll behave! Please, no! Not again!*' Joseph limped to the bars and looked through them, peering through the gloom to see where the gaoler– *named Dennis?* –was taking the con but he failed to see anything apart from the opposite cell and the glowing torch casting its flicker up the grime-streaked walls.

A strange and uncomfortable silence filled the block– all knowing not to push their luck even when the gaoler had left. *No wonder he's in charge of the entire block. Everyone's terrified of him.* Joseph didn't even want to wonder what kind of things this Dennis was known for and what had given him this powerful reputation with the cons.

Suddenly a hand grabbed his collar and yanked him from the bars, pushing him against the wall. Before he could question who or what, a knife was against his throat; its blade pressing on his Adam's apple. A hand grasped around his throat too, so that if he moved either way he'd be cut or strangled: it was clear this offender was experienced with this type of introduction. Thin but toned arms held him with a surprising force, but darkness concealed his face, hiding any notable features apart from narrow predatorial eyes. His voice was so sharp and clear, dominating, that Joseph didn't need any light to know his cellmate was going to be an issue. With the shadow of an obvious accomplice standing behind, the man declared the situation. 'You're a shit-filled sack of worthless waste and nothing else. You an't got no friends in 'ere, no one to help you. Your side is this one, you dare cross it you'll be stabbed. I don't care, I done it before. What's another life in here to a life out there, eh?' Joseph didn't answer, sensing it to be rhetorical.

His eye adjusted to the gloom and he could see the man's eyes now– crisp and blue. The knife pressed a little harder, 'I own this cell and I says what scum can and can't have. I say scum sleeps on the bottom bed on your side, and I say you an't 'avin' no niceties in here that you'd have out there– like that cane o' yours.'

The man behind reached through and took it from his sweating hand. Joseph struggled and tried to reach for it back, but the man only pressed him into the wall harder making his ribs burn in pain. Joseph watched with his one good eye as the other shadow raised his knee and brought the cane down on it, snapping it in half.

His eye welled with tears, he wanted to yelp. *Not my cane* . . .

'What's your name?' The blue-eyed man continued.

'J-Johnathon.'

'Best you get to bed Johnathon and get a good sleep on all what I've just told you.' His knife pulled away with his hand. Joseph clutched his throat instinctively, breathing deeply with his ribs crackling.

There was nothing he could do. He was a newcomer again, and this time his welcome was rougher; newcomers always were picked upon and prodded, but that was only so the others could determine what kind of person you were; that was how he remembered it anyway. Times had changed; it was the murderers, rapists, thieves and gangsters who ruled this prison and Joseph was going to have to find his place in the pecking order– or be ready for the worst.

Powerless against the ruffians who already ruled the cell, he limped around to the lower bunk on his side of the room and laid his battered body down on a weak-framed bed, the wood riddled with worms and the straw mattress infested with lice and fleas; a flat stained pillow offered the only comfort. The other cellmate he hadn't seen yet was on the top bunk, his heavy breathing a sign that he didn't want to be involved or disturbed; Joseph didn't blame him, he would've kept out the way too if he had the chance. He turned to face the cold wall of stone, his body already beginning to itch and ache, missing the feel of Lucy's comforting embrace as she snuggled beside him.

A sharp shake of the shoulder roused him from a restless sleep. He forgot and tried opening both eyes, but his right was fused shut and ached dully, still painful, so it was up to his left to look around in the darkness. *What was that? Was that even real?* He wasn't sure. What he could tell was that the prison was a lot quieter now, and darker too; the light of the torches seemed brighter than light beyond the window bars. He turned over and gasped at the sight of a silhouette crouching beside his bed. 'Wake up,' the figure whispered with the hint of an accent.

Oh no . . . oh no, no, not this. He'd heard tales of poor souls who had been unfortunate enough to share the company of promiscuous men in their cell who cared for neither men nor women, as long as there was a heartbeat and a hole. He'd even heard of strange ones who cared not even for a heartbeat, which was a certain distasteful notion. Instinct pulled him away, shuffling back from the side of the bed, praying for this not to be what he thought it was.

The figure raised his hands and whispered. '*Easy, boyo, take it easy. I'm not what you're t'inking. I only want to talk is all; it's hard to get a solid word in edgeways when you've got those two eejits breathin' down your neck.*' Is that an Irish brogue? He noticed.

Still suspicious, his one eye strained to see through the dark. This wasn't either of those two who had given him a red line across his neck earlier– then he realised this was his other cellmate from the top bunk. This one seemed friendly, and he smiled through the dark. '*I'm Billy, what's your name?*'

'*Johnathon,*' he murmured, trying not to wake the others up.

'*Alright. And what's your name?*' Billy repeated.

The con found himself smiling, *he knows the game.* '*Joseph Winter.*'

Billy looked surprised, '*Blimey I didn't recognise y' with the pillow face y' got goin' on there. You look like a blind cobbler's thumb.*' he smiled and held out his hand, '*Billy Baker, but t'ose two over there know me as Andy so when mornin' comes it'd be grand if y'shook my hand as Andy Turner, for the sake of poor Billy's safety, if you take my meaning. Sorry if I'm gettin' mixed up here, but are you the fella they call "Trace"?*'

Joseph took his hand and shook it, '*the one and only. But, somehow, I left one this time, else I'd be back home right now with me arms around a lady instead of these fleas.*' *If she'd still have me after she hears what I've got myself into.*

'*Where'd you leave a trace then?*'

He sighed quietly, *'at a job I think, or perhaps with a false friend.'*
The thought angered him so much it sent the pain away a little.

Billy pointed to himself, *'Ah. Me, I'm innocent. Wrong place at the wrong time.'*

'Of course. Keep telling yourself that if it'll make you feel better.'

Billy chuckled. *'Alright t'en. I stole two baskets o' sweet buns, but then got caught when I had my arms around a woman eating the buns from between her lovelies, and might I say she had a fine pair of cupid's kettle drums on her too.'*

'The peelers followed you after the buns?' Joseph asked.

'Nah, peelers got involved later about my gambling debts. It was me wife that caught me instead.' He winked. *'Anyways, couple of t'ings to look out for over the next few days; the stook with the knife's called Ed and the ot'ter is Pat. Mind where you walk outside and mind where y' looking. Some o' these muppets are about as mad as a box o' frogs. Always keep your t'ings with you and don't go gettin' involved with the sweet whisperings from Fat Fred's gang; they aren't nothing but fools and liars who want to get us cons working the Crank and Treadmill day and night. They'd try an' sell ya the eye outta' your head if they could.'*

Joseph remembered the Treadmill well enough, having once spent two days on that loathsome contraption and climbing a never-ending staircase. *'Thanks for the advice.'* He nodded, *'I'll bare it in mind.'*

'Good. Make sure you bare it in practise too.' Billy stood, taking a quick glance behind him at the sleeping pigs, then looked back to him, *'see you in t' mornin' Joe.'*

'See you in the morning.'

Billy nodded, smiling, and climbed up onto the bunk above him, the wooden frame creaking as he got himself comfortable.

Joseph turned over, pulling the fusty sheets up to his chest and closed his eye, trying to get back to sleep.

A minute passed in silence, then he heard Billy whispering above him. *'Seek far, seek wide, lose yourself . . . and find. Oh, this sounds good!'*

Joseph ripped his eye open, stunned. *Shit!* He felt along his back around his belt where he'd tucked the map earlier on, on his way to the prison desk in case of circumstances leading to a loss of his cane.

The map wasn't there anymore. It was gone.

A shadow of a hand holding a scroll of parchment then appeared from above him. Joseph quickly snatched and tucked it back in his trousers. '*Billy! That's mine, don't you ever-*'

'*-Joe, what is that? Is that a treasure map?*'

The owner paused. *He's read it now; he knows about it.* '*Maybe.*'

'*Just like in the old fishwife tales?*'

'*Perhaps.*'

Billy's head appeared hanging upside down, '*I won't tell anyone, on a cellmate's honour. I'll seek far and wide, and I'll help you find it . . . if I can. We'll have a look at it soon an' see if we can figure out where it leads first.*' His smile was so bright Joseph could see it in the dark, '*I'm in.*'

Chapter Six

The next day Joseph and Billy kept close and waited for a time when they could examine the map more intently, but a chance never came. Eyes watched them wherever they went, stares and glares that told them a slip up would go noticed and they knew better than to make any mistakes, so they waited and hoped for a better opportunity the following day.

Joseph had some discoveries of his own regarding his new Irish friend however, whereupon Billy told him his past as they walked around the courtyard. The man had a boyish face with scraps of a light brown stubble peeking through freckles and brown curly hair loosely bounced underneath a small brown bowler hat, faded and flecked. 'I'm from a small town near Dublin over in Ireland so I am, lovely scenery, lovely birds; of both sorts,' he winked, showing a slightly crooked front tooth in his grin, 'but by the time I was enterin' me teenage years the famine hit hard, the potato one, and my family upped sticks and moved over to this shite-hole of a city where I started mixin' with "uncouth individuals" shall we say?'

He nodded, understanding completely. Billy shrugged, 'grew up with it all. I like a drink and I liked a gamble y' see, I like a good craic and the two don't go well together when you also mix in with the wrong crowd. That's when I found out me girl was pregnant; baking a bun in her oven so we ran away together and tied the knot; but it ain't all it's cracked up to be let me tell ya'. I got a job as a docker, hauling off barrels and boxes and the like from ships. We were doing fine for a time with the new babe before I started getting a taste o' pickpocketing for a few extra pennies, and t'en that began to snowball and got me back to the bad crowds again.

'Then the complainin' started and wouldn't bloody stop– moan, moan, moan. She finished with me after I started getting good at the gamblin' as well as pilferin'; I was bang up to the elephant, but I nearly lost everyt'ing so I did. I was gamblin' our lives away . . .' A flash of sadness crossed his face and he scratched his sandy brown curls, 'that was all back nearin' on five years ago now, and I'm wiser for it,' he paused and smiled, 'but none the luckier.' He said chuckling as he motioned to the walls around him. Joseph also found out he was thirty years old and his daughter, Bessie, was now six and didn't know of him. He could understand, most people didn't want to get caught up knowing cons like them, but it made him realise to live a life of crime was safer to do it alone, to not risk hurting those close by. *Maybe I should've broke it off with Lucy sooner.* He mused as he looked out at the courtyard full of criminals.

Not many chances presented themselves to the pair over the course of the next day either; the environment was too risky with snitches eyeballing their every move, so they waited until lockdown in the middle of the night to look at the map fully. *'All's we need is a starting point, t'en all the rest will follow from there.'* Billy whispered.

Joseph scanned over the paragraphs again, sifting through the words as if he were sieving through soil looking for a nugget of gold. The nugget of gold didn't show itself easily though, this soil was hard-packed. *'It's like a bloody safe and we don't know the combination. I can't figure anything out from this.'* He hissed, trying to keep his voice as low as possible to not wake the two pigs opposite.

'Well I'm sure there's something t'ere, Joe, there's got to be. Why go through the trouble of makin' a riddle-like map if no one can figure out where the devil the treasure is. Whoever made the map wanted it to be found and wanted it to be found by someone "worthy", someone who won't give up. Lookie-' he pointed to the line, *'it even says "Hope is something you must not lose".'*

Joseph read through the words again, trying to find anything that gave a hint of a clue away. Scratching at the fleabites, he tried to focus. *'I can't find anything. Let me get some more light.'* He quietly pushed himself from his bed, wincing at the sharp pain in his ribs, and limped over to the moonlight shining through the iron window bars, finally being able to use a crack of sight as his other eye began to deflate.

He peered, scanning, and flipped the paper to the other side whereupon a glimmer of something new caught his eye. Brows creasing, he turned to the bunk and the silhouette looking to him. *'Billy, there's something here.'*

Chains rattled and clanked around Joseph's ankles as he plodded toward the wooden pedestal in the centre of the circular court room. It made such a racket– with each step there was a constant jangle and scrape as the metal dragged across the stone slabbed floor; he almost felt self-conscious about the sound in the unpleasant quiet of the room. Apart from slight mutterings, everything was so quiet any sound would've been a cacophony, but the chains would not stop rattling and the manacles would not stop digging into his ankles.

No one made his announcement as he made his way down the aisle, and he was relieved by it. He wanted to retain as much dignity as he could without hearing his name echo in this godawful silence. *These chains are my announcement, they'll do the job better than anyone else could.* Bodies turned around; more people were here than he'd anticipated, and all manners of glares daggered into him with icy blades; every person's focus as sharp as the edge. Eyes laid into him, bore into him, judged him from the different benches in front and behind; blue pairs, green pairs, brown pairs peering through spectacles, bearded faces, women's faces, long faces of dismay, or was that disgust, or both? *Have I really affected this many people? Surely, they can't all be here for me.* Half of the benches were empty, but the others were full of onlookers all following his every move; not seeing a human but an animal, a prisoner who was now facing trial. *They're judging me and I haven't even got to the stand yet.* Joseph kept walking, trying to hide his limp and wondered if Lucy was in here too.

The past two days had been tough there was no doubt about it; especially with his attempt at adapting to the sheer quantity of bodies all confined within those brick walls. The sheer density was astounding and claustrophobic, the stench unequalled. Having no freedom was an even harder task to accustom to, but he was glad to have made a friend amongst the rats– what fate lay waiting for Billy Baker was a thought he had to press from his mind. The wooden pedestal he now stood on required all his attention, as well as the Judge in his powdered white wig, looking down at him from the high bench that sat proudly in front of the great panel displaying the golden coat of arms.

The look of it was intimidating. He rested his hands on the wooden barrier, the manacles wrapped around his wrists clunked. The cuffs felt heavy to carry around, a solid burden of linked metal reminding him of the freedom he had not meant to trade in. *Let's get this over with.*

He splayed his fingers out openly, making sure that no matter what they were going to pin on him he was going to keep these two hands clean by the end of it. This was the day of his judgement, but after everything he felt strangely confident and subdued; he hadn't killed or raped anyone, been involved with a murder, threatened the innocent or damaged anything in the process of his crime; all he had done was steal a scroll of parchment and a compass. *The necklace and ring have been taken from me already, I can't count those.* In all honesty, he wasn't sure why he needed a court like this, his crimes were not grievous; Joseph hadn't hurt anybody, not even a tug of an earlobe, so what *could* they condemn him for? Innocence and freedom were just a short distance away, hidden within that polished wooden gavel.

The Judge had a sharp face, lean, clean shaven with a narrow chin and curved nose. Pallid, gormless and motionless, he could've been mistaken for a corpse under his welsh wig. *Christ! Someone needs to check his pulse.* His grey eyes glared coldly down, unblinking, as if he was looking down at a cockroach that would not seem to die no matter how many times he crushed it. Joseph looked from the Judge to the two welsh-wigged magistrates either side of him through his one good eye and half of the deflating other and tried to keep calm. No matter how much confidence he thought he had the silent eyes gave such an icy front that he could feel a chill coursing through his veins, and a frost nipping at his face like a harsh winter breeze. Words were not needed to be spoken for the condemned to know what they were thinking, until finally the silence was broken.

After the petty jury had been sworn in, a man walked out from the side of the Judge's benches. 'Good morning.' He projected to the court. Despite his small height, the black flowing gowns and powdered white wig gave him a dominating authority that made him appear much taller and much more powerful. Joseph hadn't seen him there but then remembered the man's role– *ah yes, the prosecutor, how could I forget. What dish is on the menu for you to serve today?*

He addressed the courtroom and petty jury with a loud clear voice, 'we are present today to pass judgement upon a Mister Joseph George Winter for his recent crimes against the public that include theft, maim against officials and undermining the law for his own gain, in the sight of the Holy Father, our Lord, who watches and judges us all. A defence lawyer has not been supplied, which means the defendant is able to defend himself. There are witnesses present that have agreed to give statements to the following session. Do you have anything to add before we begin today's proceedings, Mister Winter?'

All eyes turned to him again. *Maim against officials?* He shook his head lightly. The prosecutor took that as an answer, even though Joseph guessed he didn't care what he came out with. 'Mister Winter, on the first day of the third month you burgled a well renowned jewellery store and stole a handful of valuable items that were for sale, necklaces and diamonds to name a few, only to sell on to the criminal underworld for more money than the original price. Do you deny this?'

How could he possibly know that? The peelers didn't even catch me, I could've been anyone! 'Yes, I do.' Joseph said loudly.

The Judge interlocked his fingers on the desk above. 'You are aware that to lie in court is to lie in the eyes of God above, who judges us all?' said the prosecutor.

'Yes, I am. That's why I'm telling the truth.' He lied. 'There are a lot of poor people in this city, sir, a lot of people who live in abject poverty because they are underpaid and undervalued and will lean toward a life of crime because it gives them a chance to keep some food on the table that they wouldn't have had otherwise. The person who burgled that shop could've been anyone, so I think it's quite unfair how you pin it on the first convict to come in here. Just because I have chains around my hands and feet doesn't mean I'm responsible for all the crimes that happen in London.'

The prosecutor prickled slightly, 'you are in chains because you are a thief and a criminal and a liar who takes advantage of our laws to reap your own gains, the very laws that are put in place to protect society from despicable cases such as yours.' He stepped over to his table and pulled up a small case, opened it, and showed the court a collection of jewels, rubies, necklaces and rings. 'Do these look familiar to you, Mister Winter?'

What – how . . . how is this possible?! He gulped, eyes widening slightly, stunned. 'No,' but his hesitation told otherwise.

The prosecutor left the case open on the table and looked toward the ceiling, taking a step back. All eyes focused on him. Then he looked back to the convict. 'My apologies, I'm just minding the lightning bolt. It should be here any second. The Lord is usually quick to smite those who continue to sin before Him. I may be a few feet away, Mister Winter, but I can tell when the mouth spews falsehoods because the eyes,' he raised a finger, 'they always tell truths. The tongue can manufacture vices yet the eyes, when clear, show the true virtues. And right now, your eyes are as big and as bold as an infant who has claimed they didn't knock the vase over.'

The bastard's playing games with me. Joseph turned to the jury in a bold effort to spin the perception, 'he could've bought those jewels himself not a day ago.'

The prosecutor looked to the jury, then to Joseph, 'I didn't buy these jewels Mister Winter, and neither did you. Your Honour, might I ask up the owner of the jewellery store– a Mister William Newson?'

The Judge allowed it and a tall man walked up and out from the crowd. He was dressed in a formal suit with top hat and cane and looked the spitting image of the rich aristocrats whom Joseph was trying to impersonate earlier on in the week. The prosecutor offered him a look inside the case, then asked him to sit and was sworn in. 'Mister Newson, do you recognise these jewels?'

'Yes.' the prim stick insect chirped, 'Of course. Diamond rings, studded necklaces and precious gems and rubies. These valuables were for sale at my jewellery shop but were recently taken. My business has been running for almost two decades and has already upheld royal appointments and is entrusted by our gracious Queen Victoria to create her infamous Victorian Cross, so for a thief to burgle us is not only an insult to my business but also to the British monarchy.' His eyes rested on the accused, 'it is a disgrace to this glorious Empire.'

'Oh, I am sorry to hear that.' A glance at Joseph, 'by taken, do you mean stolen?'

'Indeed. The thief stole near to two shelves worth of fine jewellery and gemstones. At the worth of over three hundred pounds. As much as he could get his grubby little paws on.' He paused, 'pardon my lack of decorum, fine sir.'

'That's quite alright, Mister Newson. It must be hard to deal with, to stare in the face of the criminal whom has taken not only your finery but your sense of security too.'

The owner sent daggers to Joseph through his glare. 'It is.'

The prosecutor nodded, 'no more questions, sir. Thank you, Mister Newson. You may return to your seat.'

His lanky legs lifted him, his gangly arms straightened his jacket and he walked back to his seat with his nose held high. Joseph watched him walk back with a fresh bead of sweat tracking down his brow, *this isn't looking good.* In his mind he could hear the bang of a hammer hitting a nail. Suddenly he felt the stare of the prosecutor. 'You've been busy Mister Winter, haven't you?'

'The past few days have been pretty slack stuck behind some metal bars.' Joseph replied coolly, and for once, truthfully.

'Which is where you should be kept, for an exceedingly long time.' The white wig retorted, 'they say a thief will always be a thief; and I'm afraid your recent actions prove this to be true. Days after the jewellery raid you plundered a house within a renowned district, stealing a necklace and ring and frightening the mistress sending her into a fit of anxiety. Her servants also were victims to this paranoia. One of which claims to have seen you.'

How could she have seen me? I was a ghost, not leaving a trace. He didn't reply and kept quiet.

The prosecutor pulled a pouch from his pocket and pulled out the contents, holding them up for the judges and jury to see. There, lying innocent, were the necklace and ring Joseph had taken for compensation. 'For the sake of evidence, the mistress of the house has given me permission to use her stolen jewellery to support this case.' He was right, they were the exact same.

Joseph bit his lip, *looks like the peelers didn't take them back after all.*

The lawman spoke clearly, 'unfortunately, the mistress of the house is unwell and could not attend this session today,' Joseph exhaled in relief, only for the prosecutor's eyes to twinkle as he looked up to the Judge. 'Your Honour, permission to call up the kitchen-maid, a Miss Sylvia Brooks?'

The Judge nodded and out from the benches walked a young woman dressed in her uniform. The same woman he had bumped into on the street. The same woman who saw him that morning . . . and saw him now not as a rich gentleman but as a common thief who had not only lied to her but had burgled her home and place of work. 'Please, sit.' She was then sworn in too.

Sylvia sat and looked to Joseph's bruised face and half swelled eye. He noticed her eyes were glistening. 'Miss Brooks, how long have you been in service to your master and mistress?' asked the welsh wig.

She nodded and tried to swallow her emotion, 'nine years, sir.'

'Therein you would know the people, neighbours, community?'

'Of course, sir.'

'Miss Brooks, have you seen this man before?'

'No.'

Oh God bless you Sylvia, thank you, thank-

'Not like this. When I saw him, he was dressed differently, formally and his face wasn't bruised as it is now. He is almost another person, but I recognise him. I began to see him walking around the street regularly; a few times over a few days.' A slight blush crept up on her cheeks. 'As a kitchen-maid, it's my job to pick up the fresh produce, you see, and, knowing the people around the street, I didn't recognise him. It was on the Friday when I came out with my basket and saw him again and this time, I bumped into him; he looked nervous about something, so I asked if everything was alright-'

No, Sylvia, please don't do this . . .

'-and he said he was thinking about moving to the district, asked how many servants are in service at my house and thanked me. He wasn't dressed like this; the man I met wore a fine jacket with a bowler hat, high collar, necktie and shined shoes.' She gave a look of confusion. 'He was dressed as a rich gentleman, so I obviously trusted his word.'

Joseph looked at her sadly, feeling the air deflate from his lungs. *Oh Sylvia, what have you done?*

'Did he tell you his name?'

She paused, remembering, 'Yes. He said his name was Charles Pettering.'

The prosecutor turned to Joseph and smiled coldly– his eyes bright. 'Well, Mister Pettering, it seems to me like *winter* has come early for you.'

The jibe was as well executed as the witness' statements. Dumbstruck, Joseph was speechless. In his head, the hammer hit the nail again, driving it into the wood- of what? There was nothing he could say, nothing he could do to defend himself. They had everything spot on. Had he really been that careless? That amateur? Suddenly he began to doubt the art he thought he'd mastered. Doubt the career, the reputation, the life he'd built for himself around these dank streets. *I don't understand. I planned everything. I'm Trace, I'm the ghost, not some worthless rat.*

'I saw him again, not long afterwards.' Sylvia Brooks chirped up again and looked to the prosecutor. 'It was early in the afternoon; I was walking back with the groceries from the market when I passed four peelers-'

'Policemen?'

She nodded, 'policemen– carrying a well-dressed man through the streets close to the house. It was peculiar; we never get drunkards or vagabonds around the neighbourhood, yet here these policemen were taking him, dragging him, more like, as he wasn't walking normally. His hat was pulled down, but I could see his face was beaten and broken. Now that I look at his face again, I can see the resemblance.' She paused, 'this is the same man.'

Just stop, Sylvia. Please. Just stop talking . . .

The prosecutor turned and looked at Joseph again, his eyes burning brightly, like a child waking up on Christmas Day. 'Thank you, Miss Brooks. You may return to your seat.'

Sylvia got up and hurried over to the benches where Joseph saw her in the corner of his eye dabbing her eyes with a handkerchief, clearly upset. His attention was then drawn back to the man who was ruining his life, or was he himself the main contributor to that? 'It seems to me you see no difference in lying to a common kitchen-maid than to the Judge, and worse yet, God Himself. Never have I seen such sin. How do you sleep at night, knowing that the crimes you commit hurt others and your venomous pride ruins lives? What is it you feel if you can feel anything with such a heart of stone? I thank the Lord the four policemen apprehended you in time, and I pity the one you maimed whilst they were doing so.'

Joseph frowned, a twinge of anger pulling. '*Maimed?*'

The prosecutor shook his head indignantly and glanced to the jury, his teeth grinding against each other. 'His own face gives evidence of a brawl and still his reptilian tongue continues to weave these lies.' He looked back to Joseph, 'I am ashamed to be in your presence. When will this act come to an end, pray tell? I am tiring of your ill-founded slander. Do you really wish for the policeman you injured to come and face the crowd?' His tone was frank, tiring of Joseph's attitude.

'Yes, I do.' Joseph said resolutely, 'I harmed no policeman, I never have.' Suddenly he understood why his case had resulted in this; usually there would be a minor sentencing, it was only major crimes that ended up in the courtroom. *It'll be fine,* he said to himself that morning, *what have they got to pin on you? It an't nothing major.* Oh, but they had found something, whether he did it or not. Something like this would end up in the newspapers.

'Your Honour, I have Constable Nicholas Lockley in the courtroom.'

The Judge allowed it and a heavy thudding footfall made its way out from the benches. The constable arrived at the front, fashioned in his complete uniform looking proud to be at the front; or was that look of pride to do with finally getting the best of the infamous Joseph Winter? Eyes narrowing, it was one of the policemen who chased him from the jewellers and who raised the baton when they caught him exiting the tunnel. The only thing he didn't recognise was the black eye and swollen cheek marking that proud face of his. *How . . . did he get that?* It looked fresh, the vessels beneath the skin prominently raised within the blue welt and there was a fresh cut on his lip.

The constable, Nicholas Lockley, glanced at Joseph and a sly smirk appeared on his lips but like an outdoor candle it was quickly snuffed out before anyone noticed, but Joseph did. It was meant only for him.

'Please, sit.' The prosecutor motioned to the chair and the policeman sat down, his black eye drawing all attention for its harshness was hard to miss. He was then sworn in before the pros-ecutor asked, 'please recount your experience with Mister Winter, to the best of your recollection.'

Wanting to close his ears, he feared what he was about to hear.

Lockley sighed and pursed his lips, as if the memory were a strain to push onto his tongue. 'Constable Bill Peters, Jim Fawn, Guy Smith and I first came across him skulking through the streets of the district. We recognised his face; he wasn't doing anything wrong, but it confused me; only the other day I'd seen him in beggar clothes whereas that day he was well-dressed, as Miss

Brooks previously stated, dressed like a fine gentleman of wealth. To me, he stuck out sorely. Sensing he was up to something, we followed him, keepin' a wary distance and saw him sneak into an alley near to a residence. We just turned the corner as a large slab in the ground was coming down and we knew where he'd gone. These old houses have many escape routes you see, tunnels; many that the owners don't even know about. Somehow this rat had found one though, and he'd scurried down it before checking to see if he were bein' followed.

'We waited a long time, must 'a been an hour and a half before we started hearing echoes of a scuffle and footsteps coming from the drain and we knew he was comin'. The slab then opened, and he came out into the light. Constable Peters went to grab him, but he was angry at being found out. He threw punches and kicks and gave us all sorts of curses and blasphemies that would bring shame right up to heaven's loftiest ceiling, making the angels blush and wince. Some even I had not come to terms with, and to me it sounded downright vulgar. Gutter-rat spittle. I jumped in to help Constable Peters who was on the floor howling in pain but Winter jumped on me then and gave me this,' he pointed to his eye and cheek, and continued with a croak in his voice, 'I cried for mercy but he wouldn't stop, he was like a feral animal on prey, a fox on a rabbit. It was cruel, relentless, and I was powerless against his might. That was when he threatened to kill me and my innocent family.'

Joseph watched him recount this wretched fabrication with a rage slowly simmering. *I ought to have killed you. The whole lot of you. Slashed your veins and broke your necks.*

'Thankfully Constables Fawn and Smith were there and they defended me with their batons to stop him,' he continued, 'the wrath of their weapons seen upon his face is nothing more than self-defence, for if not I do so believe I would not have much of a face left for my dear wife to kiss, or a life left to live, after his ferocity.'

Joseph had heard enough. With a reddened face and gritted teeth, he gripped the edge of the wood and pointed to the lying policeman as if he were readying to strike him down. *'You lie! Lie! You sell me a dog and I'll send you down to the Old Scratch! You beat me within an inch of my life and watched me bleed! I did nothing to you! To any of you, and you know it!'*

The Judge hammered his gavel against the block once, twice, thrice; its bold knocks a punctual reminder of the power he had over this courtroom. *'Order! Order I say!'* he cried, 'I will have order in my court! Mister Winter, calm yourself or you will face the consequences!' the Judge looked down at him, the glint in those cold eyes giving away his hope that Joseph did continue.

The convict bit his tongue and pursed his lips, breathing through his nose harshly. He relaxed his arm and tried to compose himself, but his reddened face showed him doing anything but that.

The courtroom was silent. Stunned.

Suddenly Joseph regretted his outburst, now realising what he had shown.

'You see Your Honour, this is a prime example of the rage and ferocity this convict displayed to Constable Lockley and the rest of the heroic band of policemen, causing them grievous bodily harm. I for one, am glad those chains are keeping him over there elsewise he'd be showing no mercy in his vile murderous intentions for us all.' The prosecutor said calmly with his hands folded over each other, eyeing Joseph carefully, seeing which nerve he could pluck next. Then unexpectedly he turned back to the constable, 'is that the truth of it, Constable Lockley, did he beat you to the ground?'

Lockley gave a slight smile and answered with a question. 'As a man of the law and of God, do you really think I would lie in this fine courtroom?'

Bastard. Pigeon-livered hornswoggling skilmalink. I wish I had fucking killed you. 'I'd stand back if I were you, prosecutor, if you're afraid of lightning bolts from the sky.' Joseph said coolly before a reply could be made. 'I am an honest man, my Lord, and I will admit to many things but hurting those policemen is something I *cannot* admit to, because I *never did it.* What you're seeing here before you are weak attempts at framing me. He's a fraud. Look at that eye, that's as fresh as a daisy, whereas mine is days old now and starting to heal. If these wounds happened on the same day, then surely they'd *look* the same?' Joseph scowled at Lockley plain to see but the policeman was quick-witted.

'Everyone's different Mister Winter. Some of us heal fast and some slow, some of us are policemen protecting the streets and some are criminals that we catch.' Joseph noted how he used the word "catch". There was pride in it.

The prosecutor walked a few steps toward him, his black gown flowing, 'of course you recognised his injuries, because you're the man that gave them to him.'

'No. I'm not.'

'You took him to the ground, laying in blow after blow, not giving him a chance to recover, to defend himself-'

'*No. I didn't.*' he emphasised.

'Of course, you did! Look at his face! This man has faced violence!'

'*Look at mine! Look at what they did to me!*'

'I *am* looking at your face but all I see is a filthy dog who cannot obey commands, even simple instructions a child could understand. To tell the truth. Now tell us all and tell us frank, did you rob Mister Newson's jewellers?'

If he wants to play this game then fine, I'll play this bloody game! 'Yes, I did.' *Two years' sentence?* Another hit of the hammer.

'Did you sell those items on at a higher rate?'

'Yes, I did.' *Four years?* Another hit.

'Did you lie to Miss Brooks about your identity so you get her to trust you, even when all you wanted was information about her house– her house you were about to break in and burgle?'

'Yes, I did.' *Six years?* Another.

The prosecutor took a step forwards, revelling in the triumph. 'Did you enter the house through a concealed tunnel, steal the necklace and ring and frighten the lady of the house and her servants?'

'Yes, I did.' *Eight? Maximum.*

There was a pause. *Did you beat the policemen upon your exit, giving Nicholas Lockley the injuries we see here before us today?*

The question ran clear through Joseph's head and he waited for it to be spoken. The prosecutor inhaled and stopped, leaving Joseph dangling with peering eyes.

But the question never came.

A sly smile tugged at the corners of the prosecutor's dry lips, then he swiftly turned and smiled at Lockley, then looked up to the judge. 'No more questions, your Honour. I have said all I need to say. This man is guilty of all crimes and has confessed to them. Let the jury decide this dog's fate.'

Joseph's eyes widened. *He knows I didn't do it. I gave him all he wanted. Confessions to each crime, and evidence of contempt against the peeler and the rest he's leaving to the jury. Oh, you are a stupid, stupid man . . . what have you done?*

The Judge motioned for the jury to retire and one by one they descended from the benches and left the room in a foreboding silence. No one spoke, not one sound was made, apart from the quiet jingle of chains as Joseph shifted his weight nervously. *Eight years most likely, or ten, in prison. They won't hang me for this. No way. Then after a while I can be released if I behave well, that's how it always works. The prisons have enough mouths to feed. Just a few years, that's nothing really; then I'll be out and home with Lucy again. That's if I don't escape first, I've done it before I can do it again . . .* The thought of Lucy pained him; he had heard nought from her ever since he left the morning of the burglary. He turned and tried to find her in the crowd but there were too many faces looking at him, and their glares were bitter. He faced the front and wiped his sweating hands on his trousers. *Just a few years, that's all it'll be.*

A few minutes passed before the jury re-entered the courtroom and found their way back to their benches and sat. One then stood, a middle-aged man with grey dusting through his black hair, and spoke loudly for the courtroom to hear, 'we find Mister Winter guilty of the crimes he has committed and should be sentenced to-'

Eight years in prison: was what Joseph wanted to hear. In truth, the outcome was far worse than even that.

'Hanging from the neck until dead.' The speaker sat down, and a haze fell over Joseph Winter as the words drifted into his ears.

No . . . no. He felt the colour drain from his face, he gulped with a dry tongue as if he were swallowing dust. But there was still hope that the Judge might disagree. *Might.* He looked up earnestly for the final words; the words of the wigged man who now ruled his future. *Please . . . say it won't be so.*

The Judge leaned over to his magistrates either side of him and heard their decision before sitting up boldly and grasping his polished hardwood gavel. The Judge no longer looked like a judge; he now looked like a gypsy and his gavel a crystal ball, but instead this time the words that were to come forth from his thin lips were not going to be a guess or an approximation: it was going to be a solid and absolute truth.

He opened his mouth and the official judgement was called. 'Mister Winter, you are a cold-blooded monster who enjoys inflicting brutality upon others, and you appear to revel in ruining the lives of the innocent people who are unfortunate enough to encounter you. You have thieved, lied, conspired and inflicted violence to the officers protecting our streets. Your case is a solid one, with substantial evidence and insignificant defence.

'I myself would not hesitate to agree with the jury, such are the depths of your crimes, yet the magistrates here have identified this as an easy way out for the likes of you and I am now inclined to agree. For your numerous crimes, you deserve to rot and fester and to be forgotten behind bars for the rest of your miserable existence; it is indeed a worser fate for someone who clearly lives by their reputation and thrives on theatrics and false fame. To hang you now would only add to your reputation and I do not want that. You shall not become a martyr for the criminal network. Therefore, after due consideration from myself and the magistrates, it is within my power from the almighty Lord himself and my pleasure of a man of justice and virtue to condemn you to serve thirty years, confined and caged, within the walls of one of the finest prisons in the country at maximum security. Once your sentence is complete, if you have not yet perished, you will receive another trial to determine where your future lies. My magistrates agree with the verdict and the motion carries. May God have mercy on your damned soul.' He raised his gavel and slammed it down onto the block; the final hammer hit, driving the nail into the wood of Joseph's coffin, its echo reverberating around the chamber right into the heart of Joseph Winter.

Thirty long years confined within brick walls, trapped inside metal bars with criminals not afraid of death or to give it. Foul stenches of faeces, filth and decay would be his new scent of home. Rats would be his pets. Murderers, rapists, addicts and vagabonds would be his fellow neighbours; chained and bound to travel the same journey of time in the same place, living the same life not to rehabilitate them, but to confine them until death snatched their meagre existence from that hell-hole and freed up another cell to be filled. His life was not his own any longer, as of now he was a part of the system. A statistic. A number to be erased.

That was his future.

All for a scroll of parchment with a few words written upon it, that and an old compass.

The sentence didn't seem to stick well, the words were not agreeing with him. He looked around the room feeling light-headed and nauseous, everything a daze. Was this reality? He hoped to god it wasn't. But it was, and his course was now set whether he liked it or not.

Guards came up and dragged him off the pedestal and away from the Judge and the looming, haunting coat of arms. He hobbled slowly, his body still aching but now not nearly as bad as his heart did. Each step felt heavier than the last. The room felt hazy, the floor trembling beneath him, unrecognisable, like the shimmering haze of the summer sun as it beat down onto London's tall buildings. Joseph looked up as he walked past the benches, past an elderly woman, a young gentleman, a bearded man with a hat, and suddenly saw Lucy Bolts standing, staring at him from the benches, weeping. Her hair was knotted, her face white. The red rings circling her eyes showed her stress; she'd been crying, for days.

Then unexpectedly she shook her head and mouthed, '*go.*' She then scurried from the benches, her head low, not wanting to know him.

Joseph bit his lip, trying to hold back tears, and headed for the door; knowing that was the last time he'd ever see her. He didn't need any other form of confirmation to know that their relationship had reached a bitter end, but for now his emotions were running too wild to focus on it. Anger? Sadness? Concern and foreboding? Hatred? Shame and guilt? Betrayal? Loss? Dread and self-loathing? He felt them all in a giant mesh of tangled feelings, each tugging hard at their own strings. *Is this enough of a thrill for you now, Trace?*

Suddenly a woman bumped into him. He'd been too encased in his head he didn't even notice her in front. The guards didn't seem to notice her either. Joseph faced her and barely recognised her in the daylight without the shouts of the punters or the acrid smell of wine, damp and vomit. 'Charlotte?' Her hair was neat with a centre parting, tied to chignons at the nape of her neck with ringlets of hair just covering her ears; she wore a high-necked dress with a buttoned front, the bell lost at the front and emphasising at her back. He did not know why he saw such detail, perhaps it was the surprise at seeing her here. Surely his favourite prostitute had not come to watch his trial. She smiled at him and held out her hand. 'I was sent to give this to you,' she muttered and brushed her hand against his, discreetly passing him a slip of paper, and then suddenly she was gone, moulding into the exiting crowd just as a natural criminal would do. She'd learned the tricks of the trade well.

He hobbled toward the exit and out into the light, into the fresh London air. Joseph breathed it in, savouring the gasps of this lovely stink before he was thrown back into the cesspit where it festered alarmingly. As the guards escorted him his chains rattled loudly, and he looked down to his hand to the note Charlotte had given him, and suddenly clarity stabbed deep.

In a blind fury, he scrunched up the note and threw it to the ground, stepping on it and pressing it into a pile of horse shit, or human shit; he didn't care. The city was full of the foul stuff. He pressed hard, but no matter how hard he stepped the words were now etched into his brain and would never leave. Would never be forgotten.

> *That were nice jewellery you stole, now time to find*
> *yer own diamonds.*
> *Always remember: yer only as good as the things you steal.*
> *Enjoy the new chains.*
> *M.V.*

Chapter Seven

Thirty years.

Three decades.

When he thought about it, a generation would be born, grown and have children of their own in that time . . . and he would still be here, stuck behind these walls. Locked behind these bars. No home to return to. No wife to love. No children to raise as age slowly took its toll. Nothing of worth at all. His reputation, although impressive, was now permanently dented and would soon fade as years washed his legacy away, the world continuing to turn. Soon, given a year or two, it would be as if he had never existed; as if he had been given a death sentence. Despite not wanting to prove the judge right, the thought of being forgotten was agony. *Thirty years is a long time. No one will know you. No one will remember. All the hard work for nothing . . . Thirty years, and even then, I won't be released, but I will have a chance at it,* he thought at he stared through the darkness at Billy's bunk above and listened to D Block sleep.

Thoughts spiralled in his mind like a sink emptying water, yet the more it emptied the more thoughts came rushing in to fill the void; and would not allow him to sleep. For the past five nights it had been like this; no rest, no peace– was insomnia creeping in or was it just a terrible case of hopelessness? He didn't know, he couldn't tell the difference.

A vicious conflict battled within him. In a way he felt glad that he didn't have to suffer the crowds or the barrage of social obligations that pushed him to marry and have children; just so he could complain like everyone else, yet a feeling of sheer isolation deepened and a helplessness of which he'd never known. The friends he thought he had had been wearing fraudulent masks; fakers out to crush any rising powers that threatened to topple their high seats. As he delved, he found the only feeling powerful enough to rival his isolation was his rage at the man he thought he knew. *Vincent fucking Jenkins, a wolf in sheep's skin. A leech in a man's clothes.* Grinding his teeth and tensing his muscles, he tried to control his temper and put his mind to other issues. A different task, yet it was that or cause more trouble and stir the pot further. Optionless, his mind pounded with the impossible.

Despite his disgust for people and society in general, he couldn't help but to feel a loss that he was apart from it. *Why do I feel like this? You always risked everything to not be there; making a living on the brink, in the niche where money could be made illegally. Every day was a risk of getting caught. You're now away from those docile vagrant ratbags that choke the cobbles. You should be happy.*

The plug was pulled, the sink drained, to then be filled again. *I'll be sixty years old. White hair, white whiskers and wrinkled skin; I'll be an old man, as bitter as my old grandfather.* A realisation dawned on him, *what life will I have once I leave here? What chance do I have in society? Who will take in a sixty-year-old ex-convict with a history? I'll be homeless, a vagabond– too weak to steal, too old to continue where I left off, too wretched to better my odds in this cruel unforgiving world. And that's if I don't die in here first, which sounds like the better option. I'm happy to grin at the daisy roots from in here.*

He sighed and turned over, closing his eyes; only to see the image of his beloved Lucy weeping: "*go.*" That was what she'd said to him, and she had meant it as she hurried away. Go back to prison, go back to the streets, go from her life and never return; what was the difference in the meaning? Either way she was done, and this time there was no bringing her back to loving him again.

In time, given a few years, he would just be a hazy face of someone she used to know; a figment of memory that only served as a minor point in her life. She'll move on, find another, have children and live her life whilst he– he would own nothing and be nothing more than a convict merely existing in the system as an example of corrupt justice. Their lives had parted, and Joseph doubted he would ever see her again and, truth be told, he wouldn't want to. For his sake and for hers. Their future no longer shared the same path: they were two different people. Nonetheless, the memory of her face still hurt to think on, her face a fresh wound not yet ready to heal.

Turning again, he pushed Lucy from his mind only to find the bruised face of the lying policeman in her stead, smirking at him with more pride than a self-portrait. *He* was the reason he had to go to trial, to have a large sentencing; framing Joseph to get him locked away for good, as well as pumping up his own name as the policeman that took Joseph Winter down. Joseph could even imagine it: "*all it took was a good old one-two from Bill, a bit of theatrics and there you have it– the man's in chains. Locked up behind bars. What can I say? Get us in another round o' the oil of victory! Apple ladies for everyone!*"

The thought was poison, so he turned again and found himself staring at the man himself: Mad Vinny Jenkins. Bald, fat and branded; a pawn dealer, a father figure– a traitor who had given him the sour tip, knowing fully well what it would lead to. He'd probably sent those peelers too, to the exact spot on the pavement. They'd have had to have known; they were there, waiting for him. An ambush, who knew Vinny had it in him. Vinny was harmless, always had been and was never a one for brains yet alone tactical eradication. *He must've had help, or maybe he's been leading me to believe he's had a dull wit all along when in truth he's a criminal mastermind.* Before him, the image of Vinny grinned and laughed madly. *Enjoy yer chains, Trace!*

His normal life was gone, traded in for a scroll of parchment; a few words written on a scrap of paper. How legitimate it was he didn't know, but it was all he had. The map and the compass, but neither would bring his life back. Nothing would. No one was out there to smile for him, to remember him fondly; it had all been for naught, the money he'd earnt losing all its worth; everything had toppled. *I need a rope. A long length of rope. And a chair, a chair to kick out from under me. What is there left to live for?* And yet, amid this despair, Joseph remembered the scroll and compass and suddenly saw in them more value than any figure printed on paper. *They're all I have left . . .*

The possibility was becoming an apparent form, a one that Joseph decided to reach out to. A new path. His only path. *What have I got to lose? I have nothing.* He closed his heavy lids and for the first night since receiving his sentence, the crook found a slim chance at peace and slept sound.

The next morning Joseph woke refreshed and rolled on through the daily routine until they were allowed outside. Stepping out into the cold morning, he buttoned his jacket, pulled his newsboy cap down and rolled himself a cigarette with stiff fingers and lit it with a match, puffing as he scanned the courtyard, peering over the masses of people in the swathing cloud of coal smoke. Bedraggled, pale and lice-ridden with scars, red blisters and ugly welts, they were not a pleasant sight to behold, yet behold them he did as he searched for the Irishman. Eyes narrowing, he took a drag and found him around a table in the courtyard watching a game of cards unfold; he walked over, motioning him to a quiet corner. 'Billy, I think it's time we start making a few new friends.' He quietly said, checking they were not being watched. He took a deep drag and held the roll-up in the corner of his lips.

'Why, don't like our cellmates, no?' He folded his arms and looked concerned, before breaking out into a smile.

'Oh, they're great, hunky dorey. I'm just not sure I can hack sleeping next to them for the next thirty years.'

'What're you talkin' about? Are y' swappin' cells?'

'No, I'm swapping fates. Billy, something got to me last night and I can't shake it.'

'Aw, man, have you got the lice too?'

'What? No. I'm talking about escape.' He whispered the word as if it was a taboo. 'Billy, we have a treasure map to keep us busy and a compass to keep us in the right direction and to be frank, I'm tired of squabbling over the thought of legitimacy; I reckon there's treasure out there and I'm willing to put my faith into this map because, let's face it, what else do we have left to put faith into? God certainly an't looking after us. We'll follow the pointers, chart a course and find whatever this leads to. We already have the first point; all we need now are new friends and a chance.'

The Irishman smiled, showing off his slightly crooked front tooth. 'Fifteen years is what I got, and I never was a one for long commitments. If it's escape you're telling me, why, I'm up for it– I've escaped from one marriage and that's basically a prison so I've done it already boyo.' He winked. 'Now, escaping from here would be piece o' piss but out t'ere, that's where it gets harder. Peelers everywhere; you'd be caught and t'rown back in here before the day's done.'

'I don't mean escaping just from here.' He said solemnly, sucking in the tobacco, 'I'm talking about escaping Britain altogether. Escaping from this poxy country. That'd be the only way we can be free. We have a map that points further than the docks.'

Billy nodded as he began to understand what he spoke of. 'Aye. Why the new friends though? And who? Cons in here aren't exactly lookin' for friends.'

'They might not be looking for friends but they're looking for someone to trust. Everyone needs someone to watch their back, especially people with fingers in the wrong pies.'

'You'd trust a con?'

'You trust me, don't you?'

'Aha, well played.' He poked a finger at him then looked out at the crowds, 'who would you pick to involve in this then? I'm not bein' funny, fella, but this nest is full o' pricks and rats.'

Joseph pursed his lips and looked around at the decrepit congregation, slipping his hands in his pockets. 'I'm not sure yet, not many; just a few who's wits are sharp and who're willing to risk everything for a new life outside these walls.'

'Risk, well I'd say half the prison would jump at that– risk is what got em' in here. As for wits, now that's a different thing. See, most are wily but not witty, they can't t'ink on their feet and they crumble under pressure. Ot'ters, well they got a head like a bag o' spuds. It'll be harder to find the ones who can get through it. Why not just us two, eh? Less people to worry about, less mouths to feed.' He suggested with a shrug.

He shook his head, 'we're going to need about seven new friends. Anymore and we'll struggle to get them all out and away. You'll see mate, I've got an idea.'

'What is it?'

Just then a large pot-bellied man walked by with a large rounded head and a tiny bowler hat and eyed them up with black beads squished into a fold of facial dough. *This is too dangerous to talk about freely.* 'I'll tell you when we've found the numbers, but for now we just need to find them. Put some feelers out and see what you can find. I've already got one person in mind.'

'Who's that?' asked Billy.

'Just someone I know who likes to run.'

Over the next two days Joseph didn't see much of his accomplice, only when they returned to their cells for the night, but they did not talk about their progress; the risk of the others overhearing was too great. The less people knew, the better– this was intended to be a small affair after all. Joseph knew, and suspected Billy did too, that if word got out prisoners would be hawking them for a chance at escaping, so they kept as quiet as they could. Instead they waited for the next day and found each other in the courtyard and Billy noticed Joseph had a guest. A young lad was with him. 'Alright sonny?' He nodded to him and the boy nodded back.

'This is Robert Epping, or Hare, whichever you choose but he knows the deal and has agreed.' Joseph mentioned.

'Ah, spot on. How d' you do mate?'

Rob replied with a simple, 'I'm well thank'ee.' And kept quiet; it was clear he was a more of a listener rather than a speaker– there was no wonder why Joseph had thought him appropriate.

After finding a quiet corner, Joseph got down to business. 'Any luck?'

Billy nodded, 'Some. I saw a few people and gave them some words; but I didn't tell them fully what's goin' on. Instead I told them a story; puttin' the feelers out, see who would take to it.'

'Wait, so what did you tell them then?' Joseph asked, intrigued.

'The story of the Leprechaun and the Magic Mask.' Billy Baker grinned, 'I wasn't about to go blurtin' out everything 'cause then word would really spread so I made up a story of our intentions, like a disguise.' Their looks begged the answer, so he obliged and began his tale.

'There once was a lucky leprechaun who was skipping along a country path when suddenly he came across a lake. Across the lake there were woods, and the lucky leprechaun loved talking to the trees, but he was unhappy for he had no boat to sail across. He thought on it and picked the magic mask out from his pocket and asked it what to do. It advised to build a bridge.

'"Now there's an idea, to get across this lake! A bridge of bows is what I'll make!" So, he kicked his heels, threw some dust and made a bridge of colourful bows. Skipping across it, he entered the woods, singing a merry little tune with his brown curly hair bouncing and shiny black shoes clopping. A happy little leprechaun was he and he smiled to the trees, but the trees did not smile back. The trees, see, they were angry with him and thought him a cheat, for he had skipped over their lake using a bridge of colourful bows where he was meant to swim.

'"A cheat? Not I," says the leprechaun, "I am a lucky Irishman you see, for I have a magic mask with me. I only came t'rough for my gold at the end and then I'll be off, gone, around the bend."

'The trees, they did not agree, so they set a trap for him; a hole in the ground and as he skipped and sang, sang and skipped he fell and landed in the cold dark earth. Looking sadly up to the surface, he saw the trees and knew they didn't believe his wish. Out of options, he took out his magic mask and sang to it in a woeful tone.

'"O Magic Mask, Magic Mask with terrific powers meant to last; I am in a hole, dark and cold– will you help me to my pot of gold?"'

'Suddenly the wooden mask opened its blank eyes and sang back to him. "Unlucky leprechaun, unlucky leprechaun, I will help you cope– if you will but not lose hope. A rope, a ladder, a coil of spring, and yet none will be able to lend a wing. This is my advice should you choose to heed; it is friends that you really need.'"

'"Not I,"' says the leprechaun, "I am a lucky Irishman you see; I do not need friends here with me– when I have you.'"

'The mask opens its eyes again. "Friends have arms, have legs and will help– all the unlucky leprechaun need do is yelp. Whistle, sing, or tell a tale– and in the end you shall prevail.

'"If they find out what I'm trying to reach– they will take my treasure and ignore my speech. O Magic Mask of might and must, how will I know who to trust?'"

'"Tell them of your shiny amount and if they believe you, their trust will count. Witty and risky they must be, your friends are out there, wait and see.'" The magic mask sang.

'The leprechaun skipped in the air. "Well twiddle-dee-dee! Friends are out there for a lucky Irishman such as me! A share to each I shall give if they will help this leprechaun live! Help from this hole is what I need; this is the message I choose to heed. Who will be out there, I wonder, when I whistle a tune to out and yonder? Thank you, O Magic Mask, powerful and great; for you have changed this leprechaun's fate!"

'He lifted his head to face the hole, breathed in the air and whistled the finest of tunes to the woodland above . . . and waited for his friends to come to him.' Billy paused as he glanced at a woman passing by. Then he found Joseph's eyes again and smiled, 'that's what I told them.'

'So how does the story end then?' Rob chirped, his eyes bright with wonder.

'We'll find out soon enough boyo. I paused the story and told whoever wanted to find out the ending to find me this morning in the courtyard around this area.' He turned and spied the crowds, waiting for the friends to reveal themselves.

People passed by, some in groups and some alone but none were interested in them. A few people glanced around yet their eyes were not curious; they had no care for the three of them. No use for them. *The ones who can sift through the story will be the friends we need– they'll be the smart and risky ones. Billy's much sharper than I thought,* Joseph mused, impressed at the allegory as he stood scanning the passing crowd.

Suddenly a man in dirty trousers with mishap stitching, a grey shirt and braces came wandering up to them and eyed the Irishman up, before his face contorted into recognition. 'You! The Irish bloke who told the story! I've been doin' some thinking, and to me it seems like something else is going on here. Either with the story, or with you; I can't put my finger on it. It just sounds more like a riddle and I want to know the ending. What happens? Do the friends come and save the unlucky leprechaun?' He stood with his hands in his pockets and a glint in his eyes. He had black stubble and untidy sideburns stretching out from underneath his cheap scally cap.

Joseph looked at Billy and Billy looked at Joseph. 'What's your name?' Billy asked.

The man eyed them suspiciously, 'Dave James. Why?'

'Because Dave,' Joseph spoke up, *'you're* the friend we've been looking for.'

He took a step back, 'I don't get it. I don't want to be part of no gang. I don't like what's going on here.'

'Dave, how would you like to be one of the friends that helps the leprechaun escape from the hole to go and get the pot of gold?' Billy asked, smiling coyly.

Over the next hour, several people found them and came asking similar questions about the fate of the leprechaun until six people had joined Dave in waiting. Harold Arms had been the next man to join, and his name was more than appropriate seeing as he reached a height of six feet. The sisters, Tess and Poppy Mills, followed; Tess, the eldest of twenty, had a petite young face with long dark hair but had eyes of sharp grey like flint and Poppy, the younger sibling who looked to be twelve, had freckles and an overbite with tight curls spooling to her shoulders.

Benjamin Smith arrived next and talked quickly for a man with so few teeth left. Aged, wrinkles lined his weathered face and an old scar marked his right cheek and down the side of his nose and upon them looking, gave a brief overview of his adventurous past. 'I ran away from home at thirteen and stowed away on a merchant ship. Instead of tossing me, the Capt' kept me and installed me as a cabin boy. After I got a taste for the waves, I worked me way up to become a master rigger. Spent me life at sea, I have. I've travelled the world, fought off buccaneers and at one point was captured by cannibals on a tropical island and managed to barter my freedom with a spare bit of black tobacco I had in my pocket. That were a sticky situation, let me tell ya.' He grinned as they all looked to him in amazement, Joseph especially, knowing he was perfect for what he had in mind. He wore a stained shirt and a jacket with a large tear at the sleeve with a belt made of string holding up his faded trousers. A faded and holy *Boss of the Plains* hat sat atop his head and with the white frizzy hair that grew out from under it, Joseph would've put him at late fifties to early sixties.

A woman approached them next after spotting the Irishman through the crowd. 'I was just wondering about that story of yours,' she paused and thought, 'that I think you told me yesterday.' She was tall, slender and pretty, wearing a flowing yet old dress with no bodice and had her long light brown hair up into a loose chignon with small ringlets hanging around her ears; a lovely portrayal she gave, which begged the question of what on earth she was doing in this hellhole. 'The unlucky leprechaun, was it? A magic mask he had too, didn't he?'

Billy nodded.

She gave a slight smile, 'A fine tale, but I have questions. To me it seems odd how he didn't see the hole coming, if he had the mask that gave him prophecies.'

He shrugged, 'the mask could only give him advice on what to do, not what to expect.'

The woman didn't seem to buy it. 'Either way it seems like there's holes in the story and it means something other than its appearance; an allegory, I think it's called, but I do wonder about the ending. What happens next?' Victoria Penning was her name and she was asked to stand and wait if she wanted to discover the truth behind it.

Lastly, a man named Hugh Jackson found them and wanted to know how the story ended, as well as how much one of the friends got in the share of gold. He was a small man with a scruffy ginger beard and seemed to see through the story. He didn't know what it was, but Joseph couldn't help but think him to look like the leprechaun from the story– all he needed was the magic mask.

At length, once he'd tallied their number, Joseph nodded to Billy and they turned to their new friends who stood wondering. Their inquisitive minds had been agile enough to see more than a story, to come asking what it meant and more importantly, why Billy had told them it.

'Right,' the Irishman started, 'you're all here cos y' want to see what happens next in the story and what it means, but first my good friend Joseph needs to run over a few t'ings.'

Looking at them all with his cool greens, he gazed at their blank faces one by one and knew this was a start to something, depending on their answer. It was crucial; he had to know who was willing and where they stood with following directions from an age-old treasure map. Taking out a pinch of tobacco, he rolled it into a strip of newspaper he'd managed to pilfer and lit it with a match. 'Faith is a funny kind of thing,' he took a drag and kept the cigarette in the corner of his lips, 'you have it, or you don't. Some people choose to put their faith in God and believe he will sort everything out. Some people choose to put their faith into shiny coins and folded notes, believing money will get them out of any problem and solve their woes. The leprechaun had faith and believed that friends were out there to come to his aid and help him from the hole to find the pot of gold. My faith . . .' Lucy sprang into his head suddenly, memories of his home he hadn't stepped into for weeks, and he paused. Her hair, her arms, her embrace, her face . . . her face? It was red and crying, yet its clarity was blurring. He was forgetting her, slowly but surely, and he had to let her go.

His gaze falling to the ground, he took a drag and looked back to them. 'My faith is in a treasure map I found, and, in the moonlight, I saw different words written in a different ink; a hidden pointer to the first part of the hunt. The map is old; I have a vague idea of who wrote it and set the trail, but I don't know if the treasure has been found already, so don't ask, but I choose to believe that it's still out there waiting for a shovel and a pair of hands to bring it out into the light once more.' Joseph looked to them all, trying to reach out to them, 'I've been framed for a crime I did not commit; I've been set up for failure by friends I thought I had. I've been dumped by the people that I loved, and I've been leading a life I can no longer be proud of.' He paused, 'I've got to believe it. I need to believe in something. I'm putting my faith into this map, into this venture and treasure, whether it exists still or not,' he shrugged nonchalantly, 'I've nothing else to lose.

'My life in London is gone. In this urban sprawl of decadence, I find naught but ghosts; in the beating heart of the Empire I find nothing but hopelessness; a vacant vessel void of fibre, filling its lungs with the stench of horse shit, coal smoke and rotting death. A disgusting habit, yet this city *needs* its fix and won't stop. It's up the pole with its flaws. After standing back, I can't do it anymore. I can't play the fool. This city . . .' he looked to the ground, *this city has rose me up and tore me straight back down. This city has destroyed me. I'm worthless.* 'This city is nothing more to me than a hovel of waste and a metropolis of corruption; granted I played my part in it, Christ knows I'm no saint, but I an't a sinner either. There's nothing left for me here. Everything I had I lost and I'm to remain behind bars for the next thirty years for something I did not do; but I'm not going to do that. I don't plan to. I'm prepared to follow the trail wherever it leads, which means escaping from this hinterland and getting away from this damned country as fast as possible.' He took another drag, the orange tip burning inward, 'this an't something I can do alone though, and I need a few helping hands.

'*I* told the leprechaun to find friends and he whistled a fine tune and here you all are. So, the questions I ask you all are these: are you willing to put your faith into another life outside these walls and help me find whatever lies at the end of this map? Are you willing to trust each other, to help each other and to put yourself at risk? Are you ready to escape from here and set sail into the unknown?' Joseph examined their faces, waiting to see their reaction, waiting to hear their response.

Their faces each told different stories– some were confused, some indignant but most were intrigued. It was Rob who stepped forward first, 'Aye. I'm ready, I think.'

Joseph smiled and nodded, 'good lad.'

'Aye, I's spent most a' me life at sea,' Benjamin spoke up, 'it would be good to sail it one more time. I know I'm an old man now, there's nothing left for me here.'

He nodded in approval. *That makes three.*

'Well,' Hugh Jackson chirped, and Joseph's ears pricked up, 'I got a girl in here.'

He pursed his lips, 'Alright mate, thanks-'

'-but she hates me, and I hate her so I could do with a trip away.'

Joseph smiled, 'welcome to the crew.' Giving a nod, he sucked in another breath of smoke.

Tess and Poppy took a minute to talk it over and came back. 'We'll help you find the way; you seem like a nice man, and honest, which is hard to come by.' Answered Tess with Poppy nodding.

'You do,' added the woman, Victoria, 'almost too nice. How can I be sure you're not just scamming us? There are plenty of gangs in here who play games for their own gain to get us winding that Crank, or for revenge or something else. How can we trust you?'

Joseph paused; she had a fair point. He hadn't thought about that, he was asking them to trust each other when they didn't know if they could trust him. *Just show her the map, that's the only way you can get them to believe you.* He considered the options and saw no other alternative. Reaching around to his back pocket he pulled the scroll out and kept it close to him, hiding it as much as he could.

All eyes were drawn to the paper he now held, and there was a moment of silence. They slowly crowded around and, when he was sure no one else could get a peek, he opened it and let those who could read have a quick glance over. Then he rolled it back up rapidly and tucked it into his belt. 'That's what I've been talking about. Take it as you will, but I believe it's real.'

'How do we know you didn't just make that whilst you've been in here?' Victoria asked, penning him with more possibilities. She was clearly a bright woman.

'I can't write like that, and I an't pulling your leg, but where in here could I get a quill, or ink, or paper that looks as old as this?'

She considered and concluded. 'Alright, fair enough. I'll be a part of this.'

Joseph smiled. *Seven. Now to know about the last two.*

Dave James eyed him and Billy up, his face turning into a frown. 'I don't know, it sounds pretty dangerous to me.'

'It will be, it's a risk and that y' can count on but I'd sure as hell want to be a chancer and live me life rather than spend it in here for the next fifteen years.' Billy added.

He played with his braces, stretching them out as he weighed up the options. Eyes narrowing, he thought it through. 'You two seem friendly enough. I don't think you're messing us about, and I don't think you've made that map up– but what do I know? I'm just another criminal in here and I can't even read the bloody thing. Thinking about the result, what happens with that? When we find this treasure, the pot of gold, *if* we find it, how can I know you won't all take the money and run?'

'Dave – it is Dave, an't it? – I give you my word, if you help to find it you will get a share of the gold.'

'Shake on it.' He held out his hand.

Gestures mean more to this guy than words do. Joseph took it and they shook. 'Alright, I'm in.'

Eight, and could be nine. The last man's word counts. 'Harold,' he said slowly, trying to remember his name. 'What do you say, possum?' All eyes turned to the tall man in a thin waistcoat, frayed tweed jacket and a rough comforter wrapped about his neck. Fine sandy hair was receding yet pulled forward as his forehead crinkled whilst he pondered his options.

Harold felt their stare and blushed awkwardly; his breath visible as the chilly air caught it. 'Well, I just-I just, well . . . I never been on a boat before. I never been out of England, I never even been out London.' He looked to the ground timidly, 'I've always been around buildings, so to set out to sea– that just frightens the life out of me, so it does. So vast, so empty, I wouldn't know what to do with myself. And I wouldn't want to get in the way.'

'I've never been out of London before either. I've never seen an open field, a hill or a mountain in my life. These buildings are my home and I wouldn't want to leave them, if it wasn't for the feeling they give me now. To tell you it straight, I don't feel comfortable anymore; I'm in a place where I shouldn't be, and I'm forced to stay here for the next thirty years. By then the buildings will feel like they're craning over to watch me slowly wither away like a plant at the end of autumn. It already feels like that now. It's not as if the buildings will care anyway, they'll move on with or without me and by the rates of things I'll be forgotten by the morrow.

'That's why I've got to face my fears and set sail out and away, and I'll have my new friends with me so that when I eventually do begin to wither, or falter, or lose hope, they'll be there to support me instead. Not like the people here. For the past month, I've been nothing but vermin to them; a rat they've caught and trapped. No one's cared.'

'But that's what we are. We are just rats.' Harold reminded him.

'Yes, but we're rats with a treasure map and a chance to change our fates. How long is your sentence for?'

'Ten years.'

'Do you still want to be here in ten years, or would you rather be somewhere else with the sun on your face and a chance to breathe fresh air?'

He thought about it for a moment then nodded. 'I'll help you find what's at the end.'

Joseph smiled, smoked the last of his cigarette and looked at the group; a variety of ages, heights and characters yet all sharing the same aim. They'd all agreed to join, yes, but the next hurdle would show their true differences. Escape– its difficulty would be high, Joseph knew.

'Who was it that set this trail?' Tess asked curiously, 'you said you think you know them, would we?'

He pursed his lips as he looked to his feet, wondering whether this would dissuade any. *Tell them. They need to know.* 'You might. I believe the people who left this map are Eve and Henry Scott; the legend that left behind a treasure that no one's found. The Lost Loot. Some might know it as Scott's Trove.'

Suddenly the young girl, Poppy, stepped forward. 'Why did you ask us for help if *you* wanted to go so badly? Why didn't you just go by yourself?' Her sister then abruptly pulled her back and started whispering harshly.

'Because I wanted to give others an opportunity for a new life,' he replied with a friendly smile, 'and because I need a hand with sailing a ship. That's something I can't do alone.' With a flick, he tossed the blackened end of the cigarette away.

Chapter Eight

It should work; if everything goes to plan, Joseph thought as he lay staring at the bunk above. *They said they're all good to go and can manage this, all I've got to do is get used to trusting their word.* Experience had taught him to doubt, to consider before placing trust in someone– it was almost as valuable as a rare jewel; not something to give away easily. After all, he didn't know them outside these walls. They could be anyone. Uncertainty plagued him like a virus, or was it concern? Either way, he wasn't sure what the next day would bring; after all, escaping from this high-walled cage of brick and metal wasn't meant to be easy.

After their first meeting, the group had joined again the next day and then once more a day later to discuss the escape plan. There wasn't much to it – he knew it wasn't fool proof – but it was the best he could come up with under the circumstances they were all in. Now that a week had passed since they all last saw each other; Joseph's doubts were high.

It was necessary for them to not meet, he kept telling himself; to not arouse any suspicion from the other cons or guards and yet now instead of arousing their suspicion he'd aroused his own. Could he trust their word? Would they remember the steps he and Billy had put in place? Should he have put faith in them? Joseph turned over, pursing his lips and ignoring the lice; he just didn't know. Overthinking was preparation and being a part of his meticulous nature, it couldn't be helped– it was a gift, a skill he'd honed but it was also a curse that took away his chance to rest. Soon, not only was his issue with trust belittling him, his faith in the plan was too. *Five steps. That's all there is, five steps to go through. Easy enough to follow. Five steps and we'll be out of here.*

The convict rolled over and faced the cellmates who were snoring soundly. Thankfully, he hadn't crossed them much since his arrival and had gone to bed straight away after lockdown nearly every night. Only once had they tried to interfere with him, but he had made sure with his own newly acquired knife they were not to touch him again. He looked at them and remembered his first night from what seemed like an eternity ago and realised this was to be his last night in this bed. *I'll be sleeping somewhere else tomorrow night, if the five steps work. If not; I'll be sleeping well at the end of a rope.* The thought had been omnipresent in his mind since they created the plot to escape but instead of letting it haunt him, he used it as a reason to be even more precise with planning.

'*Johnathon?*' Billy whispered from above.

He looked up to the wooden planks and dark mouldy straw mattress. '*What?*'

'*Havin' trouble sleeping?*'

'*Yeah, you?*'

'*Yeah, but I'm not worried about what'll happen tomorrow. I got something else on me noodle.*'

'*What's that?*' Joseph asked.

'*What if we travel this distance and reach the end only to find the pot o' gold empty. What if the Lost Loot's already been found? The people we've befriended, they're expectin' something.*'

'*We'll be giving them something, don't worry. A new life, freedom, a chance: if not for the gold they'll have that.*'

'*What if they don't want that? What if they'd rather have the gold?*'

Joseph considered it, '*then we'll just have to see what happens. We've only met their surface, it's out there where we'll meet who they really are.*'

'*True, true.*' Billy paused, '*Joe?*'

'*What?*'

'*What did the map tell you that night?*'

Joseph hadn't told him, hadn't told anyone. That information he'd seen in the moonlight he'd kept to himself, just as insurance so that if anything did happen to the map, he'd still know where to go first. Considering, he looked over to the men on the other side; they were sound asleep. It was safe. *'After I turned it over, I saw a large circle drawn in the centre of the paper; it was cut into quarters and in the bottom right quarter there were four lines that said:*

'Seek the beach, the sand, the roots of the flying trees,
The next part is hidden there, in amongst the leaves.
A bright sun and good tide will bring you on,
To the good Cape of the good Gabon.

'It'd been written in a different ink, that's why we couldn't see it before– it only showed itself in a different light.'

There was a pause. *'Oh, blimey that's it, ain't it? That's where it's buried.'* Billy shuffled over to the side and looked down to Joseph.

He shook his head, *'I've no idea what we'll find there, but I don't think it'll be the end. I reckon this is just the first marker.'*

'It might be matey, it might be. What is that place though? What's Cape of Gabon? Where is Gabon?' he said the word slowly, unfamiliar with it passing his tongue.

'I don't know. We need a world map, I'm sure it'll be on there somewhere.'

'How're we gonna' know what direction to head in if we don't know where to go?' Joseph noted the concern in the Irishman's voice.

'We do know where to go, it's given us our heading.' Joseph said.

'It has?'

'Yes.' Joseph answered, *'south-east. I'll explain it soon.'*

After an uneasy night's sleep, Joseph only nodded to Billy in the morning; giving nothing away of any conspicuous activity and went to breakfast. The food was abysmal as always, half rotten and maggoty but Joseph ate and ate, filling his stomach until he could eat no more. How much good it would do him he didn't know but he thought it better if his belly were full– for he didn't know when or where his next meal would be. *If* he were to have a next meal. The thought of the noose was like a spider in his mind; no matter how many times he swept it under the carpet it still came scuttling out trying its best to scare. *No. It'll work and I will not hang today or any other day.* Despite the reassurance, he knew that spider would return before this day was done.

He wandered out to the courtyard and squinted. The sky was a clear watery blue and gave no protection from the blinding sun. A chilling breeze blew through the shadows, sweeping away the dense clouds of smog, tugging at his clothes; he felt prickles rise along his back and down his arms– he buttoned his jacket up, pulling his cap down and planting his hands deep into his pockets. In amongst the expanding crowds he saw people wearing hats and comforters and holey gloves to brace against the cold; winter still seemed to not budge. *Winter won't be here for much longer though; Winter will be out on the breeze.* The thought was relieving, and he walked out and around, craving a cigarette even more now he'd ran out of tobacco.

More fresh faces were now mingling in amongst the crowds; new criminals trying to fit into the pecking order. Some were already in with Fat Fred's gang, although Joseph guessed they wouldn't last long– the fresh fish were always picked on and within a day or two would be locked up walking the never-ending staircase or winding a continuous crank. Criminals like Fat Fred were here to stay and had made their life on the inside. *Not for me, I have other plans.* Joseph scoured the scene and picked out the sisters Tess and Poppy sitting against the wall, looking around just as he was. *They're waiting for the signs; they're watching for the first step.* He wondered how many others of his gang were doing the same, watching, waiting, hoping.

-    Step one.

'Alright,' said Billy as he and Hugh approached a group sitting on a table playing dice.

The laugher and banter stopped, as well as the play. Together, they turned and looked up to them. They didn't look friendly and didn't try to be. 'Mind if we join?' The Irishman asked.

The men looked to the man sitting on the other side and he shrugged lightly. He was stocky, with his waistcoat struggling to keep itself buttoned around the obtuse curve of his waist. Lines marked down from under his hat, making them guess he had a tattoo on his bald head; he had stubble though, but that was as far as hair went on his head. 'Shift over boys, let 'em sit. The dice don't judge nobody, they only ask full payment.' He nodded, and two men shuffled along to make room.

Billy and Hugh sat and watched them. 'Set point is six.' He told them, 'if the dice add up to lower– y' get nothing and higher– y' get points depending on how close you are to the set point, but if you guess the number right y' get five points. If you get twelve points after one round you get the money. What say you, Pete? Start us off.' said the large man.

'Hmm. I say eight.' Said Pete, the man next to Billy.

'Four.' The next man said.

'Ten.'

'Nine.'

'Eleven.'

Eyes turned to Hugh. 'Oh, erm, three.'

Billy chose five.

The man rattled the dice together in his palms and blew on them before casting them upon the table. The dice rattled and landed. One read three. The other read five.

Eyes turned to Pete until he realised what had happened. 'Eyy! Nice! Go on then, keep 'em rolling!'

The dice were collected up again and the bets were given. The caster blew on them and threw; the dice rolled and landed; one read four and the other read six. Points were awarded and the system rolled on again.

'Five.'

'Nine.'

'Two.'

'Eight.'

'Twelve.'

'Seven.' Hugh said.

'Twelve.' Billy said.

The tattooed man blew on the dice and cast them. One read six and the other read the same. 'Tie!' he called, 'Tom and . . .'

'Billy.'

'Billy, you two face off. What say you?'

'Six.' Tom gave.

'Four.' Billy said.

The man handed Hugh the dice. 'You roll 'em, there's a change of hands for the tie.'

Hugh took the dice, rattled them and threw them to the table, just as Billy moved his arm and knocked their path. One landed on three, and other landed on one. 'Four!' Billy said. 'There it is, four!'

'You moved your arm! You forced them to stop!' Tom exclaimed.

'They'd already stopped mate. Come on then, cough up y' pennies to the lucky Irishman.' He grinned and held out his hand, but none moved.

'I an't coughing up nothing, you stopped 'em! They would've landed on six!' cried Tom.

Billy shook his head, 'they were landing on four an' they landed on four, Mister Tommy. If I didn't know any better, I'd have thought you were calling me a liar. No point tryna' act the maggot, we all saw what happened.'

'I am calling you a liar!'

Billy pushed him off the table, 'I am not a liar!'

Tom scrambled to his feet and Billy stood. The rest of the table stood and made to move to prevent what was to occur. 'Come on then. If y' t'ink you can!' Billy antagonised.

Tom yelled in anger and threw the first punch, but Billy blocked and smacked him hard around the jaw.

-     Step two.

Halting, Joseph looked up to the sound of a scuffle beginning to arise over near the tables. The sound of men punching and hitting, grunting from blows and shouting in protest was slowly becoming audible. Attention from around was being drawn to that area, people were turning to see what was happening; interest was growing, and people began to slowly gravitate toward it.

Following the crowd, he hurriedly moved toward the area and saw four people pushing, punching, kicking and screaming over the heads of the onlookers. The noise was amplifying; the yells were bouncing off the walls, chatter and shouts were spreading through the people.

'What's 'appening?' He heard someone say.

'Is that a fight?'

'Get away 'fore we get pulled in!'

Some pushed through the crowd, eager to taste violence once again, jumping into the thick of it without any second thoughts. More and more people were pushed into it, jumping in or trying to flee but it was too late– the ferocity was spreading, and the fight was escalating into a brawl of many bodies. *It's not moving fast enough; more people need to get in there.*

Joseph pushed through the crowd, acting as if he was trying to get a better look but instead shoved two more men into the fray and continued to push more in until fifteen, eighteen, twenty – he lost count– were in the fight. It looked an ugly battle too; blood was running down faces and teeth were being kicked out. If anything, it was more of a release of tension for the more violent folk, especially after trying to keep straight in here for so long, but it was something Joseph didn't want to partake in. Scarpering from the centre of the crowd, he slipped into a different setting where the sound of shouts replaced the cacophony of pain and wonder.

Scanning the courtyard, he saw guards running and yelling, waving their batons in the air, and looked back to the crowd. 'Come on, get out of there quick.' He muttered as he began to move against the flow of people.

Here, he noted that some had not moved from their spots and took little or no interest in the ongoing brawl. It was understandable– the less they got involved in anything, the better; *old timers– they must've seen it all before.* Suddenly he noticed he was not the only one jostling away from the crowd. There were four people also joining him; people who were moving almost as if they'd anticipated the fight.

Which they had.

A figure moved through the crowd, swiftly and quietly, until he reached the gate at the end. There, he looked to be fiddling with it for a second until the metal grill swung open slightly. The figure was short, nimble-looking and turned around to check who had seen him, and more importantly who was coming.

Two men then approached him. They exchanged something and then both slipped through the gap, running through the dark archway that led to the front courtyard. Yet the smaller figure didn't join them and instead stayed where he was.

Joseph saw it happen and his eyes widened. He broke out into a run, heading straight for the open gate; it was not in desperation that he ran though, for he recognised the identity of the smaller figure and knew he would keep the gate open.

As he had told him to do.

'Good lad, Hare! Now go, I'll keep it open for the rest.' Joseph huffed as he grabbed the gate and ushered Rob through it.

A moment later the two sisters approached him and quickly ran through, before Victoria who gave him a quick nod as she passed by. The old man came up to him next, wheezing, 'me legs ain't what they used to be, lad.' And looked to be struggling as he came to the gate.

Joseph had no time to waste. 'You'd best use what you've got left of them then, Ben, and bloody use 'em well if you want to keep off the gallows.'

Benjamin nodded, 'Aye.' And quickly scrambled through as quickly as he could.

Come on Billy, hurry up Hugh. Don't get too caught up in the fight. We haven't got the time for delays, he prayed, grinding his teeth together, spying the crowd that was beginning to disperse. The sound of yells could still be heard, and batons could be seen flashing above the heads of the watchers. It looked like the gaolers were sorting the scrap out harshly, which was no surprise. Soon people would start to notice the gate had been unlocked; soon people would start to gather around him to let them through too. *Hurry up lads, come now!* Then suddenly two figures appeared from behind and skirted around Joseph to get to the open gap.

'No, wait!' he exclaimed, but when they turned, he saw bruised but recognisable faces. Hugh had a red blotchy eye and scratches lining his cheeks and was limping but not badly and Billy smiled through a bleeding lip and bright red cheek. A clump of his hair had been torn out. 'Tis alright Joe, we're here mate.'

Urging, time was of the essence, 'lovely stuff. Now go!' They quickly shot through the gate, shutting it behind him.

The three of them bolted through the length of a dark archway and for a brief minute all they could hear was their harsh breathing and clopping footfall bouncing off the stone walls. A fresh breeze swept through the tunnel, but their blood was running too warmly to let them feel it. Adrenalin kicked in and pushed them onward to the gate at the other end. The gate that had been left open . . .

Hugh ran through first, followed by Billy and Joseph who slammed it shut behind him. His heart was racing, thumping loudly in his head– he liked it, its beat was a familiar one, a pace he hadn't heard in a long time. Once more he felt like he was Trace again and longed for the pursuit, giving him a glimpse of comfort; for a moment he felt normal, for the moment he felt free.

- Step three.

The front courtyard was of a different layout to their usual one– this one was smaller, compact, which made the number of prisoners in here look even higher. People were everywhere, the courtyard choked and those closest to the gate looked stunned as the escapees came bursting through and weaved through the crowd.

'*Walk-er!* Wot' are they doing?!' Joseph heard from a person he passed by.

'How'd they get the keys?'

'Blimey! What's goin' on here then?!' cried a man as he jumped out the way of the string of runners.

Joseph paid them no heed, he had not the time to. *Just get to the end where the main gates are. Just get to there.* He glanced ahead to the great walls of drab bricks and metal, to the tall entrance he was never meant to see again. Once more the atheist prayed, prayed that Dave and Harold had managed to hinder the gaolers enough for them to unlock the gates.

Following the slithering Irishman as best as he could, he squirmed his way through the shocked inmates. They were all new faces to him; it seemed odd to be in a different area, it almost felt like being in a new prison, and suddenly doubt crept in making him question his judgement of direction; was this the right way that led to the entrance; or was this the one that led to the rear? Despite the haste, a sickness swelled in him. To be caught now meant death.

Suddenly Billy halted and Joseph almost crashed into him. 'What's going on, why've you stopped?' he urged with sweat running down his face.

The answer was more of a visible kind and had far more of an effect. In front of them was a clearing where the people had spread from the centre, and in the middle was a gaoler holding Harold in a headlock, his baton raised high ready to crack skulls. Beside was another gaoler restraining Dave. The gaoler shot daggers with his glare at the crowd, his eyes set on the criminals. *'If any o' you lot tries it, you'll all be facing the gallows!'* He declared loudly, and the surrounding noise dimmed. 'I an't having no one try to get to me or my men– am I clear?! Word has already been sent to the others, alarms have been raised; they'll be here soon and he's not moving until they do, if not this baton's coming down on his head! I'll do it, I don't care! I couldn't give a toss about you lot o' piss-pots!'

Joseph noticed the gaoler restraining Dave was fumbling as he tried to get the manacles out to clasp onto his wrists. The hope of the flight was dwindling, the image of escape was soon to be thwarted. He felt as if someone had kicked him hard in the stomach. *No, not now, not when we're this close.* Behind the gaolers was a thick wooden door lined with metal braces; its purpose was to be impenetrable: *that's the door. That's the one!*

The gaoler was still fumbling, clearly new to this.

The moment had to be now.

'I'm getting the keys.' He whispered to Billy and he turned his head in surprise.

The gaoler holding Harold suddenly cried out, released him and fell to the ground, just as the other let go of Dave and scrambled at the arm that was crushing his throat. There, in the place of the uniformed guards, stood Victoria holding the baton and Rob holding the gaoler with a tight grip.

At once, the crowd rushed forwards all thinking the same thought. The gap of the clearing was closed in a matter of seconds as the prisoners swarmed for the gaoler with the keys. They didn't care for the back-up that was to come, they cared not for the unconscious gaoler either; there was only one key that snatched their attention in unison. The key to the door. However, none of them had anticipated a scenario such as this to happen, none of them . . . except nine who had planned for it and knew what to do.

Joseph, Billy and Hugh rushed forward to the bodies on the ground, but the scram of people denied them from reaching the guards in time; they were already being overwhelmed, so many were piling up, so many fumbling and crying out but still they pushed for the chance. '*Keys!*' cried Joseph, 'get the keys!'

Just then someone tugged at his shirt and pulled him back. Instinctively he went for the hand to pull it off him, until he turned and saw Poppy who was neither rushing nor desperate. She pointed forward. 'Door!'

Looking up, the door had already been unlocked with four people nipping through. The situation hit him. *Victoria took the keys when she got the bloke!* He grabbed Billy and Hugh by their collar and shoved through the crowd to where Rob stood standing with his hand on the keys to keep them from sight. Time was ticking by; some observers had already seen and were making their way toward him too.

The four of them reached the door and started slipping through the gap. Poppy jumped through, then Hugh and Billy but Joseph pushed Rob through next, just as he snatched the key from the lock and stole through the gap, slamming the door shut behind him and locking it before any other con could get a foot through. He breathed hard, now realising the film of sweat on his forehead and the hammering within his chest. Bile lingered at the back of his throat. *The rats are out the cage, but we haven't escaped the nest yet.*

- Step Four.

At the door, shadow was thick, but daylight managed to stretch to it and as Joseph turned, he saw the source. Beyond the portcullis at the end of the tunnel, London's streets bustled with daily life. Life of normal people, free and innocent, a part of society– not apart from it. From this dingy hole he spotted a mother pushing a pram and a businessman taking a stroll as hansoms rolled by on two wheels; the sounds of horses trotting the roads and chatter of society was a welcoming relief after being shut from it for so long behind the high brick walls of the incarcerated. A welcoming relief, as well as an opening for the stale memories that rushed back in a heaving surge. *I must not linger here any longer. I've got to get out.*

There was one more obstacle to hurdle first though, before they could run free. Ahead the portcullis stood looming from floor to ceiling, stretching across from wall to wall. This time they couldn't use keys; this was a portcullis and had to be lifted through chain and effort.

In the sheltered daylight of the tunnel eight silhouettes were reaching the defence and figuring out where it lifted. Joseph skipped ahead, running for them, seeing what he could do to help. *It'll have to be lifted if we can't find the crank for it.* Out of breath, he stopped behind them and scanned the metal grate– up close it looked menacing, a real medieval artefact from an age long gone. *This should be in a castle, not a prison,* he thought, a *good way to keep people on the outside and enemies on the inside.* Gazing up at the web of engineering, he wondered how it could be overcome. 'Is there a crank nearby?' Joseph asked them, huffing as he caught his breath.

Tess spied the gloom, 'the crank is on the other side, through that door. I saw the people inside it when me and Pop were brought in.'

'Well I hope everyone's arms are ready. We're lifting this bastard.'

Pairs of eyes looked around incredulous.

'If we lift it enough, a few people can slip under to get to the crank.' He clarified.

Suddenly banging erupted from the other side of the door and the handle jangled around in its place. The noises were loud and angry as they rumbled through the tunnel. They all turned to look at it, expecting to see it fall down any second. Joseph was glad to have left the key in the lock, hindering a second key.

'They're trying to get through.' Hugh said quietly.

Seeing no other option, they moved along the length of the portcullis and Rob and Hugh were told to slip under once it was far enough from the ground. No one argued with the decision. Hands gripped the metal and heaved upwards. At first nothing happened, but then a judder rumbled through the grate and it rose from the ground an inch before they let it go with a huff and groan. 'We've got to do this,' he reminded them, 'it's heave this up or hang from a rope.'

Sore hands now gripped the metal and they heaved once more, pulling the mechanism up with nothing but sheer might. There was a judder, a rumble and squeak and it lifted from the ground, then dropped. They tried again and this time it lifted higher, this time Rob and Hugh managed to scramble under it and get to the door before the portcullis slammed down. Quickly they opened the door and jumped inside whereupon sounds of a fight ensued as the two men overthrew the guards on watch.

The banging coming from behind the door intensified. A thought occurred to Joseph, a daunting prospect. *Surely that door can't be the only entrance. There's got to be more.* Nerves began to tangle themselves like too many fingers trying to perfect the cat's cradle. Images ran through his head of officers bursting through the door, hurtling around the corner of the exit or appearing out of a hidden cubby hole they hadn't seen. His heart skipped faster; fear pumping through his veins quicker than any venom could. It was almost instantaneous. With a hardening tone in his voice, he ushered, 'if it's in there, get cranking, we can't waste-'

Suddenly the portcullis juddered again and began to slowly rise into the ceiling. They didn't need any sort of trigger, as soon as the gap was big enough to crawl under, they clambered past it and immediately made a run for the exit at the end of the tunnel.

Benjamin was the last to waddle under and he was no further from it than when the portcullis dropped with a clang and Rob and Hugh emerged from the door, sweating profusely. 'Well done lads,' Joseph said to them all, 'now go. Run. Run for the nearest docks and don't look back! I'll meet you there!'

A concern suddenly made itself known; *do they all know the way to the docks?* But then the answer came to him out of common sense; *of course they do, they're Londoners. They'll know the back routes better than any peeler.*

He watched as each of his comrades burst forth into the light of day and onto the street, startling the people nearby, and made a dash into the crowd. The mission of blending into the crowd no longer applied; yes, they were going to be looked for and hunted by the police but as Joseph had made it clear to them: they were not going to stay in the city for much longer, so camouflage wasn't necessary.

'Run,' he'd told them, 'run any way you can, find any path, find the fastest route. Find your pace and stick to it and whatever you do, don't hang about. Haste is what you need so don't go waiting for everyone– once you get out there, it's every man for himself, just bloody make sure you get to the docks – the nearest one to here – you all know it. Once you get there, hole up and wait for us all to arrive. Don't bother trying to blend in; that'll just waste time – if you can grab a coat or something to throw your tail off then fine, do it – just get to the docks. This city an't our home anymore, we've got to remember that.' They had listened intently, but the moment to prove their worth and word was now.

Joseph was the last to exit the tunnel. The daylight seemed intense, blinding, but the sights of buildings, streets and people was so refreshing he instead opened his eyes instead of squinting. The streets were already beginning to clear; pedestrians had scattered and scrambled away from the entrance now seeing that nine criminals had managed to escape. The street was in a frenzy– people were running and squealing like a flock of hens after a fox had just got in. He couldn't help but smile. *Thank you, proud people of London,* darting through the conundrum to the nearest back street, *you've helped throw off any attention that would've been drawn.*

Down the alley he ran, heaving in the cold morning breaths, listening to the sounds of panic lessen as his footfall and heartbeat amplified. This time he was not gripping a bowler hat. This time he had not any stolen goods in his possession. Policemen were not the enemy this time– he wasn't running from them. Instead it was the city in general, escaping from this country that now haunted his dreams and sickened his hopes past the point of damnation.

Not only had he taken part in the corruption of society, he'd also seen its ugly powers from the other side; now the once beautiful city he called home was nothing more than a rotten apple with wormholes to run through. There was nothing for him here, and as he bolted down familiar streets and scarpered down old alleyways, he felt nothing but a longing to be away from them, to live a life outside of bricks and mortar and stone. The happy memories that once gave him hope were now sour, fully ripened with loss and loathing and gave a bitter recollection as he fled through the lanes he once trod. Fresh memories had to be made away from this hostile environment, far from this warren of treachery, lies and deceit, far away from this condemned place that wanted to keep him locked up to age and wither until he forgot what life was.

The more back streets and short cuts he ran felt like a start to something else, something new. It was when his legs began to burn hard that he started to not think on the memory of each place and saw the street names for what they were– simple directions leading him to his final destination in this ugly urban town. A one-way trip of which he was in haste to say goodbye. With each sign he passed, the more excited he was to leave.

He jumped out from a shady alley onto a street and bustling market. People were everywhere, browsing and buying; they seemed to not even notice him as he hurtled through. The smells of the fresh produce were delectable after the foul odours he'd been smothered in; he sucked up the scents as if he were eating them. His pace was interrupted though, and Joseph found it difficult to gain speed. *Oh move! Move out the way god damn you! If I slow now, I'll be too tired to push on.* Despite a life of running, he knew his limits and knew if he were to stop now it would be tremendously difficult to keep the pace. This game of stamina was a fickle thing.

Joseph slithered through the crowd as best as he could, ducking and dodging, skipping around tables and women carrying baskets. Then suddenly two peelers walked around a hidden corner and onto the main thoroughfare of the market.

Startled, he scrambled forward– there was no time for hiding, but as he passed a table, he realised there was a chance for camouflage. With light fingers, he pulled an old navy-coloured overcoat from its stand and slipped it on, pulling the collar up high to hide his face. As fast as he could manage, he manoeuvred through the crowd and passed the policemen before they could notice who he was and where he was supposed to be.

'Oi! You 'aven't paid for that! Come back here!' A man shouted from behind him. He turned and saw it was the owner of the stall selling preowned clothes. Eyes suddenly swung at him, he felt their glare, so cold and hard it was like being pelted by rocks; he glanced to the policemen and saw their approach. *You fool Joseph! What were you thinking?!*

Without a second thought, he fled from the scene with the peelers trailing after him. He pushed through the crowd, bowling people over and shoving them to the ground until they began to clear a path. There was no care anymore; he felt nothing where he knew he should've done. Joseph tried to find sympathy but instead felt frustration; *Why should I care about them when they don't care about me?* 'Out of the way!' he cried, 'Move!' he urged his legs onwards.

'Stop! Halt!' One of the policemen cried.

'Stop there, thief!'

He did not.

Joseph kept running, skipping down another alley with his new coat flapping in his wake, flying through the rat-runs of this godforsaken nest. *Don't stop until you get to the docks. Keep running, stop for nothing.*

A left, right and a long straight took him to the sign he wished for, informing him the docks were half a mile away. He ran on with legs burning and lungs heaving. He ran on, until the smells of salt and sea greeted his nose and replaced the dense scent of filth and shit; until the sights of masts, rigging, dock workers, shipyards and warehouses became more distinguished. He ran on, into the shimmering light reflecting from the waters of the Thames; the river that was to take him out and beyond, across seas and through storms, to seek and to find the treasure that lie waiting.

Chapter Nine

Step five.

Slowing to a walk, Joseph made his way toward the docks, heading for the silhouettes of berthed ships with their sails hauled and flags fluttering in the breeze. Jetties were choked with dockers and officers manning them, taking the tax and checking the cargo when needs must. The shipyard nearby was bustling with shipwrights and carpenters repairing ships with others building them. The air was alive with swarms of seagulls cawing and complaining, the cacophony of sounds and unfamiliar lingo passed his ears in a jumble of movement like waves. His eyes darted as he flowed into the thoroughfare, moulding into the busy crowd.

People were coming and going, shaking hands, eating, drinking, laughing and joking. A variety of characters filled the wharf, smelling of fish and salt as if they'd just walked from the waves. Fishwives were selling the day's catch of fish, eels, clams, shrimp and crab; oyster-catchers were hollering about their haul and sailors swung drunkenly from the taverns singing their maritime shanties and sharing their tales of voyage in a language Joseph could not comprehend. Beefy dockers hauled barrels and rolled them into warehouses, some hauled sacks as others heaved them, offloading ships and loading them under the watchful eyes of the captains and officials. Amongst the throng, crisp businessmen sealed deals and traded their goods for money, looking odd in their black and white suits amongst the weathered salt-stained clothing of the sailors and captains.

Spotting the sailors was easy; their faces were lined, tanned and rough; the climate beyond the coast sculpting their complexions to give a more appropriate look for journeys out at sea. The sun and wind had chipped away the soft clean curves of youth leaving the hardened man underneath to not only prepare for the elements but endure them and understand their ways. *I wonder what we'll look like a month into our journey,* he imagined. There were a variety of ages around; the docks yielded to none– if you could walk, could work and could wake early you were hired.

Joseph wasn't looking for a job though, he already had one and was willing to take any means to make it happen.

He wiped the sweat from his forehead, his hair feeling thick and unkempt, and tried to calm his racing pulse. His legs ached terribly, and his joints squeaked, not prepared for that kind of alarming exertion. Breathing deep, he tried not to look suspicious as he passed stalls and pubs and warehouses that lined the main thoroughfare. No one paid him any heed. No eyes judged him or recognised him, and therefore didn't know he had to be anywhere. A slight feeling of freedom touched him then and lifted him past the stress of the morning. *We had to get out for this feeling, here and now.* Yet caution still nagged: he was not away from the city yet; the shackles were still supposed to be on him, and he knew if he made himself known, the law would do its best to clamp down on him again.

'Oi, mate! Is that you Joe? Joseph!' A voice called.

He turned and saw a man peeking out from an alley. Without making any sudden change in composure, he walked over to the alley and into the shadows to see four people loitering, looking bedraggled, sweaty and tired. *They're here!* He thought in relief but tried not to show the joy.

'Blimey I'm glad to see you made it!' cried Harold, 'Me and Dave took off in different directions and I lost him, lost everyone.'

'He'll be along soon mate, I'm sure. Especially if he knows the back streets as well as he said he did.' Joseph replied. It was cool in the shade of the alley, making his throat pine for water, wine or cider or better yet, all the above.

The other arrivals turned out to be Hugh, Rob, Tess and Poppy; each looking as tired as the next, each with a small relieved smile on their face as if they couldn't believe their plan had worked. In all honesty, he couldn't believe it either, but they were not on a ship yet, so he saved the cheering. He sat down against a wall and rubbed his face tiredly. Decisions had to be made, and he found out he was not the only one thinking about it.

'What happens now?' Rob asked, sitting opposite him on a wooden box.

Joseph had thought about it, just as he had with everything else. 'We wait here for a bit, an hour maybe, until the rest join us and then a few of us scout ahead, seeing what ship looks like its near ready to leave. When they come back, we run hell-for-leather and get on. When Benjamin gets here, we'll get some advice on how best to stowaway since he managed it before.'

'When he was thirteen though, a small boy, and there was only one of him. This is a bit different.' Hugh reminded him with blushed cheeks.

'What if people stop us and catch us before we get on the ship?' Tess asked, pushing a lock of damp hair from her face and looking to each of them with blushed cheeks as she caught her breath.

'They won't. No one will be waiting for us. No one will know what's going on.'

'What about if the rest don't turn up, or if some don't make it to the docks within the hour? Are we leaving without them?'

'They'll make it. Don't worry, if they've lived a life within these streets, they'll know all the routes to get here.' He reassured.

'Dave don't know this area well– he's from the other districts; other side o' the city.' Harold chipped in.

Why didn't Dave mention it before?! He frowned and sighed. 'We'll wait an hour and *ten* minutes then but after that we really need to make a move. We can't stay skulking in an alley for too long. Peelers love looking for loiterers.'

They quietened down and waited, sensing the tension. In the meantime, concern began to take hold. *How many of the others didn't mention if they knew the way? They should've said something beforehand.* He suddenly felt the weight of responsibility laying heavily on his shoulders; when it came down to it, he would have to be the one to give the final word to decide whether to leave the stragglers behind.

And he knew he would do so, regretfully.

With Harold keeping an eye open they were announced of every arrival. After twenty minutes Victoria Penning strode down into the alley, red-faced with ringlets of hair clinging to her forehead. After that, Dave James made his appearance, grumbling at the distance and tripping over twice; he sat and wiped the sweat from his head and the back of his neck. Ten minutes passed before the old man Benjamin heaved his way into the alley, surprised he'd made it with everyone present. 'I was starting to think you'd huv' left by now.' He said with a chuckle in between breaths, leaning as he held his back, 'wouldn't have been the first time; old Ben's been left behind a few times before. I tell ya, these legs an't for speed, these here are sea-legs and serve me better on deck.'

'Well it's a good job we're getting on one.' Victoria said with a quick glance at Joseph: *you bloody well make sure we do get on a ship else this will all be for nothing.* Joseph knew women well enough to know what that look meant.

He nodded to both, 'we're making a move as soon as Billy turns up. He's the last one.'

The last few minutes ticked by until the hour was up. Deflated, Joseph stood and was about to announce that the time had come to move on when Billy Baker finally came into the alley after a call from Harold. A fiddle was in his hand. Joseph smiled, 'took your bloody time mate, we were just about to leave!'

Billy smiled tiredly, 'it's been a rough mornin' I can tell you that for nothin'. I'm feckin' knackered.' He wiped the sweat from his forehead. His eye was bloodshot, rimmed in red and his cheek was starting to show signs of colour, exhaustion was also making an appearance, but he tried not to show it.

'What's with the fiddle?'

He looked down to it as if he'd forgotten it was there, then smiled, 'I used to play it as a bye', quite a fine fiddler so I was; thought a long journey could give me a chance to flitter the ol' fingers again.' It was clear from his expression he was excited to use it again. 'Right, so what now?' he asked them.

Joseph recounted his plan, but Billy's face was flat; he was not impressed. 'Not bad. But can I suggest an alternative? Either way it's six o' one, half a dozen to the other.' The Irishman said, as he spotted what lie strew down the alley.

Holding his head high, Joseph Winter walked out from the shade and into the light of the early afternoon sun, heading for the river, ships and jetties at the bottom of the street. A spot was empty now; the jetty had been cleared; one ship had already left the port. *We should've been quicker; they're already beginning to leave!* Holding his nerve, he scanned along the line and saw three more berthed ships with their cargo being hauled on. One had a sail unfurled and the rest were being worked on, as well as flying different flags. He eyed the unfurled one; its great sails were filling with air– it looked to be leaving at any moment. He changed his pace from a stroll to a brisk walk, planting his hands in his pockets holding onto the compass for good fortune.

Billy, Dave and Hugh walked out a moment later, none of them talking; all knowing their role. This was their one chance and they all knew it.

It was either this or the last-ditch attempt, which was now what Joseph's plan had been reduced to, much to the relief of the others.

They walked on in silence. Each man confined to the space of his own head thinking of possibilities of what could go wrong, hoping for the end they wanted to be right. The last stretch passing the remaining stalls and a blacksmith's felt even longer than the distance they had ran earlier on, for they knew this was the final hurdle to the five-step plan Joseph had vaguely outlined before. The final hurdle that most of the group believed to be near impossible. The four of them reached the bottom where most of the bustle took place, holding their breath; tense to the atmosphere they'd created.

Joseph stopped and looked around at the commotion as men lifted sacks, rolled barrels and heaved boxes from the end of the warehouses to the jetties and gangway planks that led up to the main deck. With a keen eye, he spied through the bustle to seek the man he hoped was here.

Standing nervously beside a cart of barrels, Joseph found Harold Arms. He stood frozen and looked lost. *Act natural Harold for Christ sake, you're standing out like a sore thumb.* He turned to the others, trying to make this ordeal look more like a casual affair. 'Alright lads, just go and help him out over there, would you? I'll be back in a tick.' Nodding to them, he hurried over to the merchant ship with the unfurled sails, now spotting it flying the Blue Peter flag in the breeze; the flag that indicated a departure.

Hurrying along the jetty, hearing the flop and splash of the water beneath the wood, he scurried up the gangway plank to the deck where tired men were emerging from the hatchway. A man busied himself about the deck, checking everything was in order, and at the sight of Joseph he quickly walked over. The man was sweating underneath his sailor's hat and his grey moustache wiggled as he spoke. 'Hullo, this ship's about to lift anchor, can't you see the flag-'

'I just got five more barrels to come. The men are bringing them up now.' Joseph cut in, sounding out of breath as if he'd just been loading cargo all morning and stood to the side to let the other men depart, their boots clomping down the wooden planks.

'And who might you be, eh? I 'aven't seen you on the docks before.' The boatswain scrutinised with sharp steely eyes.

'Do you ask the name of every helping hand?'

'Only the ones I never set eyes on before.'

'Fine. I'm Joseph and I've been sent from the centre to deliver five barrels of wheat and barley from the warehouse. Now, if you won't mind, we really need to get this cargo on.' He made to move forward, but the boatswain held a hand in front of him.

'Wheat and barley, says you? Now why in the name of the sweet Lord would we want to waste space for that when it's France we're sailing for? They grow wheat and barley there. Now off with you, get off this ship before I call the captain.' He said aggressively.

It was then that Joseph noticed a man moving about the quarterdeck above. It was the Captain. *Think quickly now, time is running out.* He glanced behind him and saw the men already climbing up the gangway plank carrying a barrel each. They hadn't waited for his signal; they were coming aboard the ship whether he was ready or not. They too, it seemed, were not intending on wasting time. *Act now Joseph!* 'Right, that's it. Off with you! Off the ship, go on!' the boatswain ushered.

Joseph shot a look at the captain and saw he was looking down at something in his hands. He was not watching what was going on. With a sudden flash, he smacked the man hard in the face and quickly took the hat off his head and placed it upon his own, before catching him in his arms and hauling him to the stairs where he took him into the shadows.

'All good down there, Mister Johnson? Ready to make sail? The tide's up and ready for us, we best not make her wait!' the captain called as he looked out to the mighty river.

Giving a cough, he tried his best to impersonate the boatswain as he kept his face facing the other way. 'Aye sir, just a few more barrels and she'll be ready to go.'

Billy jumped on deck first, carrying his cargo and Joseph pointed him in the direction of the hatchway and he carefully made his way over. Hugh huffed red faced as he boarded and followed Billy down the stairs. Next came Dave, nodding to Joseph as he walked past and last of all Harold came aboard, muttering, 'Rope's untied, we're ready to go.'

'Good man. Follow the others.' He replied quietly and lifted the plank and used it to push them away from the jetty before letting the mooring rope drop into the water.

The rope slipped away from its post and with a flop it fell into the water. The deckhands winched up the anchors of the stem and stern and the edge of the jetty gradually moved away from them. Drifting, they were leaving the dock and moving into the flowing current of the meandering Thames.

Sails cracked as they suddenly ballooned with air and the ship tugged forwards, slowly inching further away from land. As the crew busied themselves upon the deck and rigging, Joseph stood at the side of the ship and watched as the docks, shipyard and the people on it moved away. The remaining ships now looked stationary; the buildings moving, sliding past. Alas, he felt no foreboding in the loss of his hometown– only a magical feeling of excitement and inspiration as the ship drifted away from the rising towers of grey concrete and drab stone. *They'll only get taller as the years go on,* he reflected, *there'll be no stopping them grow. The city will keep getting bigger and more people will flock to it, there'll be no more room left for people like me. People like us.*

Immediately he felt as if he could breathe freely again; the hands of brick and mortar were losing their grip and soon, in the next few days, even the thought of London and the shores of England would be but a memory. Like the ship drifting down the mighty dividing river, his mind, too, drifted and brought him back to the first marker; their first heading. Of course, the crew had to be dealt with first, but he had the heading that would set them one step closer to the end.

Joseph picked the compass from his pocket and opened it, watching the arrow wobble and waver, starting to spin, forever pointing around four quarters of a circle, reminding him of the circle drawn on the back of the scroll. As he saw it, south-east was their heading, for that was the quarter the poem had been written in.

Seek the beach, the sand, the roots of the flying trees,
The next part is hidden there, in amongst the leaves.
A bright sun and good tide will bring you on,
To the good Cape of the good Gabon.

Chapter Ten

Sailing on the Thames' steady current with a swift breeze filling their sails, the ship drifted through the city passing busy docks with jetties stretching out into the river and, on those that were not in use, fishermen fished at the edges and on the banks hoping to catch a free meal. Despite the calm water there was a flurry of activity taking advantage of the conditions; flocks of rowboats bobbed up and down the river ferrying goods and people at cheap rates and tugboats chugged thick clouds of smoke as they powered through the meandering channel, smothering the cries of the gulls that soared overhead.

Amidst the shroud of smoke, the buildings slid by like great tree trunks as they navigated through the stone jungle; the native fauna quickly bypassing the river to avoid its stench. Onlookers were few and far between; those who had enough time to spare enjoyed watching the movement of the great ships as they bore out to countries way beyond the horizon, far from sight and imagination. Although, for the watching pedestrians a certain sensual neglect had to be held for the river was a dirty mud brown, the churning waters emitting a foul reek. In addition to being the main trade route to enter the heart of the city, the Thames was also the sewage disposal for an overpopulated area. Already those on deck had seen pots being emptied out of the neighbouring windows and had sailed through streams and swamps of raw faeces.

Captain Robertson breathed, and gently turned the ship's wheel around the meander of the river and emerged onto the course that would bear them steadily out to the English Channel where sets of "examples" hung from gibbets. Hanging from hempen ropes or trapped in cages, pirates and criminals alike shared the same swing along the banks of the river as a warning to any daring enough to push the limits of the law. The brutish scene seemed paradoxical compared to such a fine day, perhaps even heightening the monstrosities with their ragged flesh and eyeless sockets and rows of blackened teeth stretching into an eternal grin. A beautiful ugliness. A deterrent to the unlawful people coming into a lawful city.

Squeaking with the cages against the breeze, the ropes of the ship tightened as she sailed along the river. Named after their fair queen, *Victoria* sailed fairly; even in the harshest of storms she skipped the waves as if she were playing hopscotch, so this small hop across the sea was going to be quick. The captain was optimistic as he licked his lips looking out to the river ahead; if the conditions stayed as such, he could be back in time for breakfast the following morning. He enjoyed sailing her; her balance was admirable, and her responses were always finely tuned. She was of fine workmanship from the shipwrights of London, perhaps the finest, especially after what he'd had to sail before in his career.

With her sails taught, they filled not just with air but with gold as the afternoon sun bathed them in a rich brilliance that only a clear sky could give. The conditions were perfect, light winds and clear air were an omen of good fortune. The bowsprit and jibboom pointed onward, a long finger forever reaching out to foreign waters away from these placid English shores. He smiled through his trimmed black beard. Like all adventurous women, she was always eager to break out of constraint. 'All hands to deck, Mister Johnson!' He commanded in a powerful voice.

There was no answer.

'Johnson! Pull your tongue out from that bottle and get on deck, front and centre!' he tried again, but to no avail. 'Drinks like a fish and takes orders like an old dog.' Muttered he, shaking his head.

Frustrated, he scanned the deck and spotted two of the crew ahead on the forecastle, watching the cast off, but there was no sign of the boatswain. 'He was there but a moment ago, I'm sure.' He frowned and tried again, 'Johnson, you old flapdoodle! Get your arse up here!"

'Sorry, sir, be right with you! Just counting up the cargo is all.' The reply came from the hold.

Oh, I'm sure that's what you're doing, I know your problems with the neck oil as soon as you're away from the wife. 'Alright, front and centre as soon as you're finished.' Captain Robertson called back.

'Will do sir!' Joseph yelled from the darkened shadows and glanced over to the corner where the boatswain was bound and gagged. His heart hammered, his chest felt taught and his palms felt itchy, *god I need a cig. I need a smoke, even if it is from the chimneys of that dire town. A smoke and a drink. A strong one to knock back and burn away this godawful craving.*

Poppy clambered out from her barrel and eyed the man up, 'are we just going to leave him there?' She asked, looking round to Joseph and her sister.

'For now, yes,' he replied, trying to keep his hands still, 'until we figure out what to do next but first, we need to find something to eat. I'm famished.'

'Christ so am I; I could eat the twelve apostles.' Added Billy in his Irish brogue.

Everyone agreed and began a search of edible goods. As they scoured, walking through small pathways searching the brands that labelled the necessities, Tess, Victoria and Benjamin pulled themselves out from their barrels and brushed themselves off, suddenly gazing around at the long wooden room. Barrels upon barrels lined the sides, lashed together in packs of six each with a blackened brand burned onto their sides; boxes were stacked on top of each other toward the front, filled with dried goods. Despite the reality their look was indignant, as if any moment they expected to wake up back in their cells. Joseph had to admit, even he found their success overwhelming as he looked at where they were now.

Even though the river was smooth, after transferring from land to water they felt every movement under their feet and heard the creaks of a sailing ship about them constantly. It was all alien and strange and made them feel nauseated, especially on empty stomachs. It was like nothing they'd experienced before but they knew they would be used to everything before this journey reached its end, seeing as their journey would take them out to the waves where naught but blue could be seen on the horizon.

A musty smell of straw laced with spices wafted around the wood from previous hauls and made their mouths water; they hadn't eaten anything all day, so even the faintest of remaining scents caused their tongues to long for more. 'Aha! Here we go now! Apples, fish, cheese, bread, biscuits. And there's a barrel here for water too.' Billy cried and started picking out food and ladling water to his lips.

The rest of the company joined him and picked their meal out. Although the food was limited, the freshness was astounding, not one maggot or patch of fur could be seen, and they remembered how enjoyable and important taste was when it came to eating. A muffled cry then came from the corner of the room and a clunk and thud followed. Eyes turned and saw the boatswain wiggling across the floor heading for a rack of dark sticks that leaned against the wall. Poppy giggled at him as she took a bite from a biscuit.

'Maybe he's hungry too.' suggested Harold.

'I don't reckon he fancies a munch wid' us though mate, I'd say he's got something else in mind.' Billy eyed the sticks and saw they had triggers.

Joseph jumped from a barrel and walked over to Mister Johnson, seeing that Billy was right. They were muskets. He'd spotted some on each deck as he descended to the hold at the base of the ship. *Must be for emergencies,* he thought, *just in case something bad happens . . . just in case the ship gets any . . . stowaways.* He smiled to himself and hauled the boatswain back. 'Listen here, that's enough of that. We can't let you get to those muskets and we can't let you go.' Johnson's eyes were bulging as he writhed, sweat beading under his receding hairline. He ignored the struggle, 'I've a few questions first and I want you to nod or shake in answer.'

There was a pause. He glared at him with animosity before giving a small nod.

'Lovely job. Does this ship have a map on board?'
Nod.

'Will this ship get any more cargo when it reaches France?'

Nod.

'See, we're off to a flying start mate. Proud of you. Hunky dorey. Will you get off at France, never speak of us again and board another ship home?'

He wriggled angrily and shook his head, trying to shout, trying to scream. There were flames of fury in his eyes.

Joseph kneeled on his stomach hard and spoke forcefully. '*Will you get off at France, never speak of us and get on another ship home?*'

Pause. Then nod.

He smiled, 'Ah you're a diamond Mister Johnson, absolute bull of the barn. Now, one last question: are those muskets loaded?'

The boatswain shook his head proudly.

'Well I an't got a clue why you were trying to get to them then, you old muff. Never mind.' He looked up at the four of them, lined up against the wall. 'They don't need to be loaded.'

Standing, he walked back to the others who watched on not with concern but with intrigue. They were all thinking the same question; what were they going to do next? They couldn't stay in the hold until France, that much was clear. And Joseph hadn't planned for them to. 'I have an idea.'

The sun sank into the horizon, slowly vanishing under the line like gold melting through the fingers of the earth. Afternoon was waning, the evening was nigh. Eyeing the landscape, the Thames was widening as they passed Gravesend and sailed around the curve of east Tilbury, soon to be out on the open sea . . . and Mister Johnson was still nowhere to be found. Captain Robertson ran his fingers through his long hair and put his hat back on, breathing out steam in the chill of an English dusk. 'Johnson! I've had enough of this! Ten more minutes and we'll be out on the open water and you haven't even shown your face!' he cried, 'I'm coming down and if I so much as find you drunk and wasted you'll find yourself sailing to France in a longboat with naught to paddle with but your empty bottles!'

Robertson left the wheel for the helmsman and thumped down the ladder to the main deck and descended to the berth then to the orlop and then to the hold at the bottom. Stuffy air stuck in his lungs and he breathed hard, trying to accustom to the smells of the cargo. 'Johnson?' he called out in the dark. 'Johnson, you useless pig of a man, pick yourself up and attend; heed me.'

Silence. The boat creaked; the faint sound of waves lapped up the sides of the ship.

'Johnson?' quieter was his volume. Concern was his tone. Slight fear was his mood.

A footstep quietly shuffled beside him. He turned and saw a dark hole staring at him, a lidless black eye, its size was small but the fear that struck was profound. A gripping punch. Something he hadn't felt for years. It was then that he looked down the barrel. It was then that he saw a strange man holding the gun to his face, wearing a tattered navy jacket and Johnson's hat. He gulped, and suddenly heard a click from his left.

Another hole was staring at him and, holding the shaft with a finger on the trigger, was another man with a bruised face, curly hair and eyes dead set on him, boring into him menacingly with evil intent.

A cold metallic finger pressed into the nape of his neck. He froze. He didn't even need to turn to know what that was. Robertson's head emptied of thoughts; his arms emptied of strength; outnumbered he knew he didn't stand a chance. *How many more are there lurking in the dark?* Slowly, he moved his hand to the pistol hanging from his belt and tried to calm his breathing.

'I wouldn't do that if I were you.' The man in the navy coat said coldly.

'And I wouldn't try hollerin' the others either. Our triggers being pulled will reach their ears faster than your words can.' The other man said with an Irish brogue.

'Al-alright, alright.' Robertson stuttered, 'I won't call. I won't shoot. Just put your guns down, or at least out of my face, so we can talk this over. Please. Lads, please.' He let go of his pistol, standing straight and raised his hands.

A man's voice said sternly from behind, 'you an't in the right position to tell us what to do. I'd say we hold that power.'

Robertson gulped nervously, *don't break. You're in control.* 'You're right. You're right. I'm not. But how can we move this forward without moving?'

'Our triggers won't pull whilst we're getting answers.' The stowaway said.

'I don't want to talk when I've got guns in my face.'

'Well that's a shame, because we're the ones with the guns . . . and you're the one at the end of them, so I'd say you'd best start spilling words before we start spilling blood. There's things we need to know.'

Captain Robertson licked his lips nervously. His mouth was dry, throat parched. Gulping, he tried not to show he was afraid. 'What might that be?'

'This ship; how much food is on it?'

What? He thought of the cargo and answered, 'enough for a month at sea. Too much for a short voyage.'

'How much edible food if we *didn't* unload in France?'

There was a pause. *How does he know we're going to France?* 'Two months at sea.'

'Two months.' The man in the coat muttered to himself and paused in thought, 'and how many longboats do you have aboard?'

'Two.'

He paused again, then asked, 'how much do you like your job?'

'What?'

'There's going to be a change of plans. We an't stopping off at France anymore. We're dropping your crew off in a longboat near the coast, then we're off again.'

The captain had a worrisome, surprised look in his eye. '*We?*'

'Yes.' He replied, 'you're staying aboard. You're the only one aboard who knows this ship and how to sail her.'

This time the captain was perplexed, 'how am I supposed to sail a ship when you've just abandoned the crew to the French waters?'

This time the man smiled, 'we have my crew.' Then, one by one, six people stepped out from the shadows and into the murky light at the bottom of the stairs. Two men, two women, an old man and a girl; all scruffy, all bedraggled and haggard and in need of a wash and yet their faces– their faces were solemn, grave . . . and desperate. These were not skilled personnel. They were gutter rats that had somehow managed to scurry out of the run and onto the ship. How were they to know how to manage *Victoria*?

He looked at them all and reacted instantly. 'This voyage is ill-fated now anyway; everyone knows it's a bad omen for a voyage to have women aboard a ship yet alone working one. We must turn back.'

One of the women prickled, 'why? Are you afraid we'd best you at something for once?'

The main man cut in before Robertson could reply. 'They're staying whether you like it or not, superstition or no. We need all the hands we can get on this ship, don't we?' He looked as if he was about to reply, then he cut in again, 'let's not forget who is holding the musket here.'

Robertson pursed his lips and narrowed his glare. '*Fine*. Has anyone been on a ship before?'

'None of us have.' The main man replied for them all.

The captain shook his head, 'No one knows how to sail? No, that's far too dangerous, way too much of a risk to take. No, I can't do it. I *won't* do it. There'll be nothing but death out there with an inexperienced crew.'

The Irishman spoke up, 'Oh, we're fast learners don't you worry your little sailor's noodle. How else do you t'ink we've survived living in such a city? If we can manage the streets, we can manage the sea– either situation there's always bigger fish eatin' the littler fish. Oh, and before I forget, you don't have a fuckin' choice.'

Suddenly his anger flared, 'don't have a choice? I am Captain of this ship and you are stowaways demanding me to abandon my crew and replace it with a bunch of street urchins who got lucky. I don't even know where you plan to go!'

There was a clatter as the man behind dropped his gun and grabbed him and before he knew it a knife was at his throat. Eyes bolting, he held his breath, fearing that thin cold kiss of sharpened steel leaving its red mark across his neck. Only now did his brow sweat.

His eyes trained on the man in the coat, wishing for him to say something in disagreement but his face was unchanged. Calm and unwavering, the leader looked at him in slight dismay under the shadow of Johnson's hat, then declared, 'the way I see it, I am the one in control. These people, these "urchins" as you call them, are my friends and they've taken this risk and followed me on this ship. They trust me and I them, whereas you; I find doubt. Not in your skills as a captain and sailor, but in your word. That's why I'm hoping that knife will draw out your true colours. Captain, I hold your life in my hands; I might've been your fate all along, or I might not be, depending on how you handle this. Before you do, don't even dare judging us as everyone else does. You have no idea what we've all been through and have risked getting here so if I say they can sail, they can sail. The Cape of Gabon is where you'll lead us and then from there; we do not yet know. You see, we're not out to pillage or steal or kill– we're treasure hunters and we're following a map. Now, will you guide us out to sea?'

The knife loosened slightly, allowing him to reply. He breathed deeply through his nose. The steel was cold. The Irishman was right, he didn't have a choice. 'One condition: may I see the map first?'

The man hesitated then pinched the scroll from his belt and unravelled it before the captain's eyes. He read through the poem, and with each line his heart thumped faster. 'Wait . . . this? This is your map? It can't be! This, this is the one! The map! This is it, *the* map! Scott's Trove!' he squirmed, finding a grin above the steel.

With a loosening grip, he pulled himself free to speak. 'Nearly every sailor knows of the legend, has grown up hearing of an undiscovered treasure known as the Lost Loot and the map that is unlike any other, that is written instead of drawn. My good man, who are you? How on earth did you come by it?!'

Joseph lowered his musket slightly, 'you said so yourself, I'm just an urchin that got lucky. Now, will you help us? I need your word.'

There was a fire in Robertson's eyes, of slight anger and a flicker of amazement and wonder as he gawked at the map and saw evidence that the myth he had been told stories of was indeed fact. It was no longer just a story of fiction told by the fireside he'd hoped to believe; it was material, formed and stable. There was a lost treasure out there waiting to be found. But how could this be the one? The map had been lost for over a century, and with this realisation came indignancy. 'I want to believe this is it, but how can I be sure? How do I know it isn't a fake?'

The Irishman spoke up sounding less hardened, and in fact he'd lowered his musket too. The tension of the hold seemed to have dissipated with the revealing of the parchment. 'If it were a fake, we wouldn't have risked everyt'ing to get here. Not everyone can write something like that, not where we come from.'

Robertson nodded in agreement. 'Just as well, I have my duty to consider; what do I say when we return? Say I've been out galli-vanting the seven seas searching for lost treasure? No one will believe me. They'll think me a shirker, I'll be killing the canary, they'll say.' Robertson said ruefully.

He smiled, 'who said we have to return? All of us boarded this ship hoping not to. We left our old lives behind; our future is out there.' *I've got him, I can see it in his eyes.*

There was a moment of silence as the captain considered the opportunity. His job was a merchant, no, a sailor was what he was. The rising waves, the flowing tide, the wind through his hair and the spray of the sea in his face– that was where he belonged. *Victoria* was his vessel, his second home; her rocking as she rode the waves felt comforting and she rocked his hammock like a mother would rock her baby's cradle. The world was out there past the ports and shores, and now out yonder there lie something else his spirit of adventure had always dreamed of, yearned for ever since he'd heard the of the trove. The lost chest. Deep in the earth with worms for company, hidden away from sun and wind and the prying eyes of man, lost beneath the surface of this eager, confused world . . . until now. He looked up to the man, the gleam of hope to uncovering this antique fable. 'I will help you, sir. With the right tide and wind, we'll chart our course and find the end to the map, wherever that may be.'

He nodded and gave a tired smile, or was that an expression of relief? 'Welcome to the crew, and you don't have to call me sir or master or captain– Joseph will do nicely.' Lowering his musket, he tipped his hat up slightly so light could touch his eyes. He turned to the gloom, 'you all *chose* to follow me anyway, I'm not a superior.' Then he faced the man again, 'keep your role as Captain, you know more about sailing than any of us but the map I keep with me. Though you must understand; this is a dangerous journey and I cannot guarantee your safety.'

He nodded, 'understood. And call me James. Or Jim.'

Joseph held out a hand and shook Jim Robertson's, sealing their pact. 'I have one more question. Do you have any tobacco on this ship I can have before my teeth drop from my gums?'

As the hour passed, the calm breeze rose to a swift easterly gale that swept down the Thames as *Victoria* sailed around the last curve and flowed down into the remnants of the great river where its width was its widest. Here, she passed more ships coming in from the Channel and joined the stream of vessels that were heading out to the open water to do business abroad.

The evening sky was crisp and colourful, a beautiful blend of orange, pale yellow and a fine white, like a flame of fire that was slowly extinguishing to the west; throwing wild embers out to the twilight for them to burn on through the dark. The azure looked like a painting of watercolour; waning yet wonderful with small stretches of cloud weakly spreading over the stratus, long searching fingers reaching out, trying to grasp the gold before it disappeared and sunk below the cooling earth.

By dusk, the banks of the river were so far away it was difficult to tell them apart from the dark stretch of water that now took up all remaining sight. The last lands of England; the shores of Britain, now shrinking steadily away. Captain Jim Robertson buttoned his jacket and took another sip of warm broth as he looked out to the darkening horizon upon the forecastle. Steam rose from his mug and blew from his nose as he shivered against the chill of the night. Stars were appearing one after the other in the gaps between the clouds, peppering the black sky with dots of pure white light. He spied the hauled sails and noticed a calm about them, not a creak of a rope or a clunk of wood; the *Red Duster* flag hanging limply. The breeze that had borne swiftly had slowly ceased leaving the night still and unwavering and a healthy glow from the oil lanterns spread about the deck cast gentle shadows upon the tarnished wood. All was calm, apart from the captain's mind.

Alone afore the ship, Robertson's thoughts whirred. The deckhands were eating and laughing down in the berth; he'd only been on a few short voyages with them and they were friendly lads, but he could not help the feeling of apprehension. It began to burden him, for he knew what the morning would bring. The plot. Gazing up to the dark streaky clouds above, the feeling subsided into caution and excitement, knowing he had to be patient. Yet still the thought continued to gnaw; *have I made the right decision?* He took another sip of broth and leaned against the railing.

Below decks in the dark hold, a lantern had been lit for everyone to see by yet still they stumped their feet on barrels and numerous cargos and tried to keep their curses quiet. Above them they could hear the crew; any loud noises and their plans would scupper. They circled the light carefully, huddling together and holding mugs of broth that the captain had managed to smuggle down. Although the gesture was generous, some of the company felt unsure of the predicament and had voiced their thoughts soon after their plotting with him and he had departed to the main deck above.

Amongst them, Hugh, Harold, Victoria and Benjamin thought it unwise to place so much faith in the man they had just met. 'I just an't sure mates,' Hugh Jackson had shrugged, 'he is the Captain after all– come morning he might change his mind, get the crew down here an' toss us on a boat in the middle of the sea. How can we know he'll hold his word?' The uncertainty was halved however, as the others deemed it to a lack of solid trust after their time in prison, which was true of course; trust in peers was hard to generate when a whole life had been lived with nought but deceit. Nonetheless, his gesture was appreciated. The warmth of the broth was a comfort to the cold hands and nippy fingers and the taste of freshly cooked food was exquisite; that was something they all could agree on.

'Let's see how tomorrow pans out.' Joseph muttered, a dot of orange glowing in the gloom as he took a drag. Other dots were also aglow, relishing the tobacco after a stressful day.

Mister Johnson was given a mug too, though his hands and feet were still bound. They laid straw for him to lay on and bundled a hessian sack beneath his head, letting him know this was a far better treatment than they ever had. They themselves made beds as best as they could from other materials, finding as many soft things as they could to go with the straw and hay. Some padded out their barrels whilst others emptied hessian sacks to sleep in. No one complained; they were used to hard beds and awful conditions yet getting to choose their own bedding seemed a luxury. Prison no longer held them, Britain could get to them no more: they were on a ship bound to other places, new locations, places with undiscovered trials and treasures. Hardships were out there; this they knew and were prepared for– apart from a certain ordeal that came with unexperienced sailing.

Incarceration could be adapted to quite easily, yet such a simple thing as the tide seemed much greater. It lapped up the sides and pushed the boat this way and that, rocking it, shaking it and swaying it uncontrollably. Presently this tide was a good one, to a sailor this was a calm night but to a city slicker who had never set foot off land it felt like the water was heaving hither and thither and had found a firm grasp; tugging the ship continuously and churning their stomachs, making them yearn for a solid flea-infested louse-ridden D Block bed.

The night felt long and restless and despite the organisation for the morning the darkness felt brooding as if the light of day had suddenly become sheepish and was tentative in coming forth. The abandoning of the crew was the last hurdle, after that the ship and captain were theirs. They had gone from prisoners with lengthy sentences to stowaways who had persuaded a captain to sail them out to sea in less than a day– so their nerves were unnecessary, and yet still deeply rooted.

At last faint pastel colours of morning scraped across the night sky, a moody white, grey and navy blue. Clouds had spread overnight, snuffling out the last few stars that were late to depart and smothering chances of a clear sky with a blanket of grey, like sea foam rolling over the tide. The air was cold and moist, clammy like nervous palms. Forlorn and disapproving, the breaths of light wind that curled around the sails were more akin to sighs.

The morning bell chimed; breakfast was served, and the hands hauled up anchors to continue the journey. By sunrise *Victoria* was riding through the choppy waves of the channel, heading for the French coast.

Tipping downwards, *Victoria* split through another large wave, causing those below deck to hold onto the barrels and mast. Harold and Rob had already emptied their stomachs during the night and the rest of the company, save Benjamin, were feeling ill at ease. Even Joseph was as pale as the morning cloud. 'It's alright my chuckaboos!' Benjamin had told them perkily, 'the more time yer spend at sea the more time yer get used to how she treats yer. She can be angry and temperamental, but it makes yer appreciate the times when she's 'appy and calm. Yer'll find yer sea-legs soon don't you worry. When I's a lad it took me nigh on a week to get used to the rock n' tumble o the wood beneath me feet.'

'Shh!' Tess suddenly hissed, 'someone's coming.' In the quiet, footsteps thudded down the steps and they ducked down behind the barrels and melted into the shadows.

A man, a stranger, stepped down into the gloom. He had a bald head, save for dark bristles rounding his chin. He walked forward, checked a barrel, heaved it up and started up the stairs again. On the second step, he stopped and turned back, eyes searching the murk . . . for what? A noise? Was that a noise? He wasn't sure and turned to continue the stairs. The company breathed in relief, and realised they had to be more careful. One slip and their plans could go awry.

What felt like hours passed before they heard another set of steps coming down into the hold. 'Someone's coming!' Hugh whispered harshly. Everyone darted for cover and peeped out to the bottom of the stairs.

The man stopped and looked out into the gloom and scratched his black beard. 'Joseph?' The captain called out, 'France is nigh, we're two miles out from the coast.'

Joseph stepped out from the shadows to meet him, 'are we still good to go?' he asked.

'Aye.'

He nodded, picked his empty musket up again and turned to the rest. 'Then let's go.'

Thud, thud, thud, thud. Heavy footfall climbed the companion-way from the berth, from many feet. But the captain had gone by himself? The rest of the crew were on deck; a puzzled look spreading through them. Pair by pair their eyes turned toward the hatchway in concern until the captain staggered to the deck, wild eyed and frightened with a gaunt-looking man pressing the captain's very own pistol to his head, scowling at the crew with unfriendly eyes.

More people came out from the stairs behind him. A scarred old man growled as he dragged netting up from the stairs and a tall man with a blank emotionless face thumped up on the deck braced with a stick of wood ready to wield. The other man and woman both had muskets and had them aimed at everyone. It was immediately clear what was going on. 'Captain! Jim!' a man cried out, the man who the stowaways had seen earlier. 'Good god!' The crew jumped and scrambled, shouting to each other and trying to reach the hatchway to grab their weapons but it was of no use. The stowaways were blocking the entrance.

'Out of the way, filth! I'll 'ave yer grinning at the daisy roots when I'm done with yer!' One of the crew spat and tried to attack Billy, who shoved him back and smacked him with the butt of the musket.

'Back! Get back y' rank maggots! The lot o' you!' Billy yelled, and for a moment they heeded him.

A moment of silence fell, and Joseph took his chance. '*Get back now or the Captain will die!* I've killed before and I'll do it again. I an't afraid,' he spat on the deck, 'I an't afraid o' death, dying or forcing others to it!' he hissed menacingly, hoping they'd take to his lie.

The five crew members stopped advancing and stopped movement altogether. The waves crashed against the sides; the sea sprayed high. No one else was around. It was just them, just the ship, alone on the Channel. Outnumbered, the crew knew they had no way to call for aid and upon hearing the plea of their captain, knew they were powerless to this assault.

'Do-do as he s-s-says.' The captain stammered, eyeballing them all franticly. 'Get b-back, please lads, it'll be alright.' Colour drained from his face as he gripped hold of Joseph's arm around his neck.

The men halted, but then a lad ran forward in fury; he must've been no older than Rob. 'Captain Jim! No!' he yelled.

The crew leapt forward to stop him, seeing that force was futile when the opposition were armed, and their captain's brains could be splattering the sea if they trod wrongly. All muskets turned to him, Harold raised his plank of wood and Joseph cocked the pistol, pushing it hard to the side of the captain's head. 'Stop, boy!' Joseph snarled, 'do you really want me to do it?'

Seeing the predicament, the boy stopped, and his flushed cheeks drained to a pale white. This situation was not like the tales of the typical heroes and villains he'd been brought up with. No, this was real, and life was not so easy. 'Heed me now, all of you!' Joseph called out loudly in competition with the waves, 'I'm not a merciful man, if I had it my way there'd be blood spraying this deck– not seawater. But we've agreed to give you ugly mumbling coves a chance, but first I want a longboat lowered into the water, and I want you all in it. Then row. Row yourselves to the nearest port and in return for not killing you all, no one speaks a word of what happened here to anyone. *Anyone.* As far as you're concerned, we're nothing more than ghosts– and we don't leave a trace. Now, fetch the longboat.'

The sailors stared blankly at him. 'Fetch it *NOW*!' Joseph exclaimed. The men jumped and quickly went about getting the longboat and lowering it to the undulating waves that licked the keel with great wet tongues. One by one they climbed down the ladder and into the boat until all five sat, staring up to the faces that overlooked the sides; their heads looking dark, featureless against the grey sky. Ghosts who had overthrown their ship.

'What about the Captain?' One man called out.

The leader shook his head. 'He's staying with us. He's needed. Now row on, and I'd row quickly by the look of those waves.' Joseph replied, as he hauled up the ladder and left them bobbing on the rising tide amidst a shroud of bubbling foam.

Rising from the bulwark, he glanced around to their relieved faces, before rambling to the other side to heave up his guts to the seawater.

Chapter Eleven

Captain Jim Robertson pulled the thin curtains of his cabin apart and let the grey daylight struggle inside to the table, desk, bed and chest of drawers. The cabin was still dim from the dank cloudy sky, and for a moment he wondered why he'd bothered opening them. Joseph thought the same and turned up the oil lamp that gently burned on the cluttered table. Now was the moment, the time where everything was ready. They had the ship, had the captain, all they needed now was the course.

The rest of the crew stood watching and waiting, excited at the freedom that had now become available. The air was thick with enthusiasm; everyone wanting to goggle at the map, to make sure it was still material and not a part of some wild fantastical dream, wanting to see where it was to lead them on their journey onward. That was the only way they could go now. Onward. There was no turning back, and not one person aboard wanted to; they had left their old lives behind.

The door squeaked as it opened. Joseph turned from rolling up a cigarette and smiled at Rob, Tess and Poppy as they entered the Captain's Quarters. As a safety precaution, he'd asked them to stay below until after the overthrow since they were the youngest. The last thing he wanted was to get them killed before their lives had even began. Nevertheless, their want and drive for adventure matched even old Benjamin's and they were soon on deck as soon as the longboat was out of sight. 'Looks like it all went well then.' Tess noticed as she found a place around the table.

With everyone now present, Captain Jim made room on the table and unfurled the map of the world upon it; the blank shapes of the continents looking inviting, ripe for exploration. Everyone gathered round, their eyes glued to the land masses, the quarters, segments, latitudes and longitudes, searching, wondering which was the good Cape of the good Gabon. Joseph waited no longer; he plucked the scroll from his back pocket and opened it, placing it over the world for all to see.

Once more, those that could, read through the poem; once more their imaginations exploded with fresh ideas, new possibilities. 'Where does it mention Gabon?' Asked the captain.

Joseph turned the scroll over to the blank side. 'I held it to the light of a moon, and I know it sounds iffy but it an't, so keep with me, and a different ink seemed to rise, to glisten like a spider's web in a morning mist. So fine, you'd question yourself whether it was even there, but there it was.' He took a drag; the tip burning bright orange and drew with his finger. 'A circle appeared cut into four and in the bottom right quarter was the poem saying the first marker is in the Cape of Gabon. That's where I figured we had to head south-east since it was written in the bottom right. I don't know, I assumed it had something to do with a compass and on a world map Gabon would have to be in the south-eastern corner.' He gave a slight shrug.

Captain Robertson picked up the scroll and examined the emptiness of the page intently. 'The moonlight, you say. Well the poem did say "days will not illuminate". The poem on the back must've been written in luminescent ink or something of the like, to rise like that but not at any other time.' He mused, 'it's definitely a sailor that wrote this. On clear nights, moonlight and stars aid in navigation better than the sun can. More accurate points to look at. Although bringing darkness with it, the moon can be a reliable companion on the dogwatch, too. Night is the main clue it seems to me.'

'So, do you know where Gabon is?' Victoria asked, less interested in the paper.

Robertson nodded and pointed to the world map. 'There. West coast of Africa. South-east to Britain on a world map, as Mister Winter suggested.' Eyes were drawn to his finger, which had landed on a small nodule that bulged from the side of the west coast underneath the grand head of the vast continent. 'No occupation is held there, only ancient tribes. Most ships don't venture that low to Gabon. Their interest is more with the north of the continent as its easier for trading to the Americas and Britain.' He nodded, 'the triangular trade; it's convenient for the slavers and has easier access to the Atlantic, so I doubt they sailed lower to Gabon unless they needed to.'

'There's no people like us there?' Poppy wondered, standing beside her sister.

'No, not white people anyway. In fact, I'm not sure whether we'll even meet anyone. The tribes who live there aren't as developed or as populated. We might meet a fishing boat or two, but I doubt it.' For the city-dwellers who had known nothing but dense crowds, to hear a place with little to no one sounded peculiar, almost alien.

'My turn for the question,' Hugh jumped in, 'how long d' you reckon it'll take to get there?'

The captain looked down to the world map and scratched his beard. 'I'll need to do some calculations first, charting a course, but it'll all depend on the water, wind and weather.'

'And food.' Dave added from a stool in the corner of the room.

'And food.' Robertson nodded. 'But if we do run short, we can stop off at the nearest port, buy some stock or trade the remaining uneatable cargo for fresh produce.'

Joseph nodded, impressed. He hung over the two maps and scanned them with fresh eyes. *Bottom right quarter, that's where the poem was written.* Picturing the world map cut into four, Gabon was in fact in the bottom right quarter of it. Just south-east of the globe on a world map. He nodded 'Let's not let slide we'll need to get used to our new jobs, and you'll have to be patient– we've never been on water before.'

'I have lad.' Benjamin chirped, 'I used to be cabin boy once in me youth, then when I was a man grown I was a rigger and I's still quite handy when it comes to knots; right from the Full Carrick Bend to the Highwayman's Hitch.'

Robertson smiled and took his hat off revealing long dark greying hair underneath. 'Well, if you like. . .'

'Oh, er, Benjamin Smith, sir.'

'If you like, Benjamin Smith, you can keep the same job on here. Rigging is an important business, perhaps one of the most important; it's not safe but out here nothing is particularly safe.'

The old man smiled, showing his few teeth, 'Aye Cap'n. A rigger I shall be.'

The captain then assorted jobs out to his new crew and explained what the jobs entailed. Dave and Harold were to be riggers hands, Benjamin's apprentices and to lend a hand wherever needed about the ship. Master Gunner was given to Hugh, in charge of ammunition and weaponry, and to help where needed, and Victoria was to be the new Boatswain; required to supervise the maintenance of the ship from sail to keel and stem to stern.

'And you are?' he asked.

'Robert Epping, sir, or just Rob for shortness, like. But you can call me Hare if you want; everyone does.' He said and stood out from the shadows, the light from the window catching his acne and highlighting his adolescence.

'Alright then Rob, you can be the Cabin Boy and Mate, as well as you, Irishman.'

'Billy, Billy Baker is my name.'

Robertson nodded, 'Billy, how are you with woodwork?'

Billy shrugged and ran his fingers through his curls, 'eh, drobes. Bit rumbly but clean on. Somewhere in the middle y'd say.'

'Right, that'll have to do. You can take the role of Carpenter and take care of anything that needs fixing; if you haven't noticed, the ship's made of wood so you'll be hot on your feet but by the time we reach our journey's end you'll be carving me snowflakes out of splinters, and you can teach the two young ladies too.'

'Aye, and they're Tess and Poppy Mills.'

Captain Robertson shook their hands. 'Nice to meet you.' Then he addressed them all. 'All will be Swabbies since you're all able-bodied-sailors, which means any task at hand must be done to the best of your ability. If there's a mess, clean it up. If there's a leak, plug it. If there's a tear, sew it. This vessel is our only way of transportation; if one thing breaks, we're stuck until it's repaired, which means stress on food and resources. This ship is our home; we'll be working on it, sleeping on it and living on it so it *will* be clean. Snouts and sties are for pigs; not us. I will not be rolling in shit for this voyage. Our grand *Victoria* here is a fine lady; treat her with respect and she'll give you what you want and lead you where you need to go. Have faith in her.'

He stood straight and looked at them all seriously, 'I won't sugar-coat this, so I'll be frank; life aboard a ship is hard work, especially for new sailors. There's a lot to learn very quickly and since there are only a few of you, everyone will take turns at each station to scrub up on that area, so if a problem arises everyone will be able to assist. You'll all muck in together whether it'll be with rigging, cleaning, maintenance, caulking; what have you, and you'll each be taking watches overnight. Days will be long and there'll be no podsnappery or work not up to dick; and I won't be dealing with any skilmalink business either– we've all got secrets and shady doubts so let's not spread new ones. You will get wet daily; waves come in all shapes and sizes and catch you when you least expect it, groan as much as you want and soon you'll be praying for a nice gentle sea spray. You will get cuts, bruises, welts, sores and blisters and possibly more; she's a safe ship but that don't mean she's covered in cotton and wrapped in wool. Wood is hard to knock into, so be prepared for the first few days to be *unbalanced,* shall we say?' he smiled, 'getting your sea-legs working with the tide is a tough game, is tough for everyone– waves will always be pulling the ground from under you so don't fret; you'll all be foozlers and as clumsy as each other.

'You're out of the city and you're now on the sea– two completely different environments; it'll be hard to adapt to but be patient, time will tell and by the time we reach the destination at the last point of the map, you'll all look upon this day and wonder why on earth you tripped so much. I know I do. Look at it as this: the sea is your new horse and this ship is your saddle. Learn her ways, breathe her air, feel the way she feels and soon you'll ride the waves with her white mane spraying in your face as she rears readying to gallop. Be patient with my ship, be patient with the sea; learn to work with them both.' He surveyed them all, wondering if they were taking this all in. In here or out there, one way or another, they would. 'Now, I'll be the Sailing Master, the Captain, as that's about navigation and directing the course, and I'm the only one aboard who knows how to work the apparatus properly. As for the Quartermaster, or First Mate, this role must be voted by the crew, so I'll leave you this to decide.'

To his surprise, they grouped together and muttered for a minute and then opened back out to him. 'We vote Joseph to be First Mate. He's the one that found the map, he's the one that gave us our lives back. We followed him into 'tis an' it worked, and I t'ink I speak for all of us when we say we trust his decisions.' Billy spoke out.

The captain smiled and showed a glint of a gold tooth hiding shyly behind those other grey molars. 'Then so it shall be. Joseph, you shall be our Quartermaster.'

Billy smiled and lightly punched Joseph's shoulder, 'First he's Trace the master criminal and now he's Quartermaster of a sailing ship; Mister Winter, the man of many roles.'

Suddenly Robertson stopped short, 'wait, Winter? You're a Winter?'

Joseph nodded; he'd been waiting for it. 'Joseph Winter.'

'What? What is it?' Victoria inquired.

But instead he fired another question, 'are you in any way related to Frederick Winter? The explorer?'

'Yes, he was my grandfather.'

Robertson smiled and placed the map on the table, giving a slight surprised chuckle, 'I can't believe it. And so, the legacy continues! No doubt you'll find your sea-legs in no time, your name is quite renowned among the waves. I wonder, was it adventure that called you out here, or was it destiny?' he winked.

'What is it? Joseph, your grandfather was an explorer?' Tess asked, a few others had wondered at that as well.

But instead it was Robertson that answered, 'aye, he was indeed, a famous one at that! Sailed upon the *Endeavour* with our very own James Cook, and had a few other adventures after that too I hear.'

The company looked at each other in surprise. 'You never mentioned this before mate, if I'd have known I would've cut down my suspicions the moment I met you.' Hugh smiled and folded his arms.

Joseph took Johnson's hat off and laid it on the table and took another drag; the tobacco was of a different blend and tasted strong. 'Then it would've been my grandfather's name you'd have been following, not my request for help. I didn't mention it because I didn't think it was important. My dear old man enjoyed his time out and away, all beer and skittles, but it cost him and cost him dearly and he never spoke of what truly happened. It seemed he lost parts of himself out there in the world and ended up back in London only a fragment of the man he once was– and not in a good way. Something gnawed at him, he wouldn't let it go, and I'm not just talking a bad case of the morbs. If I'm being completely honest, I only met him three times before he died, and he was an old weathered man, suffering from a loss of spirit. Melancholy. I don't know, he just didn't seem like a hero to me.'

Silence filled the cabin, the waves rocked *Victoria* mildly as the tide began to change. 'It's your grandfather's name as well as yours,' said Victoria, 'his past doesn't change your future. What's done is done.'

Poppy spoke out abruptly, 'what was it that made him lose parts of himself? What was it that he couldn't let go?'

Her sister then squeezed her hand, '*Poppy! You can't ask questions like that.*' She whispered harshly and turned back, 'I'm sorry Joseph, she-'

'Ah it's alright Tess. It's a tale for another day, at another place.'

Captain Robertson sensed the lull coming, so picked up his compass and map, 'speaking of places, I'd say it's high time we start heading toward ours. My new crew, are we ready?'

Out in the sea air with Joseph standing beside him, looking out to the main deck and to the rolling grey landscape, Captain Jim

Robertson turned the wheel and the great vessel turned parallel to the coastline, using the remainder of the Channel as a funnel that was to send them out to the open sea. A swift south- easterly wind caught their sails and pressed against them almost in frustration, as if they were struggling to shift around the wide sheets. They soon picked up speed, and before long waves were crashing against the stem and water was spraying over the deck, for the tide was not a smooth one. To a sailor these were mild conditions, not the best but all seamen could shrug and agree it could be worse. To the city-dwellers, this was a howling wind with waves crashing and beating the bow in an endless stream, a storm like none they'd experienced.

From the helm, Joseph spied three masts; the one directly behind the wheel was called the mizzenmast, then the mainmast stood in the middle of the deck and the foremast at the front, and each had two extended spars called yards climbing up them that square-rigged sails, called the mainsail and topsail, flew from. Additional strips of canvas were attached to the sails that Robertson called the "bonnets", since "all fine ladies wear them and deserve them, and our *Victoria* is a particularly fine lady." Robertson also told of two more sails called the topgallant and royal sail that could be attached by rigging an extension mast called the topgallant mast into the crosstrees, but for now these were all stowed. Behind, attached to the mizzenmast by a long spar and extending beyond the taffrail was a fore-and-aft sail called the spanker which provided additional balance and stability.

Each square-rigged sail was intricately connected to their mast by a web of ropes called the rigging that ran down to the belaying pins neatly ordered along the pin-rail on the inside of the bulwark on each side of each mast. All lines were tied secure in a figure-of-eight knot. Other ropes called "halyards" were used to hoist a spare spar or yard. "Sheets" were used adjust the position and angle of a sail and "stays" were thick ropes connecting each mast to support them. These lines were called forestays and backstays depending on their location on board, and these ran vertically down each mast and coiled around another pin-rail called the "fife rail" at the base of each mast. Stays, he was told, could also be used to fly staysails when connected to the bowsprit and a spar extension called the jibboom. Other ropes that looked like ladders were called "shrouds" and these were used not only to add further support but also to climb up to the yards or platform above the mainsail called the "maintop" or "foretop", depending on which mast had been climbed. All of this, from masts to rigging, could be called by its collective term of the "tophamper".

Ropes, ropes, ropes. They were everywhere and connected everything, each having a specific use, each having to be maintained. Joseph observed the hemp web and gulped at the enormity, wondering whether he should've bust more cons out of jail; suddenly their number didn't seem enough to tackle such an enormous task.

Robertson said there were two types of rigging; the running rigging that could be adjusted to control the shape and position of the sails and the standing rigging that supported the masts and bowsprit and when struggling to move that lot of rigging, the capstan helped to multiply the pulling force to haul that bulk-load of rope. *Dash my wig, there's so much to remember . . .* large triangular sails were strung tight from the foremast to the bowsprit and jibboom, sails that Robertson said helped to keep them straight and give extra velocity. *The forestaysail, I think it was called, and then the jib. It had queer name.* That was about as much as he'd managed to take in from Robertson's barrage of information before they'd set off. *And the grate that leads to the stairs are called hatches and the stairs leading to lower decks are called a companionway!* He blinked, hoping to remember the names should he need to call upon them as First Mate and Quartermaster.

Observing the busy deckhands at their new stations, Joseph admired their determination; they were finding their feet then losing them, metaphorically and physically. The rocking conditions were hard to stand up on, everyone was swaying and tripping, grabbing hold of the masts as they tried to manoeuvre along the deck. Before they'd cast off, Robertson had given each a brief rundown and demonstration of their jobs, giving demonstrations where necessary, yet he knew, as did they all, the education would come the hard way. Robertson had only shown them the basics, leaving them to figure out the details themselves.

At the mainmast base, he spotted Benjamin in his element examining the ropes and knots tied around the belaying pins, reaffirming himself with them as well as showing Dave the names and functions of each line. About the deck, Victoria slowly strode, trying to find her sea-legs, wearing her grey dress as she examined the row of sturdy poles called stanchions, familiarising herself with how everything should look. Rob and Hugh stood upon the forecastle holding onto the rails spying the end of the bowsprit as it pointed ahead, dripping seawater. Waterlogged, their trousers and long-sleeve cotton tops clung to their bodies but still they did not let go, perhaps out of fear.

'Where is it you all came from then?' Captain Jim asked, his hands holding tightly onto the rungs of the wheel as the waves continued their assault.

Behind bars, locked up for numerous crimes, he was about to answer but hesitated and thought against it. All of that was in the past now, and there was no use in looking back. 'Bad places with small rooms and poor conditions.' He answered.

'You are criminals?' He paused, understanding, and Joseph struggled to gauge his reaction, until he finally said, 'how did you all manage to get out?'

'Planning and coordination.'

'How didn't you get caught? There's a rise in policing of late.'

'With keen eyes and light feet. Look, it doesn't matter where we came from. I'm sure you'll get to find out our stories soon but right now the mood is high and we're looking forwards, not back.'

He nodded, understanding, relating. 'Everyone has their own story to tell Mister Winter. Although from the looks of it, I wouldn't like to know Harold's at the minute.' Robertson nodded his head down to the side of the deck to where Harold leaned over the bulwark convulsing.

'Give him time, he'll find his sea-legs soon. We all will. It's this water, it's choppy and to be frank, I an't feeling up to dick myself.'

The captain looked to him, then chuckled, 'Christ, you're as white as a pair of virgin's knickers. Go and find some ginger, there's always a stash in the hold. Any ship will have one to help with things like that. Eases the stomach. Whilst you're at it, get some for Harold too, although I don't think his tongue will be fancying much right now. Failing that, keep your eyes on the horizon; simple tricks work wonders– it's the only thing that doesn't move when everything else is seeming to.'

He nodded and tenderly made his way down to the hold, passing Billy, Tess and Poppy in the . . . *what was this deck called again? Something strange. The berth, was it?* His legs were rubbery and weak, and his stomach churned like a farmer working butter. In the gloom of the hold the motion of the ship seemed to lessen but the creaks and groans of the wood were now louder, *Victoria*'s complaints were excessive. Searching through the darkness he found a labelled hessian sack and retrieved a stick of ginger, snapped it in half and began to suck a segment. It was sharp, he winced and pursed his lips as he felt his mouth salivate. *Bugger me, she's got some spikes with her!* He was about to turn when he noticed some barrels had been pried open, some boxes had their lids removed. He frowned; *someone's been raiding our stash.* Turning, he stopped short, seeing a shadow in the corner of his eye . . . and was suddenly struck in the nose by a shaking fist and felt it crack. Blood jetted from his nostrils and he backed up, crying out at his broken nose, almost falling over the sack of ginger and choking on his piece as he saw the encroaching figure in the shadows. A pistol was in the man's hand as he hissed wildly, '*Joseph bloody Winter!*'

Joseph passed back into the darkness, blending in with the cargo but the figure was hasty, he moved fast and darted forward with a fierce growl and his arm outstretched. In a desperate move to not be cornered, Joseph leapt forward and tackled the figure to the ground, knocking over boxes and barrels. The figure was strong though and wrestled mightily with a blinding fury blazing in his slate-grey eyes. Before the figure could get a clean grip on him, Joseph slipped from the clash and made a dash for the stairs, vaulting them two by two.

A hand grabbed his ankle and he lost his footing, crashing to the wood and thumping down painfully. Rolling over, the thin red face of Mister Johnson snarled from the bottom of the stairs with his hand clawing for Joseph's throat. His lips were split and bleeding, his wrists were swollen and bruised, his face was drawn, and his moustache had been half ripped off; a web of burst blood vessels mapped his cheeks, yet the liveliest thing about him were his shot animalistic eyes. 'Forgot about me, did you? Still here, bound and gagged for two days you cruel uppity fuck! No food. Hardly any water.' He pointed the pistol to Joseph's face. With eyes narrowing, Joseph saw the pistol was cocked and loaded. Hornets were buzzing within their nest, waiting for the trigger to release them. 'Up. Now.' The madman ordered.

Awkwardly, Joseph raised to a stand and stood in front of the gun unwavering as he sucked on his ginger. He looked down it coolly, calmly, unafraid, even though deep inside he was a jittering fly caught in a spider's web. Johnson grabbed him and turned him around, holding him tight, pressing the pistol to his temple. 'Walk.' He instructed and Joseph slowly ascended, trying to think of his options.

They reached the berth, all was quiet; *someone please step out! Where's Billy and Tess gone? Poppy?* But no one did. Johnson marched him up the companionway where they arrived on the main deck and into a light rain that had begun to fall from the dreary sky, marching him in front of an astonished crew.

Benjamin's face dropped, 'Joseph . . .'

There was a cry from Victoria as she grabbed the netting from earlier and came hurrying forwards. Dave and Hugh turned and made to move.

'Not another move!' cried Johnson, 'From anyone! If anyone even takes a step, I'll pull this trigger and splatter his brains up the mast! I know he's the leader of you all, I know what your plans are! I was listening! I was there!'

The crew stood motionless, except their wobbling as they steadied themselves against the rocking ship. In a sharp U turn the gleeful atmosphere had now become a tense silence. An ugly silence, an apprehensive quiet with nought but the splashing of the waves to listen to. Everybody waited; the rain falling harder.

The captain spoke out from behind as he descended the stairs from the quarterdeck. Joseph closed his eyes and tried to keep calm; if anyone could subdue this maniac it would be him. 'Walter. Calm yourself, please. No shooting. No triggers. Just take the gun away from his head and we'll talk this through.' He kept his tone soft, soothing.

'Well dash my wig if it an't the traitor himself!' Johnson turned and glared at Robertson, 'you're one of them. I heard the plan, the plot. I heard it all! You're no better than they are, and you're the captain of the *Victoria!* Shame on you, you an't my captain!'

The captain gently pulled out his own flintlock weapon and aimed it for the previous Boatswain as the waves rolled the vessel and foam splashed to the deck. 'We mean no one any harm. We aren't out to kill, to pillage or shed blood. Look at us, do you think we are a danger?'

'Don't sell me a dog, Jim, 'nough of the lies. All I see is the waste of London, the scum scraped from the back of the city.'

'The scum that overthrew your ship.' Added Victoria with a scowl.

'We're treasure hunters, that's what we are.' Benjamin said from the shrouds.

'Ha! Treasure hunters.' Johnson spat on the deck glaring at the old man with his bloodshot shards of slate. 'There an't nothing out there worth the trouble. It's all a fable, a lie, a bedtime story to the children doomed to die in the city, where you all belong!'

Captain Robertson stepped forward; his barrel trained on the man. 'If that's how you feel then take the other longboat and row yourself to shore, but if you harm my crew, you'll be getting to shore in quite a different fashion, trailing red colours in the sea. We don't need you aboard this ship.'

Johnson scowled at the captain, and for a moment there was a fear in his eyes. Then it passed. 'Your threats won't work on me, *Captain.* I've sailed with you twice before and I know an empty threat when I hear one. I an't going anywhere.' He tightened his grip on the gun, his finger tense.

'Let me give you a threat then. If you don't let 'im go, I'll pry him from you and break every one of your fingers and toes until there aren't any piggies left to go to the market. I'll batter ya' an' toss you to the water where you can try swimmin' how the fish do it, how does that sound?' An Irishman said from behind. 'I t'ink you forget, there's ten of us an' only one o' you.'

The madman turned and looked at Billy and gave him a seething smile. 'The only one who knows how your stores fare.'

'We spent a night down there; I think we know what's there and what an't. We've got 'nough to last us a while.' Hugh said stubbornly, his dirty ginger hair still dripping from the foredeck spray.

'What have you done?' asked the captain with a hint of concern, rain dripping from the rim of his hat.

'You'll see, Jim. Then there won't just be empty threats but empty stomach's too.'

'Bastard!' Hugh cried, 'Captain, shoot him and be done with it!'

Robertson went to pull the trigger but stopped, seeing how close the shot would be to Joseph.

Suddenly Johnson doubled over, and his arm moved away from Joseph's head. Joseph slipped from his grip and fell to the deck, where he grabbed the bundled netting and turned, flinging it out over the madman, tangling him like a trapped fish.

The pistol went off involuntarily with a great bang. The bullet flew wide and thumped into the mast. The ship split through the unpleasant waves, everyone found their footing, except for Johnson, who wobbled and wavered trying to pull the netting from him.

In a mad flurry, the crew leapt forward to save Joseph and arrest the prisoner but in a sudden jolt he turned the wrong way, walked backwards and caught his foot in the loose netting and toppled over the bulwark, falling from the ship into the waves. A cloud of bubbles rose to the surface, although when Dave, Hugh and Victoria peered over the side they only saw the bubbles of sea foam and froth from the curling waves. A body did not float up; swallowed by the current. Suddenly the rising waves looked treacherous, more menacing than before: a cold brutish trap of no return.

Whilst the captain and three others rushed down to the hold to find out the meaning of Johnson's final declaration, Billy rushed and helped Joseph to his feet. 'Joe! Are y' alright boyo?' he asked, spotting the stream of blood from Joseph's crooked nose.

He nodded and took the handkerchief Billy offered him and wiped the blood from his spittle. 'I'm fine. I think my nose is broken, but I'd rather deal with this than have his fate.' He replied in a nasally tone.

Billy smiled, showing his crooked front tooth. 'Aye. Well done, you've officially conquered your first sea skirmish.'

'Ah! I can already taste the victory.' Joseph smiled, revealing a red set of teeth from where the blood had spread. Suddenly he frowned and looked down to see something poking from his chest, it looked like a rib. 'I think I've broken something else.' He opened his jacket and pulled out the stick of snapped ginger, which he handed to Harold who nodded and gave a weak smile upon his ghostly face.

Robertson, Tess, Benjamin and Hugh rushed back on deck. 'He's ruined our food!' Hugh cried.

'Poured lantern oil right over the tops of the barrels of edible food, he did. Bread is soaked through, biscuits are mush, meat's enough to get you orf chump. It's ruined.' Benjamin added, 'how many days' worth did ye say we had left, Cap'n?'

Captain Robertson looked pale. 'Four days, if we ration. We'll have to make port sooner than I thought.'

'The next and nearest port, do you mean?' Tess asked, placing her hands on her hips. Her dress was soaked through from the spray and rain, clinging to her body and showing her undergarments.

'I hope so.' Added Dave.

Joseph chipped in his opinion. 'We'll see how far we can get with what we have. Then, when there's no other option we'll head to land but first we really need to gain some distance. Jim, how far can we get in four days?'

'I'll check the chart, just to make sure. Benjamin, take the wheel. The rest of you, to your stations.' He ordered and hurried off to his cabin with Joseph and Billy following.

Inside the cabin, Robertson turned up the lamp on his desk as Billy closed the door and they crowded around the table, looking at the map. Compared to outside, the cabin seemed quiet and sheltered which gave them a chance to think clearly. 'Four days . . .' the captain muttered, 'four days . . . with rations . . .' he pointed to the French coastline on the map, looking intently. Picking up his divider and compass, he placed it on the map and charted how many miles they could cross and calculated the mouths to feed and how much each mouth would need. After a minute, he spoke clearly without looking up, 'with full stock at eight to ten knots a day, we should've made it to north Africa in about a week and a half to two weeks, three at the latest, give or take, but with four days' worth of food, hmm. If we keep at a speed of eight to ten knots and stay with the prevailing winds, keep to the Canary current and play nicely, we should be able to make it to southern Spain, or the tip of northern Africa and make port there where we can sell some stock we would've sold to France to buy some more. Of course, this all depends on circumstances which a sailor can speculate, and a good sailor will forecast.'

'How many days until we reach Gabon then?' Billy asked.

Another scan of the map and a scratch of the beard, 'Another five days from Spain, or six. A week at the latest. By then you'll really have to acclimatise, Gabon is at the equator and there, the sky forgets what clouds are and the sun will be brighter than it ever has been. The heat will be unbearable, scorching; not to mention that is the place of calm waters where prevailing winds drop and currents slide past each other mercilessly without taking or giving anything– they are named the Doldrums. It's a relentless force of nature, it does not cater for the weak.'

'We'll be fine.' Joseph said, 'we're sailors now, we'll be ready.'

Captain Robertson smiled at him; a smile of faint hope laced with sorrow. 'I admire your optimism Mister Winter. You'll need it for the journey to come.'

They exited the cabin and walked back into the rain to see the rest of the crew working at their stations, learning the new skills and adapting to the strict requirements. All dripping wet, all beginning to shiver. Joseph pulled up the collar of his navy jacket and buttoned it. At the sight of them exiting, Tess, Poppy and Victoria swiftly walked over. 'What's the news?' Tess asked.

'We're hoping to reach southern Spain where we can sell stock there.'

'And if we run out of food before then?' Victoria folded her arms.

'Then we'll discuss that when the problem arises, for now we'll just keep our heads and spirits up and pick up our pace.'

Tess braved a smile, her grey eyes probing for better news. She was shivering, her hair dripping. 'Alright. Thank you.' She took her sister by the hand and headed off down the companionway to get out the rain.

Victoria sighed and looked down to her feet, before pulling a lock of wet hair back and tucking it behind an ear. 'I could help with that, you know. Your nose. Captain's told me as Boatswain, or Bosun as he keeps calling me, I need to also be a surgeon. Now I don't know about that, but a good place to start is with that crooked question mark you've got below your eyes.'

He shrugged, 'give it a go.'

She quickly grabbed his nose and cracked it back into place without warning. He cried and pulled back with blood splattering over the deck.

'Oh yes, I forgot the warning. Sorry, it might hurt.' She smiled, 'if anything else crops up, let me know.' Joseph looked up with his eyes streaming and nodded.

'She's quite a woman, ain't she.' Billy said when she'd gone, although Joseph wasn't sure whether that was a question or statement.

'She is indeed, we'll keep an eye on her.' he said, snivelling; his face feeling sore.

He laughed, 'she'll keep her eye on you more like. Surely y' must've seen the way she's been looking at you?'

Joseph turned to him, wiping the water from his eyes. 'What? No? I don't think so. She's been looking at me?'

'Aye matey, eyeballin' you as if you were a lovely iced bun in the window of a baker's shop.'

He smiled, flattered, and nodded, 'She's a lovely woman. Fine bit o' raspberry.' A flash of Lucy's face sparked before his eyes and he gulped, feeling a rush of confused emotion. Looking to his feet, he decided to leave the topic of conversation there.

Billy smiled, 'That she is, fella.' They fell back into silence and looked out to the crew working hard. It had only been a day, and all looked near to a common sailing crew, albeit slow, but perfection would come with time. Experience was not credited by a hashed effort. Looking at them, not one looked to be sad, to be missing their home or past lives; the good-byes had already been said long ago, in fact, Joseph wouldn't have been surprised if everyone had said their farewells to their homes and families the moment the bars closed, shutting them in their dark dank cells. Everyone looked focused, glad to have purpose again. Billy seemed to have been admiring too, 'you t'ink we've made the right choices, Joe?' he said, folding his arms.

'I think so. We'll see.'

Billy turned to face him, but Joseph continued to look out to the crew. After a moment, he spoke. 'When I was a boy, before I became Trace, I used to help around the markets. Running errands for the bakers and fishmongers and butchers, collecting things for a halfpenny, fetching for a farthing. I met a lot of people, new people every day although there was a man, an old codger, I can't forget. He turned up to the market wearing the business: the deep-set black against the whiter than white shirt, clean-shaven and barbered and clean as you ever could see. Necktie, waistcoat, top hat, velvet collar; the whole shebang. I admired him for a start. I thought he was rich, perhaps the richest and it was odd to see the likes of the uppity about the nest. I spoke to him once or twice, nice enough bloke. Then as the days wore on, so did he. Within a matter of a week his black jacket scuffed in places and then began to tear; his white shirt greyed and faded and turned mouldy, his shined black shoes turned brown with filth.

'Day in day out he walked the streets, buying the same things and smiling to the same people but soon even I started to notice that his smile was the brightest part about him. Eventually he didn't turn up one day, or the day after. A week passed with no sign, and on one of my errands I passed an alley and saw a lump against the wall. I stopped running and walked up to it, recognising it was the man in the flousy tattered suit with grey stubble and brown stumps for teeth. A bottle of rum half-drunk was in his callused and crooked bony hands, bottles lay all around him and smoked cigarettes were scattered around his feet. His skin was all drawn and he reeked bad. He didn't look up to dick, and it was clear he should be six feet under grinning at the daisy roots. Instead he lay against that brick wall with rum in his hand smiling that gap-toothed smile. No one was there for him. He didn't care.

'If you want to know what I think, Billy, I'd say we found a good group of people with the right appearance, but their true colours are yet to be seen. We've seen loyalty, yes, but I won't be too quick to judge their honesty as being a wholly pure thing. We are criminals after all, and we know how to change appearances to suit a setting. You said so yourself– who'd trust a con?'

'Why didn't that man just buy a new suit when it started getting tatty?' Billy asked, more intrigued about the tale than the answer. 'Surely he knew what he was starting to look like.'

'Oh, I think he knew, but I don't think he cared. And if I'm being honest, I've thought about this a lot, I don't think he was a rich man and he knew he was going to die. That's why he bought that expensive suit, so he could see what it was like from the other side in his last few weeks; so he could experience how people look at the rich and treat them as such, and then when his money eventually ran out he spent the last of it on the things he enjoyed most so he could die a happy man.'

Billy shrugged, 'well, sure, if booze and fags make you happy then go for it. I myself wouldn't mind poppin' me clogs in a brothel with satisfied women around me. I guess that's what we all want in the end though ain't it? Just to be happy.'

Joseph chuckled and wiped blood from his nose. 'I reckon that's what we all want. Happiness and perspective. At the end, I'd want to see the other side of things, like what that man did. When it comes down to it, the only thing that he really wanted was-'

'A decent drink and a chain o' smoke?'

He shook his head and looked around at the new sailors, looked out to the bowsprit, gazed out to the horizon locked from all movement and suddenly felt the seasickness pass. 'A fresh perspective on things, so he could die with that smile on his face because he saw the way people looked at him and it made him feel something he'd never felt before. A new experience. That's what we've given these people, Billy. A fresh perspective, and a hope that in some way it will change us into better people.'

'Sometimes the world doesn't work like t'at though Joe, sometimes people are who they are, and no amount of freshness can change that. A vegetable can grow lovely with sun on it, it can grow and grow but no matter how much sunlight it gets, in the end it'll still be a vegetable.'

Joseph smiled, 'a big vegetable though.'

'Juicy one too.' Billy licked his lips. Just then Tess and Poppy came up from the berth and waddled uneasily as they tried to walk with the waves.

'Sorry,' Tess started, 'Billy, just wondering if you could come help us with some of the wood downstairs? It needs shifting and our poor mother didn't grace us with the strongest hands.' She gave a tired grin, trying to supress the pain from the splinters.

He cracked his fingers confidently, 'well, let's see what we can do.' He winked and turned to Joseph, 'see you in a bit.'

Joseph nodded and smiled to the girls before walking along the deck, gazing up at the bellying sails and to the bullet hole in the mast where but an hour earlier it was readying for his own head. He shook his head, indignant to his own luck, or was it fate? Destiny? He didn't know. Perhaps just coincidence. Striding up to the forecastle he viewed the scene ahead. The remainder of the French coastline was to his left and the open water to his right; miles and miles of wobbling grey and blue, stretching to a rigid line cutting the sky and sea in two. *That's our heading,* he thought, *onward to the end, to the strip where the sun finally touches the land and to where the treasure lay buried. The chest, the answer to the legend. Or are we the answer, those who are going to find it?*

Chapter Twelve

Days passed in slow progression with watches taken each night, and unlike in the city, they could witness the movement happening. The sun seemed brighter, hotter and stayed out late into the evening until it sunk below the horizon almost unwillingly; a sunset of which they'd never seen before and the weather seemed more distinguished as well as uncontrollable. Clouds swept in on big grey rollers or scraped across the highest blue; they brought sheets of rain or cleared altogether to leave a tepid warmth to the air; an air that felt clearer to breathe and cleaner on the lungs; apart from the cigarette and pipe smoke Joseph, Billy, Benjamin and Hugh continued to inhale. Harold had some too . . . when he managed to pull away from retching over the bulwark.

Their eyes accustomed to viewing the world unobstructed; there were no buildings in the way, no people, no horses or carts and for the first time the earth felt open and wider beyond imagination. To them, the only thing that was the same as city life was the constant stream of activity from the water. The sea was forever changing, the tide turning and waving and thrashing and slowing in an unstoppable motion. Flopping and spraying, rising and falling, calming and glistening as the white spring sun shone through a pale watery blue. As well as the water, the company watched as the rich coastline constantly changed its shape; at times it curved and jutted in great cliffs and rocky outcrops, other times it straightened out to a gravelly beach, then sand, pulling further away from them yet they kept it within their sights. Cabins and houses could be seen too along the coastline and they passed numerous sailboats and fishing tubs out for the day's catch.

As with the distance, their confidence and knowledge in their new jobs grew daily and soon they could understand the sailor's lingo associated with their current role. The more Captain Robertson yelled about the "footloose" of the sail or an "even keel", the more they could discern what he really meant, although "swab it" was a universal term they got the gist of almost immediately and began to dread hearing it. Although not as much as "dressing down" the sails or "paying the Devil"– to caulk the longest seam of the ship known as the "devil's seam".

The days were long and hard with everyone working tirelessly, finding aches and pains they never knew they had, yet these only helped to ease the smoothness of their slumber. To begin with the ship jolted and listed, tossing hither and thither wildly as the new riggers were forced to learn how to control the rigging and sails; mistakes were made often as everyone was thrown into the deep end and forced to learn quickly. As the first few days passed though, the crew settled into their stations and the ship sailed smoothly. Bumps and scrapes lessened as each found their sea-legs whilst their hands began to fill with splinters like a pincushion, giving Victoria plenty of practise with her tweezers. Soon the creaks and groans of the wood were like soft lullabies from a mother rocking the cradle. Nothing could better the feeling of the final bell though, when the anchors were put to bed in the shallows near the coast and the sails were hauled and tightly stored for the night, then they could enjoy the final hour of daylight with free time.

Dice was played on deck whilst sipping the warm broth cooked up by Benjamin on the cast iron stove in the berth, or cards were folded, flipped and exchanged as the evening sun slipped lower to the edge of the starboard bulwark. Stories were shared of their experiences in the city or on the waves and laughter was enjoyed atop barrels on the main deck, and as the bowsprit danced in the evening light, Billy's fingers made deft work upon the fiddle strings making them reminisce old times listening to the Irishman play *Old Joe Clark* as Rob and Poppy danced and laughed together before the masts. They passed the time freely and how they wanted; either spending it quietly upon the poop deck looking out to the horizon or carving bits of wood with a sharp knife. Most sat and smoked the rich tobacco listening to the ship breathe, the ends of their cigarettes and pipes glowing like fireflies, like embers floating up to the darkening sky.

The good evenings ran short due to a powerful southerly gale on the fifth day, forcing them to venture out to open water and lose sight of the coast completely. Fears resurfaced, and tensions thickened upon deck and arguments broke out, boiling and crashing like the raging waves of that tumultuous day. Alas, their captain was a man of his word and handled *Victoria* with a stern grace that managed to uproot her from the patch where the winds had planted them and continue along the coastline, sailing as the crow flies. Unfortunately, the mood aboard the ship did not rise as edible food was running short and all were feeling the effects of hunger that no amount of grog could help.

As instructed, rationing was put into place to conserve as much as they could, but it was depressingly plain to see their stores and how they dwindled as each day passed with stomachs continuously groaning along with their owners. After four days since Johnson's departure, his legacy continued to press. Their stock was running dangerously low, so now there was hardly enough for two people to eat this evening yet alone ten. Biting his lip in frustration and clenching his fists at his own mistake, Captain Robertson climbed to the top, 'All hands to deck!' he called, just as the day was almost done and the evening dimmed to a dull orange to the west and an inky stretch followed by a sallow grey looming to the east. The clouds were rounding and looked murky, miserable and ready to douse them with a cold shower.

'My crew,' he addressed, deflated but defiant from the railing of the quarterdeck. Everyone looked up at him expectantly hoping to hear something good. 'I have miscalculated and made a mistake. The food we have left will not be enough for us to reach southern Spain.'

A chorus of sighs and moans passed through the hungry and forlorn crew. 'Where are we now then? An't there any port we can reach nearby?' Hugh tried, scratching his forehead in fatigue. His ginger scraggly beard looked thin, he licked his dry lips and gazed at the captain with squinting eyes and a fading hope. A weakly rolled cigarette hung limp from the corner of his lips.

Robertson looked down at his tired crew. Their clothes were showing signs of the sea: fading and thinning, tearing and crusting with dry salt. It was in their hair too, and faces were reddening with sunburn and drawing in as their bodies tried to adjust to a lack of food and more physical work. It was clear to see they'd got the morbs as the truth of travel sunk further. He pursed his lips, *how am I supposed to tell them this?* 'The next port is in southern Spain and we are close, but another two days.'

'You're 'aving a laugh?! There must be one sooner than that!' Dave cried.

'There are but they're only small, not a major port or any place we can sell our stock for food. If we land, they won't want our stock, they won't need our stock, so they won't buy our stock. We need a main port for that. We'll end up stealing for our food and, although there are many here who can,' eyes narrowed at him, 'you won't be able to steal enough to last us another long journey. Plus, because they're small docks, they'll wonder why a big merchant such as ours has moored there– they'll know exactly what's going on. It won't be how it is in the city– for one thing it's not easy to hide an argosy ship such as this.'

The answer did not seem to settle well with the crooks from the London gutters. 'Then we'll anchor away from shore away from view and row to a quiet spot, steal what we can, fill our bellies and take more to last everyone until we reach Spain then.' Hugh suggested with a hint of irritation in his voice.

Harold and Tess nodded their heads in agreement and Victoria added, 'that does sound like a fair plan to me. We can't just wait until we get to the next port, else there'll be *no one* left to get to the port!'

'I agree.' Rob said, holding his torso trying to stave off stomach cramps.

'Aye, she has a point.' Benjamin nodded folding his arms with his pipe softly smoking, hooked in his lips. 'We don't want to end up like that ol' Nantucket whalin' boat all those years ago. I'm sure that story has been written into a book, now, what was it called?' he squinted his eyes as he looked to the deck in thought.

Eyes turned to him at a loss, not sure what the tale was but patience was wearing thin and interest was decreasing steeply. No one asked. 'Everyone's hungry, Captain.' Billy said puffing out cigarette smoke, 'we'll run out of food and soon run out of hope. We'll be down to eatin' rats in the hold.'

'I don't want to eat rats!' Poppy cried; her voice hoarse; she looked the weakest of them all. Her face, instead of red, was a sharp white, drained of blood.

The sails flapped as they caught a lost breeze and small droplets of rain began to fall from the grey sky, but none felt it, their minds were busy considering the possibility of consuming rodent flesh.

'Quartermaster.' Captain Robertson called to Joseph, redirecting the barrage, 'your thoughts?'

Sitting on a box leaning against the main mast Joseph sat forward and placed his bearded chin in his hands, sucking in a drag. He needed a shave. He needed a wash, and a change of clothes wouldn't go amiss. He felt dirty and weak, and yet hardened to the situation, as if just a week out at sea had already chipped away some of the features of urban life. Resolute, he blew out smoke and replied, 'I reckon we should head for the next small port and steal what we can, anything is better than nothing. We all need to eat. I'm hungry, you're hungry, we're all hungry and that'll only lead to more collie-shangles and skilmalinks. No one wants more arguments, so I say we go and get something to get us by until we reach the main port where we can sell the stock.'

Eyes turned from Joseph to the captain, awaiting his judgement. 'Although risky, it's necessary. As of tonight, we will have run out of food, so tomorrow we'll head for the nearest dock or port and see what we can do but for now, drop anchors and haul the sails. This wind is picking up and it's raining, there is nothing more this day has to offer us.'

The decision seemed to settle everyone's minds and after a quiet chat in the berth to avoid the rain and a very small bite to eat between them all, they settled down in their hammocks for the night to an uneasy sleep, hoping tomorrow would bring more fine food than fine fortune. Joseph struggled to find rest along with them too, his empty stomach groaning and popping like the rocking keel, cramping up and not letting him find peace. He shivered in his long-sleeve cotton top. In the gloom, he tossed and turned before getting up and lighting a candle on the table. He picked out the scroll from his pocket and slipped back into his hammock as carefully as he could manage without dropping the candle. His body ached from the exertions, or was it hunger? He couldn't tell anymore; the pain felt the same now, so he immersed himself back into the parchment to keep his mind distracted.

Reading the map in bed in the dark again reminded him of his cell; the prison life that felt like a year ago already, although he had the steady groans of *Victoria* to listen to instead of the snores of cellmates. He smiled shallowly and read through the stanzas once more in the soft glow of the candlelight. Turning the page over he saw it blank. *How does the message rise and fall with moonlight? The message is there, I just can't see it. What type of ink can do that?* The paper glowed above him, empty and featureless, yet yearning to reveal what lie hidden. After a moment, he considered going up on deck to catch any moonlight to see the message again now that it had stopped raining, but then something caught his eye.

Suddenly words began to rise on the paper in reaction to the heat from the candle he held below it. Words formed into a sentence. A sentence became two. Sentences surfaced one after the other, rising like corks in water. His head swam, reeling at the newfound discovery. The words were new, the information was fresh, a clue activated by heat. *It's been written in a different ink!* Joseph read through the piece again and again, his eyes striking down the words like a viper lashing out to its prey bite after bite. His mouth dried and he sat up, flinging his legs out the hammock and dashing up the companionway to the captain's cabin before anyone could wake to catch him.

The deck was wet and the lanterns were out, making a trip across the ship a slippery one, especially with the rocking waves battering the portside hull nearly driving him into the capstan, but

Joseph ran through it and with a clenched fist he banged on the door. 'Jim! Jim! Captain! Wake up!' Sweat ran down his face even though he wasn't hot. He looked around and saw Billy fast asleep against the mast, clearly doing a fine job on his watch, but Joseph was relieved. This conversation could be a private one.

He looked back to the door and stared with wide eyes, struggling to swallow. He rose his fist again ready to bang once more but at the sound of hurried footfall he stopped. The door was thrown open, the curtain fluttering inside. Captain Robertson threw his head out, his long slick-back hair now straggled, his eyes searching in the darkness. 'What?! What is it? Have we run aground, fouled up?' he said in alarm with a crispness that was hard to miss.

The man before him smiled and held up a scrap of paper and a blackened candle. 'Message. New one. I'll show you.' Joseph pushed past him and placed the scroll on the table, sitting ornaments on the corners to stop it rolling back. The page was as blank as before.

Captain Jim joined him at the table eager to see but saw nothing. He lit the oil lamp but still saw an empty page. Itching the worn cotton top he wore, he asked, 'A new message, says you? Joseph, are you sure it wasn't a trick of the eye?'

Joseph looked at him desperate for belief, 'I'm sure of it! Hang on.' He remembered how it happened before and snatched the paper up, lit the candle again and held it just above the flame.

'*What are you doing!*' The captain exclaimed and reached for the page that glowed bright orange ready to combust.

'Hang on!' he pulled the page away from the flame and placed it back on the table and turned the lamp up higher, as well as the other that sat at the other end. The cabin illuminated slowly, its shadows growing and flickering, yet it did not compare to the illumination of the two men who both stood dumbfounded, reading the bright words that but a moment ago were non-existent.

> Stay on the coastline but seek for the Lake,
> 1755, that is where the earth shakes.
> Questions you have but answers you must find,
> Here, where Tagus meets the tide.

𝔗ell 𝔴hom and ever: virtues and vices, 𝔴hat is lost
is not always lost.
Psalm 16:11

Their eyes burned brightly like smouldering hot coals; the cobwebs
of sleep brushed free; their minds now coaxed back into action
by a riddle written by the founder of this legend. Perhaps even
the people that buried the chest. Joseph swallowed with a dry
tongue. 'Jim?'

He answered as if he were miles away and had just about heard
him, 'what?'

'Is there any neck oil in this cabin? Scotch, whiskey, schnapps;
any, I need a tipple. A tot. A glug. Any you've got.'

Captain Jim didn't even look up from the paper, 'in the cupboard
over there. Bottle. Whiskey. Pour two.'

Joseph walked to the cupboard in a state of delirium. *How many
more clues are hidden on that page? Which is the first marker;
Gabon or this place described here? Have we passed it already?*
He retrieved two glasses and a bottle of Old Pulteney and poured
the whiskey. Seeing his hand, it was shaking. *New course. New
heading. New journey. Where will it lead us?*

Passing the glass to the captain he saw the message was fading
back to nothing, but Captain Robertson had sensibly made a note of
it on another scrap of parchment. His eyes narrowed as he thought
on something, running his fingers through his stupefied hair. Then,
strangely, he picked up the paper and held it to his nose, smelling it
and smiled. 'Oranges. Here, smell it. It's very faint but you can get
the tang.'

He held it to Joseph's nose, and he was right, there was a slight
fruity scent. 'Writing in orange juice or lemon juice is basically
writing in invisible ink.' Robertson described, 'only through heat
will it reveal the message. I should've thought of it before. It's
basic steganography.'

'What?'

'Steganography. The study of hiding messages using different
inks and revealing them through different reactions. Sailor's use it
sometimes.'

Joseph nodded, not really understanding what he was talking about, and not exactly caring at this moment in time. 'Have a drink, Jim, and let's go over this.' He took the sheet of paper and read through the message again. 'Firstly, I don't have a tallywack what any of the first part means although I reckon it's giving hints to the location to find . . . something, but what and where . . . the only thing I understand is the last word. Psalms. That's from the Bible, an't it?'

Robertson took a gulp of whiskey. 'Aye. That's a passage from the Good Book, but I don't have one aboard. Never have done. I'd rather put my faith into experience out on the waves rather than a man I've never met.'

'Right. Well looks like we can't get the meaning from *that* then. Unless that *"Tell whom and ever: virtues and vices, what is lost is not always lost"* is the passage?'

'No, I don't think so, it doesn't sound very godly.'

Joseph had to agree, which meant he'd ran out of options already. He sighed and scratched his jaw; his beard was coming through and itched terribly. 'Shame there an't a Bible here. It might've given us a clue.' He read through it again and scrutinised. *"Stay on the coastline but seek for the Lake."* How can there be a lake near the coastline? Unless it means a lagoon or mudflat; something like that, would that count as a lake?'

Robertson shook his head. 'Lagoon's a lagoon mate, and a lake is inland away from the coastline. That's where they mainly are anyway, but I don't know of any lakes near the coast if I'm being honest. Read on.'

"1755, that is where the earth shakes. Questions you have but answers you must find, here, where Tagus meets the tide." Joseph read, only seeming to get more confused a second time round. 'Tagus, what's that? That's capitalised so it's got to mean something.'

'Tagus.' The captain pulled out a chair and sat down rubbing his eyes tiredly and thinking. In his glass the whiskey rolled up the sides as *Victoria* rocked. After days of rocking, Joseph hardly felt it anymore. 'Tagus . . . doesn't ring any bells for me, but it must be important. It sounds Latin. Latin's always the language of important things.'

Joseph thought logically. 'It's a name of something, names have capital letters. And it "meets the tide", so it's got to be near to the coast. Do you reckon Tagus is the name of the lake it mentions? Something could be hidden near the lake that we've got to find.'

'Tagus meets the tide,' Robertson pulled his long hair from his face and muttered to himself, his eyes slowly opening. 'Tagus meets the tide. Joseph, what do you get at coastlines?'

'Oh, erm, docks, ports, beaches, ships, seagulls . . .'

Robertson stood, 'What do those ships sail on to get to the docks or out to sea?'

'Rivers.'

'Rivers!' he smiled with a light in his eyes, 'they run out to sea, they *meet the tide*. That's what Tagus must be. A river.'

'Right, so a river called Tagus– where?' Joseph asked, hoping he might know.

Captain Jim walked around the table, pulled out a drawer and picked out a scroll. He rolled it out, pressing down the corners and hung over the large detailed map that not only had the countries but also their capitals and trade links. Squiggly lines also indicated major river networks that were handy if ever a sailor needed a suitable way into the coastline without docking at a main port. Joseph walked around, his eyes pinned to the map, searching for the mentioned river of choice.

The oil lamps burned quietly, the waves buffeted the hull, rocking it in a pendulum motion. All was silent. Robertson pointed to the map abruptly. 'There! Tagus, it runs through Spain and Portugal, the main river actually so it's a busy one.'

Joseph looked at the end of his finger and saw a line squiggling through the Iberian Peninsula, a tributary branched from it creating a fork in the river but other than that it was a solid line that ran all the way to the coast. *Here, where Tagus meets the tide.* 'Where does it meet the tide?'

Robertson pulled the drawer out again and scuffled around some loose items before retrieving a magnifying piece. He placed it on the map, following the line of Tagus right up to its merging with the Atlantic. 'Lisbon. Tagus meets the tide near Lisbon, capital of Portugal.'

'Are you sure it's Lisbon? Not ten minutes ago you didn't know what Tagus was.'

The captain looked up at him, 'I'm just reading what the map says– and the map is saying Lisbon.'

'No, what I mean is are there any lakes near Tagus in Lisbon?'

'No, not that I can see.'

Joseph sighed, pulled a chair out and sat down, reading through the poem again. *What does the second line have to do with anything?* 'I don't suppose you have a book or anything to do with Portugal or Lisbon on this ship, do you? We've got Tagus, but this second line must be involved somehow, and if this is Lisbon the clue is talking about then it's got to be referenced in one way or another. They've all got to link.'

'What's the line?'

'"*1755, that is where the earth shakes.*"'

Captain Robertson gave it some thought. '1755. It's not written as if it's a code, do you think? Like a combination?'

'It sounds like its written as you see it and say it. As in the year 1755.'

'1755,' he ran his fingers through his hair again, puzzled, trying to remember any key things of that year over a hundred years ago. Nothing came to mind. 'Earth shakes. You don't reckon that means an earthquake?'

The sailor was beginning to think the same thing. 'An earthquake in Lisbon in 1755?'

Robertson smiled, 'Now that sounds more logical. It must mean that.'

'That would support the clue leading to Lisbon, the river and the earthquake. These an't things you can make up.' He prodded the paper, 'these are facts.'

Captain Jim drained his glass and poured another tot. 'Aye, a historical event and a location– they aren't works of fiction. I'd say our next stop is the port of Lisbon, Mister Winter. There, we can restock and find what the end part has to do with anything.'

He read through it again, '"*Tell whom and ever: virtues and vices, what is lost is not always lost. Psalm 16:11.*" This bit must be for when we arrive.' He paused though, and said hesitantly, 'the lake near the coastline though, that still doesn't fit in. It's got to be important because that lake is what we've got to seek.'

Nodding, he replied, 'Aye, that doesn't seem to fit but maybe that's something we find out when we get there, along with the last line and Psalms passage.'

Joseph shrugged, 'perhaps.' Another thought occurred to him, 'wait, how long will it take to get to Lisbon with our food situation. We've ran out now and we an't even at southern Spain.'

'Lisbon isn't far from southern Spain, three days at the most. Two days if we pushed and had a good wind behind us.'

'How about a day?'

'You're pushing your luck there.'

'You'd have a very hungry crew if we waited three days, Jim.'

'And a hungry Captain, let's not forget.'

He sighed, shaking his head, 'what other choice do we have?'

'We could stop and steal from a small port like what we discussed, or we could push on until we get to Lisbon.' Robertson suggested.

'What do you think we should do?'

'Hmm,' he considered, weighing up options, 'A few hard days won't kill us, I say we head for Lisbon.'

Hard days won't kill us, but starvation might. Yet we need to get there if we're to sell stock and find the next clue. Joseph nodded slowly, knowing the hardship that was to come. 'Lisbon, it is.' He stood and clinked glasses with the captain, draining Old Pulteney in a single gulp.

Chapter Thirteen

The cawing of seagulls floating on the warm morning drafts awakened the quartermaster back from his thoughts. He peered up from the note in his hand and spied the seabird against the pastel-blue sky– a blatant sign that they were approaching the coast. Racked with fatigue and hunger, he gazed out to the calm turquoise Portuguese waters and reminded himself that this was better than being locked in a cell. *This is better, this is better. Clean air, sea . . . breeze . . .* This was not the first time he'd had to revisit the thought and each time it became harder to believe. This was what he'd chosen after all and what the others had chosen too. This was adventure, pros and cons included. Whilst his stomach cramped, and his fingers tingled, his thoughts wandered past like a lost friend, *perhaps we never should've . . . left, we would've been . . . better off in the gaol.* He remembered the busy streets; the dirt, the grime, the smoke and shit and filth and neglect, the life of crime and dear Lucy sobbing as she headed for the door. *Go.* It all seemed like a lifetime past. He sighed, his mind now paining him as much as his stomach. *Lucy.* Shaking his head to rid of the thought, his bloodshot eyes fell back to the note in his trembling palm. *I need a smoke, something to clear my head.* Unfortunately, they'd ran short of tobacco two days ago, and he was feeling itchy.

> *Stay on the coastline but seek for the Lake,*
> *1755, that is where the earth shakes.*
> *Questions you have but answers you must find,*
> *Here, where Tagus meets the tide.*
>
> *Tell whom and ever: virtues and vices, what is*
> *lost is not always lost.*
> *Psalm 16:11*

Joseph read through the note once more and bit his lip nervously as he looked up to the port of Lisbon, each wave bringing them ever closer to the port where already the bustle appeared daunting as well as opportunistic. A reminder of the life he'd left behind. *I'll need to be a rat again, squeaking around in strange runs.*

From what they could see from the bulwark, the port was already busy at an hour past sunrise and as the heat of the day rose so did the Portuguese punters. The humid streets were waking to the cries of merchants flogging their maritime wares from seafood to ornaments, to the crows of cockerels and bleating goats wandering through the stalls. As well as the jetties and ferries already beginning their bustle, the stalls were eager to get a full day's business and, hopefully, profit. People were heeding the call too and buying the goods for the day whilst commuting to work, if they had steady employment that is, which already they could notice most did not. Vagrants wandered in rags with thick shaggy black hair followed by clouds of flies; lost and hopeless, reminding them of home. *What home?* Joseph thought as he observed the port's activity.

Two ships were docked at the port, their sails hauled, halyards tied, the men on board shifting cargo on and off their vessels. To a sailor coming from abroad, exasperation would be the appropriate response as he'd have to detangle his way through the crowd but to the ship of starving criminals this bustle meant their business would be far easier; after all, they were experienced in the art of moulding through a crowd. The more eyes that see, the less of them there are to see you.

The crew crowded the stem of the ship scrutinising the new scene with eagle eyes and itching fingers. Anticipation was hot in the air, tensions were tangible; the starvation setting in. Already bones were beginning to prod through pale and drawn skin and conversation was a mere one-word affair. Eyes sunk into sockets and hair thinned along with gums that had begun to bleed. As they saw each other haunting their stations, each became a grim reminder of the poor people they had left behind squatting in the London Mud. The captain's miscalculation had turned a one-day journey into two and a half due to a spell of poor weather and every person aboard had felt the minutes tick by. Attitudes were common ground and sarcasm with irritable responses were the main reaction to orders from the captain if there was a response at all. Dave, Hugh and Poppy hadn't uttered a word in over two days, and it was clear to see several of them growing weaker; their work ethic and attention span thinning just as their bodies were.

It was true Joseph prayed this was the place of the clue, but half of him was more relieved they had managed to make it to the port regardless. He looked back down to the note and read it through again, still trying to comprehend the meaning of the lake. A dull throb of a headache settling above his eyes again as he rocked with a bewildered mind. Suddenly he found it hard to prioritise information over food.

'Remember your role everyone.' Captain Jim called out to them from the helm as he steered the ship to the nearest free jetty. 'Tess, Poppy, Benjamin and Harold, you're with me helping to sell stock, buy it and load it on the ship. Dave, Hugh and Victoria, do your best with stealing as much as you can: clothes, foods, replacement materials. Rob and Billy, help Joseph with figuring out the rest of that note and see if you can get any answers. Now, to your stations everyone and prepare to moor. Harold, use those arms of yours and hoist the Red Ensign and the flag of Portugal below; it's green and red with a shield emblem on it.' It was obvious he was trying to sound strong in the face of the current predicament, but a hoarse voice prevented him from doing so; in fact, he sounded just as weak as everyone else. Starvation was not picky with its victims, like an infection it could claim everyone.

A few of them looked around to him, their faces gaunt and impassive as they managed to peel from the sides and man their stations. Benjamin hobbled over to the pin-rail and began loosening the sheet lines from the belaying pins to adjust the sails as Dave and Harold climbed the shrouds and ratlines (or as Robertson and Benjamin called them: "rattlins") to draw the sails and slow them. Hugh made for the anchor and Rob and Victoria left the sides to gather the cables and gangway plank. Meanwhile, Tess and Poppy went down to the hold to prepare the cargo they were to sell. Not a word was said between anyone, the silence that had fallen was tense and, paradoxically, relieving; they were minutes away from land and food, which was the main reason for everyone's effort.

Victoria edged further into the port and beelined for the vacant jetty where the uniformed officer stood awaiting their arrival, and for their docking bill. Entering shallower waters, the ship slowed and was close enough for the heaving lines to be thrown to the waiting dockers who pulled their vessel to the jetty. Amid the tension Joseph allowed himself the excitement that came with arrival– they had reached Portugal, a place where crooks of London never should've been and yet were. A smile found its way to his dry bearded lips, and as Captain Robertson scooted down the deck to approach the officer patiently waiting the crew seemed to queue up behind him.

The gangway thudded to the wood as the captain, trying to look as confident as he could under the conditions they had just faced, walked down and greeted the officer, whilst Dave and Harold tied the hawsers to the bollard using a newly learned bowling knot. Standing before him in the queue, Billy turned back to him, 'y' ready matey?'

Joseph nodded, 'four hours; we won't have long, so let's do what we can.' To extinguish the excitement he'd felt not long ago, a harrowing concern continued to constrict his mind; a bleak doubt that a mistake had been made; that they had arrived at the wrong place and were far from its true definition. The feeling of guilt that he'd pushed them to a port furthest away when they could've stopped earlier on ransacked his emotions to a crippling point. He pursed his lips and retained his wild thoughts and moved along, boarding the plank and exiting the ship to the outstretched jetty. *Does Lisbon have a lake?* Despite his empty stomach and stepping back onto solid land, Joseph felt nauseous.

'See you all later.' Victoria waved to the remaining crew as she, Dave and Hugh walked toward the port. Tess waved them goodbye and the group began to scatter, each knowing their purpose in Lisbon, each knowing their stay would not be long. Especially since those who entered the port wouldn't be using the traditional means of trade.

The wooden jetty rumbled as footfall stepped across it, it sounded strange to them after being at sea for so long. What sounded stranger, however, was the native language; the company had never heard anything like it– no English vowels or adjectives, just a rabble of foreign tongues talking unbelievably fast. They couldn't understand a word. As they came to the end of the jetty and onto hard ground, Billy looked at his companions and gave a perplexed shrug. 'Damfino what they're about.'

Joseph gave him a tired smile and looked to Rob, who was beginning to look frightfully skinny. 'Right lad, would you be able to see what you can do about food as we move through these here streets? And if you can, keep your eye open for any signs of a lake at all.'

Rob nodded and scratched at the healing blisters on his palms from his swabbing and rope burns. 'Food, I'll have no problem with, seeing how busy the streets are. But Joseph, an't lakes big, like huge? Why would one be near the sea?'

Good question, he thought but couldn't give an answer. 'Damfino, Hare. Damned if I know, still working on that one. Just keep your eye open anyway.' He replied as they crossed a road and merged into the main street that led further inland. Ahead of them, Dave, Victoria and Hugh had already disappeared into the throng of tanned Mediterranean people.

'Aye, will do mate.'

Strangely enough, being surrounded by a crowd of people made them feel comfortable and almost homely. Weaving through person by person, all walking and talking and selling and buying and paying them no attention felt natural despite being in the capital of Portugal, a country they'd never set foot on. It was bizarre, though; everyone looked so different, wearing thinner and colourful clothing and having jet black hair with tanned skin and dark eyes. Suddenly Joseph felt out of place wearing his torn and worn dirty shirt and the salty navy jacket, with his milk white skin and shaggy unkempt hair and beard. He could feel eyes on him as he walked and felt a tang of exposure and an immediate threat that they knew him. As well as the heat, anxiety made him sweat. *They don't know me, I'm not a crook anymore. I am a sailor.* But the truth, he knew, was both.

The language was an exotic code and these people seemed to scream it; perhaps it was because of their time at sea in absence of throngs of people or maybe it was a rise in volume, they didn't know but everything seemed amplified. *Surely London wasn't this loud, was it?* Billy walked ahead and stopped to let people pass, stepped short to avoid a donkey and a group of children laughing behind it, minded a waddling goose and stepped around a woman carrying a big basket of fish and a man drawing a cart behind him; he turned back and to Joseph's surprise, he smiled.

Suddenly he found himself smiling too, until they passed a weathered old beggar against a wall with a skinny dog looking up with puppy eyes as he held out a wrinkled hand for spare coins, then passed another vagrant woman; skin and bone with the pox hidden under her tatty shawl, holding a wailing baby, crying herself. His smile disappeared when he stepped in piles of shite along the road and felt his pockets being patted by the opportunistic Portuguese pick-pocketers. *The robins will be there anywhere you go.* He reminded himself as he saw the sights he used to see in his hometown, especially with the vast spread of horse, donkey, goat and human excrement lining the streets, feeding the flies. People hid in the shade of the alleys; people that had lost limbs, scarred and pocked faces, spying the crowds with wary eyes. Clouds of fetid smoke, spices and pollution drifted through on the humid air; true it was not the scents of London rot but after breathing in clean sea air for weeks now the horrid smell and density made his eyes water. He coughed, his head reeling, and pressed on. *Jesus, get me back on that boat.*

There was a tap on his shoulder. He looked back and found Rob discreetly handing him an apple and a palmful of round small pellets called olives, and in a light step he did the same to Billy. Joseph nodded to Rob and took a bite from the apple, letting the juice flow into his scraggly beard. He moaned with relief as the taste hit his tongue and before he even knew it the apple was just a core and the olives were gone. No meal had ever been so flavoursome. Apples he'd had but olives, he'd never had one, yet his stomach yearned for more.

Rob worked his magic and ferried legs of crab, mussels and oysters, nuts and more olives to them as they walked; hands that struggled with his knots on deck were snakes upon the tables. Joseph was impressed and was reminded of his early days. He eyed the street signs, but they were illegible and saw nothing of a lake nearby. Whether it was because there was finally food being added or because of the lack of idea where to turn next, his gut began to sink. *What now? Where do we go now? I see nothing of a lake.* Again, the doubts resurfaced, and he felt his food knocking at the back of his throat.

'Joseph, me boy,' Billy slowed to talk to him, 'I don't see anyt'ing, are you sure the clue leads to here? To this place?'

He frowned, 'Tagus is the river that runs through Lisbon, and there was an earthquake here over a hundred years ago. This has got to be the place.' These were facts, they couldn't be changed, so why did the clue mention a lake when there clearly wasn't one here?

'Maybe the lake is inland, somewhere in the country itself?' he said as he swerved around a group bartering at a stall.

'No, it says to stay on the coastline.'

'Well, bugger.'

'Yep.'

'No, I mean bugger as in our Hare's running and throwing his arms out.'

Joseph looked back and saw the lad running as hard as he could, threading through the traffic to reach them. *This can't be good.* 'Run!' he yelled to them, people turning to his outburst. 'Go! Go!' His eyes were frantic, and Joseph spotted behind him a bald angry merchant giving chase with his fist in the air and a knife in the palm.

They wasted no time in heeding the call and immediately kicked their feet back into gear, running as best as they could through the crowd. Keeping their feet light, they managed to thread a path through the people and dodge the obstacles, but not enough ground was being covered to warrant an escape and as Rob soon caught up with them, so did the stall-owner.

His hollers reverberated through the streets and soon everyone ahead could see them, could see what they were, and knew what they had done. It wouldn't be long before someone who thought themselves brave would stand ready to stop them. *Then we'll be done for,* he knew, *running in a straight line an't bloody working.* 'Next turn.' Joseph nodded to the turn-off to their right.

'We don't want to get lost now.' Billy remarked tiredly, his cheeks red.

'We don't have a choice.' Joseph darted for the junction with Rob and Billy close behind and ran down the street, quickly making a left down an alleyway and then another right back onto a street until suddenly his legs stopped running; ceased moving entirely and he crumbled to the shit and stones in front a crowd of people.

Billy and Rob grabbed him by the arms and hauled him to his feet, which trembled weakly and refused to carry his weight any longer. Looking down to his body, he realised how frail he was. 'Joe, you alright?' Billy asked.

Exasperated, he uttered, 'we need to stop. My legs, they can't do it.'

Rob looked back and couldn't see their pursuer any longer, nor hear his bellowing voice. 'He's an't chasing us anymore.'

Drained of strength, they collapsed against a wall near the road. There were less stalls here and more shops, which meant less of a crowd, but people could see them clearly. *Bollocks to 'em, let 'em look.* Their pumping legs gave a dull ache as they tried to catch their breath. The truth had to be faced– *if* there was a lake in Lisbon, how could they find it with the little strength they had, and little time? 'Maybe we're in the wrong place lads.' Joseph said looking down to his legs in denial and disappointment, 'I'm starting to think I made a mistake. Maybe it wasn't leading us to Lisbon at all, maybe it wasn't leading us to anywhere. It could've been a fake clue to throw us off; a diversion,' he stopped short, 'to throw *me* off.' He was the one who recovered the map after all, he found the clues, wouldn't it be his fault? Realisation of a fake clue became ever more real as they sat there; Joseph sinking into self-pity and desperation.

'Maybe mate . . . or maybe not. Have a lookie over t'ere.' Billy said and nodded to a sign of a shop just down the street on the corner to another alley.

B LAKES e FILHO
TAPETES

Joseph narrowed his vision to read the sign, 'What? I can't read Portuguese.'

'Neither can I, but there is one word I do know that's up there. Lakes!'

'You think that's it? That's what we're looking for?'

'It's the first and only feckin' thing I've seen so far that has anything to do with lakes.' The Irishman stated, and he was right.

'I'm not sure,' Joseph replied dubiously, 'the clue said *seek for the lake*. It means a lake, a great area of water.'

'Not havin' a gas boyo but I don't t'ink we're going to see any lakes around here, and that's the closest thing we've got to link with the clue.'

Rob spoke up, 'let's just have a gander inside the shop, see what's what and maybe ask a question in there and then see where that takes us.'

Joseph looked at the parchment in his hand again, his hand that quaked, *lake is capitalised, that means it's the name of something. This might be the lake we're looking for.* He ground his teeth together as he felt another craving grip him. *Jim better make sure there's a hefty stash of 'bacco on board. I'm dying for one!* He nodded, 'let's do it.' He rose to a shaky stand and stepped across the street toward the shop followed closely by his accomplices.

Resting his hand on the handle, he turned and looked at the two weary travellers giving a hopeful smile. They nodded, and he swung the door inward, chiming the bell to signal a customer.

Despite being situated in the colourful and busy streets of this Portuguese city the shop itself showed little impact as they entered a gloomy room where lamps had to be lit along the walls and at the back where the sunlight failed to stretch. Carpets and rugs hung in limp rows along the walls, each displaying a vibrant woven pattern yet giving the air a staleness that was hard to miss. They breathed it in and had to draw their breath short, the fustiness being unpleasant to the lung. As they viewed the exquisite patterns of the carpets, Joseph made a slow walk to the desk at the end of the room where in the musty glow an old man sat reading a newspaper. A money bank was beside his arm and a mug was beside the other. His white bushy eyebrows did not look up from the paper, and his bushy white moustache trembled slightly as his mouth moved to the words. His deeply tanned skin suggested a life outdoors, yet now; *bloody hell, he looks like part of the furniture.*

The owner looked up from his newspaper and over his rounded glasses that sat on the bridge of his nose. He sat up and placed his hands on the desk, '*Olá senhores, posso ajudá-lo?*' he asked in a gravelly voice. *Hello gentlemen, may I help you?*

The three men looked at each other, and one of them walked up to the desk wearing a thick navy jacket. 'We don't speak any of the language. Do you own this shop, is this place yours?' the thin man queried, almost nervously.

English sailors, the old man thought, thankfully he knew some and nodded.

'Do you, er – are you-'

Just then a short elderly woman burst through the door behind the desk yelling nonsense aiming for the old man, and they instinctively saw a husband and wife. '*Eric, quando você vai limpar os tapetes nas costas, eles estão cheios de poeira e precisam de bater. Eu disse para você fazer isso-*' *Eric, when you are you going to clean the rugs at the back, they're full of dust and need a hit. I told you to do this–* she stopped short, seeing the customers at the desk who looked lost, in a place they did not belong. '*Desculpe por interromper, Eric vem para trás quando terminar.*' *Sorry to interrupt, Eric come to the back when you're done.* She gave a short smile and was about to exit when the man spoke up in English.

'Look, I'm sorry for not having correct manners but we're in a rush and we need answers. Is your surname Lake?'

The old man nodded and replied in accented English. 'Mine is not. Lake is my wife's.'

What have I got to lose? He pulled the note from his pocket and read the final line, the line he hoped would make some sense in this strange land.

'Virtues and vices, what is lost is not always lost. Psalm 16:11. Does this mean anything to you?'

The three of them watched in surprise as the old couple gasped and looked at each other. A stunned silence settled over the shop. The elderly man, Eric, took his glasses off and rubbed his eyes, smiling at them. 'So, the legend continues,' he said and gestured to his partner, 'my wife, follow her. She will explain. It is nice . . .' he paused and struggled, '-to have meet you.'

Joseph hardly heard him. His heart pounded in his chest, his palms slick, and in what felt took a long time to do, he nodded kindly to the man and stepped forward, following the old woman through the door and up a set of stairs. Billy and Rob moved along as well, all not knowing what to say; they were shocked.

The stairs creaked as they took the weight of the men, and the fusty smell seemed to worsen as they climbed. Gloom set in and when they arrived at the top and followed the woman around to a quiet room. They were relieved to see she'd entered a room with an open window and daylight pouring through.

She gestured for them to take a seat at a table and she sat opposite, folding her flowing ankle-length skirt beneath her. With her hair tied and hidden beneath a folded red bandana, her face was open for all to see. It was evident that age had left its mark; wrinkles tugged at her features, mapping her face like a guide through her past, a display of age that indicated the wisdom collected through a life lived fully. Liver-spotted hands spread out to gnarled fingers and two missing teeth amongst yellowed others gave her smile personality whilst the faint line of upper lip hair bonneted her mouth like her bandana. Her eyes were blue and clear, sharp like ice, and although they were the relic of her attractive youth, they now gave her the ability to look innocent and fresh as well as sharp and secretive. Yet it was her large rounded ears that were the source of her tales and secrets, for they heard the legend passed down through the generations and told her of her part to play in it.

Pulling her chair up to the table, she placed her hands on it, interlocking her twisted fingers and smiled at them expectantly. 'I am glad to have met you all. I am Elanor Lake.' She started, her Portuguese accent thick but understandable. 'My husband and I, for most of our lives have been waiting for this moment here and now.' She chuckled to herself, 'I learned English for it, to convey the message. We wondered if we would live to see it.'

Joseph was surprised at how well she knew her English, and placed the note on the table, 'so you know what this means then; the line I read to you?'

She nodded, '*sim, sim,* yes. It is important line my grandfather once told the two explorers when they passed through Lisbon: *virtues and vices, what is lost is not always lost.* It is the line my grandfather passed to my father and then down to me, so that when their map would next be found, and the clue discovered, our family of Lake would know whoever next read it back to us is the one taking on the voyage and picking up the pieces to the end.'

'Wait, so you know who t'ey are then? The two explorers?' Billy blurted out.

'*Sim, sim,*' she replied, 'Man and woman, Eve and Henry Scott. They are the two who had special chest and took it with them wherever they go. They make small markers in the places that were important to them along their travels that eventually led to the last place where they buried the chest and finished the map. Eve and Henry came through Lisbon on their travels and became good friends with my grandfather, and so used his saying as a clue in their infamous map.'

Rob spoke up quietly at first but then grew in confidence, 'did they mention to your grandfather where they were going next?'

Elanor turned to him and smiled again, 'sweet boy, they did not. They never knew where they were going until they arrived. They never had a plan; like leaves in the wind they were as free to fly and fall wherever fate destined them to be.'

Joseph furrowed his brows and dug out the scroll from his pocket and unravelled it. 'Elanor, we've found another clue but there's something that doesn't seem right. I found the other first and *then* found the clue to Lisbon. I'm not sure whether this was meant to be the first place, the first marker. I mean, is there an order to the clues?'

Her blue eyes lit up and she pulled the paper scroll to her, scanning the words, feeling the paper between her crooked fingers; almost sensing its age and value. '*oh, santo senhor, esta aqui na minha casa.*' Oh, my lord, it's here in my house, she whispered to herself. After a moment of reflection, she looked up at Joseph, 'what else did you find?'

'The next clue is leading us to the Cape of Gabon. Is that a place of significance?'

Suddenly a look came over her face, a shocked expression that slowly moulded into a clear understanding. '*Oh, meu Deus, sim!* Yes, this is the place they first meet each other; Cape Lopez!' She exclaimed.

'Cape Lopez an't Gabon though. The clue said Gabon.' Joseph said, not sure she understood him.

'No, no, no, Cape Lopez *is* Gabon. Lopez is the bay in country of Gabon.'

Joseph's eyes widened as he understood. One by one things began to make sense. 'And as well,' Elanor continued smiling, 'there are more links that are tied to this Cape; it plays important part in our histories. It was discovered by Lopes Goncalves in fifteenth century.'

They paused, waiting for her to explain but she only sat there looking at them with pride. They couldn't see it. Finally, Billy asked the question that was on their minds, 'A'right, what's the link? Who's this Lopes?'

'He is a man who explored and discovered in the age where sailors went out to make their mark in history. And Lopes Goncalves was Portuguese.'

The next clue leads to Gabon and Gabon was discovered by a Portuguese man, and we're here in Portugal. Jesus. Joseph almost shook his head indignantly, as if the fates were lining up.

'*Desculpe, estou esquecendo-*' she shook her head and grunted in annoyance at her language confusion. 'I am sorry, I have forgotten my manners. Would you all like a drink?'

It was a question they'd all been yearning for. 'Yes please, just water if you have any.' Joseph replied for them, although he sounded casual about it their thirst was formidable. *And a big wad of 'bacco please love, a nice big wad of 'bacco for me to fill my pouch and smoke away to get this bloody itch off my back.*

Elanor nodded and excused herself and walked out the room, soon returning with four glasses and a jug of water. The three snatched a glass each and poured the water, drinking until each was empty and then they poured another. Elanor giggled, 'thirsty, yes?'

'Aye, we were.' Billy said wiping his mouth.

'Long at sea?' She noticed their tatty clothes and grubby faces, and their unfortunate smell.

'It felt like a damn long time, yes.'

'Speaking of time, we haven't got long before we have to leave so if you wouldn't mind, is there anything else you have to tell us about the clue?'

'Which clue?'

'Any that you have information on.'

She poured herself some water and drank, looking thoughtful. She wiped her mouth and scratched her hairy chin, until she gaped at them with surprise. '*oh meu, como eu poderia esquecer!* How could I forget. There is something else.' With her liver-spotted hands she pushed herself from the table and tottered out of the room with a swirl of her skirts, leaving the three men in a tense silence.

A moment later she returned holding an object, but the way she held it, Joseph noticed, was like that of a piece of delicate china as if she were carrying a priceless family heirloom to them. Sitting back at the table she placed the object in front of them. A small wooden box. Joseph gulped and gawked at it, before reaching out to it and stopping himself, remembering he wasn't Trace. 'May I?' he asked politely.

'This object has been in my family for three generations now, and before I die I was to give it to my eldest son so that when the day came he may pass it along to his own kin or to the one to repeat the line only the family knows. Alas, my son was not destined to possess it, for it is I that can now play my part in the story and give this object to you, as was planned.' She smiled, 'it is with great honour that I allow you to open it.'

With tentative hands he reached to the box and gently pulled it closer to him. Chairs scraped softly beside him as Rob and Billy pulled themselves closer. He pulled the latch out and lifted the lid.

Inside was another smaller object wrapped neatly in a fine cloth. His pulse quickened; he licked his lips in anticipation. Delicately, he picked the object out and set it in front of the box . . . and slowly began to unwrap.

There, in the middle of the cloth, were a pair of oddly fashioned glasses and a small key. Their age outnumbered everyone at the table, their value was sensed amongst all– it was a piece of unknown history, an artefact from a bygone age; a relic from a lost legend laid before them waiting to share their secrets with the criminals from the backstreets of London.

With shallow breaths, Joseph picked up the glasses. They were light, as if he were holding a feather, and neat; handcrafted. The wire earpieces looked flimsy but would give a challenge to anyone trying to bend them and the lens the wire held was a questionable thickness. The glasses looked like they had been crafted not for everyday sight but for this purpose only; to convey a message, to allow for the next clue to be unravelled. The more he inspected them, however, the more he saw a major flaw. Confused, he looked up to Elanor who stared in wonder at this passing. 'Elanor, there's only one lens in these glasses.'

'*Sim,* yes.' She nodded as if that explained everything.

'Where's the other lens? Do you have it? Did it break?'

She shook her head. 'It was given to my grandfather like this. The other lens is in a different place, hidden at a different time. Only with both lenses can you see the next clue, I presume. It is something I have been thinking on for a long time, and now I know the answer to it. Now I know where the other lens is concealed.'

It began to make sense. There was an empty slot where the other piece should be, it had to be found and slotted into the wire frame in order to see the next clue and chart the following course. He picked up the small key that came with the glasses, 'this. This must be the key for the box where the other lens is hidden.'

Elanor linked her crooked fingers together, 'it is possible.'

With a fire burning in his eyes, he knew where the lens had been left. *Gabon. That's where it's hidden. Cape Lopez.* He wrapped both items back up in the cloth and placed them in their box and stood. 'Elanor, I can't thank you enough. When I'm done with them, I'll make sure they're delivered back to you. They're your family's after all.'

She smiled and wiped a tear from her eye. 'Thank you, kind sir.'

Billy stood behind Joseph, 'Thank ya' for the glass of water there, and for the box. You've no idea how much it means.' And she smiled and nodded in return, but Rob didn't rise.

'There's still something I don't understand.' He said as he slowly got to his feet, looking confused.

'Yes?' she eyed him curiously.

He scratched his hair, 'Well I don't know me letters, so I don't know what it says properly but didn't the clue mention something about a verse from the Bible?'

Joseph's eyes widened, remembering. 'Psalms 16:11. Does that ring any bells?' he asked eagerly.

Elanor frowned and shook her head. 'Not for me, no, but Bible I have. I bring it to you.' With a quicker step she toddled from the room again and returned a moment later, flicking through the old Book.

She placed it on the table and the flicking slowed until she stopped and looked at them. It was written in Portuguese, but she translated well enough. 'Psalm 16:11.

> '*You make known to me the path of life.*
> *You will fill me with joy in your presence,*
> *With eternal pleasures at your right hand.*'

Looking up from the book, she spotted Joseph and closed her eyes, marking the cross upon herself, whispering an *amen*.

He frowned, not understanding . . . until he looked down to what he was holding in his right hand.

The box with the glasses and key inside.

With those two items, their path to life was now known and all four inside the room were filled with joy.

Although what they lacked was time.

Chapter Fourteen

Before they left *Victoria,* the captain had given those venturing out into the city four hours to search for their required aims, be it food, materials or information, as that was the average time it took to restock a ship for a long journey. Four hours; that was all, and as they bade farewell to Eric and Elanor they checked the clock on the church tower and saw fifteen minutes now remaining. After a curt curse was shared, it was time to move.

With his feet pounding the streets, Joseph rounded the corner narrowly missing a man carrying a woven basket full of shellfish. His legs burned already; his lungs were aflame but the sheer necessity to reach the jetty in time overpowered the pain.

Ducking, dodging and weaving a path through busy thoroughfare reminded him of home, of the smoky cobbled streets strewn with litter and grime, instead this time he was not carrying his bowler hat or being pursued by the city's persistent and corrupt peelers. With him now were his two close partners, those that had helped to build this venture. Billy was a few paces behind, and Rob was out in front: his legs quick, his step light. *No wonder they called him Hare,* Joseph thought as another drop of sweat ran past his eye, *he'll need those legs to get him to the ship. We all need those legs.*

Despite a fast pace, he was struggling to manage it whilst trying to keep the wooden box stable. The last thing they all needed was to reach the ship and sail away to sea only to find the one lens inside smashed and broken by the small key that shared its company because he thrashed too hard. *Keep your feet moving, not your hands.* Suddenly the voice of Mad Vinny echoed through his head, *keep yer feet light and yer fingers lighter, Trace my old chuckaboo.* If he had the air to chuckle, he would have; for it was that fat bald vagabond who Joseph had to thank for giving him the job to find the map that led him here.

They bolted down the main straight; beginning to recognise the stalls and people, beggars and scatterings of shit they had seen earlier but their hastiness prevented any relief. Yes, they were back on the same route, but this time was much worse as their time and chances were slimming with every passing second.

'Move!' Joseph began to yell to the people, knowing fully well they wouldn't understand him but having no other alternative. 'Out of the way! Hook it! Hook it! Be off with you!' Faces turned to see the commotion but those who's reactions were slower were suddenly bowled over and shoved out of the way. Manners forgotten, they raced pass without a thank you. The smell of the sea wafted down the street, pushing another cloud of smoke and fetid air through the alleys. Merchants selling fish, mussels, shellfish and sea sponges became frequent and the familiar sound of seagulls cawing told them they were near. Joseph tasted bile in his mouth from the exertion, and from stepping in what had looked like human waste. At least he hadn't slipped. Down the street they jostled until sight of the *Victoria* came into view; her hull bronze in the late morning light, her sails unfurled– her rigging taught, her Blue Peter flag aloft, waving them goodbye. They pushed harder, and saw Poppy and Victoria pulling the gangway plank back up to the deck.

'Wait!' Billy cried, but his voice fell upon deaf ears. 'Wait ya' bastards!'

They scrambled by the busy dockers and onto the jetty, leaving the officers shocked and unable to catch up to investigate their hurry. Their boots thudded against the wood as they ran, a rumble that ousted the smooth lapping of the calm waters that curled up the feet of the jetty. 'We're here!' Joseph exclaimed, waving an arm in the air. 'Fuck sake, *we are here!*'

Victoria began to move with her sails catching the breeze; her hulk sliding past the wooden platform as Dave, Hugh and Harold hauled her away from the mooring jetty by rowing her in the longboat. *No, no, someone look! See us!* Joseph pushed harder, paying no heed to the burning pains spiking through his legs.

Suddenly a person appeared astern upon the poop deck; a woman; Tess. She stood at the taffrail underneath the creaking spanker sail looking back to the port, when her eyes caught sight of the three men hammering down the jetty, flailing in desperation. She quickly darted away and rang the bell, and more faces appeared at the sides.

'Throw something! Anything!' Joseph called to them, now almost running beside the moving ship.

A hawser was thrown over, thudding to the wood and unravelling rapidly. 'Get it, Rob! Grab it!' he cried.

Rob reached over and jumped onto the rope. He climbed a short way before turning back, reaching for the box. Instinctively he passed it over, 'the scroll too!' Rob exclaimed, and he passed it over . . . before understanding the reason why the extra hand was needed.

His legs seized and buckled as they found no ground to land upon, his stomach dropped as he didn't find something he expected to be there. Joseph and Billy fell off the end of the jetty, splashing into the Lisbon waters. Despite being enveloped in liquid; the truth was harder than stone: neither could swim.

The rope dragged off the edge as well, flumping into the water with a soft splash. Their legs kicked weakly and found no ground, no propulsion. They bobbed in the water, arms up, flailing, floating, sinking. Joseph opened his stinging eyes and saw the end of the rope sliding past like an eel.

Without thinking he grabbed it and took hold of Billy's arm and the tug instantly pulled them along. They sucked in water and coughed, spluttered, the saltiness stinging their eyes, but with great strength he managed to pull his friend up to the rope to find a hand hold. Hand after hand, they fought hard against the drag of the water and climbed to the keel where they were careful not to be sucked under *Victoria*'s swell. They clambered up the rope with their remaining strength, hooking their hands around the rails and, with help from those on board, flopped onto the deck in exhaustion.

Everyone hurried to them. 'Joseph! Billy! Are you alright?' Victoria ushered as she gave Joseph a towel and Tess wrapped another towel around Billy. She tried to get him to his feet, but Joseph only stumbled and dropped back to his knees again spluttering up seawater as Rob watched on, clutching at the scroll and wooden box.

Benjamin knelt beside him, smacking his back. 'Aye, lad, get it all up. You'll be a'right.'

After a time, Joseph looked to Victoria with red bleary eyes, his hair and wiry beard dripping and clothes soaked through, then turned back to the deck to cough up water. When he'd finished, he breathed deeply and managed a, 'thanks Vic, how did you get on?' It was then that he noticed she was wearing different clothes; a fitted shirt complemented her figure; it looked to be a man's garment but she'd tucked it into a pair of trousers and tied it off with a belt suiting it to her style and giving her more freedom when working the ship. She'd also swapped her thin heeled shoes for a pair of leather boots to give a surer step on deck.

She smiled and for the first time he noticed she had a slight gap in her two front teeth and, if anything, it made her more attractive. 'Good. We got more food, a few more materials and managed to get a bundle of clothes too, enough for a few of us to change I think.'

Dave joined her, visibly sweating after rowing the ship out from the busy port. 'We grabbed as much as we could, not sure whether the clothes will be enough for everyone though.' Harold and Hugh were at the bulwark hauling the lines to bring the longboat back in.

He nodded and lifted himself up to a box to sit on. 'It's fine. We'll try and wash the ones we do have.' He glanced around at the crowd but struggled to discern detail through his shot eyes, yet he could not find the captain amongst them. Instead he spotted him upon the quarterdeck steering the vessel around the bay and approaching ships and out to sea. *Why did you try and leave us behind?* It was a question that could wait until later.

'I know what you're thinking,' Dave lowered himself and sat on a barrel beside him, 'he tried to stall as much as he could, tried chin-waggin' to the officer but he wouldn't have it. They'd already restocked and were taking up valuable space. The tide was right. If we stayed any longer, we would've been fined so he decided to leave. The four hours were up anyway. Captain *did* say four hours before we left.'

Joseph turned and shot daggers, '*we were almost there*. We were running and calling you.'

'Mate, I don't know if you've noticed but it an't easy to stop a moving ship.'

'Where was you in the crow's nest, then? That's a station of yours, an't it? You would've seen us coming. We were only late by a few minutes. You could've waited.'

'I was towing this bloody ship thank you very much. Why, if I had of been in the crow's nest whilst still moored, I'd have been wrist-slapped for shirking.'

'Dave,' Victoria chimed, sensing the tension, 'why don't you go and help Harold with the rigging?'

He took his hat off almost mockingly as he got to his feet, 'as the Bosun commands.'

When he'd left to join Harold at the pin-rail, she muttered, 'he's been a bit funny ever since we arrived at the port back there.'

'He's been a bit funny ever since we left England.' It was clear Dave had been souring by the day.

She sat next to him, 'The sea's already starting to change us.'

'Well it can only do two things; make us or break us, and with what we found in Lisbon I'd say the sea will help us a lot. I need to speak with the Captain. We need to sail for Gabon immediately.' He stood and swayed a little, his legs rubbery, he steadied himself and turned back to her smiling. 'Thanks for the towel.'

She nodded and returned the expression, and he kneeled to see how Billy was doing. 'Come now my Irish possum, we need to have a chat with Jimbo.'

Billy looked up at him with red-rimmed eyes, his wet curls dripping water down his face. 'Now?'

He took his hand and pulled him to his feet. 'Now. He needs to know.'

The wind filled the sails, pushing them further out to sea. *Victoria* sailed with a stern grace back out to join the cold Canary current that was to take them to northern Africa, riding the waves like a jockey racing his white horses. Sea spray billowed across the deck, dampening the crew at their stations but the splash of the water as the stem split through the rounding swell fortunately did not reach the four men on the quarterdeck; something Joseph and Billy were especially pleased of as they dried off. Standing next to the captain, they moved with the sway of the ship as they'd learned to master.

Jim Robertson held onto the rungs of the wheel and turned it slightly, feeling the tension of tiller ropes turning the rudder as they streamed out from the port to move with the coastline. 'Gabon it is then?' he glanced at them, giving a quick smile that exposed a glint of his gold tooth.

Rob nodded, 'Yes, sir. And we now know what we have to look for.'

'Sounds like you found what you went out to seek?'

'Aye we did and get this; the lake wasn't a lake. What the clue meant was a *person* with the surname of *Lake*.' Billy added, some colour returning to his face.

Joseph recounted a summary of what they learned at the carpet shop from Elanor. 'It's the missing lens from the pair of glasses we need to look for, in a box probably. Then we can see what the next clue is on the map.'

Robertson nodded, his eyes facing forward to the deck and sea as the sails netted the coastal gale. The ship began to turn in a wide arc to run alongside the rest of the coast of Portugal. He said to them in a rather odd tone, 'you did well then.'

Rob nodded, not picking up on it. 'We did, she also gave us the key to the box when we find it. Her family have been holding onto it for a long time.'

'Rob, lad, how's your knotting coming along?'

'It's . . . not too good.'

'Experience comes with practise and to practise you need old Smith. See if he's busy, old boy.' The captain said.

Nodding, he handed the box and scroll back to Joseph and scurried down the stairs to find the old sailor.

'Something amiss, Jim?' Joseph asked inquisitively.

There was a long pause; seeming as if he was trying to generate the words, or perhaps wanting to avoid it. Again, the captain spoke with the strange tone that even Billy frowned at. 'Joseph, how is it that you never cared to mention the crew that I now have working on my ship consists of rapists and murderers? The thieving and vagrancy I knew about, I guessed as much from how quickly some of your hands can work, but raping? Killing? You really were testing the fates breaking them out. *Who* was it you found in that gaol to follow you?' It was now that he turned to him, and Billy took a step back. 'I abandoned my crew and have endangered my career for this, only to discover the people who work this ship have slipped from their punishments after committing such atrocities.

'London is strife with injustice and inequality, I know, but I'm now helping those who have slaughtered the innocent and raped poor women to freedom and a life void of consequence. You've all managed to shrug off those sinful crimes for a new life at sea, to do what? Rape and murder again? Please, Joseph, tell me you didn't go under the hammer for those crimes as well.' His eyes were angry yet yearned for truth.

Joseph had never thought to ask why his company had been locked away. If he was being honest, he didn't think it was his business. That was their past and they were in prison paying for it. All he saw was that he was helping people escape a condemned life, to escape dying in a cramped and dangerous place just as he was doing. He hadn't considered how it would look from an outsider. *How did he find all this out?* 'Hand to heart, I did commit crimes, but it was only thieving.' *And maybe setting up a few hits to get rid of a few others for a few extra pennies in the pocket,* 'I never killed or raped. I knew people who had but I thought not to mix with that crowd. I just wanted to help the people who wanted to help me.'

'You'd take aid from a killer then; you'd shake hands with a rapist and forget all what he'd done because that was his past and he said it was so?'

'I wouldn't recommend the second one Cap'n,' Billy interjected, 'not with where they've been and what they've done.' Joseph couldn't tell if he was being serious or not, but he hoped he was. Now was not the time to joke.

Captain Robertson switched target, 'And you, Baker, what were you in for?'

The Irishman's face set hard suddenly, his eyes stiffened. 'I couldn't pay up my gamblin' debts and people came for me. I didn't kill em', but I protected myself as best as I could. Peelers found me with one man at my feet, one with a broken arm and me kicking the third on the ground. I was a mess too, so I was, a face like a blind cobbler's thumb with broken ribs and collarbone, but I was the one that got done for causing grievous bodily harm to others, although if I hadn't done that I wouldn't be standing here now, and that's a fact y' can take to the bank.'

The sailor looked at his friend. *That wasn't what you told me in our cell.*

The captain's mouth shut, seeming to let some of his anger out. Joseph started, 'I'm sorry for their past, for all our past's and what you've heard, but we're trying to make amends for that now. We're trying to become better-'

'-Don't. Winter, if I were you, I'd stop there. Dry yourself off and get to work. We'll need all hands to work *Victoria* if we're to arrive in Gabon.' Captain Jim turned his back to them and focused on the waves, not saying another word.

Despite already having his sea-legs in order, the deck felt uneasy once again. In silence, they stepped down the ladder to the main deck and down the companionway to the berth where they dried and rummaged through the pile of clothes for something their size. Joseph picked out a clean long sleeve cotton top and slipped a shirt over it, then clipped on a pair of braces and slipped a waistcoat over that and fitted a newsboy cap on his head. Billy picked out a vest and a grubby *Boss of the Plains* hat. Once they'd changed, they descended further to the hold to look for a drink and something to eat and found the deckhands Tess, Poppy and Hugh checking over their new stock and tallying it up as Robertson had instructed by the light of an oil lamp.

No one spoke. No one seemed to want to. Joseph wondered what words had been shared whilst they were away; the atmosphere aboard *Victoria* seemed even more awry from when they'd landed in Lisbon. At length Billy spoke up as he took a handful of mussels and a crab leg, 'the restocking went well then I see? We couldn't really get much out of the Captain, he started getting a bit shirty; I don't t'ink he's in t' mood for talking.'

Tess lowered her finger from pointing at the barrels and turned to him, smiling faintly in the gloom. She wore a change of clothes too and had pinned her hair up, revealing her pretty features. 'We got on well, all restocked.' She turned to her sister, 'Pop, how about you go and see if Victoria needs a hand?'

'You're going to talk about adult things, an't you?' she asked, 'well I'm almost a woman now, I'm not a child anymore, Tess.'

Her sister eyed her sharply, 'you are *almost* a woman, but not yet. You're still young and I am still your older sister, so you'll heed me; now go and see to Victoria.'

'It's just so you can talk to Billy, an't it? I know you eye him!'

Billy grinned, and Tess blushed but tried to remain calm, 'Poppy. Go to Victoria.'

Huffing, Poppy Mills whirled her skirt and stomped from the hold. When Tess made sure she'd gone, she turned back to the men and forced a smile, 'the joys of having a sister on the edge of her teenage years. Sorry about that.'

Still grinning, the Irishman nodded, 'oh, tis fine Tess, no bother at all.'

She pursed her lips then joined them to talk. 'Captain found out,' she said, 'I don't know how or who by, but he found out about the crimes we've committed, and I think it struck a nerve. I've been hearing stories, not from his lips of course but whether it's simple deck blather I don't know; either way he's disappointed in us.'

'Why? What did you hear?'

'His wife . . . well, a few years back they were caught in the middle of a gang and mugged and beaten, you know what those gangs can be like, we all do. There's not a lot you can do before you're betty fanged. She never recovered from her injuries and died soon after.'

'He did though, he recovered.' Hugh interjected, 'his bruises healed, and he now has that gold tooth and a few scars.'

She nodded, 'his wife died because of people like us. Ever since he heard that some of us are, well let's just say sourer than others, he went quiet and started replying with short words.'

'I know what you're thinking– I was thinking it too; we weren't the ones to do that to his wife so why should he be taking it out on us?' Hugh added, sitting atop a cask eating bread and cold meat. 'Since he found out what we were capable of and have been locked up for he just doesn't want to talk to us at all.'

Confused, Joseph folded his arms. His mood was irritable enough as it was without his tobacco; this was not helping. 'He knew we were criminals though; he knew we came from a gaol in the city so why is he so surprised at how we got there? Surely he could've guessed we didn't go in there by choice.'

Tess shrugged. 'I don't know, I think he assumed we were all doing time for petty crimes; it's what got me in there anyway, stealing food for Poppy and I and the other family we were living with. I suppose the fact that we had the map helped to smooth him over to our side when we first came aboard; must've made him forget.'

Shrugging, Joseph sighed, feeling tetchy and ready to snap.

'Fuckin' hell, I didn't realise we were aboard a ship o' milk; within four bleedin' hours the whole boat's curdled.' Billy looked down to his mussel, cracked it open and supped at the gelatinous insides.

He didn't say it, but Joseph thought the same. Something had shifted whilst they were away. He nodded in silence, grinding his teeth together. 'It'll blow over, we're all getting a bit hot with the new climate. We'll try and sort it out.' He tried to sound as positive as he could, but Tess could see through the thin veil.

'I hope so.' She said and turned and went to climb the stairs out of the hold but then turned back. 'Oh, there's a stash of 'bacco by the way, Joseph. Just over there.'

He looked where she pointed and made haste in pinching some, rolling it and lighting it. The first drag was blissful, and he immediately felt his jangling nerves soften. Looking round to the stairs, he gave a thumbs up. 'Thank'ee sweetheart. You're a doll.'

She smiled and nodded and continued up the stairs. When she was gone, Billy wondered what Hugh had done to get into the gaol and asked him, since the topic had now been breached his curiosity weighed more than his manners. Hugh shrugged and scratched at his ginger beard, pinched some tobacco and rolled up giving a lopsided smile, 'let's just say I was being too friendly with ladies that didn't want to be friendly with me, and it got out of hand. I like me some female company, perhaps too much and me hands wander freely without me knowing.'

'There's pleasure houses for that, y' know, Hugh. Brothels a' plenty in London. You got to pay em' but it's got to be better than raping around.'

He nodded, 'I know. I know, and I did visit a' plenty, even one when we were in Lisbon and I tell you, there's some fine hedge-croppers in there.'

Joseph glanced at him, the short ginger man and suddenly saw him as one of the criminals who needed to be kept in the gaol, a man who deserved to spend time behind bars. *You're one of the rapists, my god.* He knew his company were not all thieves and petty criminals, but he was coming to the realisation that that was just what he wanted to think. They were not all like him. Some of them had incited and participated in travesties he would never want to indulge in and were what society would call monsters. An abrupt guilt wrenched at his gut as he looked down to the wooden floor and saw that he had helped these people escape from prison, helped to give them a new life. *A new life, but did they deserve another chance?*

It was a question that spiralled around his head over the next week and a half as the ship left Europe behind and began rounding the northern head of Africa sailing upon the Canary current. It was a question that rattled around his mind as the sun started to beat down upon them with a wrath they had never felt before. The

London summers were hot, everything dried and cracked, and the shit of the city baked in its cobbled grills, but this heat was something else; mercilessly, it zapped their energies and strength making their work harder than before.

Trying to clear his head, Joseph paced his daily routine inspection of the decks and found himself praying for something an Englishman would've never prayed for. A cloud. The heat was relentless, an unforgiving blast that had to be endured whilst nearing the equator; it seared them as if they were standing under a magnifying glass, it baked them as if they stood in an oven. He wiped his thick dry tongue over his cracked lips and longed for air, a simple breeze. None had felt humidity like this before. This heavy air they sucked in was false and fraudulent; all oxygen had scarpered away seeking scants amount of shade to hide under.

Spying the coastline from the portside bulwark, it had transformed from rocky outcrops of the brink of southern Europe to beaches, white and sandy with huge green trees lush with life. A few ports and coastal settlements could be seen, as well as a few passing ships sailing nearby; yet these were tiny in the distance. As they sailed, it became hard to distinguish detail in the rising heat as the pressure compressed distance into a haze of blurred colours; an untidy spread of yellow and orange with flecks of green smeared over the horizon letting them know they were still in sights of land.

The only other rival of change was the tone of blue in the sea beneath them. It appeared clearer, cleaner and as they ventured out to deeper waters it became a palette of blues from azures to periwinkles to a deep rich royal shade that looked so thick it could've painted the barnacled hull. The African waters had more to offer too. On one occasion a small pod of dolphins leapt and dived in front of the stem, dancing before the bow to the rhythmic flap and crack of the jib and forestaysail as they caught spontaneous southerly gales and tugged them along the head of the vast continent, edging down the bottom of the North Atlantic.

The bubbles and froth the ship whipped up looked whiter than before; if anything, the sea was looking desirable and inviting. Although, all temptation was soon erased from their heads when

Captain Robertson instructed them to all stay back and keep their wits about them. 'Heat can do funny things to your mind,' he'd said that morning, 'back in England we all beg for a few rays, but this is not like that, oh no. This type of sun doesn't just get you a bit hot and sweaty– this one drains you of all strength and feeds on your will to live. It dries out everything including the air in your lungs, making you feel like you can't breathe and if you let it in it'll suck sense from your head making you believe that the water of the sea is drinkable and refreshing. Legends make you think the waves make you mad and yet the sun is the biggest siren of the sea.

'Do *not* believe those sweet nothings it whispers. Do not let it take you for a fool. To listen will be the last thing you want to do; if you jump in this here tide the temperature will shock you into submission, the current will suck you under and the sharks that live out in these clear blues will eat you alive. They're monsters of the deep that'll pull you under in a second, whereas that,' he pointed to the sky with a dry finger, 'is the monster of the sky trying to tempt you *into* the deep, so all of you listen closely and heed me: keep an eye on each other, keep drinking water and try and keep to the shade as much as you can.'

Joseph was surprised, those were the most words the captain had said to them, apart from barking orders, in five days. *He must've had others from a previous crew jump in because of the heat,* he pondered as he watched Robertson browse over the rigging and sails, before heading back to the shade of his cabin leaving Victoria at the helm. He sighed and cast his eyes back to the deck where he perused the figure-of-eight knots tied around the belaying pins and eyed the shrouds leading up to the mainmast, maintop platform and crow's nest. 'Harold my fine possum,' he called, 'double check these knots and turnbuckles on the stays and make sure they're secure enough. We don't want any tension of these masts to come loose when we got this gale blowing us forward.'

Harold lumbered over with a wet towel wrapped around his head and tied with a length of string, wearing a vest with trousers cut at the knee. He had a faded and smudged tattoo on his shoulder, he noticed. 'I checked em' not long ago, Quart'.' He replied.

'Good man. Give the starboard sheet of the mainsail a heave to keep us south by south west and attach a bonnet, then get Benjamin and Dave to help you rig the topgallant mast to fly the topgallant sail and royal sail of each mast to give us a few extra knots. Be careful, it'll be windy. Then, rig the jibboom and fly another forestaysail, the outer jib, to catch all the wind we can. Captain's said there's corals in these waters, we don't want to breach the keel so best to keep her to the deeper waters.' *My god you sound like a sailor now,* he thought with pride in his ability to adapt.

'Aye, I'll see what I can do.' He said, glancing down to his red and blistered fingers from swabbing the deck with the holystone. Each of the crew had come to know that there was nothing holy about the holystone.

Joseph nodded and was about to turn away when he stopped short and looked at the man; throughout the voyage so far, he had no hidden intentions, no malice behind his brown eyes. An honest, hard-working man, a what-you-see-is-what-you-get type; he wondered why on earth he'd ended up in the gaol. 'Harold, what did you do to get a ten-year sentence? You don't seem a criminal.'

Harold Arms shrugged, as if he didn't know himself. Itching his thick brown stubble and salt sores on his face, he replied, 'I had a woman once. A fine lady she was, even though she was only a cobbler's daughter. I loved her, and we were to be married. When she found out I was good friends with another woman she got jealous, accused me o' cheating and blackmailed me for a year. She controlled me, from everywhere I went to everything I did until I cancelled the engagement and she accused me o' rape and abuse as well as other things; I found out she'd hidden diaries o' lies about the lot. I thought I was the Jonah; I was hexed, bloody jinxed. Now I'm a simple bloke sure 'nough. I'm a worker. Hauler. Labourer. Call it what you will, I got my hands dirty and earned a living lifting and moving things. Never did learn my letters, although if I had I would've seen the scandal she'd created and testified against the lies.' He shook his head, 'they read the diaries, saw the bruises and matched them with my hands since they're roughened by my career. I should've learned to read when I went to them churches as a boy, but at that age I didn't care much for it and saw my future in my hands. If only I knew what those hands would get me into, or what a simple cobbler's daughter was capable of. 'Fore I knew it I was locked up with a decade to wait, that's if I didn't go down to the Old Scratch first.'

Joseph looked at him pitifully. He'd been in relationships with women as such, but never had been afflicted by them in the way that Harold had. If anything, this man was the victim. 'I never was fond of cobbler's or their daughters. They had deft fingers but sour hearts.' He said lightly, as if to console.

Harold nodded, 'mate, they're the sourest. Like sucking juice from a lemon, it was to be with a person like that.'

'Ah well. The sea's the only woman you need to please now.'

'From a sour one to a salty one, and both do well to keep me on my toes.'

Joseph chuckled, 'at least this one's good at rocking your bed at night, even if she is cold to the touch.'

Up in the crow's nest, Dave tensed and fixated on the horizon. Another shape was moving across the water, heading west away from the coast and into the Atlantic. 'Ship!' Dave James cried, 'ship out to starboard, heading out to sea!'

Heads raised and mutterings spread through the crew before they flocked to the railings. It was the first sight of other life they had seen in days: other human activity. Another water-bound vessel manned by another crew heading for another destination– a swell of excitement moved from one person to the other as they watched the square-rigged craft slip into the horizon. Poppy clung to the railing next to Rob, her hair tied back and her forehead sweaty. 'I wonder where they're going.' She asked no one.

'I bet they're off to those exotic places you hear about with coconuts and rum.' Rob stipulated.

'To America lad, that's where they're going.' The captain said from behind them, lowering his spyglass and looking off colour. 'We're now crossing the Middle Passage, or that's what it used to be called, and that ship's cargo is carrying more valuable things than just spices and sugar– down in the hold there'll be Africans off to be sold illegally. It used to be like this all the time until it was abolished but it still happens all these years later. I'd like to say it doesn't but there are still dirty criminals,' he paused and gulped at his words, '-who ignore the law and keep doing what they're doing for profit. I can tell from their colours they're slavers. That ship's a guineaman.'

'Sold to do what?' Poppy asked, not even seeming to hear his remark.

He looked down to her, *surely, she must know; she's got to be old enough, what is she? Eleven, twelve?* 'Some to work on plantations, some to serve as housemaids, some to do other things. I an't never been to America, but I've heard it's the land of freedom.' *Which is more than what I can say for those poor buggers.*

Poppy smiled, her buck teeth on full show, 'I want to go.'

He forced a smile back to her, 'when you're old enough, you can. I wouldn't go anytime soon though; I hear it's gripped in the throes of a vicious civil war.'

She watched the ship sail off to the blue, 'I'll go when it's done then. Once I can get off this ship.'

'Indeed.' He muttered, gazing at the horizon, before turning and climbing the stairs, taking the wheel from Hugh and steering the ship onward, praying for speed to get them through this dark corner of the Middle Passage.

Victoria sailed on through the afternoon and as the golden African sun lowered, they looked forward to the evening bell. After a day at eleven knots their spirits were high, and rose higher when Robertson made his calculations and announced if the wind continued to blow as loftily as it had done they could round the great head of Africa by the morning and arrive in Cape Lopez by the early afternoon, free to row to the quiet shores of Gabon by dusk for a few hours treasure-hunting. Joseph grinned as he smoked, knowing what that meant: another milestone in the journey complete.

The news was a welcome relief and when the evening bell chimed, and the anchors were lowered in the shelter of the coast, they admired an African sunset with the joyful tunes of Billy's fiddle and witnessed a dusk they had never seen the likes of before.

Larger than they'd ever seen it, the red sun sank to the western horizon dripping flames onto the line of the sea, setting a promising ambience the crew wanted to grasp hold of. As they ate their evening meal in the shadows of the rigging, they observed the sky glowing bright with an orange fire, making the waves of the sea look like scattering embers blowing in a lofty gale ready to catch the tinder-like froth to set the night's tide ablaze. To the east the sky gathered gloom, but to the west the great sun cast its final warm colours to the evening sky like a fantastic net out to snag the first few early stars, ever hopeful to catch one and discover the truth behind its twinkle.

Along with their meals, they each enjoyed a cupful of grog and enjoyed the warmth of the evening and the coolness of encroaching nightfall, and at last they felt something akin to freedom.

Joseph dipped bread into his bowl of vegetable broth and bit into it, feeling the juices flow; the flavours wetting his tongue, he wondered if food had ever tasted so good. Glancing up to the trimmed sails from the forecastle as he had done so many times before, he saw that even though they were blank, colourless, they displayed a grandeur of shine, as if the sheets had been sewn with golden thread as they caught the evening sunlight. *Blank and yet full of colour,* he thought, *just like the sea.* An hour or so and the sails would be furled for the night, so he took an extra glance of admiration before letting his gaze fall to the crew sitting on boxes and casks surrounding a lamp that glowed brighter by the minute. Even Robertson was there, leaning against the mast, eating and listening to the chatter. Surprised, he let slip a slight smile.

He walked over to them and caught Benjamin talking about an experience to the group between mouthfuls of broth. It was the first time in a long time the crew were talking and laughing amongst each other about something other than work aboard the ship. 'They didn't know each other then, them two, this was way before when they just met!' the old sailor was saying, 'Me dear ol' mother hadn't even met me father at this point in time, but I reckon me grandparents were knockin' about somewhere over a hundred years ago. Anyways, I'm gettin' off the plot again . . .'

Joseph found a space next to Victoria and sat down quietly. She turned to him and smiled, subtly inching closer by a fraction. 'What's he on about?' he asked her.

She swallowed a mouthful of soup, 'the legend of the Scott's Trove everyone keeps going on about. The one how your map ever came to be. To be honest, I don't know the story.'

He frowned, neither did he. He knew there was a story surrounding the map, he knew of a legend created by a couple and they had buried a chest before they vanished but of the tale itself, he was not familiar. He shook his head, 'neither do I.'

'Pop asked him first if he knew any good stories and Rob followed it up with the question that's all been on our minds– what this poxy legend is. Well, we all know *of* it, but you get what I mean– what did these two people actually do, how did they meet?' She whispered, not wanting to interrupt.

Joseph suddenly noticed how close she had got to him, he felt himself reddening but he hoped his beard was hiding it. His heart found a faster rhythm and he abruptly lost appetite. *Don't think of Lucy, come on now. She's miles away, probably moved on already. Don't make a fool of yourself Joseph, just sit quietly and listen. And enjoy her company.* He took a last swig of the soup in his bowl and opened his ears to the sound of lapping waves and a sailor recounting an old sea tale in the light of a glowing lamp by the tall mainmast.

Chapter Fifteen

The old sailor dipped the last of his bread into his lukewarm broth and passed it between his lips, feeling the juices flow onto his tongue. That wasn't the only thing he was feeling though; all eyes were on him, staring at him patiently waiting for him to begin. *This takes me back,* he thought, as he remembered the days of his adulthood when he told stories to those eager for one, back when joints didn't ache so much. Taking a swig of grog, he wiped his lips and looked at them all intently. 'Everyone's heard of this here tale, knows of the two adventurers and their chest o' treasure that's now become known as the Lost Loot, or Scott's Trove, and fewer believe in it. Tis' true, the tale, as most sea stories are– although some might be exaggerated one way or the other as all tales are when passed through so many ears and passed on by so many lips. This one of Henry Scott and Eve, though, this'uns as gospel as words from the Bible. You all listen to ol' Benjamin, he's got the true version to it.

'1722, that's the year they met. Some'd say "oh, they met at a pub over a pint" and others would say "it was at a Christmas dance listening to the music of the finest fiddler", but they're wrong. This an't a love story, and they might've been brought together by fate, but it certainly wasn't what either were expecting. Even though they fell in love, it was within disaster that their paths crossed. Tragedy,' he shrugged, 'y' could call it that, but I's not sure many people would agree. Even though the death of the one Black Bart was wished upon, he was also missed; a hero to some, aye, and a pirate to others.' He took another gulp as the sun sank lower; the lamp becoming ever more illuminating.

'The sun dawned on the tenth of February 1722, spilling its fine colours across the sky, slowly pushing the stars to the other side o' the horizon. Light crept over everything once again, so much so that the darkness had to hide within the shadows of those things left exposed. It was to be another normal day. Where was Henry Scott though, you ask me? Captaining the ship anchored on Cape Lopez? Waking to begin the day swabbing the decks of the ship as a cabin boy? Nay,' Benjamin held a crooked finger up, 'his morning was anything but peaceful, or bright. Aboard the *Royal Fortune* . . .

. . . Henry Scott suddenly jumped to his feet and looked around in alarm, along with the seven other prisoners that joined him in the cell. That powerful sound, that jolting lurch, that sickening creak and splinter . . . those wailing screams and shouts from the gun deck; it all sounded surreal. This wasn't supposed to happen, certainly not on one of the most famous ships of the eighteenth century.

This ship was different from the rest he'd been on; only a year before this frigate had been part of the *Royal Africa Company* named *Onslow*, yet now its new name under its new captain had brought it immense fame. There was reasoning behind the *Royal Fortune*'s impressive credibility: its captain was Bartholomew Roberts, or more widely known as Black Bart– one of the most infamous pirates of the Golden Age, whose name was known and feared even to the far reaches of the Royal Navy. Almost anyone who set foot on the prow of a boat knew his name and the shocking antics he initiated and participated in. There was a reason why there was that dark colour before his name. *Black Bart.* Henry knew it all too well; he'd heard the tales, which was why that boom and lurch of a cannonball smacking into the side of the ship caused such a stir of surprise.

The entire ship shook, as if the wood itself was bracing for the next impact. The sound of splintering wood as the hull was broken into and obliterated reverberated through the vessel; that one ungodly noise, that shattering tone– it hadn't a musical note of any sort and yet every single person aboard could hear it and understand the meaning completely, foresee the gravity of what was about to happen. Silence followed, the sheer and gripping realisation that this ship had been fired at. Below in the hold, kept in a dark cell, the sounds were muffled but the screams of the injured and the shouts of those in command trying to take control of the darkening situation were unmistakable. *It's happened,* Henry thought, *someone's fired at the Fortune.* The predator of the seas being attacked by another. Who would dare such a thing?

Mutters passed through the eight of them as they looked at the floorboards of the ceiling through the bars and listened to the carnage above. Dust was shaken free and scattered onto their heads, but they barely noticed. What was happening gripped their full attention. The attack was something none on board had expected, especially when they were sailing on the *Royal Fortune*, in a prison cell or not. '*Someone's trying to take it down.*' One of the prisoners whispered. *Jesus, someone's taking on Black Bart . . .* Henry thought indignantly.

Despite the sudden overwhelming fear the pirate's name gave; the same could not be said for his crew, Henry found, who had spent the night gambling, singing and drinking themselves into a helpless state after they had captured the ship Henry had been on. Celebrations were appropriate after their success, Henry had guessed as he lay on the sodden straw to sleep the night before, but unfortunately for them, Black Bart and his crew's apex reputation had led them astray and had sharply, almost vertically, took a turn for the worst.

'Sounds like the ball's gone right through the gun deck.' He muttered, looking to the wooden ceiling above him, imagining the mayhem that would now be beginning to ensue. He listened again to the shouts of brave and frightened sailors as they busied themselves priming the cannons and hauling the wounded men away from the immediate danger. 'Portside, would you say?' he questioned the old, weathered sailor beside him whom he'd heard the others call "Swaddle". Being only sixteen and at sea for two months, Henry had yet to fully grasp the maritime lingo.

Swaddle nodded and mumbled back through his whitening salted beard, 'Aye. I'd say so. Ball went right through by sounds o' it.'

Just then they were shunned back into silence, almost jumping, as a man screamed in agony directly above and another shouted,

'*Someone lend a hand! Tom's leg's been splintered! Shattered! Blood everywhere! Bosun, surgeon, anyone!*' There were stomps and screams, balls rolling hither and thither, gunpowder spilling and men yelling for organisation and soon Tom's screams were gone, moulded into the din that came with an unexpected attack. Suddenly there was a shift in movement, and everyone felt the ship turning.

A voice moved through the cell to the bars where Henry stood. 'If they're all up there and we're being attacked, who will come down to let us out?' the sailor said, 'if this ship goes down, we're going down with it. We can't get out of these bars. We're going to drown. Drown, I say.' Henry huffed and rolled his eyes; the deckhand was James Flynn, a fellow comrade aboard Henry's own ship when the *Royal Fortune* had made its appearance. Flynn, ever the pessimist, saw the glass in a state of eternal half emptiness. He was still wearing the uniform of their previous ship proudly, as if it were protecting him from the events taking place aboard the pirate's galleon. It almost made Henry laugh. Flynn was a prick, there was no mistaking it.

He looked to the straw beneath him, indignant that of all men James Flynn was here with him in this situation. He scratched his black hair, *why, why did it have to be him? Anyone, but him.* Rolling up the sleeves of his oversized salt-worn shirt he leaned into James' ear and muttered back, 'd' you really think we need to hear that right now, James? It's bad enough knowing we're prisoners of Black Bart.'

James looked at him ashen faced; Henry knew he hadn't heard a word he'd just said. He held onto the bars, gripping them with white knuckles, terrified. 'Help!' James began to shout in the darkness of their murky deck, 'release us, please! Let us go!' His words reverberated back to them, not even making it up the stairs to the catastrophe above. How could anyone hear them, or think of them with the current situation? No one said it but that was what they all feared– to not be heard, to die forgotten, imprisoned souls. It was an inevitability they all had to consider.

Even though he didn't show it, Henry was terrified too. Every sailor's fear was drowning; to float, blue and bloated, waiting for the final oblivion in the form of a set of shark jaws. He didn't want to die like that, not here, not in this cell imprisoned as the ship's hull gave way and she sank beneath the surface. He dug his hands into his pockets and clutched the handkerchief his mother had given him before he left for the docks just two months ago. Closing his eyes, he whispered a silent prayer as the commotion rallied on above their heads.

Suddenly they head a clunk as the hatchway to the hold opened and footsteps came thundering down. A boy, no older than twelve, appeared through the stacked cargo of boxes and chests of loot into their view, leading them all to rush to the bars. 'Release us!' Flynn cried, along with others, 'Please! Open the door!' White-knuckled hands gripped the bars and shook them in desperation and the cabin boy gave a look of confusion. Blood trickled down his forehead, his hair was thick with dust and gore from the carnage above. He'd been in the action too, it seemed, and had come down here to hide, yet in his hands was something they all desired. The ring of keys.

The boy walked up to them cautiously and nodded, before inserting a key with a shaking hand and unlocked the door to the cell. The prisoners rushed out eagerly, thanking him profusely, and, led by Henry, stampeded up the companionway past the orlop and berth to the hatchway that entered onto the gun deck. Yet he didn't open it. He stopped, taking a moment to realise how ill-equipped they were in getting through this.

Frightened? Yes. *Terrified* even? Oh yes. Worried? Brave? Wished there were another way and was probably going to die? Yes, yes, yes, Henry Scott felt all. He didn't consider himself a great swordsman, or a swordsman at all; he'd had two lessons worth of training. He wasn't a fantastic marksman either; with the musketoon his mate aboard his previous ship had given him, he couldn't even shoot the booby that landed four feet away. He had nothing to defend himself with . . . except sharp reactions, and even then, they were going to be put to the test.

He placed his hand on the hatch, yet somehow, he couldn't bring himself to open it. Was it fright? Fear? Had it got too much? He took a deep breath; he didn't think so. He'd been told before any battle to prepare before committing to it. *'Yer've got to be ready Harry me lad,'* his old friend Willy, who had given him the musketoon, had advised, *'if you an't ready yer gonna' jump in and make a mistake and get yerself killed. Take it from an old seadog who's seen too much; before you go into any battle or fight or scram, take a second or two to ready yerself, then take a deep breath and walk in –* he remembered it well, *'-At least then you'll be ready to fight, to survive, or to die.'* He closed his eyes, taking a fleeting moment to remember brave old Willy before he had met his maker by the point of a sword. Old Willy had been ready to fight and die, and now Henry was too.

'Go on Henry. Open it, let's get out of here! *What are you waiting for?'* James Flynn cried out behind him.

He glared back, knowing fully well their chances of surviving this were slim. *Why does he want to rush to his death?* He huffed, before pushing the hatchway open and bursting into the mayhem on the gun deck. It was a flurry from left to right, a panoramic scene of action, violence and gore. The sailors of the other ship had boarded and were tearing their way through the *Fortune*. It was a bloodbath happening right before his eyes, however if it were not for this disaster, he'd still be locked up praying for absolution. Should he be thanking the attack, or condemning it? He didn't know.

Swords clashed and rang, musketoons popped and banged clouding up the deck with gun smoke; cannonballs rolled freely wherever the waves took them, and cannons continued to be primed and fired, deafening all surrounding them. Yet despite the mayhem, men of different ethnicities fought together and bled together. In this moment it didn't matter where any had come from; in the end they would all end up in the same grave; be it earthen or watery. Henry ducked underneath the swinging arm of a swordsman and scurried past a pair of enemies locked in combat. Behind, he heard a scream as James Flynn was caught by a bullet and dropped to the deck to join the dead. Other prisoners clambered up to the gun deck and others, pirates from the look of them, were fleeing the scene, dodging and ducking, slithering through the fray hoping the main deck would offer a little more safety.

It was hard to think over the sounds of the madness. Men screamed in pain and bellowed in bravery; pop went the trigger, bang went the gun, steel rang and clashed as the frightened squealed in dark corners. Never had he heard such an ugly barrage of sounds before or smelled such an ungodly stench: a violent mix of blood, rum, vomit, death and gun smoke. Stopping at the mainmast, he crouched low and surveyed, only to see a bearded pirate of the *Fortune* recoil as a blade appeared through his back; the pirate dropped to his knees with the victorious sailor watching. Henry winced, gulped; shaking, and glanced back to the companionway that led up to the main deck but he only caught a glimpse before a man with long greasy hair and wearing a grubby waistcoat stumbled in front of him with a slash across his face and his arm severed at the shoulder, bleeding out heavily; his face was ghostly, his fate was sealed and he knew it; but wasn't ready for it.

Suddenly Henry felt vomit ballooning up his throat. *So much blood!* He swallowed hard and darted from behind the mast, skittering around the fight to reach the staircase. Just as he was about to take the bottom step a huge black pirate suddenly stepped out and intercepted him, he stood at least six feet tall, bald, and had muscles so large they were almost bursting through his worn pockmarked cotton vest. The black man's inky eyes recognised him. 'Prisoner! Prisoners escaping!' his deep voice bellowed in a thick African accent. Henry had seen many black sailors aboard this ship which he hadn't seen on the two previous vessels he'd ventured on which was why, standing before one now, felt intimidating. Noticing the dark brand burned onto his wrist he knew this man was either a runaway slave or an escapee of work, in fact he guessed they all were.

Just then the black pirate was knocked from his feet by a deckhand who had lost his footing on his way down the companionway, still drunk from the night before, and crashed into him. Henry seized his opportunity and darted around the fumble, wiping the clumping sweat on his forehead. 'Come back – *oof!*' he heard the black sailor shout as he slipped back over trying to get up, but it was too late. Henry was gone, disappeared into the calamity that roared upon the main deck.

The African sun blazed powerfully in a cloudless sky, beating a dense heat onto him as he ran outside. The warmth of it and the fresh air was a reviving relief after spending time down below but now was not the time to appreciate it, he had to keep moving. Looking out beyond the bulwark, he spotted the enemy ship and noticed it was not an enemy at all. It was a ship of the Royal Navy, *HMS Swallow*, which meant these sailors aboard were trained marines. Henry beamed as relief surged through him, until he realised, he was aboard a pirate ship; how were they to know he had been a prisoner? He looked like one of them. The fleeting moment of safety passed, and he knew he had to keep moving, fearing that if he were to be captured by the sailors of the *Swallow*, mercy would not be shown. Men with blood on their minds were rarely just.

Already sweat had soaked his clothes and streamed down his face. It was so hot . . .

'-I heard that battle took place during a heavy tropical storm.' Captain Robertson interrupted. 'I heard they sailed into the eye of it as they were escaping, lost their knots and the *Swallow* was able to catch up and board, and that's when the fight took place.'

Benjamin shrugged, 'Aye, it could 'o been. I heard it was just a normal day. It's only a tale after all; I an't here to tell a history lesson. The young-uns' wanted to hear a story so I tell's it. But if you wanted Cap'n I could add in the storm? Make it better?'

'No, no. It's fine. Continue.' Robertson said, and Joseph noticed him smiling.

He nodded, 'I'll add it in anyway, I like mixin' it up. Up on the weather deck, rain lashed down with such a ferocity it felt like pins jabbin' him; within a minute he was soaked through to the bone and the dust and blood had all but washed away. The wind billowed through the ship, confusing the sails, tricking them into takin' the ships this way and that . . .

. . . The cacophony of sounds was deafening; the action was just as thick up here as it was down there. Thunder rumbled along the sky in great rolling motions as lightening jabbed the sea with white forks of electric, drowning out the screams of the dying. It was a flurry of dark blue jackets and beards, dripping bodies and swords ringing against each other. *How did the Royal Navy even find us?* He darted behind some wooden barrels laden with fresh stock. A pirate he recognised from delivering food to their cell suddenly came into view next to a stack of boxes, sword fighting with a clean-shaven sailor from the *Swallow*. Both were soaked, fighting through the elements as if they didn't even know a storm was raging, since the storm was already within them.

The sailor was good; well trained, but the pirate, John, knew how to play dirty. Henry looked up at them with wide eyes and kept silent, watching as John's dirty defence began to slack and the sailor's attack picked up. Hungover, he wasn't parrying the blows anymore, he was nicking them away just before they found their mark. It was clear to see who was going to win– even a cabin boy like Henry could see that. The sailor then flicked his wrist and in a rapid movement John had lost his sword and it dropped to the deck. 'Filthy pirates,' the Englishman said with the point of his blade gently touching the pirate's unshaven Adam's apple.

John held his hands up and backed away to the bulwark, Henry could see immediate fear in his blue eyes. 'Quarters! Offer me quarters . . . sir. I yield. Please, pl-please,' he stammered, 'let m-me go, I didn't even want to come on this ship. I was a prisoner on here.'

'And yet you are fighting for it.' The sailor said, his hand never wavering. 'You don't deserve the noose, dog.'

'Plea-'

Henry jumped and squeezed his eyes shut. The sickening sound of a blade slicing through flesh and bone; the shrill squeal of a man losing his life in an instant stunned Henry to his core. Seeing it for the first time; a murder take place in such a barbarous manner before his eyes– it was something he would never forget. *Could* never forget.

The body thudded to the deck, but that was only what Henry thought it was. Slowly he opened his eyes to see the severed head of the pirate bleed out at the feet of its own body. 'No!' he yelped, too loudly.

The sailor pushed the body overboard; its deadweight splashing into the waters below. Henry's eyes held firmly on the man, hoping his involuntary shriek hadn't been heard. The sailor watched the body fall, and stopped, paused a second, then cast a glance behind him to check he had heard correctly. And unfortunately for a terrified boy crouching amongst the nets and casks, he had.

A smile appeared on the face of the sailor, although there was not any warmth in it. It was a cold glare of power. There was no doubt he enjoyed the thrill of killing pirates. He had no intention of sparing anyone, Henry could see; to him, anyone on board this ship was a pirate and didn't deserve to hang. This man wanted to see them pierced with his own blade. Mercy was a foreign word, a false word. Suddenly Henry's opinion of the heroes of the Royal Navy flipped. This was no hero before him now. He was nothing better than the rest of the scallywags on this tub, except he was wearing a uniform and would be praised for his dastardly deeds. The sailor's yellowed teeth looked bright compared to the dark grey background. He stalked toward the prisoner, dripping wet. 'Hello, cabin boy.'

In sheer panic Henry looked around for anything to defend himself with. The pirate's sword? No, it was too far away. The casks and barrels; he could roll them to– no, no, they're lashed together. *Think! Think!* Suddenly the answer struck, but he had to move quickly.

The man came toward him, arms tensed, gripping the sword in his right hand. Blood was splattered over his face from his bloodthirsty decapitation and the smile that cut through it only added to his look of insanity. Afraid of what his intentions were, Henry pushed back into the casks, reaching out and holding onto anything, his knuckles white.

The heavy footfall of his boots walking on the wooden deck were spellbinding, so loud against the cacophony of the deck. It felt like he was listening to the beat of his heart in his head in a moment of thick tension, a heavy rolling thump. The man walked closer. Henry watched closely, feeling his pace rise, his breaths shorten, his bladder loosen. The moment to save his skin was approaching. But not yet.

The man raised his arm, his sword dripping rain and blood, his eyes peering down at the sixteen-year-old lad with a murderous gleam; he had no intention of stopping.

Now! He yanked forwards, pulling the lengths of netting out and threw them over his foe exactly when the sailor's arms were open, and he had no way of preventing it. Suddenly his sword and outstretched arms did what the fins of a fish would do and tangled him up within the netting. He cried out angrily, unable to react, and dove forward in a wild attempt to finish what he started but the window of opportunity Henry had created had already passed . . . and he had taken it.

Running through the deck he skipped around another pair of fighting seamen and hurried around the mainmast and under the shrouds where a grapeshot landed in the wood of the mast sending splinters showering over him. He ducked out of instinct and headed for the ladder to the quarterdeck, above the captain's quarters. The deck was awash with blood and seawater and he struggled to keep on his feet where the ship rocked so much. Madness lay strewn around-

'*He's been shot! Bart's been shot! The Captain's dead!*' a man hollered from the forecastle and for a split moment everything seemed to quieten and pause whilst the storm hammered on. Henry turned and looked back through the streaks of warm rain and pushed the hair from his eyes. The impact of those words was like a hearty slap around the face, *what did he just say?*

For nearly everyone aboard the *Royal Fortune* this news was a shock to the system. This was Black Bart after all. Black Bart; the self-made pirate who was one of the most famous buccaneers of the eighteenth century, he was up there with Edward Teach, or more widely known as "Blackbeard", Sam "Black Sam" Bellamy and John "Calico Jack" Rackham. He sacked his way through four hundred and seventy vessels during his three-year long career as a pirate, building his reputation up to such a high standard that his name would still be remembered throughout the centuries. *Bartholomew Roberts.*

Henry had heard of him well before he took to the seas himself, and he knew that Black Bart's death would be a scandal that would spread across the seven seas right up to the kings and queens that could now have the chance to rule them. His death would be a blow to the Golden Age of piracy; a conclusion and full stop to the antics of those brave enough make a career out of adventures and living off the reputation they gave. The fearsome Welsh pirate captain killed by a grapeshot from one of the *Swallow*'s swivels.'

'What's a swivel?' Rob asked quickly before Ben continued.

Instead Robertson answered from behind him. 'Swivels are guns mounted on the bow of a ship. We don't have any on here as we're only a merchant ship, not meant for war or battle.' He quickly turned to Dave, Harold, Billy and Joseph and muttered, 'Lads, could you quickly haul in the sails?'

With a grumble or two, they got up and furled the sails in for the night, tying them tight to the yards with their legs hanging through the footropes. Night had fully reclaimed the world and the stars were twinkling brightly, along with the moon whose white face cast a pale light on the deck; it was not enough to overpower the lamp though and the faces surrounding it were glowing orange. The men quickly returned to the glow and Benjamin, licking his lips, continued the tale. 'In that instant . . .

. . . Things began to change. The pirates who were holding the upper hand almost lost their spirit in the fight now that their captain was not fighting with them. Henry saw a few of them throw down their swords and drop to their knees in submission, some of the black sailors aboard pushed their way through the hubbub, fearing for their future now that their captain had fallen.

To Henry Scott, Black Bart's death was indeed a shock, but he was still an escaped prisoner on a ship full of pirates who knew his face and could use him for other means to get themselves out of the noose. He would be a tool, a bargaining chip for a buccaneer to escape those three words that those with a reputation feared. *Hung, drawn and quartered*. It made even the hardy criminal shiver. There was no denying it; it was a nasty way to go. *I must hide,*

Henry thought, *at least until things settle and I can figure out a way to get off unnoticed.*

The rain lashed down on him; he wiped his eyes with the sleeve of his sodden shirt. His black hair plastered to his head, his clothes clinging. *Where to go?* Everywhere around him had become a new kind of fluster, less fighting and more running, fleeing and hiding. Now that their captain was dead what was the point in trying to fight for the ship; it was as good as gone. There was no one to fight for now, except themselves.

He looked around, spying any recesses, cubby holes, empty barrels or, more drastic, any spare longboats. None gave him any inspiration, until he saw the door to the captain's cabin with the curtains closed.

Not giving any second thoughts Henry rushed to the door, tried the handle and found it unlocked. '*Yes!*' he whispered as he turned the knob and darted inside, closing the door behind him. The key was in the lock, he found, and he quickly turned it, locking himself inside the dingy room. The curtains were also closed, although Henry couldn't see why. He shrugged, no wonder the attack had been so swift, it hadn't been seen until the last moment. There was still plates and food on the table from breakfast. That was no excuse for the crow in his nest though, he of all should have spotted it was not a merchant ship. But for now, he was happy with them all closed and to be out of the rain; there was less chance of being noticed.

Heaving a tired sigh of relief, he sunk down to the floorboards, dripping wet and trembling from the morning's events. Leaning against the door, he listened to the havoc continue outside feeling the ship jolt as another wave smashed into the side. Henry Scott had survived. How many of the other surviving prisoners could say that he did not know but he hoped for their sake they had somehow made it out alive, nevertheless doubt was present when thinking of their fate from their condition when he left them.

The doorknob suddenly jerked, and the door was pulled back and forth, jiggling in its framework. Henry jumped and turned to face the door, wide eyes fixed on the curtains, his face a stern surprise. Quickly nabbing the key from the lock, he shuffled backwards and slipped under the table; never taking his eyes from the turning knob. It hit him suddenly at how lucky he had been to slip in here first, if he'd have been but a few minutes late he'd be the one turning the doorknob in a jittering panic.

Harsh breathing pressed against the glass; Henry slithered further under the table, gripping the key in his hand. '*It's locked! Argh, old Bart must've locked it a'fore he went and got shot.*' He heard a grizzly voice say.

'*It can't be, I went an' searched him for the key and he didn't have it on 'im.*' Another voice replied, '*you'll 'ave to break it down.*'

The door jumped as a body slammed into it. The glass rattled, the curtains trembled on their railings; Henry closed his eyes and prayed for the lock to be of a study make. Any chance he had of surviving this ordeal would slip down from slim to none. Another body slam sent his heart hammering. Every crack the door faced felt like looking down at thin ice watching the fractures spread, waiting for that final moment when the fragility crumbled, and he fell through to his demise.

With his eyes firmly shut and sweat beading on his brow he whispered the words his mother had taught him with a trembling tongue, '*dear Lord, thou art in heaven. Listen to my prayer and take my words up to the holy light of kingdom come. I am Henry George Scott and-*'

'*It ain't budging!*'

'*Ah, bollocks to it! Leave it. Let's go an' find another place quick whilst-*'

A musket ball found its target, smashed through the window, burning a hole through the curtain and lodged itself into the wood above the rear window causing a ruckus that shattered the silence in the cabin. Henry almost leapt out of his skin at the sound. Ripping open his eyes, he expected to see a wide hole where the lock used to be and the door swinging open with the two pirates ambling inside to loot and hide. As he looked around though, he found a small shaft of light lancing through the bullet hole of the curtain, with the door still shut . . . and a red splatter against the smashed window and the weight of the assailant leaning against it. It seemed God had heard him after all.

He heaved a sigh and rubbed his watery eyes, wanting to weep, wanting to vomit and let his emotions flow. The events of today were hard to grasp, it felt like a dream he could not wake up from, a reality that was too incomprehensible to accept. But he had to. This was reality unfolding its way into history, a chain of events that were scrawling themselves onto the parchment as he breathed.

A clatter and thud suddenly broke the silent cabin. Sounds of the attack were dying outside but this sound, this was coming from *inside*. He turned and looked to the source– the door to his left on the other side of the room. It sounded like something had fallen over. *What was that?*

Taking a breath, Henry got to his trembling feet and walked slowly over to the door. It looked like a door to a cupboard, but it could have been anything; he wasn't familiar with the layout of a captain's cabin. He reached for the door, his hand taking an age to make contact, and grasping the knob in his hand he gently turned it and pulled the door open.

Shelves stacked with books, scrolls, jars and jewellery filled his vision. It was hard to distinguish what he was looking at in this murky light, but he could just about make it out. Nothing had fallen over, it appeared, but as his eyes wandered down to the bottom, he gasped . . . and found the source.

And discovered he had not been alone in the cabin.

A girl shuffled back from the door, her knees to her chest, looking down in fear. A glass bottle rolled at her feet– the source of the noise, and she was regretting reaching for that drink. Her matted and unkempt black hair tousled down onto her mottled grey cotton dress; how long she had been in there, where she had come from and who she was Henry couldn't even begin to fathom, but it was evident that she was frightened. Just as he was.

His heart beating loudly, he wanted to reassure her; she looked young, perhaps twelve or thirteen, and so very lost. Kneeling down he spoke in as much as a soothing tone as he could muster, 'It's alright, don't worry. I'm not here to hurt you. I'm hiding here just like you . . . Are you hurt?'

Her head raised from her knees and she looked up at him slowly, her big dark fearful eyes assessing whether he was a threat. He sensed this and shook his head, 'I'm not going to hurt you, trust me. What's your name?'

She paused, looking deep into his eyes, making her decision. 'Eve.'

'I'm Henry.' He offered a friendly smile, 'What are you doing here?'

He had meant aboard the ship, but she took it literally. 'Keeping hidden as he told me to do.' She said and turned away.

'I am too, Eve.' *Who is she talking about?*

She shook her head unexpectedly, 'I'm keeping hidden, and am also keeping *it* hidden.'

Henry's brows furrowed in confusion. 'What do you mean?

Eve shuffled out of the way to show what was behind her. 'We have to keep it safe until the time is right.'

Behind her was a chest. Ornate, dark wood, beautiful details on the metal framework. 'What is that?' He asked, but instead she answered with an action.

She turned the key and slowly lifted the lid. Henry's jaw dropped. His eyes widened in amazement. What he was looking at was something he had never seen before, and probably would never see again, but cast a large shadow over his mind. How this strange girl had come about this, to be involved in this situation was something he couldn't even begin to understand. As he knelt there, his limbs relaxing in awe, staring into the cupboard behind the girl, he felt his adventure aboard the *Royal Fortune* was ending,' Benjamin leaned forward almost falling off the edge of his box, '. . . but another was beginning, a deeper one that, he knew, would plunge him into a mystery untold to the ages.'

The waves rolled against the hull, licking the barnacles stuck to the sides and the wind died down to a steady breeze. No one said a word, but as Benjamin looked at them satisfied, he didn't want them to. Eventually Harold broke the tranquil as he looked up from his wood carving. Shavings were about his feet. 'How does it end then?'

Rob nodded, desperate for a better conclusion. 'That can't be the ending! That can't be the whole legend surrounding Scott's Trove.'

'It's the tale of how the two met, it's the beginnin' of their adventures.'

'What are their adventures though? Is that another tale?' Rob pressed, slightly annoyed.

'And who is Eve really? Is she someone to do with Black Bart?' Tess chipped in.

Benjamin hesitated and smiled through his bushy white beard, only choosing one question to answer. 'They found each other, grew together and sailed the seas carryin' their chest with them to Lisbon, and with a wind much like this'un they returned to Cape Lopez where they buried the next clue in the sands of Gabon, writin' down a little somethin' that led to their next spot. An' from there they sailed off to their next landfall where they hid the next piece and so on until they finally buried their treasure.'

Victoria chirped, 'Benjamin, that's what we've done and we're going to do. That an't the tale.'

'Aye it is, my lady. It's their tale . . . and now it's ours too. We're taking up their adventure, we're answering their call. They lived this journey, and now we're *re-living* it and answering the questions they left for us.' The old sailor said as Polaris, the North Star, shined on above; brightening as the night darkened to a deeper shade of black.

Chapter Sixteen

The evening that Benjamin had told the tale had been relaxed and the night had been chilly, especially for the poor soul on the dogwatch, but the same could not be said for the following morning whereupon they sailed from the Canary current into the equatorial counter and were snagged in the windless waveless horror Robertson called the Doldrums. Following the initial anticipation and fear, his initiative led them to strike the topgallant mast and stow the topgallant and royal sails for preservation, then to steadily row *Victoria* forward whilst the sails were slack using a thick hawser that was tied to the stem and the longboat. It was tough work rowing a ship, but they had to get through it somehow. Four days were spent in a ruthless, painful sequence with rowing, sweating, cursing, bursting blisters, swapping deckhands and rowing some more.

With great effort they heaved the great ship through the patch of becalmed waters where wind dared not to touch. The condition of the water was the strangest they'd ever seen; as smooth as glass it sent forth no ripples, no movement at all– the tide was dead, making them question the sea itself, and the heat was relentless. As there was no breeze, the sun lashed down upon them without mercy, blasting the air from their lungs and sizzling any exposed skin until it was crimson red; cracking, peeling and bleeding. Robertson was right, the equator was a ruthless torture. Thankfully, they managed to heave her back into a slight wind and flowing tide and, after two more day's sailing, they reached the clear waters of Cape Lopez. 'Longboat to the ready!' he cried as soon as the sails slowed them enough for the anchors to be dropped.

'I thought you said we'll go by dusk?' Victoria asked whilst the others prepared the craft to be lowered. Her skin was reddened and was peeling in places, she wore a colourful shawl from Lisbon about her hair and neck to try and keep the sun at bay.

Robertson peered out through the rim of his hat. 'Dusk is what I expected, and yet here we are with the sun past the yardarm in the afternoon. We can at least spend a few hours searching so I'll rephrase; we'll *return* to the ship by dusk. I'd prefer not to spend the night on the beach, especially after hearing the appetites of some tribespeople from Benjamin. We'll make sure to take some black tobacco with us just in case.'

She pursed her lips and looked out to the coastline, suddenly hoping they didn't run into anyone. When the boat was lowered and bobbing alongside the hull, the captain, quartermaster, boatswain, cabin boy and two deckhands climbed down into it and began rowing for the white beach: everyone silent, everyone excited.

The oars dipped in the pristine waves and propelled the longboat toward the coast and after spotting a white length of surf and sand through swathes of mangrove they headed toward it. A long green strip was above it, although it appeared seemingly compressed by the haze of the afternoon heat that beat down upon the coast of Gabon. Joseph Winter wiped his sweaty brow with a sweaty sleeve and spied the beach, his heart thumping in anticipation. Turning, he glanced back at the ship anchored a mile from the shore in the same cape the *Royal Fortune* had been at on its last day in service. *We're here. We're here at long last.* He smiled weakly and looked down to his aching arms still weak from the exertion of rowing a ship, to the compass in his sore hand needling this way and that.

In his other blistered hand was the scroll and with five of the company joining him in this venture to shore, his mind revisited the first clue he found in his dark cell in that dark prison many, many miles away.

Seek the beach, the sand, the roots of the flying trees. The next part is hidden there, in amongst the leaves. A bright sun and good tide will bring you on, to the good Cape of the good Gabon. Bugger me, that feels a lifetime ago, and here we are at the centre of the world. Waves lapped up the side of the boat, rolling along the wood gracefully and the soft clunk of the rowlock and splash and plop of the oars was relaxing compared to the huffs and groans of towing *Victoria* through the doldrums. Rowing one oar was Rob and Harold had the other. As it turned out, Harold was a good rower and their time at sea, with sun and physical labour, had turned the tall lanky man into a weathered muscular sailor who'd found solace in carving pieces of spare wood into animals after the work bell. Unfortunately for him, he couldn't see where they were going or that they were approaching land.

Lighter and lighter the blue water became until it cleared altogether becoming transparent, and they could see colourful fish and rays darting through the seagrass and flitting just above the white sands beneath. They were not rowing on water anymore, but air. By then the white and green strips they had seen before had transformed into an astonishing array of detail; the beach was white and flecked with brown from washed-up driftwood and the greenery of before had become trees tall and thick with leaves surrounded by bushes and sprouts with fronds reaching out like grabbing hands. Thick vegetation of which they had never seen the likes of before grew populous and thrived with their hardy leaves, able to withstand such a violent level of heat and humidity. Lengths of vine hung from the trees and snaked across the dry ground, immersing themselves within the shrubbery and starched grasses that struggled to grow with such little moisture. Beautiful flowers of purple, orange, white and yellow scattered over the bushes, adding a variety of colour and giving the menagerie of butterflies a feast to feed upon.

Within the trees and flitting around the shrubbery exotic birds chirped and whistled from their perches and monkeys chattered and hooted from the branches as they watched the new arrivals draw closer. Within the neighbouring mangroves, reptilian eyes poked above the surface watching their movement too. It looked a tropical paradise, and all eyes were so occupied with the charm of life they didn't feel the keel brush against the soft sand.

Billy whistled quietly beside him, taking a cigarette from his bristled lips. 'By Jayzus, it's like we've found the Garden of Eden here, eh? This looks class.'

He nodded without turning back, feeling his shirt stick to his shoulders and back. 'Let's hope there's no snake out there in the trees in this one though. Come on, let's make a move before I start melting.' He got to his feet and jumped onto the beach, adding feature to the featureless sand, leaving the scroll under his jacket on the boat. The last thing they needed was for the prize to get lost out here or damaged.

The sand felt warm beneath his boots, heating his sore feet. When he looked down, he saw it was a virgin white like a wedding dress, untainted if not for the ebbing tide rolling against its surface. Suddenly he looked up, noticing . . . the silence. Tranquillity. Absolute and wholesome. He'd never heard anything like it. When in London there never was a chance for silence to take hold, the hustle and bustle was a cancer to any newfound peace; even the ship creaked and groaned and was full of its own sea noises but here– there was nothing but the quiet wash of the sea drifting lightly up the sand and the birds chirping gently. The monkeys had stopped hollering, leaving a subdued quiet. It was strange, he found himself yearning for a sound of any kind for his ears to latch onto.

A quiet scuffle of boots moved beside him. 'You'll get used to it.' Captain Robertson said in a hushed tone, 'this is the sound of a land not populated, virgin nature. Don't worry about the voice speaking in your head, it's only the sound of your own thoughts you can finally hear.' He gave a wink and turned back to the others ambling out the boat, swatting at the flies that had begun to swarm. The boy looked perhaps the most astonished, Rob's eyes were so wide it was as if his lids were stuck. He addressed them all calmly. 'Sailors, you have four hours here to explore and see if you can find this hidden box, which is . . . meant to be where?' he turned to Joseph.

'Oh, the clue states it's in the roots of the flying trees, in amongst the leaves. And it's *got* to be near the sand so it's around the beach somewhere.'

He nodded, 'there you have it. Stay near the beach, try not to wander too far and look for the roots of the flying trees. Try, if you can, to leave a trail behind you so you don't get lost but if you do just shout, it's not as if there's a lot of noise about. You all have with you a small trowel in case you do find anything worthy of a dig. You have four hours, then we meet back here at the boat. Is that understood?'

There was a spread of nods, but Harold asked the obvious question. 'How will we know when four hours have passed? None of us have timepieces or pocket watches.'

This, of course, was true. Robertson nodded and looked up and around, spying through the shade his hat had to offer and held a hand to the sea to test out a measurement. 'Hold your hand out to the horizon with an outstretched thumb. When the sun lowers and is a thumb's length from the horizon, head back to the boat.'

Tess spoke up too, 'Why are you carrying that musket? There's no one around.'

He gazed at her with tired eyes and paused for a moment before replying. 'Just a precaution. Even though it doesn't look like there's anyone around just remember, some tribespeople are very skilled at camouflage, so I brought the flintlock just in case. If that's a happenstance, I'll blow this whistle.' He held up a whistle he had hanging around his neck. And with that, the peace and tranquil soured into an eerie silence. Suddenly Joseph wished there were more people here, as the trees were whispering to one another under the rustle of each suspicious breeze.

Harold grabbed the bow and, with help from Rob, they dragged the boat up the beach away from the water's edge where he anchored it with rope and a long peg. Satisfied, the captain reminded them once more, 'a thumb's length from the horizon, remember. Now, let's explore.'

With an air of caution and heads clouded with flies, the group of six began to depart and venture along the beach and inland to the vegetation sprouting from the warm sand, seeking for roots of any flying trees.

Joseph strode to the nearest bush and began to browse through its leaves, inspecting the brush and what lie beneath, lifting the leaves and checking the shade, hoping to find something akin to a small chest or box. He licked his lips and wiped the sticky sweat from his forehead where mosquitoes were landing. The little breeze there was failed to cool anything; the humidity was suffocating, the air not wanting to be breathed or even disturbed. Another fly buzzed around his head, he swatted it away. Nothing was there, no human had ever touched it.

With the sand brushing beneath his boots he walked on further, glancing at the bushes and small flowers growing on them. Picking at a few more and looking beneath he remembered the instructions. *The clue didn't mention flowers, you wooden spoon, look somewhere else.* Changing tack, he decided to move inland to the trees and vines and browsed over more bushes and shrubbery, finding not a hint of previous human existence. *What are you looking for, Joseph? Footprints? Signs? There an't going to be nothing there, every footprint would've disappeared. There won't be any trace and you're used to not leaving any, remember? Stop looking for ghosts; start seeking . . .*

Ahead of him he saw Robertson through the trees, holding his musket out ready and occasionally glancing down to the patches of dry grass and bracken underneath the trees. It was clear he wasn't trying to look for anything from the ground; it was their surroundings he was trying to look through. Joseph pursed his lips, he knew Robertson was only trying to protect them and do his duty to the crew, but he wasn't helping with the search, or to make them feel better. He eyed him through the shadows of the trees, *I doubt there's anyone out there matey. At least try and lend an eye or hand to help us find this thing. The sooner we find it the sooner we can get back to the ship and we can all breathe easier.* He found himself frowning and shook the expression from his face, focusing on the task at hand. *Seek the beach, the sand, the roots of the flying trees . . .* turning, he walked at a diagonal line spying the ground and plants he passed over. He flicked another fly away from his head and slapped at one landing on his sticky neck. There was a continuous buzz around his head, snatching away his focus and shortening his patience. With his throat aching with thirst he muttered to himself, 'what does that even mean? Roots of the flying trees; I don't see any. There an't no flying trees here. There an't flying trees anywhere.'

Beginning to wander further now, Joseph trudged through the shadows of the trees leaving tracks through the sandy earth and glanced up to their rough bark and large hardy leaves growing from the branches at their peak. Trees of the tropics; he'd never seen one before. Anything that could survive in this intense heat was now a fascination to him, it was as impressive to him as grand architecture was in the city. How a building could be so profoundly detailed and still stand, and how this tree could prosper exposed to such ravaging heat. It was an organism that had adapted to live on such little water and hot air, and he found himself wishing he could adapt to these conditions too just to feel comfortable again, but he wouldn't be here long enough to change. For now, he had to sweat. Sweat and swat and walk. Again, he found himself gulping on a dry throat and felt a tight chest as if he needed a smoke but couldn't face sucking in more heat. *I don't even know where to look for water if I do get lost out here.* The thought scared him, and he decided to stay in range of the sea.

Roots of the flying trees. What in the name of sweet Fanny Adams could that mean? He scratched his beard and licked his cracked lips. The heat was making his clothes itchy again, his skin felt prickly and risen; every time he touched it or scratched, his skin tingled and itched. He undone a few more buttons of his mottled grey shirt. As he looked down to the sand again, trying to imagine the roots beneath it, he vowed to have a scrub when he got back to the ship. Sighing, he cursed and felt the agitation mounting. *Where is this bastard clue?!*

An hour passed of nothing but the silence. Isolation set in. Joseph gulped and peered as the trees whispered and the birds snickered, and the monkeys mocked his foolhardiness. He didn't know where from, but he could feel eyes on him, trained on him. He couldn't remember the last time he was this alone, where not one person was close by. He bit his lip anxiously and wiped his clammy hands on his trousers. With shaking fingers, he tried picking some tobacco from his pouch and rolling a cigarette, but his fingers struggled with the match. Never did he think he would've admitted, but he wanted people beside him, or a person at the least. 'Focus on what you need to find,' he told himself as he took a deep breath, trying to calm his rising pulse. 'It's got to be here somewhere; else why would the map lead me to it.' It had to be here: the map was written long ago, it would not and could not be altered. Could it? He inspected the bushes and the trees and the vines intertwining the two. The more he focused on finding the chest the further he felt from its discovery.

Suddenly there was a scuffle of footsteps behind him. Startled, he jumped and snapped back, to see Victoria Penning approaching. 'Shit! *Walk-er!*' Quickly he straightened up, trying to look as if she hadn't just shaken his soul from his bones. With her red face, damp shawl and flustered look; he could tell she was lost too, and uncomfortably hot. With her shirt untucked and her top buttons undone, she tried to create an air flow as much as she could, and he couldn't help but notice a sheen upon her exposed modest cleavage. She smiled her attractive smile; a gigglemug he loved to look at. 'Oh! Glad I found you. I lost Tess a while ago and I've been wandering like a foozler.'

He smiled back, secretly glad to have her by his side. 'You an't the only one. I've been wandering and looking but not finding anything. I just don't get it. Roots of the flying trees, there's no such thing. It's like something you'd hear from a bloke who's up the pole. Have you been winning?'

She shook her head and took off her shawl to reveal her frizzy hair and dabbed the sweat around her neck and chest with his eyes subtly following. 'No. I've been checking every poxy bush and vine I pass but I can't find anything. But I figured maybe the vines were the flying trees since they an't necessarily *rooted* to the ground but are still a plant. That would count as flying, right?'

He shrugged, 'I guess so. I never thought about it like that.' He sighed, exasperated and took his unlit cigarette from his lips and tucked it in his pocket, 'ah dash me wig I haven't even been checking the poxy vines.'

She giggled, 'it's alright. No need to beat yourself up over it, you an't shot into the brown. I only thought on it not long ago.'

They began to walk together, and a moment of silence passed, 'you know, this is the first time I've truly been alone-'

'-It's the same for me as well-'

'-With a man,' she jumped back in, 'since my husband.'

He looked at her curiously, 'you're married?'

'*Was* married.' She shook her head, 'and what a shamble that turned out to be. What a fool I'd been. He was loving at first, had the charm a woman could admire, and very quickly love. Until his time at home became a rarity and he never listened to me. At times I might've just spoken to a brick wall.' She paused, 'were you smoking that?'

Joseph gulped and reflected on her words. *No wonder Lucy was frustrated with me.* She was always reminding him how he was never home, how he never listened, never put her first. Biting his lip, he painfully pushed Lucy from his mind and listened intently as they passed under an arch of vine and drooping flowers connected by two trees. 'No, no. I'd rolled but hadn't lit. You can have it.' He passed it over with the match, 'I didn't know you smoke too, I an't seen you puffing a'fore.'

She lit the cigarette and drew in a breath, coughed, then inhaled again. 'Usually I don't. But a lungful of smoke helps to cloak words of sorrow, so I can be confident to speak the veiled woe.' She coughed again and paused, 'sorry, we don't have to talk about this. You don't want to hear of it.'

'No, it's alright. You go on, I'll listen.'

Victoria shrugged, not minding either way. 'He was a lovely man for a start, a gentleman; he treated me well. We courted for a few months then married, tried for children as all newlyweds would do, until time went by with no babe and he started getting irritable, grouchy and would back slang it whenever he got the chance. More oft than not he'd come back drunk, up the pole, tight as a boiled owl and that's when he . . .' she paused, trying to hurdle the verbal obstacle, 'when he began to find more pleasure in using his fists with me instead of the thing between his legs. It . . . I became his entertainment, I suppose, and I . . . became lost. Abuse is a strange thing to be involved in, Joseph; you're too afraid to say anything, too afraid to leave, but wanting to wholeheartedly. It's not like I could've left anyway. He was my husband, by law I was his property to do with as he pleased. What a cruel law; what grey-haired ruthless old bastard in those parliament houses thought it was a good idea to pass that law I might add!' she sucked on the cigarette angrily. 'I wasn't a woman. I was a bit of worthless dough he came home to violently knead. There was no more future anymore, no past to look back on; only the present moment where he'd return home stinking of beer and vodka and some prostitute's new perfume, then he'd . . . I . . . didn't know who I was any more. He'd taken my identity, *my* future.' She didn't look at him. She was stern, but solemn and he sensed emotion under the veil, until she ground her teeth together and growled, 'what a fucking arsehole.'

'What did you do?' he asked.

She glanced round to him, her face set. It was then that he noticed tears running over marks and small scars. 'He came back again one night with whiskey on his tongue and violence in his eye; I knew that look, I knew what I was in for, so I took the poker from the hearth and when he reached for me I struck him as hard as I could and slipped out the door and ran. I didn't know where, I didn't know who to, just away. I had to get away. Anywhere. I didn't care, I had no direction. He was eventually going to kill me, why stay and wait for it to come?

'The police eventually found me, magistrates heard the case, heard the reasons and I ended up with a fifteen-year sentence for abandoning and violently harming my husband when I was still his wife, for going against what he'd told me to do and leaving him. I was his property after all. By that sick law he could do what he wanted with me, including kill me. So, I became a criminal for saving my life and getting away from a monster. In the end, he got the marriage annulled so it'd all been for nothing, but I was still stuck, still the victim. Honestly, I don't know who is more the fiend: the man who beat me or the magistrate who deemed *me* the wrong-doer.'

Joseph wanted to stop walking and hug her, to hold her and make sure she was alright, to tell her not all men are like that; but he didn't. She wasn't seeking sympathy. 'I'm sorry.' He said, looking to the sandy earth.

Dropping the cigarette and stamping it under her boot, Victoria turned in surprise. 'For what? You didn't beat me, and I don't think you ever would. I've noticed how you act around me; you're nervous, quiet, respectful, shy and they're better qualities to have than violence. I'd rather have a nervous man scared to come forth from his shell than an overconfident fool with a short attention span. You have nothing to be sorry for. If anything, I should be thanking you. I've made more friends with good people outside the confines and legalities of the city than I ever have done, and I'm travelling the world seeing sights I never thought I would, that a woman like me never should in this twisted day and age.' She stopped and looked at him, and he looked at her, 'you're the one who got us all out here and made it all possible, you're more courageous than you think.' She smiled, wiped away her tears and smiled, 'you've made me feel like I can fly Joseph,' she leaned closer, 'just like these poxy trees.' Her lips touched his and in the silence of the coast, in the beauty of Gabon they kissed, each passing second becoming more passionate than the last.

Stuck in perpetual awe, Robert Epping gaped at the greenery and colourful vegetation unable to accustom to it. Who knew there could be so few people and yet so much life? It had its own hustle and bustle, in its own calming way. He'd never known anything like it; everything was so *still,* so *quiet* and at the same time so orderly and refined. It was strange, he struggled to remember a time when he was last alone and able to hear his own breaths, his own heartbeat. Surveying the flowers, trees and butterflies, he'd never known colours to be so bright– there was so much more on the spectrum than the dark shades of concrete and stone people had imprisoned themselves in and called home.

Passing a cluster of bushes surrounding one of these strange trees, he stopped and gazed down at their array of flowers and was stunned by the vibrancy. How could anything grow so beautifully in this intense heat, he wondered. Summers in the city were warm and refreshing, giving a rare chance to ignore the grubby smog that swathed through the clustered and dirty streets but out here where there was little water, comfort, food or shelter, with the sun baking anything and everything– it was so much better. The air, for one, was so much cleaner. He sucked it in through his nose and knelt into the sand, feeling its warmth on his knees, to stare at the flowers, at their purple and yellow petals and protruding stamens. Nothing had been so pretty. Well, apart from Mary Blackburn; she was a girl a fifteen-year old lad could never forget.

If Mary could see me now, blimey, what would she say. He didn't know, but he could imagine her expression as he told her, see her eyes light up and then narrow cutely as she scrutinised his tale of treasure maps and sailing ships. Then she'd be impressed, yes, then she would be. She was fifteen too and the daughter of a baker; she wasn't his girlfriend, but Mary was not afraid to lower her undergarments either. He missed her, and he wished she could be here as well. *Does she even remember me?* As his eyes followed the tangle of vine that wrapped around the bushes and wrangled its way up the tree, he wished he'd had the courage to whisk her off her feet and offer her a ring. At fifteen, life was a constant string of wishes and dreams with little room for regret, but here in his lonesome on the beach of Gabon he found himself regretting.

Despite the vine reaching the tree, it struggled to climb higher and had stretched over to the neighbouring trunk leaving a knotted twine dangling aimlessly. Rob inspected the offshoot curiously and got to his feet for a closer look. He gulped, his throat grating as his tongue rolled down imaginary water. He wiped the sweat from his brow with a baggy sleeve, no longer noticing the flies clouding around his head. As he looked at the tangle, he saw two thick strands had grown into each other and had grown into a very distinctive tangle. They had almost formed a thick ball in their centre, with one crossing over the other and continuing its hang and the other imitating its route. Suddenly a wandering gaze became a sharp familiarity, a recognition; this was a knot. A hand-made knot made by humans. By sailors.

A new sweat broke out over Rob as he thought back to his lessons from Benjamin one evening. He'd had just one length of rope in his callous hands and yet Rob had never seen so many things become possible, so many shapes and hoops and names. One end flicked over the other and with a few twists and turns the same end he'd been holding finished in the same place next to the other, and yet he'd created a fast, simple and secure hoop that could be trusted with weight-bearing and could be pulled apart just as easily. '*This'uns the bowline, lad. An important knot all sailors need to know. It's versatile, strong and useful in more'un one way.*' He then helped Rob with his knot and pulled his own apart to start again and with another few twists and turns he held in his hand a completely new knot, with the same rope. '*Figure o' Eight. Or a Stopper Knot. We use it on the belaying pins. Stops the line from runnin' out through a block or other line.*' Rob tried it and Benjamin smiled, '*Aye lad, that's knot half bad.*' He winked. There was also the Rolling Hitch, Highwayman's Hitch, Clove Hitch, Reef Knot and Sliding Sheet Bend but the one Rob remembered well and had even used in his workday activities was the knot where Benjamin retrieved another length of rope and began to tie them together, crossing one over the other and rolling the other over the original; connecting the two. '*This'uns classed as a bend. Now, there's a few names for this one. Some call it the Shamrock knot, or the Fisherman's knot. But I's call it the-*'

'. . . True Lover's knot; because they ought never to let each other go.' Rob reminisced with wide eyes. This was the same knot hanging before him. This was crafted by a trained sailor, and from how the two strands had grown into each other it had been tied a long time ago . . . by whom? Rob smiled. He could give a guess.

He dived to the ground underneath the True Lover's knot, below the roots of the flying tree, and ripped out the dry shoots of grass and pulled the small trowel from his belt and dug it into the warm sand, flinging it out and away. Quickly the sand became cold to touch and deepened to shade of dark brown. Soon his hands were covered in wet sand and mud and the coldness began to numb his fingers but still he kept digging . . .

. . . until he hit solidity, and his heart lurched in his chest.

With his eyes wide, he scraped lengthways and widthway and saw the shape he needed to dig around; he began to excavate, first around the surface and then the sides until he could get his palms around the lid and handles. Holding his breath, he heaved and wiggled and jiggled it free from its purchase in the cold hard earth. Sweat stung his eyes as it ran down. His arms ached, and stomach whined from the efforts until he pulled the small chest from the ground and flopped to the sand with his prize in his arms; its metal framework winking in the sun of a new day, of a new century.

For a moment he sat transfixed by the chest, unable to believe it would be *him* who pulled it from the ground. It was true he joined the landing party, but he'd only held his hand up because he wanted to see what Africa was like, never thinking he would play a major part. 'I have to get this back to the boat, to the crew.' He uttered and scrambled to his feet, grabbing the chest and running back along the line of the sea where everyone would be waiting by the craft, he hoped.

The hot afternoon was turning into a warm evening as the sun slowly curled around the sky heading for its finish line on the horizon. With its power diminishing, the air sighed with a light breeze that tugged at the leaves and trees and the clothes of those explorers who had ventured to land; it was a welcome respite. Of those who remembered to check, the time was approaching where the sun had passed below the length of a thumb from the horizon and their four hours on land had expired. Evening was approaching, and darkness would not be too far behind.

With the small chest tucked under one arm and the other pumping as he ran, Rob moved as quickly as he could with sand under foot. He didn't realise how hard it was. Every step he took seemed to slip beneath him, as if he were trying to run on a blanket that was constantly being tugged from underneath. Still, those back home had not called him Hare for nothing, and he pushed on with determination waiting to see *Victoria* out on the Cape– then he knew their boat would be close.

He ran on and still there was no sign of the ship or the boat. With his lungs and legs burning, he slowed to a jog, *am I even heading toward the-*

A gunshot exploded, shattering the silence into a million fragments, sending tropical birds tearing away into the sky and causing the monkeys to howl and wail in shock. He slowed to a stop. The gunshot was not too far away, coming from inland. Captain Robertson was the only one with a weapon; immediately his thoughts ran wild circulating the one solid truth that now had to be faced. *Something's happened. Get back to the boat, now!*

He started running again, his throat crackling as he gasped for water. The sand felt like hot embers under his boots, cooking his feet and smouldering his legs as if they were oaken logs. He was shocked at how far he'd managed to wander. The strip of sand he ran along seemed suddenly smaller as the tide began to eat its way up the shoreline, munching along the beach with each rolling wave of longshore drift. Just then, another gunshot burst into existence much closer than before making Rob duck instinctively, followed by the sharp whine of a whistle. 'What is going on?!' he cried worriedly, pressing harder into the sand as he remembered the purpose of the whistle.

At last the ship came into view squatting on the hazy, milky water a mile off from the shore. It was a relieving sight; her sails were drawn, and lanterns were now dotted along the deck to fend off the approaching shadows. Below deck, Poppy was probably helping Benjamin with cooking tonight's meal by the stove and Hugh was playing dice with Dave as they always did every evening with Harold; suddenly Rob found himself wishing he were back on board. Back to safety.

With the sand strip shrinking, Rob rounded the bend on the beach and saw the boat ahead with the waves beginning to lick its stern. Some of the others had already returned and were pulling the stake from the ground, throwing the rope back in the boat and pushing it into the encroaching tide. Tess was back, he saw, as well as Billy. Approaching the boat from the other way, Victoria and Joseph were hastening as he was– all too exhausted and distracted with the gunshots and whistle to realise what it was he had tucked under his arm: the reason for their visit.

Joseph's legs were aflame, and his lungs were spitting embers by the time he reached the portside gunwale, who knew running on sand could be so brutal? There was no grip, nothing to push off, yet surprisingly gunshots were a brilliant source of motivation. The captain had whistled, and that meant their isolation was now not strictly true. Suddenly he saw that Robertson had been right to be so cautious. Sweating profusely and gasping for water, he ran into the shallow tide not caring about his boots; there were more important things to think about. He grabbed the gunwale along with Victoria and they helped the others to push the boat further into sea.

As the water raised to waist height, Tess pulled herself up and flopped into the boat. 'Grab the oar!' Billy exclaimed.

She sat up, 'what?' Hair covered her face, sticking to her forehead.

'The oar! Grab the fuckin' oar!' he cried again as he clambered in next and sat on the centre thwart, snatching an oar and slotting it into the rowlock. Tess did the same whilst Joseph helped Victoria into the boat and heaved himself up. The boat rocked heavily and bobbed against the rising waves.

'Thanks.' She said, her cheeks bright red and her hair frizzy from the exertion and humidity, though he spotted the twinkle in her eye. He gave her a quick smile and turned to see Rob splashing into the water running hard; he was struggling but it wasn't until he noticed what he was carrying did he understand why.

Shocked, he leaned over the quarter knee throwing his hands out for the small box Rob held onto dearly. The water enveloped his waist and rose to his chest; lifting the box above his head it was clear to see he was in trouble. 'Rob! Mate, hand me the chest! I need your arms!' he cried reaching out.

In the glow of the evening, Rob was paler than the white sand they'd just left behind. 'I can't swim,' he said with a voice thick with fright at the rising cold water, yet he did not let the box drop, valuing it more than his own life.

Joseph reached out further and took the chest from him and, quickly passing it to Victoria, he then reached out for Rob's flailing hands as the currents of the sea began to pull him under. The boy slid under the waves, only his arms visible above the surface beginning to flail. Quickly grabbing his hand, he yanked Rob with all his might up to the gunwale and into the boat, coughing and spluttering, dripping wet. All were exhausted, hungry and thirsty and had had enough of exploring.

The oars dipped into the water and the longboat began to move, snaking at first as Tess and Billy could not match pace but after a pause and a countdown, they synchronised and managed to pull the boat further out. The quartermaster turned to see the faces of the passengers, and hesitated. 'Where's the Captain?' he asked them quietly as it dawned on him at what they'd done. 'Fuck! Where's Jim?'

Suddenly they heard a cry from the shore. Everyone turned.

A bearded man was sprinting through the trees, waving his arms in the air with the musket in one. 'Wait! Wait!' he hollered desperately. *'I'm here!'* Jim Robertson cried in earnest. It took them a second to realise why he was in such a hurry. Movement was behind him, snaking through the trees hollering threats and intimidating noises to get him out of their territory. Billy and Tess stopped rowing, and all were silent as they observed five – no, six – *seven* dark-skinned men chasing him and aiming their spears for the captain, some swinging clubs. They now saw the reason for the gunshots. For the whistle. The tribe's warriors wore next to nothing and had bold white tribal prints painted over their bodies, some with strange objects pierced through areas that made the sailors cringe. The tribesmen pursued Robertson down onto the beach and into the water where he abandoned his musket, throwing it into the water, and dived into the depths.

Joseph realised their boat was not moving. He turned back to the rowers, 'Turn! Fucking hell! Row, for god sake! He's our bloody Captain!'

Suddenly they saw another man stumbling through the shadows behind the savages, moving as quickly as he could through the trees, but it was clear he was weak and struggling. One leg appeared to be unresponsive and an arrow was protruding from his shoulder; the side of his shirt was drenched in blood yet still he pushed through the pain. '*Harold!*' Victoria exclaimed, as well as Billy and Rob. 'Come on, hurry! Hurry! You can make it!' They hammered against the gunwale and yelled to him.

Harold Arms pushed through the last of the trees and darkening vegetation away from the warriors and reached the beach where his leg gave out at the sight of the boat at sea, and his silhouette dropped to its knees on the sand.

'What're ya' doing Harold, come on mate! On y' feet! Swim ya' rawny bastard!' Billy exclaimed, but Joseph looked at him sternly and the boat fell quiet. The waves lapped and rolled along the wooden hull.

The warriors, realising the commotion, saw the marooned man up the beach and melted back in the brush, only to appear behind him a moment later. Harold knew it; they all knew what was to happen. Raising an arm to the boat, they sensed he was trying to wave, to say everything would be alright. To say goodbye. He did not fight. There was no use. He was too weak. Gently, sinisterly, they grasped his arms and dragged him away from the beach, back into the gloom of the tropical trees.

Knocked from their trance, Tess and Billy turned the boat as best as they could toward land and rowed slowly. Thankfully, the captain looked to be a strong swimmer and met them halfway. He took a hand from the cabin boy and quartermaster and hauled himself into the boat and collapsed onto the bottom boards, breathing hard, spilling water and dripping it to the floor.

A minute passed where no one spoke, no one moved. The boat bobbed gently on the rolling tide as the sun inched lower.

At length, Robertson pulled himself up awkwardly and sat against the rising frame, his coat, shirt and trousers clinging to him uncomfortably. Taking off his sodden hat, he ran a hand through his wet lengthy hair and pulled it from his face and wiped his eyes but left the water to drip from his beard. Gazing down to the base, to the boards, he looked fatigued. Joseph could understand– they all could, he had just managed to escape from a group of savages who, within a second of him slowing, would have slaughtered him like a pig.

Robertson slowly looked up and around, and spotted there, sitting beside Victoria's boots getting dripped on, was the object of desire: the chest. The clue. It deemed their venture profitable, giving them new opportunities to continue this quest. His eyes stared for a time, his mouth not moving, until a faint smile found his lips and he sighed in relief. 'The chest. Found by whom?'

Rob spoke up, his voice thick with emotion at what they'd just seen. 'I did, sir, I found the chest.'

'Well done lad, very well done.'

Billy spoke up quickly and snatched the topic of conversation. 'Cap'n, Harold was on the beach just now, he was right there and t' savages took him. They didn't kill him, but he was alive when they dragged him away. If we turn now, we might still have a chance to rescue him.'

Everyone turned back toward the darkening shore, the trees and beach now nothing more than murky shadows against the red orange sky. They pictured him there, scared witless, being dragged through the dark trees with the tribesmen prowling around their visitor. It was enough for Tess to start crying. 'We have to turn back.' Victoria said resolutely, 'we have no choice, we've got to go and get him!'

'Let's go back to the ship, make torches and gather what we can; we've got to go back to find him.' Rob seconded. Tess was nodding with tears streaming and already starting to pull the boat.

'Morning. We'll have to wait until morning. We've no hope of finding him in the dark, even if we do have torches. We don't know the area; we don't know where they've taken him to.' Joseph prompted realistically. *Or if he's still alive.*

'Until morning? With those savages Harold won't last until morning!' Victoria exclaimed, her face reddening, her eyes welling up with tears at the thought of what they'd done. 'He'll come to the beach. He will. He's not stupid; he'll escape and follow the sound of the sea. We'll pick him up and row back to-'

'-My crew, there is no easy way to say this. Harold is dead.'
Captain Robertson said as calmly as he could and lowered his eyes
to the boards, his eyes filling with tears. There was no shying from
the truth. 'I've heard tales of what these peoples do to white men
without means of defence. They're savages; they show no mercy
even if an Englishman pleads. If Harold has been taken by them
then I'm afraid he stands no chance. He won't be interrogated or
ransomed, he will be killed. It is a truth we must face. Now we
must stand together and finish this journey, for him, for Harold.'
Tears emerged from his eyes and rolled down his cheeks and joined
the water in his beard. He looked up to them trying to stay solid,
but he was breaking. 'I'm-I'm sorry, Harold is dead. There is no
one to return for.'

Chapter Seventeen

Dave James' face whitened, his mouth hung loose. It took him a second to register the words. The rest of the crew were the same, none knowing how to process the death of a fellow crew member. Death had been a sprawling force in their city lives; they all knew of someone who had fallen to diseases like tuberculosis or cholera, or fatal injuries; it was hard not to when living in such squalor that London insisted upon the lower classes, yet no one had experienced its cold touch out here on the waves, until now. 'What?' Dave managed to utter and shook his head at the idea. 'No. No, that can't be right, he's still out there. You were all alone on the beach, we saw you. We all did, we could see you in the trees with the spyglass. There was no one else there. How can Harold be dead?'

Suddenly Poppy burst into tears and Benjamin held a hand to his mouth, putting the other around the shoulder of the crying girl. Hugh stood sullenly with his cigarette drooping loosely from the corner of his mouth. The quartermaster tried to talk gently to them, to explain the sensitive situation but he could see the pain in their features shadowed by the harrowing lamplight. Harold was a good man, a hard worker on the ship; an honest friend they all counted on. Joseph tried to stay strong and not break into tears himself; he was going to miss seeing him sitting on a cask with a mug next to him, carving his next animal under the stars. 'There were tribesmen in the trees, it's true. We saw them chase Jim to the beach. We . . . we saw them take Harold. We weren't alone, I . . . they were there the entire time. We just didn't see.' He paused, searching for the right words, but how could there be? There never were any correct words to tell someone about death, to soften the blow when telling that a friend will not be returning. 'Harold is gone.' He said solemnly, feeling the depth of the sentence as if his tongue was digging a grave.

Rob's head hung low, and he walked off from the portside of the ship where the longboat had been drawn up, to stand alone on the forecastle. Sensing he needed time, Joseph let him be. Tess took Poppy's hand and hugged her, and the captain held his hat to his chest. 'He was a brave man, a fine sailor, as decent as any Englishman. I'm sorry I couldn't do more to help him, to protect him. At first light before we break our fast, passages will be given and there'll be a chance for us to say our goodbyes. As of now, we must cherish the memories we have and honour him as our brave friend, for him to be at peace.'

Again, Dave rejected the idea. 'Did you go back? Did you find his body, how do you know he's dead?' He was probing for answers, any *other* answers. When he received none, he scoffed at Joseph, grabbed the gunwale of the longboat and began to haul it back to the side to be lowered. 'He's still out there. There's still light in the sky, we have time.'

'Dave. Dave!' Victoria called, and stepped forward calmly as she wiped her puffy eyes and attempted to compose herself. 'I'm sorry, he's gone. We . . . we've got to let him go. Let's not disgrace his memory by making a scene here. If we row back to shore and start searching in the dark, we'll be endangering the lives of everyone else. Those tribesmen . . . they weren't coming to the beach to make friends with us; they wanted us gone. You heard what Jim said, he wouldn't have stood a chance, and neither will we. If you go back there, you won't find a body. We found not a speck of evidence those savages were even there; they know how to not leave a trace– I doubt they'd leave his body lying there for us to come and collect.' Her words were hard yet needed to be spoken, but they fell on deaf ears.

Angrily, Dave let go of the gunwale, his face stern. He suddenly raised his hand and slapped her hard around the face and raised his fist again. 'I won't have a woman speak to me like that, not of Harold. He's alive. You should've stayed in the prison, whore.'

A red mist descended over Joseph's eyes and before he knew it a fist caught Dave on his right cheek. He tackled him to the deck and smacked him hard again and again; Dave reached up, grappling to return a punch but failing. His fury was so blind it had deafened his ears too, Joseph failed to hear the cries behind him, telling him to stop. He did not. He was a Winter and had the coldest of touches when in the heat of rage.

Soon Dave's face was becoming exploding putty as Joseph reshaped it and recoloured it to a deep red. He was an experienced bare-knuckle boxer after all; he knew how to brandish bold colours. Hands grabbed his shoulders and yanked him off, and suddenly kicks and blows pummelled his side and chest. Pain racked through his torso, spiking up here, there, up and down his ribs and snatching the air from his lungs. A kick to his head sent his ears ringing and thoughts tumbling. He wheezed and cried out, and the immediate pain stopped abruptly but he knew this type of pain lasted for days. Suddenly he was back down the alleyway after coming out from the house; beaten and bloodied he was, although this time when he opened his eyes it was wood he saw instead of cobbles, and the hands that pulled him away to lean against the railings of the ship were a friend's.

Blood drooled from his mouth. He looked up hazily and saw Billy restraining Hugh on the starboard side of the ship. *It was Hugh kicking me?* He gulped down a wad of blood, tasting its familiar rusty taste on his tongue, and hazily heard the voice of the captain shouting to him from miles away. 'Joseph! Can you hear me? Are you alright?' but he was too disorientated to answer.

Robertson saw him still breathing, then turned to his boatswain. 'Take him to the berth to his hammock and clean his cuts. When he's responding, tell him to come to my cabin at once. As for Dave, take him to the sick bay and clean him up as best as you can, make sure he doesn't choke on his own blood. As for Hugh, take him down to the hold until he calms himself. Is that understood, Victoria?' The captain told her.

She nodded, her cheek a red beacon.

'Quart'master?' the voice whispered to him in the gloom. 'Quart?' The ship creaked and moaned as her hulk rocked against the swell of the changing tide, but he hardly felt it anymore. Breathing harshly with the taste of blood thick on his tongue, he slowly opened his eyes and felt his brain trying to hatch from his skull in deep rhythmic pounds. Aches tormented his side and breathing hurt his ribs. Drowsily, he lifted his head and tried to rise but ended up falling back down wincing. His eyes hurt even in the soft light of the candle. Suddenly he remembered, *was someone calling me?*

Biting his lip to supress the pain, he pushed himself up and saw a silhouette with bushy whiskers and weathered features. *That narrows it down; we all look rough and have bushy whiskers now after being at sea.* 'Sorry to wake ye. I brought you some bread and chicken, not fresh I'm afraid, and potatoes. I's about to get some shuteye an' I wanted to make sure you'd eaten. Are ye hungry?'

Ah, Benjamin. He forced a smile, 'famished, and thirsty. Thank'ee mate.'

Benjamin nodded and handed him the food and a cup of water. The sight of it made his stomach grumble; he remembered how he hadn't eaten since breakfast. 'Oh, there's something else as well. But what was it?' he paused, looking to the floor, his lips moving silently. 'Ah! Cap'n wants to talk in his cabin, Victoria, Tess n' Billy are in there waiting for you.'

'Right. Cheers Ben. How's Dave? I didn't mean to take it so far, I just . . . needed to prove a point.' He drank the water then picked a sliver of chicken up and pushed it between his lips, his teeth feeling tender, his appetite at a loss.

The old sailor smiled, 'Blimey whatever the point was, you managed to blunt it with those fists o' yours. The man has just about stopped dribblin' blood.'

Joseph didn't realise how badly he'd beat him, but despite his searching he found no guilt toward his action– or any regret. 'Ah give it a few days. He'll come around.'

Benjamin pursed his lips beneath his beard. 'Joseph, I don't think ye realise Mister Dave and Mister Harold were good chums, and you all stopped him from going back to find him. The man's a hard case but he's hurting emotionally and physically, and it might take more than a bit of sea air to tide him over.'

'He would've died if he went back there. Everyone knew it. What was I meant to do? Let him row himself to a sandy grave, or stop him and let him lay a hand on Victoria?' Joseph quizzed and bit down into the hard bread.

The old sailor paused and didn't answer, then spoke, 'I once knew a man, brash and boastful he was, who'd told us him and his brother had been in a shipwreck as lads and had lost each other. Was about the only honest thing he ever told us. Years had passed but he still believed his lost brother was out at sea, sheltering on an island somewhere, thinkin' that it was a specific one. So's, we go to it whilst passing through and found no trace of him, but he was determined to keep searching. We listened to his drunken tales and heard his rambling flotsam o' bollocks and started feeling less pity for this brother-less ratbag. Still he insisted, and we searched it again on our next voyage, but there was nothing at all.

'We all knew the brother was gone, but he never listened to anyone. "He's still out there I say!" he used to give us, "we got to keep looking, I can find anything, right down to a whore's chastity belt!" a real bastard, ye know the sort; believed himself to be at an uppity station in life, always up the pole, pickin' fights, givin' the insults but could never take em'. Begging for one solid hard case to send him to the Old Scratch. Hard worker though, that he was, until we came upon that island for a third time. "He an't going to be there." We told him. "Ye brother's gone, John. Ye have to let him go." Never did he listen though; he got all angry like an' rowed himself to shore in a sulk and we . . . let him be.'

Joseph paused between eating a chunk of potato, 'what're you saying?'

'I's saying, even though he was a nasty old prick, we still let him believe his brother was out there and on that last time . . . we didn't wait for him to return. We lifted anchor and went on our way.' He lowered his voice and turned away from the candlelight to check no one was listening. 'I's saying, maybe it wouldn't have been a bad idea to let our own bastard believe in the dead and row ashore to save ghosts, as now we have to deal with an unhinged sailor who knows people don't like him . . . and knows where the muskets are kept. Goodnight.' Benjamin blew out his candle and hobbled off to his own hammock, leaving Joseph silent in the dark wishing he had some strong stuff to wash down those strong words.

Finishing his meal, he remembered where some strong drink was. With a wobble and a palm to his forehead, he slowly got to his feet and made his way up the companionway to the main deck. It was empty save for the lantern hanging from a hook on the mast, casting a shadow on Johnson's bullet hole. Darkness had fully overtaken now, and the stars were peeping through scuds of passing cloud. Night was in full swing and a breeze played upon the rigging and tied sails, knocking them and making them squeak. Rob stood by the foremast, looking out to sea on his watch. It was nice to feel, although he wondered how long he'd been sleeping for. Lights were flickering inside the captain's cabin and he hobbled his way over to the door, wincing with every step.

Voices were talking and out of courtesy he knocked on the window and waited. The door opened slightly, and Billy looked through; a smile grew on his face and he swung the door open. 'Come on in, fella. We've some grog in here if you want a tot?' he said as Joseph walked in.

'Aye, but only a small one; my head's swimming enough as it is without any neck oil.'

Billy shut the door. 'Maybe that's the reason why you need some, to calm the head and soothe the bones.' He winked and walked over to the cask, picked up a small glass and ladled it in. The quartermaster found a cushioned chair and gently sat down on it, resting his head against the wall, his ribs crackling every time he breathed. Eyes fell on him, he could feel their draw; Victoria was sitting at the table looking at him worriedly, and Robertson glanced as he leaned against the window with his own glass of ale in a dry set of clothes. A pipe was resting between his lips, lightly smoking. Joseph nodded and gave an *I'm fine* expression, but it was Tess sitting on a chair nearby that asked, 'how're you doing, Joseph?'

He shrugged. 'I feel how Dave looks.' He gave a quick smile and exhaled, taking the drink from Billy, who then took a seat at the table. 'Where's Hugh?' he asked, taking a pinch of tobacco from his pouch and pushing it into the bowl of the pipe he'd been accustoming to in order to save their stash of cigarette paper.

'Still down in the hold. I t'ink he's fell asleep down t'ere, I don't know, he didn't answer when I last went down to check if he's calmed down, so I let 'im be. Must be tired after all the layin' boots, eh?'

'He can stay down there for all I care. What happened earlier was none of his business to get involved in. The man may be short, but his feet feel like hooves.'

Tess laughed, and Billy smiled. Captain Robertson took his pipe from his lips and took a gulp of ale, 'what happened earlier has happened,' he said, 'there's naught anyone can do to change that and on the morrow, you can all shake hands and brush this off like proper gentlemen; I've no time for sulks and despondency when we have a vessel to maintain. Today has brought enough lasting drama for my liking as it is. What needs our attention now though is this small chest and what it has locked inside.' He placed his glass on the desk and hooked the pipe back in, picked up the small black wooden case and placed it on the table. All eyes were drawn to it, all minds emptied as they tried to imagine the contents. The other lens of course, but what else? There had to be more.

'Quartermaster, would you like to do the honours?' Robertson asked as he sat down.

It's time for the next step. Joseph got to his feet and felt a pang of guilt that they'd be leaving Harold behind, then he lit his pipe, puffed and wafted the match out, trying to waft the thought away. He reached for Elanor's box on the desk, flicked open the latch and picked out the small key– a small key for a small chest, and yet its weight felt heavy, heavy with duty, heavy with purpose. With palms sweating, he approached the chest, inserted the key and turned it, feeling the mechanism tumble.

The chest clicked as it unlocked, and Joseph Winter let out a slow breath as he lifted the lid.

Inside were a pile of aged papers, curled and musty and an old sextant leaning against the side. He picked some of the papers out and glanced at them, seeing them to be notes and sketches of seabirds, plants and tropical coastlines and set them aside to be perused later, and there, sitting at the very bottom, was a smaller case. He took his pipe out and licked his lips, his throat dry. Slowly, he picked out the case with gentle fingers and placed it on the table. With everyone watching intently, Joseph opened it and found, wrapped in linen, the other lens.

Picking the glasses from the desk, he unwrapped the cloth from them and carefully slid the other lens into its place. It was a perfect fit. Custom made. His heart pounded in his chest. Picking the scroll up, he turned it over to its blank side, the side that had revealed so many secrets, and, wasting no more time, he put the glasses on to see what lie hidden on the parchment.

Words lit up bright and bold, scrawled in a scruffy handwriting on the right-hand side of the page. *How is this possible? It's almost as if the paper has two layers.* It was written in a different hand from the last clues he'd discovered; written by a different person and Joseph would bet his pennies (if he had any) on who it was. *Henry Scott, this is your hand here.* He cleared his throat and spoke aloud to the rest of the room.

'𝔖ink below the equator but float to the continent's east,
𝔘nder crux and canis major is where luck will never cease.
𝔖trange lands and strange predators there are: be warned of Tangena's bite,
𝔖eek along the eastern coast, pray and do not lose sight.

𝔥elp 𝔐erina and 𝔐erina will help you.
𝔥𝔖 𝔈𝔖.'

Again, Joseph was lost. It was as much of a riddle as it was rhyme and he had not a clue what most of the words were. One thing he did know this time though was that the capitalised words were names. Carefully, he lifted the glasses from his face and surveyed the blank faces of the cabin looking ever-more confused. Only the captain appeared clued in, as he lifted his hand from the parchment he'd scrawled a copy of the clue on.

There was a moment of silence, until the Irishman shattered it. 'Another fuckin' riddle poem– what is it with t'ese people? Once we solve one there's another fuckin' riddle waiting! Why can't they just say: "go here!"' He said exasperated and Tess giggled, Victoria found herself smiling too. Joseph couldn't deny it, he had to agree.

Looking to the scroll, it was void of all marks once more. *What ink is this? I've never seen anything like it. It's bloody sorcery!* He supposed it didn't matter, what mattered were the words written *in* the ink. Nonetheless, he was perplexed and decided to probe. He took a drag from the pipe. 'So . . . any ideas?'

Victoria looked down to the table, her damp wavy hair tied back showing off her jawline; her arms folded as she tried to conjure some sense from the clue whilst Billy scratched his head and arched an eyebrow, not giving of any answers. Tess was silent. Captain Robertson brushed the feather of the quill around his hand in thought, '. . . below the equator and to the east. I need the map.' He pushed back his chair and retrieved the world map from a drawer, the same one they'd used to find Lisbon.

Moving the chest aside, he flattened the map out and placed weights on its corners. 'Sorry, what is this *equator*?' Billy asked.

'Almost like an imaginary line that circles the centre of the earth and the closer you get to it the hotter everything becomes, since it's the closest to the sun. It separates the northern hemisphere from the southern hemisphere. Here, if you can spare an eye.' Robertson said, and placed a finger on one side of the map and moved it straight through the middle along the line that split the world in two. 'That's the equator, and what we're looking for is below it and to the east.' He pulled another drawer out and picked the magnifying piece, placing it along the equatorial line and then slowly moving it lower across Africa and the Indian Ocean heading toward the islands of Indonesia. 'That's east, the lower right quarter of the earth, if you will.'

Joseph took his compass from his pocket and placed it on the map as a reference point for those that didn't know which direction east pointed. Although, it didn't seem to make a difference; the centre refused to sit still. Billy watched the movement of the magnifying piece and asked first, 'they couldn't be sending us to those islands, could t'ey? Of *Ind-on-esia*? That's east and below the equator. It fits.'

Joseph stroked his bearded chin; the straggles and patches were joining and filling out, giving him a fuller look and the opportunity to stroke whilst he mused. Something didn't seem right. 'Why would they send us to Indonesia though?'

Victoria shrugged, 'why Gabon? Why Portugal?'

Joseph nodded, 'true.'

'What's crux and canis major?' Tess asked from the other side of the table as she read through the scribbles on the note, one of the rare few aboard who was familiar with her letters. She tucked a strand of messy dark hair back behind her ear, 'that's got to be important.'

Robertson looked up from leaning over the map and inhaled, his pipe crackling. 'Crux and canis major? They're constellations. An alignment of stars. What I fail to see is why the clue mentions those two in particular? There's plenty of constellations out there, why those two? What makes them special enough to mention?'

'Maybe the land we've got to search for is under those stars? So, if we find those groups of stars then we know we've got to sail under them to find the land? Is this Indonesia place under those stars?' Tess suggested.

Billy nodded, 'Aye, that's what the clue said.'

'It's not as easy as that,' the captain informed, 'different constellations appear at different times of the year; it's seasonal, and you'll see different ones from another country and place. They'll always be there but it's the movement of the earth that shapes their timings of when we can see them.'

Victoria shrugged, 'So why don't we go outside now and see what stars there are? We're in a Gabonese summer, there's bound to be some stars out there even if they aren't crux and the other one, the major one.'

Joseph picked out the other object from the chest as he took a drag, 'they left this in here too, I'm not sure what it is but it's been left with the other things so it's bound to be important in some way.'

Robertson looked surprised, and took it from him for a closer look, 'it's a sextant, used to measure the stars or sun and calculate your position from them.'

'It's a what?' Billy looked surprised, before his face turned into a smirk.

'It's something you're not getting, Irishman.' Victoria chipped in, then smiled and winked.

'Hang on, I'll be back in a minute.' The captain exited his cabin with the sextant in his hands.

Joseph returned to his glass and took a gulp, feeling the grog warm his chest. Thankfully, his head no longer pounded but his chest and side ached every time he moved. He felt fatigued, yet his mind felt wired into the situation. Sleep would elude him tonight, he knew. After he'd emptied his glass, he walked out into the darkness.

The night air was cool, a relief after the day's heat and the scudding clouds had scarpered leaving a clear sky with nothing to pollute the transparency. He breathed deep and felt prickles up his back. The sun packed a punch in the day but at night the temperature failed to hold its own; he folded his arms, and found the captain standing at the stem of the ship atop the forecastle, a silhouette in the pale moonlight. Motionless he stood, fixated with the tool and the night sky.

Wincing, he hoped the pain would lessen soon else the day's work tomorrow would be tough indeed, especially now they were lacking a pair of hands, *lacking a pair of Arms,* he thought solemnly. He walked by Rob who was fast asleep by the mast and, climbing the stairs, he stood beside Robertson and glanced out to the coastal scene and finished his smoke. Still, after all his time at sea Joseph was stunned by the cleanliness and clarity of things beyond the barriers of stone and cement. It was all so free. In the light of the moon's rippling reflection upon the shore, the trees and bushes were mere shells of their vibrancy from the day, having abandoned their colour and life and appeared as nothing more than simple shapes and curves standing sentinel under a pure white face. Black waves rolled darkly up a blank strip of sand, the bubbles and froth invisible in the moonlight, just as the horizon was. The only way he could tell of the sea's boundary was the bold reflection of stars that looked to have finally reached the earth. The sea had transformed into a section of space that had fallen, the stars shining and twinkling in the waves in an extra galaxy he could witness with a naked eye, that he could reach with an open hand, could sail to and over; floating, riding through the endless void to make contact with other lost masses, tumbling in an emptiness that never ceased.

'Quite beautiful, isn't it?' The captain didn't look up from the sextant as he spoke but admired it all the same. He smoked as looked through the tool, twisting the mirrors and measuring the angles.

'I . . . never seen anything like it.' Joseph replied, suddenly forgetting his pains and troubles, 'it's like the world is trying to keep the beauty hidden and only lets it show in places we could never reach.'

'We can reach them. We can sail on and on but by the time we got there it would have moved on to another place in need of its gentle touch. Beauty is always somewhere in the world mate, you just have to know where to look, and when to appreciate.'

Joseph looked out beyond the bowsprit, 'yes.' He thought of Harold Arms suddenly and wondered what he would think, his friend who he'd persuaded to join them on this quest; their first loss but deep down he knew it wouldn't be there last before their journey's end.

'They're up there, you know.'

Spirits? Was he thinking of Harold too? 'Aye, somewhere up there.'

The captain looked round to him, his weathered wrinkles prominent in the glow, 'No, I mean the constellations. Crux and canis major. We're in the right place.'

'Where?'

'Look,' Robertson tilted his head and pointed to the millions of white dots sparkling in the sky, as if he were telling him to find a specific glitter on a diamond encrusted necklace. The thought of it made Joseph's hands twitch. Old habits die hard. 'See up there,' he pointed to one star and then moved his hand along to another and another, forming a shape near the tops of the trees away down the coastline. 'That one's crux,' he pointed to another patch nearby, 'and canis major. From what the clue said the next part of the journey is under those stars, and from my calculations it's near to the south of Africa, more so to its east.'

Truth be told, even though he nodded he couldn't see the shapes or the constellations. They were just small white dots perfectly spaced apart never to move as they always had been. 'The clue did say float to the continent's east.'

He lowered the sextant, 'I don't know why I didn't see it before. The continent's east; how stupid of me.'

'What?'

'Well, what's Africa?'

'I don't know, land?'

He shrugged. 'Yes, and it's also a *continent.* All we have to do is search around the east of Africa but under the equator.' He turned to Joseph and grabbed his shoulder, smiling as he showed a glint of his gold tooth. 'We need the map.'

Both men turned hastily and strode across the deck to the cabin with clearer minds, and for Joseph, a cleaner soul. 'Find anything?' Victoria asked from the table.

'We might have.' Replied the captain as he immediately made for the map and hung over it, eyes scanning fervently. 'Tess, could you turn up the lamps a bit?'

She obliged and got to her feet, turning up the illumination of the room. Once again, a silence followed, an anticipation that left them unable to sit and watch; no, they had to be there, looking at the map too.

The quartermaster refilled his glass and took another gulp. It was cheap grog they'd managed to haggle from Lisbon; it was acidic and left a sour aftertaste, but it was the only stash they had (apart from Robertson's whiskey, but he thought best to keep that secret) so Joseph took another gulp and bit his tongue. At least the tobacco was making it bearable. Suddenly Robertson slowly looked up from the table holding his pipe between his fingers. 'I know where to go.'

'Where?' they asked urgently.

'An island to the continent's east, under the equator, named Madagascar. Crux and canis major are above it; it's got to be there.'

Billy sat back down in his chair and scratched his long curls. 'What is this place? I never heard of it.'

'It's an island, a rather large one at that, that sits off the south east coast of Africa.' Robertson informed, 'I've never been myself, my duties never led me that far out but hearing from other sailors at the pub on a Friday night I hear it's a queer land, unlike any other.'

'How so?' questioned Victoria.

'I heard tales of strange trees; I can only guess that because it's an isolated tropical island, it's now developed its own ecosystems of plants and animals and-'

'-please don't say tribes.' Billy protested.

'-tribes. It's not a quiet land, not like this Gabonese beach.'

The Irishman sighed, 'Shite.'

'Let's hope they're friendly.' Victoria said optimistically as she sat back down.

The captain picked up the note with the clue on it. '*Strange lands and strange predators*– that would explain Madagascar. *Tangena* . . . maybe that's a predator to watch out for? It's the name of something, as well as *Merina*. It says we must help *Merina* and *Merina* will help us.'

'Maybe Merina's a woman we need to help and then she'll help us find the next chest? Merina sounds like a woman's name.' Tess suggested.

The captain nodded and smoked his pipe. 'I don't think you're far off with that, Miss Mills, but we won't know for sure until we get there. And from what the clue states, we need to look along the eastern coast of the island and make another venture to land.'

Billy sighed again and turned to Joseph, 'suddenly I don't feel half as excited about makin' landfall as I was, seeing how this one turned out.'

'You don't have to come along if you don't want to. You can stay aboard the ship to look after it, but a shuffle needs to take place. I don't trust a few people to keep the anchors on the seabed anymore.'

This much was true, as everyone had been considering it. 'We'll discuss who stays and who leaves another time. I need to do some calculations but at a rough estimate I'd say we could arrive at Madagascar in seven to eight days, or more, depending on the winds and tides. We'll be moving against the Benguela current and I've heard the waters around the tropics can be temperamental. Storms and becalmed waters, choppy seas. For now, though, I suggest you all get some shuteye; we raise anchor at dawn, and I need you all shipshape. The next leg of our journey awaits.' He said, giving a flash of a smile and a glint of that golden tooth.

Chapter Eighteen

That night, after tossing and turning in a never-ending cycle Joseph finally managed to slip from consciousness, but his slumber was far from wholesome. Dreams visited him in the shape of pointed spears and daggers held to his throat; he envisioned blood falling from his neck in a wide sheet as Harold had felt. Then his face appeared; Harold's pale hopeless face rising and falling like the waves of the sea, moulding into Victoria smiling to Dave cursing to Robertson's pained face as he reported the grisly details of a premature fate. Vinny suddenly appeared in the merge, that mad old crook, to his chilling smile as he told Charlotte what to write on the note he'd sent; suddenly the face was Lucy's, red and bleary, crying as he walked out the door of the courtroom and onto the deck of the ship. He slipped underfoot, the deck coated in blood and found himself walking the plank to its wobbling end, yet he didn't feel surprised as he looked down to the cold dark waters below. One after the other his feet strode until he dropped from the edge and . . . He didn't feel an entry, but his lungs burned as he sucked in seawater, could feel the agony as they filled, exchanging gas for liquid; could hear bells and gunshots ringing in his head as he sank lower away from the surface, trying to grab a rope that dangled in the water just out of his reach. The bells were ringing, the bells were ringing, the bells were ringing loudly, ceaselessly, as he began to fade into the current, pulling him out and away to the darkening depths.

The bells rang on and on . . . until he cracked open a slit in his eyes and heard the ship's bell ringing on deck to rouse the crew. He pulled himself up in his hammock, wet from where he'd dribbled during the night, or was that sweat? and winced sharply at the pain that tore his stomach and torso in two. 'Ah fuck.' He groaned and stumbled groggily from his hammock with bleary eyes. Slipping on his shirt, he then pulled on his trousers and boots and thumped up the companionway to the main deck hardly feeling like he'd slept at all, thanks to those pounding bells.

The freshness in the air caught him off guard and he stopped his yawn short to shudder. He registered abruptly that a ghostly light had barely crept upon the darkness and only a very faint glimmer of pale blue and purple hinted at sunrise, but the sunrise itself had not yet reached them. *What hour is this?* Still the bells rang, although now louder and clearer than before. 'What?' he managed to mutter, then louder, 'Walk-er! Alright! Christ! What? What is it?!'

'*We need to move now!*' howled Captain Robertson. 'They've been aboard! *They boarded the ship in the night!*'

He opened his eyes further and saw Hugh winching up the stem's anchor, Benjamin aloft on the mainyard untying the mainsail and Rob loosening the halyards ready to hoist the sails. His face was bright red, either from the chill of the morning or of embarrassment. Hesitating, he took a moment to decipher whether this was another part to his nightmare, but when looking at the sheer fear on Jim Robertson's face, the absolute clarity of that primal instinct to flee, he knew it had to be real. 'What?' was what he managed, 'who?'

'*The savages, god damn*! *Tribesmen!* They boarded the ship whilst we slept, our cabin boy on watch had fallen asleep and was damn lucky he wasn't seen by them! I managed to get one before the others scarpered, we *need to move!*' He yanked on the bell harder, his long unkept hair hanging in his face. He wore a shirt half buttoned and untucked from his trousers– no braces, waistcoat, vest or jacket, he had clearly woken in a rush.

'Right. Yes.' Joseph said, and not knowing what else to do, hurried around the capstan and hauled himself up the ratlines as quickly as he could to help fly the sails. There was a breeze, a cold one, and it was ready to bear them away as soon as the sails were taught and tied. As he climbed, the wind whipping at his shirt, he spotted the body on the deck, a ragged hole torn through its chest, laying sprawled in a pool of blood portside near the ladder to the forecastle. *My god, we really do need to move.* He scrambled up the ropes and clambered to the yard to begin untying the reef-points– the lengths of rope that keep the sail tidily purchased upon the yard. He was getting faster with his knots and how to untie them, but he was slow in comparison to the old sailor on the other side who hardly seemed to notice him. Benjamin was old salt; he was absorbed in what his hands were doing– flicking, pulling and loosening; he knew exactly which part of the rope to pull to untie it. It was mesmerising. Wishing for his own set of callous sailor's hands, he untied a few more reef-points until the mainsail was open and flapping freely and those below could haul the halyards to bring it under control. Even though Benjamin had done most of the work, Joseph's hands ached terribly. *Christ alive I need to work on my knots, I'm shooting to the brown here.*

They clambered back to the central mast where they climbed through the lubber's hole to get onto the maintop platform to then climb further to the topsail yard when Benjamin waved him off. 'Never mind me lad, my hands will manage. The Epping lad'll soon be up anyways, and Mister Jackson and Baker are working on the foresails. It'll be enough to get us going. You head up to the crow's nest and keep a lookout for any other blighters.'

Nodding in agreement, Joseph shuffled to the starboard mainmast shrouds and hauled himself up the ratlines and landed in the nest. He'd never been up in the nest before, this was Dave's station, and he could now see why he hadn't ventured this far: his hands began to sweat as he looked around to see dark silhouettes of treetops against the pale turquoise sky smudged with cloud, and looked down to the small people rousing from the berth, realising and running to get *Victoria* on her feet and ready to catch the wind. He gulped nervously, everything was high, *so high*, and so *vast*. The ocean to his right looked immense, limitless– he leaned against the mast, listening to the bell ring on. Shouts began to emerge from below as everyone rushed to their stations to prep for a swift exit. Usually it took them an hour to prepare the vessel for travel– this morning it took them half that time.

Up In the crow's nest he tried to penetrate the gloom, to see through the dim light to shore but he struggled; it was no easy feat and he found himself wishing he'd brought the spyglass up with him. Sunrise was not far off though, and light was coming; along with a canoe full of tribesmen paddling quickly, clearly perturbed by the fall of their kindred. Rubbing his eyes, he made sure for definite that was what his vision was delivering. He felt queasy at the sight, and leaned over the side, 'They're coming! *The locals; they're on their way!*'

There was a jolt from below and for a second, he was sure it felt like men clambering up the sides. Eyes narrowing to the bulwark, the fretful quartermaster waited to see hands, heads, bodies carrying spears and daggers. Then his sight slowly changed, and his position moved along the shoreline. *Victoria* was on her way. He sighed in relief and sank back against the mast. They were leaving the unpleasant experiences of Gabon as raw memories to look back on, and perhaps learn from. Joseph, in fact the entire crew, were more than happy with that.

The pastel colours of dawn spread over the dark eastern sky, giving hints as to what the day was to look like. Pale blues and oranges whitewashed the horizon and above until faint silhouettes adorned features for the eyes to recognise. Light gradually eked its way back to the world, scraping back the folds of night to give life to a new day. Aloft the ship, Joseph watched the break of day with eyes alight with wonder, grasping the beauty and appreciating the break of dawn with a fresh perspective. Even though the cobwebs of sleep still clung to his body and his hurts ached dully, he felt a comforting peace. He leaned against the side of the nest and observed as, one by one, the stars winked out, disappearing until the moon thought it safe to reach out freely again.

Looking back, he could see the canoes thrashing the water in pursuit, but they were no match for their square-rigged ship, and he breathed a sigh of relief, glad to be back on the move again. The morning air was sharp, its coolness nipping his throat as he sucked it down; its bite was a bitter one, not a relieving sigh from last night. He shivered with his one thin shirt and was reminded of how cold London used to be, all that way back in England. *No, if I were in London I'd be stepping in piles of shit and rotting waste and watching daybreak through a haze of coal smoke between tall dull buildings of brick and mortar. But if this is the equator why do the nights get so bloody cold?* When his teeth began to chatter, he caved in and carefully climbed down to the maintop, clambered through the lubber's hole and began descending the shrouds; his hands white and numb, making his effort a clumsy manoeuvre.

When at last he set foot back on deck the crew were busy at work, keeping the ship on the move. Victoria, Rob and Billy hauled the sheets of the sails to get them on the correct course whilst Benjamin was busy with his ropes, looping the hauled halyards and securing them around the belaying pins and retying those that had loosened. Hugh Jackson kept his head down as he walked the deck with a heavy boot and a coil of rope in his hands, heading for the berth where Tess and Poppy were preparing breakfast. Joseph kept his eyes trained on him, *keep walking with your sharp hooved feet, you rapist bastard.* There was no sign of Dave yet, although he knew he'd have to face him later in the day; the thought of it was a burden, so he decided to deal with the other issue on board. Stepping to the strewn body, he looked it over with concern as Victoria, Billy and Rob joined him in surrounding it.

Seeming to know what his thoughts were, Robertson ordered from the wheel, 'Quartermaster, ask the young Hare to come up here and hold the wheel. I'll be the extra pair of hands to haul the trespasser overboard.'

Joseph nodded and collected Rob to take control of the ship's wheel whilst the captain joined the group surrounding the tribesman. The wheel could've been lashed of course, but he understood Robertson's order; no boy needed to haul a bloodied corpse overboard. The group looked down at the dead man with a bloody hole in his chest, spewing gore over the deck. Not a one for subtleties, Billy said it outright, 'Hatchet of a shot there Cap'n. Right through the chest, so it is. He'd 'ave got the lot of us in our sleep if you hadn't have heard them.'

'It was a hasty shot, but I had to do something. I heard clambering on deck, and I thought it was one of you, but when I looked the situation was far worse. Thankfully, I had some hornets primed and ready.'

Joseph looked up from the corpse, 'what do you think they came aboard for? What could we possibly have that they'd want?'

'Food, women, weapons– all the t'ings a savage man could wish for.'

'If that's the case, then there's no difference between a savage man and civilised man. That's all you lot want.' Victoria said curtly, then suggested, 'do you think they knew we took the chest from the beach? Maybe they were its protectors?'

'If they were its protectors, they weren't bang up to the elephant with it. Anyway, they're tribesmen who live in the forest; I doubt they knew it was even there.' Joseph replied.

Glancing over the body, he saw he had white strips of paint over his chest and blue streaking his cheeks; his earlobes were enlarged by hoops and a bone piercing protruded through his nose. Around his neck a string of teeth and bones hung as a reminder of his fierce reputation. Then Joseph spotted something. Something he recognised. Leaning over, he pulled the necklace from the corpse and felt himself welling with tears. In his hand was a carved wooden elephant recently completed by lamplight on deck, spattered with blood.

Joseph gulped down the emotion, cut the carving free and slipped it in his pocket. Without saying a word, he wished for the others not to either. No words needed to be said. Silently he reached for a wrist, Victoria the other; Billy took one leg and Robertson took the opposing and they lifted the body up; immediately huffing at the deadweight of an adult man and hauled the body to the bulwark.

'Is that one of the savages that killed Harold?' A rasping voice asked from behind them. Dave was standing there, his face a mismatched colour of reds and blues, one eye had swelled, and he was missing a tooth.

Thinking more of the long-term closure the man might need, Captain Robertson nodded, 'Yes. This was the one.'

That was enough confirmation. Dave nodded and, as they hauled the body up on the railing, he pushed the corpse to the waves below with a hefty splash. 'He can feed the fish now.' He said coldly looking down to the water, before turning and walking away to the hold, but then he stopped, 'whoever fired the shot, you have my thanks.' He was curt and left them surrounding the blood that was now rolling in streaks with the motion of the rocking ship. There was no doubt about it; Dave looked a state, but no one dared to say anything. A man, especially of Dave's kind, wounded of his pride can be thin of patience and tolerance.

Robertson looked down to the streaking pool and pulled his straggled hair from his face, smoothing it down against his head showing his wrinkles underneath. 'Right, well this needs cleaning before we eat breakfast and give a service for Harold; blood is harder to get out than salt. Any volunteers?' he smiled as he glanced at their reaction and saw no takers. 'Great. Winter, Baker. Thank you for volunteering.'

The Irishman looked up in surprise and was about to retort when the captain walked off back to the wheel and sent Rob to fetch the bucket and water, brushes, holystones and old rags. He hooked the wheel with rope and excused himself to his cabin to get properly dressed and looking like the master of the ship. Within a minute, Rob brought up the equipment and some sand, as it was good for collecting blood and drawing out the remnants that had soaked into the wood. They knelt and started to spray the sand over the pool until it was covered, and then they brushed the clumps up and threw them overboard. They soaked up the rest of the spillage with the rags whilst the other scrubbed the patch where it had been with the holystone. 'Ah, me poor old hands. I got blisters from all that rowing, then from rowing yesterday, blisters from the knot tying and deck scrubbin' and I got sores right down to me bones from all the knocking about on this damned wood. It cuts to the onion I'm tellin' ya'. Y' know Joe, I'm starting to t'ink this sailor work isn't as easy as I t'ought it would be.'

Victoria laughed, 'oh give it a rest Billy Baker. I thought you'd be used to sores and blisters and worse from the workhouse, as you keep telling me.'

Joseph paused and looked at him, 'you were in the workhouse?' A dismal place it was, as filthy as it was dangerous, with laborious work and inhumane hours, and the pay an abomination. He would pick the life of thieving and conning any day over that place. He would pick any place, any job, *anything*, over that hell.

'Yes, he tried to break out of it and that's when he got sent to the gaol. I thought he'd have told you that?' She replied. 'Although Tess told me you'd killed someone because he robbed you and your family, but that I find hard to believe. You're frustrating and an arse but I can't see you doing that.' She put her hands on her hips.

'Aye Vic, and I'd prefer to keep the scars and memories from ears few and far between.' He smiled to her sadly, 'go an' get some breakfast sweetheart, we've got this.'

She looked to Joseph, 'Don't take too long else it'll all be gone. Oh, and Joseph?'

He looked up.

'Thank you for what you did yesterday.' She smiled glowingly, a smile that stirred his loins and made him want to kiss her again, but he couldn't, so he nodded and smiled back. She walked off and descended into the hold.

The light of the morning becoming a crisp gold as the sun breached the horizon, a dazzling brightness– it would do more harm than good to look at the sea at this time, the reflection was too powerful. The deck and masts were refreshing to look at however, appearing more gold than brown making them feel like they were really sailing on a ship of royalty. The bright light pampered *Victoria* with pretty rays of a new day, washing the dull wood of its flaws.

There was a pause. Both men looking down to their wet rags, brushes and stones, knowing what each other was thinking yet neither wanting to speak. At length, Joseph stopped and broke into the silence with a quiet tone. 'Billy, that's four stories I've heard.'

'I know.' He replied without looking up.

'Do you want to explain why there's four versions to how you got thrown in? Have you been keeping the truth from us?'

Pulling himself up to sit on his feet, he looked almost hurt. 'D'you think I've been spreading lies?'

He shook his head lightly, not entirely sure how to answer. 'Everyone's got a story of how they got in mate. I just don't understand how you've got four.'

'It's pretty obvious, isn't it?'

Now Joseph sat back, blinking, 'you've been in prison four times?'

'Twice. Of the stories I've been telling one holds truth to how I got t'rown in; the other t'ree are fake.' It was the first time Joseph had heard him sound solemn and stiff; it was clear he was uncomfortable.

'Why make up other stories if there's truth behind one of them?'

'Because I'd rather people not know the real reason. People are bound to ask but I can't bring myself to say it all the time. I'm ashamed of it, Joe, I'm ashamed of my past and what I've done. I may not seem it but I'm quite a sad man; I regret my choices and the life I've led. By making up other false reasons brings comfort to me, that I could've gone in for something else.'

Joseph went silent and decided not to pry. It was understandable, he knew of people that did it, but he wouldn't have guessed one would be the easy-going laidback Irishman Billy Baker. He tried a different tack. 'How did you manage to escape the other prison?'

He reached back down and scrubbed some more. 'Eh, it was easy to break out of, all you need is a fast pair of legs to outrun the guards . . . and then the dogs, but by then if you get far away fast enough you're a free man again. They got that many people goin' in now they're too busy trying to prevent riots and control the other inmates they don't have the time to track down any runaways.'

'Why didn't you escape from our prison?'

'I tried. Believe me, I tried. There were so many people, so many guards, so many locked doors and lost keys. I gave up and kept myself to myself, until you came walkin' into my cell. The man that never got caught, the infamous ghost who never left a trace. That's when I t'ought thing's might be possible, because if a man can never leave a trace o' where he's been, he might just be able to break out and slip away and not leave anythin' behind. Including me. And it turns out I'd made the right choice of friend.'

Joseph was about to reply when he hesitated, not knowing whether to feel honoured or used. Lowering his eyebrows, he dipped the rag back in the bucket and plucked it out dripping wet. Slapping it on the wood, he swabbed the deck as clean as it could be. 'So, what is the story of our gaol then? How did you get in? I'm your old possum Bill, you can tell me.'

At last Billy smiled, albeit a tired one. 'I want you to decide: was I t'rown in because I slept with another woman, I fought in self-defence and nearly killed a man because of it, I escaped a horrid fate in a horrid place and became what some would call a coward, or I murdered a man because he robbed me of every penny I had. Adulterer, victim, escapee or murderer. Who do you want me to be?' He got to his feet, dropped the brush in the bucket and walked off to the hold to eat.

Sitting in silence, Joseph sat back at his best friend's change in behaviour. Never would he have thought it, he'd always known him to be laid back about damn near everything so to see him uncomfortable and not wanting to open closed doors was strange. *Not everyone wants to look back; no wonder some were so eager to join me in looking forward.* He slapped the rag back to the deck and scrubbed the last remnants away, not wanting to but wondering what on earth it was that the Irishman had done that not only got him locked up, but that racked him with guilt so deep he created other versions to spread almost as a way out of his own past.

The day passed smoothly, as did the following day until they hit the Benguela current running in the opposite direction. Still they managed to sail on at five knots, navigating their way through the opposing cold current and countering winds. Taking the jibs and forestaysail down, they used only the mast's reefed sails, pulling them hard to port and then to starboard in an effort to rid of the gusting snags. The secured spanker kept them balanced though as they continued to tack against the opposing winds.

The beach of Gabon melted away, merging with the ever-changing landscape. When the winds powered into gales, they pulled away from the coast to avoid being driven into any hidden rocks or corals and kept the coastline only within reach by the spyglass, daring not to venture too far out to the southern Atlantic. Despite the lofty gales, the sun continued to be unbearable and uncooperative. Instead of humid heat they contended with dry air, sucking moisture from their bodies like a puddle in an African plain.

The crew kept as light hearted as they could with the rocketing temperature, although Dave was quiet and subdued, impassive and only replying to people when he had to; his face looked swollen and sore yet hardly any could say they pitied him, to Joseph he deserved every fist for what he'd said. And Hugh was acting strange; over-emphasising everything to make it look like he hadn't got involved, even though there was no hiding that he had with Joseph wincing with every step and beginning to bruise as the days wore on. The work became harder, especially now they were short of a pair of hands and everyone was running ragged trying to keep *Victoria* flying as the crow does. Harold was sorely missed.

Evening came on the fourth day from Gabon and, after the anchors had been lowered to the shallower coastal waters of Namibia and the sails were safely furled, they ate and played card games in the lamplight of the berth whilst listening to the wind grow stronger above. The steady breeze they'd had all day had become an irritable gale, blustering this way and that, trying to tug the ship and play with it like a child with its bath toy. It sounded bad below decks. No one said it, they dared not to speak the taboo in fear of it, but all knew what was coming– the air had been ripe for it as the day passed.

Before nightfall took away the light, Robertson appeared down the companionway and ordered all the sails to be struck from the masts and for the set of storm sails to be retrieved and rigged. With concern, all hands climbed the ladder to the deck with a nervousness not seen before. The air that circulated the ship was ominous and energised. Robertson then ordered the anchors to be winched home as he began to steer the ship from the coast and into the open sea. As light faded from the inky sky, he called out to them once more. 'Make haste everyone, tropical storms can be upon you before you know it. I will ring the bell when it's here.'

Night came and brought with it the harshest gales the group of city felons had ever felt. As they clambered about on deck, they held onto things with white-knuckled dread as the wind strengthened to a point where they could hear the taught ropes wobbling and the rigging squeaking angrily. The ship seemed alive; things whistled and whined, moaned and groaned in a ceaseless complaint. Soon the ship began to rock, but like nothing they had felt before; *Victoria* was *tipping* from side to side, as if she were on her very toes trying not to fall into the cold waters. The bell began to ring of its own accord and water splashed down through the hatches as *Victoria* netted a passing wave. If they thought they had faced choppy waters before, this was another level; suddenly the waters of the English Channel felt like a garden pond hardly touched by the elements. The waves began to rise higher, their ferocity becoming apparent as they smashed into the side of the ship so hard barrels knocked and rolled from below and their table and other objects were knocked to one side. With eyes wide and frightful, they heard a rumble of thunder incoming at great speeds.

Their small breeze of today was no more, it had been shoved to one side like a minor skirmish to make way for this meteorological warfare. Suddenly lightening cracked and split the sky with great white forks, and seconds after, thunder clapped and rumbled powerfully above as if it was trying to purge of this dense dark cloud that had smothered the clear blue; thick and dark and energised it was, like a run of free-flowing ever-changing electric tar. Rain lashed down on the deck with such a force it sounded as if it were trying to erode the wood into helpless smithereens, into splinters to be lost in an oblivion of tumbling waves and raucous currents. They were soaked within seconds. Yet amid the utter din, the captain began to ring the ship's bell as he had done that

Gabonese morning; although this time it sounded distant, quiet, overpowered by the sheer volume of a raging tropical storm.

It was the bell to hail the incoming storm, even though its call had become redundant. The storm had already arrived, turning the chilling chime into a more sinister sound.

Suddenly their ship no longer felt like a vessel they could master; a haven they could roam in. Now it was nothing more than a large piece of driftwood they were clinging to, driftwood constantly threatening to heel, to list; to be caught at unawares by a single force, a single wall of rolling curling water. At once they knew their storm sails were too late, and knew they were in for a long night.

Chapter Nineteen

Cacophony and mayhem– when living in the world's largest city they thought they knew the meanings of the words. With an ever-expanding population and industry revolutionising at such a rapid pace, it was hard to find peace amongst so much din. New machinery coughed and spluttered, chugging foul soot and pollutants into the streets, horses neighed and galloped giving the city its trademark Victorian clop and carriages rumbled as their wheels bumped through the winding maze. And then there were the people; working, drinking, shouting, talking; people grew knowing nothing but noise until they became accustomed to it. It came as no surprise that the people of London could barely be heard, with the lower classes just able to make a squeak.

The multiple sounds of an industrious developing city resonated with the hum and energy of a storm, with its buildings blanketing the ground like dark clouds, machinery cracking through it like lightning and the hum of people its droning thunder. It held a certain power, but that was just civilisation at work– as the crew clambered about the deck and yards they were enveloped by a new cacophony, a new mayhem; and they realised they barely even knew what those two words meant. This wasn't anything man-made– this was only nature. A ferocious and furious type of nature, and they were right in the centre of it.

The hull heeled to starboard as a wave crashed portside, ambling up the next rising swell. They struggled to find a footing, realising how awful this was. The rain was of nothing they had felt before, bucketing down in heavy bloated torrents, sheeting hither and thither by the aggressive howling winds. At first it came from the bow but changed course to starboard before whipping around at their backs. They were soaked through instantly with their hair tugging their heads and their wet clothes urgently trying to join the next gust.

Robertson was still yanking on the bell, drenched through to the bone. He yelled with manic eyes; his hair wild. '*We're too late!*' he exclaimed, '*leave the sails where they are! If we strike them now, we risk losing them or damaging the tophamper! Tighten stays and sails that have loosened! Reef the mainsail of all masts hard and rig the storm sails, trysails and storm jib aback! Rig everything aback! We need to tack! As fast as you can! Halyards are coming loose, stays are straining! We could lose a fucking mast!*' he grabbed hold of the stanchions to stay upright, '*deploy the sea anchor! Get the drogue! We need drag to slow us! Unfurl the spanker! We need stability! Put your backs into it, you scallywags! Cabin boy: secure all lifelines to stanchions! Pronto!*' The stem suddenly dropped as they rode down the back of a wave, only to be caught by another that crashed on the deck with an almighty force that caught Robertson at unawares. He flailed to the deck, and the others dropped too with the water cascading over them, then he was up again. '*Storm sails! Storm sails now! Rig the bastards and get the fuckers open! We need leverage else we'll be pushed back to the coast or capsize! Get to it! We must heave-to! We must ride this storm!*'

Joseph fell to his knees but looked up, squinting at the mainmast to see the sails loosening and wriggling free from their ropes, flapping loosely, eager to join the billowing winds. *We're too late! The storm sails should've already been rigged and eased!* He pushed himself to his feet, and immediately saw the deck needed bailing, seawater was flooding their area; *oh god where's the bailing buckets?!* The ship crashed into another wave and everything lurched forward, Joseph lost his footing and tumbled to the deck. He was just about to get to his feet when a wild wave slammed starboard, but the deck cut its peak, sending a heavy torrent of water across the deck. Its force was ferocious and washed him across the wood to the mainmast, coughing and spluttering. *Up Joseph! Get up!* Quickly he pushed himself back up, his legs shaking and his balance askew; the ship felt solid, the deck horizontal, yet he could not find a focal point at which he could stand and walk. The entire ship felt as if it were rolling on barrels and they were all trying to find any footing. It was hard to move yet alone work.

Suddenly there was a lurch and *Victoria* rose the next wave, crested it, then fell sharply into the dark trough where it sagged. Clinging to the mainmast, he glanced over to the foreyard and spotted two of the riggers already trimming the sail: unfurling the foresail slightly as had been ordered, as deckhands below controlled the halyards whilst others hoisted trysails and jibs up to them to rig using the capstan. '*Rig the jib aback remember! We need to make headway!*' he heard Robertson cry from the helm. He looked up to the sails of the mainmast he was at and saw a corner of the mainsail had freed and was flapping wildly, tugging at its lines, pulling more out and freeing it. At least it was doing that itself, it saved him a job. '*Quartermaster! Get that footloose under control!*'

'Aye-aye!' he yelled back, unsure whether he was heard above the cacophony of screaming winds and thrashing waves. Suddenly there was a tremendous crack and a blinding succession of white light as bolts zapped the waves again and again. Within seconds a shattering crack of thunder split the sky asunder like the sound of a great tree trunk ripping apart as it fell to the earth whence it came, and rumbled through the inky clouds with all the rage of a thrashing earthquake. The ship rocked and bucked with the water, fighting the stampede of white horses that reared at this alien wooden craft. Suddenly he blinked, *what was that?* A white glow began to emanate from the tip and ends of the mastheads and yards, a bright blue white that sparked from the tips of the wood, seeming to fizzle and crackle like fat dropping onto flames. Perplexed, he moved onward as quickly as he could and reached the pulleys and began to yank hard on the remaining halyards, his hands cold and his eyes bleary. With help from Billy and Tess they managed to wrangle the mainsail into submission and belay it as best as they could yet focus was hard to come by, and doubts were present when resting hope on a line of hempen rope.

'*Any 'ands!*' Benjamin cried from the mainyard as he tied the sail in tight. Joseph didn't even see him up there. '*I need em' up here to ease the trim o' this! Fore and mizzen sails need unfurling and reefing as well! Someone get the trysails for the main!*'

Joseph turned to Billy, '*I'll climb up! You get the storm sails!*' Billy nodded and ran for the hatchway when the ship tipped again, heeling hard to port. Falling to his knees, Joseph grappled for things to hold onto. He spluttered and wheezed, trying to make sense of it all.

'*Any hands!*' Benjamin hollered again. When he opened his stinging eyes a film of water ran over his hands, rolling back toward the bulwark and tipping over the railing. Then *Victoria* tottered again, leaning starboard as she veered, descending into another deep trough. Thankfully, the ship no longer felt completely wild; the trysails and jib of the foremast were easing the rabidity and keeping *Victoria* to the wind instead of against it. Nevertheless, she still was a long way from being controlled. He could feel gravity on him, grappling for a purchase in which to yank him over the side too. Joseph gulped a mouthful of salt water and cursed the pissy brine; fear took hold as the ship heeled harder and crashed, hogging over another ten-footer.

'*Where's those lifelines Rob?!*' Joseph heard the captain bawl, '*Forget the bailing, lifelines are more important! Get to it! That's an order! Joseph! Get your arse off the floor and give Smith a fucking hand! Mills! James! Penning! Get to that mizzensail footloose and secure it before it tears the spars from the mast then get the trysails up and open! They're the priority!*' With a struggle, he got to his feet again and moved with the motion of the rocking ship, but it was different than the normal sailing; he needed more than just sea-legs to stay upright now. What he needed were fins and a flipper, that would be the only way to escape this havoc.

Rain and hail pounded his back and the wind tore at his clothes, wrestling with his weight and balance to try and knock him over but he fought back and made it to the shrouds and began to climb the ratlines for the mainyard. Suddenly the black nebulous clouds smote the sea again with a grand bolt of lightning, forking and splitting as it searched for sinners in the waves, giving him a chance to see a flicker of this raging storm and the almighty waves rising and curling and crashing into each other in a swirling torrent of foam. Then it all went black. Thunder exploded and grumbled through the lofty abyss, threatening to splinter the sky into shards. *'Joseph!'* a voice called just as he began his white-knuckled ascent. Snatching a look down he spotted Rob at the bottom holding out a line of rope. *God bless that lad.* Jumping back down to the deck he took the rope and began to tie it around his waist. *'Clove hitch!'* the lad cried, holding onto the bulwark for stability with water streaming down his face and the wind tugging at his wet hair, *'tie a clove hitch!'* he handed him another length of line, although Joseph wasn't sure why.

The sky lit up again and a great streak of white with three prongs erupted from the sky, bending and twisting jaggedly to reach the dark waters below. Within a second it had vanished, disappeared, but as soon as it had thunder exploded overhead in a rumbling clap that sounded more akin to a triggered bomb, and the obsidian sky crackled with energy from above and yonder, snapping and fizzling as if the clouds were alive and trying to tear themselves apart with their internal turmoil. Joseph had never heard anything like it before, had never seen anything of such ferocity and malevolence. These were only elements and yet it felt as though they had their own emotions; the air felt enraged, the winds blasting a white fury.

He found himself hearing his mother's voice again, telling him whenever there was a storm *'God's reminding people of His powers,'* she'd say, *'and how easy it is to smite the sinners.'* He gulped, believing his mother even more so now and suddenly hoping his sins were not bad enough for him to be smitten. Nearly losing his footing again, Joseph tied a clove hitch as best as he could and pulled himself up the shrouds, gripping the line with his life. He knew as well as the rest of them that one false move meant death. If anyone went overboard now, that would be it. Absolution. Oblivion. The waves would take them without even a splash.

Pulling himself through the lubber's hole and onto the main-yard, the blue streaks still jittering from the tips, he shimmied along its sturdiness. To his astonishment, Benjamin was already a good way into adjusting its trim, and he realised why Rob had given him an extra length of rope. The quartermaster abruptly realised then that this old sailor, scarred and lacking a few teeth (and wits), had been up here in a violent storm without one length of rope to save him from a fall. One slip and he'd be gone, one false move; and Benjamin knew that, but he didn't care. His priority was the welfare of their vessel, as, if the ship went down, then it was taking everyone with it. Joseph shimmied faster and handed over the life-line. '*Ben!*' he yelled above the howling wind, '*lifeline!*'

The old man looked surprised to see him so scared, as if he didn't even notice there was a storm raging around them. He grinned, '*Thank'ee Joseph, my lad!*' he took it and tied the hitch without even thinking. '*The sea, she's got a bit of grit with her tonight, an't she? My type of woman!*' he laughed, and quickly held onto the mast as another great wave tore over the deck as if it were only driftwood.

Joseph forced his mind to let go of the yard so he could help with the knots, but he struggled, and his hands dismissed all orders. He clung on, wondering why on earth he climbed up here in the first place. There had been other jobs to do, why did he think the yards and sails were a safe point of call to attend? The rain hammered down on him, his hair slick and waving in the wind, his body assaulted by sheets of wild hail. Squeezing his eyes shut he tried to let go of the yard, and slowly prised his fingers from the wood and wrapped his legs around in a vice to reach out to the reef-points to loosen them for the deckhands below to tighten with the halyards. The thrashing sail knocked against the mast in a frenzy; the stays weakening under so much pressure. The gooseneck swivelled and moved with the tumult.

'*Did ye see the fire?*' Benjamin called from the other end. The ship creaked and groaned as it tilted once more, heeling hard to port and making them grip on.

The hell is he talking about?! 'What fire?!' he exclaimed, sure that a flame could not take hold whilst the deck was awash. Had lightning struck *Victoria*?

'*Why, Saint Elmo's Fire, lad! The white flame of thunder!*'

Joseph looked round to him, rain streaming down his face. His fingers were white and numb, he was shivering; he didn't even realise how cold he was. '*What are you talking about?!*'

'*The white glow at the end of the masts and yards!*' the old sailor cried, grinning, '*tis' the light of ol' Elmo that is! Only the hardiest of storms will spark a 'fire Elmo's flame!*' Suddenly, as if on cue, a stupendous streak of forked white electric flashed a mile away, its blinding illumination offering a chance to glimpse the monstrous waves that rolled and yawned; spray from their peaks reaching and falling over their backs like fans ejecting from the head of a waking dragon spewing white foam.

Then the thunder boomed and crackled relentlessly, sending shockwaves through the troubled clouds. '*Elmo's fire only appears in a hearty thunderstorm, it's a good omen Quart'master! A good omen for us poor scallywags climbing these Dover Cliffs!*' the sailor hollered repeating himself, '*no need to fret, this'uns a safe storm!*'

Joseph let go of the yard again, realising he was clinging to it. Reaching for the reef-point rope, he loosened another, feeling the sail ease slightly and tighten as the halyards were heaved, and shuffled along to work on another. *How in the name of blessed Virgin Mary is this a good storm?!* 'Now an't the time for superstitions Ben! Now's the time for bloody prayers!' he shouted back.

The seadog laughed. '*Now is the perfick time for superstitions; work ain't the only thing that's a 'gonna get us through this, belief is too, my lad! Have faith!*' They finished trimming the sail and the trysails were hauled to them by the capstan where they immediately began to work on rigging it. It was a small, robust triangular sail, much sturdier than the normal set, and Joseph could see why these were needed. It didn't take long to hoist them with Benjamin singing Blow the Man Down, and they climbed up to the topsail to rig the storm sail upon it. Benjamin, he saw, was grappling with the free corner, trying to control it to no avail. It needed tightening using the halyard he could see . . . on deck. All other deckhands were now working on the mizzen sails. *'I got this matey, you head on down and gis' a tug on the line to tighten this bugger!'* There was no argument needed. He nodded and shimmied along the topsail yard to the shrouds where he began to descend.

Victoria screeched and reeled against the waves, seeming to fight against them and pull her weight away from the brunt of the impact of the incoming swells. Starboard bow lowered, portside lifted, then portside bow lowered and starboard rose before the bow raised, lowered and crashed into another trough where water deluged the deck and everyone on it. Despite the carnage, the ship was seeming to slow and become harnessed, stabilising from the set of storm sails, yet it was no less enjoyable sailing in the thick of a raging storm.

Joseph clambered down to the maintop platform, through the lubber's hole and down the shrouds with knuckles white and clenched. Spying through bleary eyes, he looked out to the helm on the quarterdeck where Robertson heaved and fought with the wheel as he tried to tack, spinning it to loosen her, then pulling it back to reel her in, zigzagging through the countering winds. The sky suddenly lit up and flashed in white bursts within the clouds, one here; another there, attempting to brighten the fury and break the cycle, but instead making them look ever-more sinister. He bit his tongue and climbed lower, his stomach flipping and dancing the grandest piece of Russian ballet; sea sickness returning in a plague. *Oh no,* he thought he'd managed to master the ailment, but this was not just any sea they were sailing, and the waves were too much to handle.

A great torrent of water slammed against his back then, pressing him into the shrouds with a tremendous force and within a minute it had passed leaving him dripping and shivering harder, clinging to the ratlines like washed up flotsam; a rat thrown down the drain. With a heavy foot he thudded to the deck and tried to walk but he fell to his knees, his stomach crunching, stretching, lurching and rising until it had to expel its contents. He vomited hard, his spew mixing with the seawater and running around his hands, running to the bulwark awaiting a bailing bucket.

With effort, he pushed himself to his feet and wiped his sicky mouth before running over to the halyard, his legs feeling as flimsy as a flower stem. He grappled with the line and began to pull, looking up to the mast, to the topsail yard where Benjamin was still fighting the canvas. The tip of the mast and ends of the yards had begun to glow again, white at first and then a bright blue like before, giving a faint ghostly light to the ship. Rain spattered in his eyes but still he pulled the line and glanced up to see the old sailor grinning against the light of the flashing clouds as he tightened the corner. Perhaps he was right, perhaps now was the perfect time for superstitions. Joseph hoisted the halyard harder and Benjamin Smith finally tied in the corner. 'Good omen it is.' He said as he belayed the halyard to the pin, feeling the deck roll beneath him, making him cling to the line for dear life.

Another wave came crashing down, beating the wood harshly. The ship creaked loudly as it heeled starboard, turning with the velocity of the ebb. Joseph grappled harder and held it tightly to him. Other crew members, he couldn't see who they were, had also stopped what they were doing to hold on. From the corner of his eye, he saw Robertson battling with the wheel, struggling and swearing, and suddenly losing his grip. It spun from his hands and he stumbled to the deck as the spanker slapped from left to right. The effects were instantaneous; the vessel was freed and began to amble to and fro, three sheets to the wind, waiting for the next wave to carry it asunder.

Wide-eyed, he bolted aft, slipped on the ladder, picked himself up and was thrown to the bulwark, where he held on tight, then leapt onto the wheel that spun uncontrollably. Planting his feet firm, he snatched the wheel and halted its movement, and began to heave with a might he never knew he had. Yet the ship fought back and made it difficult for him to grip, keeping him on his toes as the spanker swung sharply. The force the wheel had was insurmountable as the wild currents below wrestled him for the rudder; his arms burned, he clenched his jaw and tried to focus but it became too much. It was like trying to hold onto the waves beneath, to grasp the raging current with nothing but two weak hands. Once his fingers began to bend and he screamed did he release it and collapse to the deck, but the wheel still spun. Back on his feet he caught it again and pulled it back, heaving it around before reaching for the rope to lash it, but the current was strong, not letting him. He let it go again and caught it. Soon, he grasped the mechanics of it and understood why the captain's arms had given out.

Suddenly the man was beside him, his voice competing with the howling gales. '*I'll take this, you get that sea anchor and drogue out there! We need drag to slow us before we're thrown from these Dover Cliffs!*'

He nodded and passed the wheel over as smoothly as possible and darted back down the ladder and down the companionway to the hold to grab their sea anchor and drogue. Heaving himself back up the stairs and to the bow, he tied the sea anchor with a thick rope and tossed it overboard before rushing along the ship to the stern and tying the drogue to another thick rope and throwing it over. Immediately the ship began to slow enough to allow Robertson to lash the wheel to keep them on a straighter course.

He nodded to Joseph, '*Good man! Let's help bail!*' They clambered down to the main deck to help Billy, Dave and Tess bailing and Hugh with the snapped running rigging lines. Robertson joined Hugh with the lines as Hugh cried to Joseph with blue lips and white fingers, '*ahoy matey! We're fine here! You grab the bailer and get some water off the deck! Me and Capt' have got these knots!*' Joseph did as he was told and grabbed the other bailer and tried his best but it was a near pointless exercise, there was too much water entering the ship for him to match it, yet the mechanics were brutal and the more they caught the more the ship heeled to the lower side.

Immediately he could see they were near exhaustion, as he was. Wet and bedraggled they were, they looked miserable and tired with their cold hands fumbling as they dropped their bailers and tried to tie lines back together. '*Joseph bloody Winter!*' Billy yelled to be heard over the sound of the rumbling thunder, *'next time y' thinking of a nice little adventure to go a'lookin' for treasure you can bloody well pass my invite on!'* he smiled and chuckled half-jokingly and half serious.

Hours droned on with the exhausted crew labouring throughout the darkness and the rainfall and thunder; freezing and fatigued, but maintenance was the top priority and could not be set aside. The ship was their lifeline.

Eventually the cracks and splits of lightening became internal, only flashing within their cloudy cocoons and the thunder gradually degraded into a dull grumbling drone in the distance. Only the winds and rain persevered on their elemental course, intent on continuation but even this felt like a relief compared to what they'd had to face. Soon the clouds displayed a tint of grey to their bleak surface and began to lighten and break little by little, disintegrating as if the storm's energy had burnt itself out; its fuel now only mere embers scattering to the wind. The waves no longer wore their crowns of spray and rolled underneath the ship instead of aiming for the deck and the harsh gales subdued to a fresh wind. Soon the clouds returned to their natural rounding white-washed grey, taking back their cumulus form yet still dousing the sea with rain. After last night however, this felt like a light sprinkle. As they wandered about on deck, they relished the gentle patter on their skin after the night's bombardment.

'All hands to deck!' announced the captain from the helm, his voice hoarse. One by one they plodded their way to the base of the quarterdeck and looked up gormlessly with tired sunken eyes.

He viewed them all and slipped a bowline around a rung then stood up to the railing. 'Everyone accounted for, Quartermaster?'

Joseph nodded, 'Aye. No one lost but you have a very wet, tired and hungry crew.'

'Indeed. All of you can go and get something to eat and dry yourselves off as much as you can and, on your return, the sails can be unfurled so we can see their state.' He smiled tiredly, 'Firstly, though, allow me to congratulate you all on surviving that storm. It an't an easy task by any means and it's a tough test for any experienced sailor, yet alone a crew on their maiden voyage. You all did well on keeping her upright and afloat,' he rubbed the dripping wooden railing, 'And young Hare, good job with those lifelines; done to a turn, my boy. Now go and get out of this rain for a time and return ready for duty.'

Rob nodded tiredly and smiled, soaked through to the bone.

They all filed down into the berth and dried themselves off, changed into dry clothes and broke their fast amongst the scattered possessions. If their rocking stomachs permitted it. An hour passed before Joseph ascended the companionway back to the weather deck, forcing food down his neck. The oaten biscuits were stale, the handful of nuts were soft, and the salted fish were too salty. Not exactly the tastiest of breakfasts; everything was salty. Salt, salt, salt. He was beginning to grudge the flavour; every bit of meat was coated in the stuff to keep it from rotting; the fresh food had been eaten a long time ago and stores were gradually lowering to a point where they were breaking into the reserves and needed new stock. He hoped Madagascar offered some, if any, food. *That's if we can hold out to Madagascar. We'll have to cast our nets back in the sea or try rowing out to catch anything bigger.* The chances were a long shot, but a long shot chance seemed hopeful when everyone aboard was beginning to starve. *It shouldn't get to that . . . I hope.*

Rain dappled his dry shirt and waistcoat; it was only a shower now, but it felt as if it was hardly raining compared to last night. He spun and found the captain still wet and hungry afore *Victoria* looking to the horizon with his spyglass upon the forecastle. Walking up beside him, he stood in silence. Robertson had given up with smoothing back his hair now and instead let it hang wet and loose down to his shoulders. 'I brought you some fish.' Joseph spoke up.

The captain seemed to not hear him and jumped when he saw Joseph beside. 'Sorry? Ah, lovely, thank you. I'll be down in a minute.' He said distantly.

'Everything alright?'

Still peering through the spyglass, he replied, 'ah erm, not exactly. I can't seem to find the coastline. Nothing to fret, it is still cloudy and raining after all but it's just . . . ah, concerning.'

He looked to him blankly, 'are we lost?'

'I wouldn't say lost . . . let's just go with *misplaced* for now. The storm's blown us off course but as soon as the sun comes out, which should be soon, I can get a reading with the backstaff.' The captain turned away and headed to his cabin.

'Nothing to worry about, are you sure?' Joseph asked nervously.

Robertson paused before he replied, almost as if he were searching for the right answer to give and gave a nod. 'Nothing to worry about.' He turned and thudded along the deck to his cabin.

Standing alone in the drizzle, he pursed his lips indignantly and chewed on a stale oat biscuit, one of the last few not to be harbouring its own wriggling stowaways or wearing a wealthy coat of mouldy fur. Upon the hull and bow, the waves rocked the ship, and after last night he felt sensitive to the motion. Standing against the railings he peered out to the bowsprit and stopped chewing as another wave of nausea ebbed through him. Fighting it, he swallowed the mouthful and forced himself to take another bite.

Fatigue racked his body, every movement ached and his mind felt as if it was in a rowboat, bobbing and ready to float and drift away with the current. Everything lagged, and he could feel the beginnings of a headache pulsating behind his eyes in a sharp needle-like pain. When he was changing clothes, he noticed distinguished bones rising against his skin; he hadn't been eating the most nourishing of meals of late, and what had been eaten was few and far between. He leaned on the wood and groaned, pinching his nose as another wave of queasiness came.

Trying to take his mind off his roiling stomach, he decided to walk the ship and check for damages and hinderances. True, Victoria was the boatswain but as quartermaster he'd learned the role too and kept a check on what to look for.

Masts? All were sturdy and tall; *looks fine but we'll check the turnbuckles for the tension of the stays. Mainsails an't open yet, so I can't check them. No doubt there'll be some rips that need sewing.*

Spanker's got a tear that needs mending. Rigging? He wandered to the lines of each three masts, running and standing, and found some were loose or had snapped, and some of the belaying pins had broken and had released their lines. The fife rails were fine, which was more of a relief since they were supporting the masts. There were some spare pins in the hold, so there was no trouble there and the lines could be tied back together or replaced. The stays were loose, strained in their turnbuckles, but this could be easily remedied.

To his disappointment, their boxes and barrels they kept on deck to serve as a short cut to produce had been washed away by the storm. The cask of cheap ale was gone too, much to his disapproval. *Netting?* It usually hung on hooks on the mast for when they fished, but he found only empty hooks. *Buggar, there goes the chances of fishing for something fresh.* There were three lines and two hooks left down in the hold though; they hadn't used them, but they needed checking too. All in all, they had been successful having never faced a storm before, yet his mood only dampened at their prospects. He returned to the forecastle and tried to keep his mind off starvation by looking out to the blank horizon. Land was nowhere in sight. It was open for miles and miles, a vast expanse of undulating, daunting water. They were isolated, and he guessed then that Robertson had lied.

Perhaps now was the time to worry.

Compass, where's my compass? He suddenly remembered and began to pat his pocket when he heard a seabird call from overhead, flying through the rain, floating on warm air currents. Looking up to it, he wished for his own set of wings to soar over the waves and be free. A fish was in its bright beak, he spotted, dangling helplessly, but it was fresh, and Joseph found himself scowling with envy that it would taste of fish instead of salt. It flew overhead from stern to stem and beelined through the air from the bowsprit, knowing exactly where it was heading. He narrowed his eyes. *Why not just eat the damn fish out at sea? Why carry it?* The bird's selfless act then dawned on him, and he dashed to the captain's cabin as quickly as his trembling legs could manage.

Within an hour and after a haste they were not fond of, the exhausted crew struck the storm sails and stored them away safely before making the necessary checks of their stations. They then unfurled the sails, tied the lines and spun the wheel, hauling *Victoria* around to follow the path of the seabird on its return journey. Sailing against the current was nasty and the waves chopped up the starboard hull making the ride a bumpy one but before long, land was sighted from the crow's nest and they cheered tiredly. Closing in on the coast, they dropped anchors to the shallower waters to wait for the breaking of the clouds to determine their position from the sun.

Unfortunately, the rain persisted for a further four hours, of which the crew snatched the window to rest. Remnants of storms were always hard to rid of, Robertson told them, and after a storm like that the blankets of cloud and rains that followed were akin to a rash that formed after strokes of pain. Their fortunes were favourable though, and the rain eventually stopped at two hours past noon. The sky began to lighten enough for the seams to split and the blanket to tear revealing a crystalline blue underneath, cleansed by the great white sphere that perched at its apex in the middle of the sky.

They'd all heard the saying to be careful on what to wish upon, and now they felt the gravity of its truth; their wish for dry and warm weather had been bestowed but the consequences were harsher than they'd prepared for. As soon as the sun had a chance to peep through the cracks and sweep the clouds away, a searing tropical heat scorched the ship drying everything in an instant, leaving a layer of white crusty salt on all surfaces that needed brushing and sweeping before it weakened the wood. Within half an hour it was unbearable to be exposed in sunlight and not a drop of water lasted long; the lashing rain of the night now was nothing more than a faint memory left for questioning. Their battered bodies dried coarsely thanks to the salt and burned quicker; those that had been called upon to brush the salt away now cursed their naivety as their blind ignorance in the sky above seared all memories of the chaos of the night. Clouds were what they called for now, water; it was a blanket of grey they wistfully dreamed of to shelter them from this brutal torment.

Only one evaded the pessimism– the man who held the backstaff atop the forecastle. He lowered the large odd-looking object from his eye and shoulder and licked his dry lips, checking the angle and calculation to be sure. His beard had dried and was now crispy, as was his hair, and his voice was dry and crackling when he called out to them. 'After all the time we cursed and damned the storm last night, we were mistaken; if anything, it's done us a favour. A blessing in disguise so it was. If the backstaff is telling it true we're now nearing the bottom of South Africa.' He smiled at the irony of realising where they were, 'we're rounding the Cape of Good Hope. The storm has pushed us further than I expected. Madagascar is not too far away. My crew, we have crossed the hemisphere and two continents together and you know what that calls for?'

Heads looked up at him expectantly, too tired to answer.

'Rum.' He said, putting his hat back on. 'Let's crack it open.'

His idea was shared and agreed upon; no one could deny a cup of rum after their trauma. As they headed down to the hold, Joseph couldn't help but to think back to the peace and solitude of Gabon's beach and how blissful it would be to lie down in the shade and enjoy a rest. *You won't be the only one on that beach my old possum, eyes will be watching, you know that.* He followed the rest of the crew and stood amongst the emptying barrels and strewn boxes, piles of moulding straw and skittering rats, and picked a cup and had a tot poured into it. He took a sip and sighed. Despite the heat of day, the warmth of alcohol running through their bodies felt almost soothing and their aches and pains were numbed, if only for a little while.

Suddenly a voice called out amongst them. 'To Harold Arms. A fine sailor. A fine friend.' Dave toasted, raising his cup.

Cups raised in unison. 'To Harold Arms,' they all repeated, and they drank to the poor soul left behind. Although as Joseph looked about the hold to the empty barrels, stale food and maggots, stench of salt and decay, the scuttling rats and malnutrition and knowing of the hardships to come, he wondered if Harold Arms had been a poor soul after all. For what was to come he didn't know who to pity more; Harold or themselves. He finished his rum and quickly left the stuffy air of the hold to the heavy air of the deck and began to rig the jibboom upon the bowsprit, unable to stand amongst the crew whilst they were in such a debilitated state. If he let it get to him, guilt racked through and made him see those people differently; more as victims snared in his ploy for a better life. *His* ploy. This was not what he had promised them. He knew it, even if he couldn't bring himself to admit it– this was not a better life.

After what they had been through and what they knew was to come, London seemed comforting, pleasurable; the haven they regretted leaving and, as Joseph made to unfurl the foresail and foretopsail, he found himself angrily missing his hometown. He closed his eyes and suddenly craved the smell of horse shit and coal smoke as he walked out of his front door, out to pilfer the goods from those more fortunate, and to drink cheap ale with others who'd managed to reach adulthood in such destitution and squalor, others who still managed to smile despite the injustice of the world. *Instead I led those people out of that and into this; to be burnt crispy by the sun, starved and exhausted and killed. I can't tell which is better anymore. I've shanghaied them, bonneted the lot of them to a worser fate.*

As the crew ambled back up to the main deck, a silent tension befell them; again, they were entering another hardship, except this time they knew not of its end. Where the next port was or how far they were to their next checkpoint, none could guess. And there was now the issue of netting– they had none, which meant fishing had to be done using hook and line in the longboat when the ship was stationary, either that or row out to hunt which none knew how to do. Joseph sighed and directed his gaze to the blue horizon. *Keep hoping, that's the only way we can pull through this.* Hope was something he had to hold onto, but it would not feed him or water him and was not an entirely sustainable and supportive source on which to lean on. Nervously, he gulped.

After an hour of preparations and maintenance in which the stays were adjusted, broken belaying pins were replaced and the rips in the sails were sewn, the forestaysail and inner jib were rigged, they sailed into the afternoon hours hoping to progress with their heading.

Crashing up the stem, waves split in two as the ship ploughed onward to the Cape of Good Hope, expecting to round it by sunset and join the warm Agulhas current. Everyone was exhausted at their stations, just about managing to stay on their feet and remain as alert as they could be after their long night. They tried to sound enthusiastic, but fatigue wrung them like a wet towel and revealed their enthusiasm as nothing more than false positivity; a deceiving smile was all they managed, and even the captain looked drained. Still, he offered a warm smile to Joseph as he climbed to the helm and slapped him on the back as he steered. 'You've a keen eye, Mister Winter. A seabird carrying fish is a seabird going home. You know, despite your urban background you're quite the sailor.'

Joseph eyed the deck and nodded with a pale face, 'thank'ee Jim, but after last night's fiasco I feel like I'm back at square one.' He said weakly.

He chuckled, 'That was a rough bastard, storm's like that can rattle your bones and if you an't careful, can break them and worse. Count yourself lucky you've only got seasickness to live with. Go and get some ginger if you an't feeling up to dick.'

'We're low on food, I can't take more.'

'And *you* are low on strength lad, go and get some.'

With a following churn of his stomach, he obliged and descended into the hold to find the remnants of ginger they had left to suck on. He searched through the shadows and found the sack against the side, tucked behind empty barrels that still smelled of Lisbon's port, and picked out a stick, breaking it into the smallest of amounts.

Suddenly footsteps creaked down the stairs, a pair of them, and hushed voices accompanied the approach. Even though there was nowhere to hide, and Joseph knew everyone aboard this vessel, he instinctively ducked behind barrels and stared into the gloom; sensing that the pair did not want to be heard. He clutched at his ginger and listened.

'*What do you reckon then?*' a man whispered.

A woman replied, '*Not yet. We've got give it time. Things like this can't be rushed.*'

'*Look, there's a time between slack and haste and if you didn't notice we almost bloody well died last night after that storm! Who knows what could happen next?*'

'*I'll tell you what will happen next; we'll be thrown off this creaking tub and keelhauled! I don't know about you, but I don't know how to swim, so unless you fancy trying something new you wait for me until the time is right. Preparation is key to these sorts of things.*'

'*Oh, I'm sure you've pulled off many a mutiny in your day.*'

'*You'd be surprised at what I've managed to pull off, what I've managed to execute, who I've managed to fool.*' The woman whispered with a hint of pride.

'*And yet you still ended up in the same place we all wound up. Prison bars an't impressed easily, nor do they cater for criminals clever or stupid; they can listen to your tales of success or woe, but they still shut you in all the same.*' The man replied, and Joseph couldn't help but agree with him. It sounded like something he would say.

'*Maybe I wasn't in there because I slipped up on a job or was in the wrong place at the wrong time. Maybe I was in there because I wanted to be in there.*'

'*Eh? You got thrown in on purpose?*'

There was a pause. He desperately wanted to turn and find out who was talking but he dared not. A rat scurried around the barrels; the sound made them anxious.

'*Just wait until I tell you all is ready.*' She hissed hurriedly, '*and when the time comes, we'll overthrow this skiff and dump the corpses overboard. Come on, let's get back to work before we're missed.*' The footsteps could be heard again, and the quartermaster quickly peered over the barrels to see feet disappearing up the stairs. Bare feet; they'd taken off their shoes. He bit his lip, that was what Trace used to do when he wanted to not be heard.

Sweating, he lowered back to the floor. Talk of mutiny, he never expected it. Not after what he'd given them all. *What have you given them though?* Although, there was a part of him that was angrier at himself for not seeing it– after all, wasn't he meant to be the master criminal turned seadog? Wasn't he the ghost, the man that never left a trace? He rubbed his face and wished to be that great man again, to be respected as a man of trickery, deceit, light fingers and light feet. Instead here he was listening to talk of treachery by the very people he had recruited and decided to trust, and by the sounds of it this had not been the first meeting. He had become the fool, something he never thought would happen. *Bastards, the whole bloody lot of them. They deserve the toils. Let them work.*

He got to his feet, placed the ginger on his dry tongue to suck, and looked around the murk at the shadows of emptiness, the place where they'd first captured Johnson the boatswain, where they'd turned the captain to their cause. *What do I do now?* Tell the captain? Interrogate the crew, expose the rats and punish them? He sighed. Mad Vinny had burned him before in his own hometown; these brash snakes were not going to burn him out here. Something had to be done, but he wasn't sure what. Spying the row of muskets, he saw two absent spaces. *Wait, two?* Joseph remembered Robertson throwing his musket to the sea, but the other . . .

The mutineers had been plotting, planning, gathering followers and collecting information . . . and were armed. It seemed they had been doing more than simple work on watch. Whoever was behind all this, they had been playing a role perfectly. *Now I must too,* he thought, *I've got to get them before they begin their mutiny. But I can't do it alone.* Suddenly he found himself back where he was at the beginning of this venture– indecisive of who to trust, playing everything carefully. Perhaps he had been too slack with his peers; they were convicted criminals after all. Just as he was. Enemies were aboard this ship, that much was now clear.

Walking to the rack, he picked a pistol from the wall, the gunpowder and primer and slipped a dagger into his belt for extra security. He quickly primed the pistol, loaded it and went up to his hammock where he slipped it under his pillow. The dagger he kept. Safety on the ship was no longer paramount, not when some were spending more time plotting than knotting.

Suddenly his ears pricked up to screaming on deck. High of pitch, it aroused immediate reaction. *Oh god, the mutiny . . . it's started!* Snatching the pistol, he launched himself up the stairs, ready to fight, ready to die. Ready for whatever this journey had to throw at him next.

Glossary

Victorian slang, phrases and insults:

Apple lady – a hard cider.

Back slang it – to go out the back of a dwelling.

Beer and skittles – to have a good time.

Benjo – a busy day in the streets.

Betty fang – to thrash or beat.

Bitch the pot – another term for pour the tea.

Bit o' jam – another term for a pretty woman.

Bonneted – to have your hat pulled down over your eyes: a popular joke in Victorian times.

Bricky – to be brave or fearless.

Cabbaging – another term for stealing.

Chignon – a type of woman's hairstyle where the hair is pinned to the back of the neck or the back of the head. There were many variations of the style, but a basic chignon was popular in Victorian times.

Chin music – a conversation.

Chuckaboo – another term for a close friend.

Cop a mouse – another term for a black eye.

Comforter – an old-fashioned term for a scarf.

Collie-shangles – another term for arguments.

Cupid's kettle drums – another term for breasts.

Damfino – unsure of what is it about e.g "damned if I know."

Dash my wig! – a term of exclamation.

Dance upon nothing – to be hanged at the gallows.

Dip – a type of candle.

Don't sell me a dog – another way of saying "don't lie to me".

Dog days – the hottest days of the year.

Done to a turn – something has been completed satisfactorily.

Evening wheezes – false news, another term for newspapers.

Fancy girl – another term for prostitute.

Flapdoodle – a sexually incompetent man or woman.

Foozler – a clumsy person.

Fresh fish – a new recruit.

Frousy – another word for tatty or unkempt.

Gibface – an ugly person.

Gigglemug – a smiling face.

Got the morbs – temporary melancholy; sadness or depressed.

Going down the line – going to a brothel.

Grinning at the daisy roots – a term for death, six feet under.

Hard case – someone who is rough and tough.

Hedge-cropper – another term for a prostitute.

Horizontal refreshments – another term for sex.

Hornswoggler – a fraud or cheat.

Hook it – to tell someone to leave or move, another way of saying "be off with you!"

Hornets – another term for bullets.

Hunky Dorey – another term for terrific.

Jonah – a person believed to be jinxed or hexed.

Jollocks – a fat person.

Kenned – 'ken,' to know something.

Kith and kin – one's relatives.

Killing the canary – shirking or avoiding work.

Links – coarsely made torches that lined the streets in Victorian times before the installation of electric streetlamps.

London Mud – the streets of London during Victorian times were clogged with waste from horse and human alike that has now become known as the London Mud.

Make a stuffed bird laugh – another term for preposterous.

Meater – a coward.

Mumbling-cove – a shabby person.

Mutton-shunter – a policeman.

Nanty-narking – another term for great fun.

Neck oil – beer or alcohol.

Oil of gladness – an alcoholic beverage.

Old Scratch – a nickname for the Devil.

Open the hall – to begin a battle or fight.

Orf chump – to have no appetite.

Pigeon-livered – another term for cowardly.

Podsnappery – a person ignoring problems in belief they're too good to sort them out.

Poked up – another term for embarrassed.

Possum – a best friend or buddy.

Poxy – cursed.

Ratbag – a general term of abuse.

Riding a Dutch gal – to consort with a prostitute.

Robin – a young child beggar.

Shin plasters – paper money, pound notes.

Shoot into the brown – to fail.

Skedaddle – to run away fast.

Skilmalink – shady and doubtful, secretive behaviour.

That's the ticket – the proper thing to do.

Tickle one's innards – to have a drink.

Tight as a boiled owl – another term for drunk.

Uppity – a person who believes they're above their station in life.

Up the pole – another term for drunk.

Vazey – another term for stupid.

Wagtail – a promiscuous woman.

Walk-er! – a cockney expression of astonishment or surprise.

Welch wig – a cap knitted from smooth yarn.

Wooden spoon – an idiot.

Billy's Irish slang and phrases:

Acting the maggot – to be a fool.

Batter ya – to beat someone up.

Chancer – a dodgy character, manipulative for their own gain.

Clean on – another term for good looking.

Craic – to have a good time.

Cut to the onions/to the bone – to be fed up.

Doin' a number – to cause discomfort, upset or stress.

Drobes – another term for bits and pieces.

Eejits – another way of saying idiots.

Gas – a laugh, someone or something funny.

Hatchet – another term for brilliant.

Head like a bag of spuds – stupid or ugly.

I could eat the twelve apostles – I'm very hungry.

In tatters – to destroy or be destroyed.

Kicked and booted – to assault or be assaulted.

Knackered – I'm exhausted.

Layin' boots – to kick someone whilst they are already down.

Like a blind cobbler's thumb – something ugly or messed up.

Mad as a box of frogs – crazy.

Muppet – a fool.

Noodle – describing a head.

On the lash – to go out drinking.

Poormouthing – to talk bad about someone or something.

Racked – I'm exhausted.

Rawny – describing a delicate man.

Rumbly – dodgy job or person.

Sell the eye outta' your head – a persuasive salesman.

Shebang – the whole thing.

Sticking out – another term for doing well.

Stook – an idiot or fool.

Ship, nautical terms and phrases:

A.B.S – able bodied sailor. The backbone of the ship, they were expected to have knowledge and experience in all areas. When this was called, this meant anyone on deck.

Aback – when there is a strong headwind, to rig the sails aback means to brace them the opposite side in order to catch the wind to reduce speed. This is done to assist in tacking and heaving-to when there is extreme weather during a storm.

Abaft – toward the stern, the rear of the ship.

Afore – the front end of the ship.

Aft – the rear end of the ship.

Ahoy – a cry to draw attention aboard a vessel.

Aloft – to be in the rigging or above, to not be on deck.

Anchor – a heavy object used to slow or stop a vessel's movement, usually in the shape of a hooked plough.

Anchors aweigh – this term is meant to be said when the anchor has cleared the seabed and is no longer anchored.

Anchor ball – a small black floating object that indicates the ship is still anchored.

Anchor home – when the anchor has been winched above the water allowing the vessel free movement.

Anchor winch – a small capstan that is used to winch the anchor up from the seabed.

Argosy – a type of merchant ship.

Aye-aye – a reply to an order to confirm the order has firstly been heard and secondly will be carried out.

Avast – to stop or cease what is being done.

Backstaff – a navigational instrument used to measure the altitude of a celestial body, such as the sun or moon.

Backstay – a stay or cable reaching to all the mastheads from the foremast to the mainmast and the mizzenmast, which then runs down into the lower rigging. This stay supports all masts of the ship beyond the forestay.

Belay – to fasten a line around a fixed fitting such as a cleat or pin.

Belaying pins – a removeable wooden pin in a rail which running rigging and standing rigging are fastened to.

Bend – a knot used to join two ropes together, or to attach a line to a fixed object.

Berth – the deck where hammocks and bunks are stowed and hung, where the crew sleep.

Bilge – the bottom flooring of the ship.

Blow the Man Down – a classic sea shanty sung to give motivation.

Blue Peter flag – a flag that indicates a ship is about to sail.

Bulwark – the railing of the ship; the sides above the level of the deck.

Boatswain – the role on the ship charged with supervision of duties, maintenance and inspection of sails and rigging as well as supply stores. The Boatswain also is charged with deck activities such as hoisting sails and where to drop anchors. Also colloquially known as "Bosun".

Bonnet – a length of canvas attached to a sail to increase surface area in order to catch more wind.

Boom – a spar extension that can be added to a yard on a square-rigged ship in order to give more length for the sail. On a sailboat, the boom is a spar that greatly improves the angle and shape of a sail.

Bosun's chairs – a short board or strip of canvas secured by winches and ropes that is used to hoist a man aloft or over the side of the ship for maintenance.

Bow – the front curve of the ship, also known as the "stem".

Bowsprit – a spar running out from the bow of the ship. With the extension of the jibboom, the forestay, forestaysail and jibs can be fastened to this.

Cabin Boy – an attendant to the crew, who is charged with menial jobs such as tidying or swabbing and maintenance. Usually a young man with little or no sailing experience.

Cables – a band of tightly woven ropes used for heavy lifting.

Capstan – a wide revolving cylinder powered by spars used for hoisting objects from the deck or winding rope or cables.

Captain – the master of the ship, in control of navigation, discipline, setting duties and general seamanship.

Careen/Careening – maintenance such as ridding of barnacles, caulking or painting, usually performed when the ship is beached but can also performed when the ship is afloat.

Carpenter – responsible for the repair and maintenance of all woodwork aboard a vessel.

Cut and run – cutting the anchor in order to make a quick getaway or cutting loose a hinderance such as a rogue sail.

Companionway – a set of stairs leading to a lower deck.

Courtesy flag – a flag that is hoisted when entering foreign waters as a sign of respect and to show there is no threat.

Crosstrees – a cross of struts at the top of the topmast used to rig the topgallant mast for the topgallant sail and royal sail.

Crow's Nest – a small platform, usually a barrel upon a nineteenth century square-rigged ship, attached to the main mast near the masthead for use of a lookout for other ships or nearby rocks.

Deck – the top of the ship which is worked on to keep the ship sailing. There are at least four decks on a ship.

Deckhand – the role of the deckhand is anything from supervision and maintenance to swabbing to helping another role; anything that needs an extra pair of hands.

Devil to pay – an expression on deck for unpleasant and impossible tasks, usually known as a punishment for sailors with bad behaviour. Usually associated with caulking the longest seam of the ship known as the garboard seam or devil's seam.

Devil's seam – also known as the garboard seam, a long and difficult to reach seam.

Dock/Docking – to moor a ship in order to transport goods to the port or for maintenance purposes.

Dogwatch – a watch period, usually the nightshift.

Doldrums – a patch of becalmed water where the wind and tide are absent and only drifting on the passing current can move a ship.

Dover Cliffs – a slang term for rough seas: high waves with whitecap peaks.

Dressing down – to treat thin and worn sails with oil or wax to renew their effectiveness.

Drogue – a type of sea anchor to slow a vessel, usually comprised of a small parachute, or an earlier version consists of largening slats of wood around a pole.

Dutch courage – false courage induced by alcohol.

Even keel – a vessel floating upright without listing or heeling.

Equatorial counter – the belt of the equator where, due to the earth's polarity, currents are forever shifting leading to harsh weather or becalmed waters.

Fathom – a nautical measure of depth of water equal to six feet.

Fife rail – a horizontal fitting rail located below each mast with which belaying pins are used to belay the mast's stays and standing rigging securely.

Figure-of-eight knot – a type of stopper knot that prevents the rope from running through or out of certain devices.

First Mate – usually the first officer below the captain, with the same responsibility as the captain and quartermaster.

Flotsam – floating debris after a shipwreck.

Footloose – the foot of a sail that is not attached or secured properly.

Footropes – ropes connected to a yard on a square-rigged sailing ship for sailors to stand on or put their legs through whilst furling or unfurling a sail.

Fore-and-aft – a sailing rig that sets its sails along the line of the keel, such as yachts or sailboats.

Forecastle – a raised deck at the front of the ship.

Fore tophamper–

- **Mast** – the mast closest to the stem of a ship.
- **Masthead** – the top of the mast.
- **Sail** – the larger sail of the mast.
- **Sheet** – the line that adjusts angles and positioning of the foresails.
- **Shrouds** – the standing rigging connected to the side of the deck to the foretop platform that gives access to the yards and higher foremast tophamper.
- **Stay** – a long taught line or cable connecting the bow of the ship to the masthead to support the foremast. This then

connects with the standing rigging and fife rail at the base of the mast.

- **Top platform** – the platform giving access to the foreyard as well as shrouds leading up to the foretop yard.
- **Topmast** – the upper mast set above the foresail and foretop platform where the foretopsail and foretopsail yard are rigged.
- **Topsail** – the smaller sail rigged above the foresail.
- **Topsail yard** – the shorter yard or spar that the foretopsail is rigged upon.
- **Yard** – the longer yard or spar that the foresail is rigged upon.

Forestaysail – a triangular sail that is strung with the other jibs upon the forestay.

Fouled up – when the motion of a ship or a line aboard is obstructed, entangled or collided with that hinders further movement and effectiveness. For example, a rope gets tangled or an anchor gets snagged on hidden obstruction.

Furl/Furled – to roll up or stow a sail against its mast or yard.

Garboard seam – the longest seam of the ship that is the hardest to reach when caulking, also known as the "devil's seam".

Gangway – an opening in the side of a ship's bulwark to allow passengers/crew to enter and exit when docked.

Gooseneck – a swivelling connection for the boom to attach to the mast, allowing better movement for the sail.

Grog – rum diluted with water.

Guineaman – a type of ship slavers use.

Halyards – Ropes used to unfurl a sail, or to hoist any other object to the mast's yards.

Hatches – an opening in the deck of a ship where cargo can be loaded and accessed.

Hawser – thick cables or ropes, usually used to moor or tow a ship.

Headstays – stays rigged between the bowsprit and foremast.

Heel/Heeling – a lean on a ship caused by strong winds on the sails.

Helm – the steering apparatus of a ship; either a wheel or tiller.

Heave to – to rig the sails so they will catch the headwind to slow the vessel, as well as lashing the wheel of the ship and deploying a sea anchor and drogue (depending on the speed of the ship.) This tactic is a usual manoeuvre when sailing through a storm or harsh weather in the open sea and shelter cannot be reached.

Hitch – a type of knot used to tie a rope to a fixed object.

Hog/Hogging – when the peak of a wave is in the middle of the keel, causing the hull to bend as the weight of the stem and stern are unevenly distributed, sometimes resulting in the keel to be warped.

Hold – The bottom deck where majority of the cargo is stored.

Holystone – a block of sandstone used to swab/scrub the decks with. Named after the kneeling position sailors adopt that looks like praying and the stone itself is rectangular in the shape of a Bible.

Hull – the body of a ship.

Inner jib – the next jib after the forestaysail.

Jacob's ladder – a rope and board ladder used to climb the side of a ship.

Jetty – a wooden platform extending into shallow waters allowing easier access for ships to moor/dock and for the crew to enter or vacate a vessel.

Jetsam – floating debris from a shipwreck.

Jib – a triangular sail set ahead of the foresail, attached to the forestay between the foremast and jibboom, used for extra velocity and to give additional accuracy to steering.

Jibboom – an extension spar connected to the bowsprit to give extra length for additional jibs to be attached and rigged.

Keel – the base of the ship around which the hull is built.

Keelhauling – a punishment for any sailor by which one is dragged under the keel of a ship whilst still attached by a rope to the bow.

Knots – one knot equates to one nautical mile, used to measure the speed of a ship.

Ladder – all stairs on a ship are called "ladders".

Laudanum – an alcoholic solution containing morphine and opium, formerly used as a painkiller.

Line – all ropes upon a ship are called "lines".

List/Listing – a large tilt on a ship when there is an uneven keel.

Lodestone – a mineral with natural magnetic qualities.

Longboat – a rowboat a ship carries to act as a tender, to either transport goods or people from ship to ship or ship to shore.

Lubber's hole – a hole built into the top platform of all masts to allow access to the platform as well as onto the yards or shrouds.

Mess deck – the deck where crew eat, or if there is no mess deck aboard, the berth becomes the mess deck.

Main deck – the open deck of a ship, also known as a weather deck.

Main tophamper –

- **Mast** – the middle and main mast of a ship.
- **Masthead** – the top of the mast.
- **Sail** – the larger sail of the mast.
- **Sheet** – the line that adjusts angles and positioning of the mainsails.
- **Shrouds** – the standing rigging connected to the side of the deck to the maintop platform that gives access to the yards and higher mainmast tophamper.
- **Stay** – a long taught line or cable connecting the foremasthead to the mainmasthead to support the mainmast. This then

connects with the standing rigging and fife rail at the base of the mast.

- **Top platform** – the platform giving access to the mainyard as well as shrouds leading up to the maintop yard.
- **Topmast** – the upper mast set above the mainsail and maintop platform where the maintopsail and maintopsail yard are rigged.
- **Topsail** – the smaller sail rigged above the mainsail.
- **Topsail yard** – the shorter yard or spar that the maintopsail is rigged upon.
- **Yard** – the longer yard or spar that the mainsail is rigged upon.

Man the yards – a term to have all the crew of the vessel off the deck and aloft to spread along the yards.

Mast – a tall vertical pole with an arrangement of horizontal spars in which sails and rigging are attached.

Mate – All deckhands or A.B.S are called mates aboard a vessel. Mates are charged with maintenance and routine daily inspection, reporting any errors to the Quartermaster, First Mate or Boatswain. Also, they take care of hoisting and dropping anchors and all duties when arriving at a port.

Middle Passage – the section of the triangular trade in which slaves were transported from Africa to the Americas.

Mizzen tophamper –

- **Mast** – the mast closest to the stern of a ship.
- **Masthead** – the top of the mast.
- **Sail** – the larger sail of the mast.
- **Sheet** – the line that adjusts angles and positioning of the mizzensails.
- **Shrouds** – the rigging connected to the side of the deck to the mizzentop platform that gives access to the yards and higher mizzenmast tophamper.

- **Stay** – a long taught line or cable connecting the mainmast-head to the mizzenmasthead to support the mizzenmast. This then connects with the standing rigging and fife rail at the base of the mast.
- **Top platform** – the platform giving access to the mizzenyard as well as shrouds leading up to the mizzentop yard.
- **Topmast** – the upper mast set above the mizzensail and mizzentop platform where the mizzentopsail and mizzentopsail yard are rigged.
- **Topsail** – the smaller sail rigged above the mizzensail.
- **Topsail yard** – the shorter yard or spar that the mizzentopsail is rigged upon.
- **Yard** – the longer yard or spar that the mizzensail is rigged upon.

Moor/Mooring – to dock a ship upon a jetty.

Ninth Wave – after a build-up of high waves, it is said to be the largest wave in a storm.

Orlop deck – the level below the berth deck, also known as the "tween deck."

Old Pulteney – a type of malt whiskey.

Old salt – a slang term describing an experienced sailor.

Opium – a widespread drug in the nineteenth century for its use in treating pain, dysentery, diahorrea and other illnesses. Contains high levels of morphine and originates from poppy seeds.

Outer jib – the next jib after the inner jib.

Poop deck – the highest deck aft on a ship, also forming the roof of the cabin below.

Port – nautical orientation to turn left.

Quarter deck – a ship's upper deck, usually where the helm is located.

Quartermaster – the role on the ship charged with maintenance, discipline and navigation. During the Age of Sail, this role was voted on by the crew and was one rank below the captain.

Ratlines – the rungs fastened between the shrouds to act as a ladder so the shrouds can be climbed. Also known as "rattlins".

Red Ensign – a British flag insignia flown by merchant ships to show they are part of the United Kingdom's civil ensign. Also known as the "Red Duster."

Reef/Reefing – to reduce the area of a sail exposed to the wind, either to slow the vessel or to protect the sail against strong winds.

Reef-points – lengths of rope attached to the sails, used to furl and stow sails when they are not in use or to secure a reefed sail.

Rigger – charged with maintenance and control of all rigging and sails from keeping tension in the stays, adjusting angles and positioning of sails and hoisting and trimming sails. Perhaps the most dangerous job on a ship since they were always aloft on high slippery yards without any safety harness.

Rigging – a system of ropes and cables which support the masts and adjusts the angles and shapes of the sails.

Royal sail – the highest sail of the topgallant mast. This would only be rigged when there is fair wind and would speed up the ship considerably.

Rudder – an attachment at the very base of the keel connected to the wheel by tiller ropes, used to steer a ship through the water.

Running rigging – rigging that is used to control the spars and sails including the shape, size and angle as well as the raising and lowering of the sails in order to give the best conditions for a ship's movement.

Sag/Sagging – when the ship is in the bottom of a wave's trough, forcing the shape of the hull to warp as the stem and stern of the keel are higher than the middle.

Sail-plan – a set of traditional sails that can be changed to adapt to the changing weather. For example, a working sail plan is changed to a storm sail plan in rough weather.

Scally cap – a cap worn by sailors. Otherwise known as a flat cap or newsboy cap.

Scuttlebutt – a large barrel with a hole in it containing the ship's drinking water.

Sea anchor – a stabilising object, usually in the shape of a small parachute, deployed in the water to provide drag to slow the speed of a ship whilst heaving-to in harsh weather.

Sextant – a navigational tool used to measure stars to calculate latitude and longitude whilst at sea.

Shanghaied – the involuntary service of a crewman working upon a ship; to be forced into service.

Sheet – a line, used to control and adjust the angle and positioning of a sail in relation to the wind direction.

Ship's bell – a bell fixed to the main deck, rung when there is a change in shift, to draw attention or to make an announcement.

Shrouds – standing rigging attached to the side of the deck to the mast in order to climb to the yards or upper tophamper.

Sick bay – a sectioned off part of the berth where crew or passengers with injuries or ailments would be taken to be treated.

Skipper – another term for the captain of a ship.

Spanker – a fore-and-aft sail that is rigged upon an extended spar from the mizzenmast at the stern of a ship, used to keep a vessel stable and balanced when moving.

Spar/s – horizontal wooden poles set upon masts used in the rigging of a ship to carry and support the sails.

Spar deck – a temporary deck constructed of spare spars and canvas to provide shelter for watchmen during rough weather.

Spyglass – a small extendable telescope used to see over a distance.

Square-rigged – a sailing rig that sets its rigging and sails across, or "square", from the line of the keel and line of the masts.

St. Elmo's Fire – a weather phenomenon in which luminous plasma is created upon the tips or ends of sharp and pointed objects within the vicinity of a strong electric field in the atmosphere, usually generated by a storm, causing them to glow a bright white or blue colour.

Stanchion/s – a sturdy row of vertical posts used to support lifelines and other lines.

Standing rigging – rigging that supports the masts and spars, including shrouds and stays. These are not usually manipulated or adjusted apart from their tension.

Starboard – nautical orientation to turn right.

Stay – a strong rope running from the bowsprit to each of the masts to support their weight. Jibs can also be rigged from the stay between the bowsprit/jibboom to the foremast; these are called headstays or forestays.

Staysail/s – sails that are rigged upon a stay line. For example, jibs and headsails.

Stem – the front of the ship.

Stern – the rear of the ship.

Storm sails – a set of sails that are smaller and more robust than the usual sails and can withstand harsh weather. Also known as "trysails".

Stowaway – a person/s trespassing on a ship.

Sun's over the yardarm – a phrase aboard a ship to describe the appropriate time of day for lunch or to begin drinking.

Surgeon – a medically experienced sailor charged with treating ailments and injuries.

Swabbie – although not technically a job, this was a role that every deckhand took part in which consisted of swabbing decks and keeping everything as tidy and clean as possible.

Tack/Tacking – zigzagging through the water when there is a strong headwind. This manoeuvre is usually performed whilst heaving-to or whilst sailing through harsh weather or strong winds.

Taffrail – the rail of the poop deck at the very rear of the ship.

Tender – a smaller vessel, usually powered by an oar, to transport goods or people from ship to ship or ship to shore.

Topgallant mast – a mast extension that can be rigged from the crosstrees to make the topgallant sail and royal sail available for use.

Topgallant sail – a smaller sail rigged above the topsail, rigged when there are light to moderate wind speeds in order to gain more knots.

Tophamper – a collective term for the masts, spars, sails and rigging that stands above deck.

Three sheets to the wind – when the bottom three sails are loose resulting in a drop in speed and for the ship to meander. Also, a phrase for a sailor who has drunk too much and is stumbling.

Tiller ropes – ropes connecting the ship's wheel to the rudder, enabling the ship to turn in any direction.

Trim/trimming – adjusting the area of a sail to boost its efficiency.

Trysail – sails that are part of the storm sail plan. These sails are smaller and more robust, able to endure harsh weather conditions.

Turnbuckle – a small device used to adjust tension in stays, lines or shrouds in the standing rigging.

Unfurl/Unfurling – to open a sail from its purchase upon a yard ready for use.

Weather deck – the highest deck exposed to the weather, also known as the main deck.

Wheel – a device at the helm used to steer a vessel by use of tiller ropes and rudder at the stern of the ship.

Working sail plan – the normal sail plan that is in use regularly when there are variable weather conditions.

Yard – a horizontal spar from which all sails are hung from and attached to. All spars upon a ship are called "yards".

Longboat terms –

Bottom boards – the bottom flooring of the boat.

Centre-thwart – the middle plank of the boat where the rowers (usually two) would sit on to row.

Gunwale – the lip of the boat.

Quarter-knee – the stern corners of the boat.

Rowlock/oarlock – a curving device that allows free movement of the oars as they move but will not allow them to slip out

Stem post – the post that joins the inner frame (rib) at the front forming the bow.

Stern sheets (stern thwart) – the board that curves around the quarter-knee giving the stern passengers a place to sit.

About the Author

I have a full-time job as a qualified bricklayer and builder and have a passion for creative writing, with years of experience. When I'm not building houses or on the trowel, I'll be writing books. I like to write gripping stories with a range of interesting characters with their own tale to tell but who are also relatable. It's something I find therapeutic; almost like slipping into someone else's perspective to see the world through their eyes. It gives me courage and freedom in day-to-day life, enabling me to find the power to shape my own future and fate.

I live in Cambridgeshire with my family (not to mention the dogs, cats and chickens) and love to get home in front of a warm, crackling fire after a cold winter's day working on site. I also love to travel, always seeking new adventures and discovering different cultures and ways of life.

Seadogs and Criminals is a series of two books (so far) and is the first work I have had published.

Lightning Source UK Ltd.
Milton Keynes UK
UKHW011844290821
389672UK00002B/59